THE LAST DITCH

More Sandy Mitchell from the Black Library

• CIAPHAS CAIN •

CIAPHAS CAIN: HERO OF THE IMPERIUM
(Contains books 1-3 in the series – *For the Emperor, Caves of Ice*
and *The Traitor's Hand*)

CIAPHAS CAIN: DEFENDER OF THE IMPERIUM
(Contains books 4-6 in the series – *Death or Glory, Duty Calls* and
Cain's Last Stand)

Book 7 – THE EMPEROR'S FINEST
Book 8 – THE LAST DITCH

Dan Abnett novels from the Black Library

• GAUNT'S GHOSTS •

Colonel-Commissar Gaunt and his regiment, the Tanith
First-and-Only, struggle for survival on the battlefields
of the far future.

The Founding
(Omnibus containing books 1-3 in the series: FIRST AND ONLY,
GHOSTMAKER and NECROPOLIS)

The Saint
(Omnibus containing books 4-7 in the series: HONOUR GUARD,
THE GUNS OF TANITH, STRAIGHT SILVER and
SABBAT MARTYR)

The Lost
(Omnibus containing books 8-11 in the series: TRAITOR
GENERAL, HIS LAST COMMAND, THE ARMOUR OF
CONTEMPT and ONLY IN DEATH

Book 12 – BLOOD PACT
Book 13 – SALVATION'S REACH

Also

DOUBLE EAGLE

SABBAT WORLDS
Anthology includes stories by Dan Abnett, Graham McNeill,
Sandy Mitchell and more.

A WARHAMMER 40,000 NOVEL

Ciaphas Cain

THE LAST DITCH

Sandy Mitchell

For Kelly, Tess, and the class of 2010. Inspirations all.

A BLACK LIBRARY PUBLICATION
First published in Great Britain in 2012 by
The Black Library,
Games Workshop Ltd.,
Willow Road,
Nottingham,
NG7 2WS, UK

10 9 8 7 6 5 4 3 2 1

Cover by Clint Langley.

A CIP record for this book
is available from the British Library.

UK ISBN 13: 978 1 84970 124 2
US ISBN 13: 978 1 84970 125 9

Distributed in the US by Simon & Schuster
1230 Avenue of the Americas, New York, NY 10020, US.

Printed and bound in Great Britain by
CPI Group (UK) Ltd, Croydon, CR0 4YY

See the Black Library on the internet at
www.blacklibrary.com

Find out more about Games Workshop
and the world of Warhammer 40,000 at
www.games-workshop.com

It is the 41st millennium. For more than a hundred
centuries the Emperor has sat immobile on the Golden Throne of
Earth. He is the master of mankind by the will of the gods, and master
of a million worlds by the might of his inexhaustible armies. He is a
rotting carcass writhing invisibly with power from the Dark Age of
Technology. He is the Carrion Lord of the Imperium for whom a
thousand souls are sacrificed every day, so that he may never truly die.

Yet even in his deathless state, the Emperor continues his eternal
vigilance. Mighty battlefleets cross the daemon-infested miasma of
the warp, the only route between distant stars, their way lit by the
Astronomican, the psychic manifestation of the Emperor's will.
Vast armies give battle in his name on uncounted worlds. Greatest
amongst his soldiers are the Adeptus Astartes, the Space Marines,
bio-engineered super-warriors. Their comrades in arms are legion:
the Imperial Guard and countless planetary defence forces, the ever-
vigilant Inquisition and the tech-priests of the Adeptus Mechanicus
to name only a few. But for all their multitudes, they are barely
enough to hold off the ever-present threat from aliens, heretics,
mutants - and worse.

To be a man in such times is to be one amongst untold billions. It is
to live in the cruellest and most bloody regime imaginable. These are
the tales of those times. Forget the power of technology and science,
for so much has been forgotten, never to be re-learned. Forget the
promise of progress and understanding, for in the grim dark future
there is only war. There is no peace amongst the stars, only an eternity
of carnage and slaughter, and the laughter
of thirsting gods.

Editorial Note:

This extract from the memoirs of Ciaphas Cain might strike some as a whimsical or even bewildering choice, concerning as it does his return to the world of Nusquam Fundumentibus, when the details of his previous visit have yet to be disseminated. His activities on that occasion, however, relate only peripherally to the material at hand, and, for the most part, whatever is germane can quite clearly be inferred from context. Where this is not the case, I have attempted to remedy the deficiency by the interpolation of other material, or the provision of my own supplementary comments.

I've done the same throughout Cain's account of the events of his second visit, which, as ever, glosses over almost everything which doesn't concern him personally. Since he was serving with the Valhallan 597th at the time, one of the primary sources on which I've been reluctantly forced to rely remains the published reminiscences of the celebrated Lady General Jenit Sulla, who, at that time, was a far less exalted officer in the same regiment. Suffice it to say that, as before, the Gothic language capitulates early against her sustained assault, and I've endeavoured to restrict the use of the resulting literary casualties to a minimum.

The bulk of what follows is Cain's own account, however, and so far as I've been able to ascertain, as truthful and accurate a record of events as he habitually provides.

Amberley Vail, Ordo Xenos.

ONE

I'VE BEEN TO an awful lot of places I'd rather not go back to in the course of my long and discreditable career, but every now and then fate, or the hand of the Emperor, has decided otherwise. Returning to Perlia[1] would turn out to have a definite upside, apart from the odd interruption by Chaos-worshipping loons with ridiculous moustaches[2], but the prospect of another visit to Nusquam Fundumentibus most certainly didn't.

My dismay at the prospect never showed on my face, of course, a lifetime of concealing my true feelings replacing it with the all-purpose neutral expression which most people seemed to take for polite interest.

'Haven't been there in a while,' I said levelly, staring at the regicide board between me and Lord General Zyvan as though it were of far greater interest than the news that he was proposing to send me back to a freezing hellhole I'd been more than happy to turn my back on twenty years before. In the decade or so since our first

1. *The site of his less than peaceful retirement.*

2. *Varan the Undefeatable, Warmaster of the Chaos invasion of 999 M41, whose no doubt self-ascribed nickname fortunately proved to be a little on the optimistic side.*

encounter on Gravalax we'd fallen into the habit of socialising on the rare occasions it was possible to do so, finding one another's company tolerably pleasant, and I had no wish to introduce a note of discord into the evening. Neither of us expected to remain on Coronus[1] for long – no one ever did – and I'd rather my future access to his table and exceptional cellar remained unimpeded by any bad feeling which might linger at our departure.

'Since you saw off the greenskin invasion,' Zyvan said, as though their defeat had been entirely my doing, rather than that of an Imperial Guard task force over ten thousand strong. Truth to tell, I'd spent the entire campaign trying to keep warm, and as far from the orks as possible; but the reputation I'd picked up on Perlia as an ork-fighter *par excellence* kept getting in the way of the latter ambition, to the point where I'd once again been credited with breaking the back of their assault almost single-handed[2]. Pointless quibbling about it, though; the legend had taken on a life of its own by now, and Zyvan would undoubtedly think I was merely being modest anyway.

So I simply shrugged, and muttered something about having had a lot of good men beside me (which was almost true, as I'd done my best to make sure they were a pace or two in front most of the time, especially when the orks were around), and Zyvan smiled in the manner intended to convey that he hadn't been fooled for a second.

'The point is,' he said, leaning across the board to refresh my goblet of amasec, 'you know the place. You've fought over the ground before, and your regiment will feel right at home there.'

Well, I couldn't argue with that. Being deployed on an iceworld would be the next best thing to a holiday as far as the Valhallans

---

1. *A world, and its surrounding system, given over entirely to the resupply and redeployment of the Imperial Guard regiments active in the Damocles Gulf; if you think of it as the Munitorum equivalent of an Adeptus Mechanicus forge-world, you won't go far wrong, although on the whole it was rather less grubby.*

2. *As so often in his memoirs, Cain appears genuinely unaware of the magnitude of his contribution to the defeat of the Emperor's enemies. Had he not been there, the forces of the Imperium would undoubtedly have been victorious in the long run, but at considerably greater cost in both time and lives.*

were concerned, and the prospect of orks to kill when they got there the icing on the cake[1]. So I nodded, and flipped one of his Ecclesiarchs, setting up what I hoped would be a winning move in another couple of turns. 'They'll be pleased,' I conceded, with carefully judged understatement. 'Particularly if it lasts a little longer than our last sojourn on an iceworld.'

Zyvan smiled tightly. The 597th and I had only been on Simia Orichalcae for a day or two before being forced to withdraw, losing the promethium refinery we'd been sent to defend to the emerging denizens of a hitherto unsuspected necron tomb. Blowing up the installation had buried them again[2], and preserved our little corner of the galaxy from an onslaught of the hideous machine creatures[3], but indisputably failed in our original mission objective. The Adeptus Mechanicus had not been pleased to lose one of their precious shrines, not to mention the chance to loot the tomb they fondly imagined we'd cost them, and Zyvan had been left to face the wrath of the senior tech-priests; at least until I got a message to Amberley, whose retroactive sanction of our actions by the Inquisition had finally got the cogboys off his back. 'I'm sure things will go a lot more smoothly this time,' he said.

'They could hardly go worse,' I agreed, equally inaccurately, and sipped my drink, relishing the sensation of warmth as it slipped down my gullet. I might as well enjoy it while I could; there'd be little enough to take the chill off where we were going.

'AN ICEWORLD?' COLONEL Kasteen asked, not quite managing to conceal her enthusiasm at the prospect. She exhanged a brief smile with her second-in-command, Major Broklaw, whose expression remained as taciturn as ever, but not enough to fool someone who knew him as well as I did. 'Which one?'

---

1. *Valhallans retain a visceral loathing of greenskins from the time of the failed invasion of their home world, and particularly relish the chance to bring the Emperor's retribution to their ancestral enemies.*

2. *Probably.*

3. *Possibly.*

Two identical expressions of polite enquiry faced me across the table between us, if a sheet of flakboard and a couple of trestles could be dignified by such an appellation. Like pretty much everything else on Coronus it was temporary, the stark room we'd requisitioned for meetings just as likely to revert to storage space, administrative matters, or a makeshift kitchen as soon as we vacated our assigned barrack blocks in favour of the next regiment to pass through here *en route* to another war. The afternoon sun was paling beyond the grime-encrusted window, casting a faint pall of darkness across us, too slight as yet to require alleviation by the luminators, but sufficient to make the pallid complexions typical of iceworlders stand out in even greater contrast than usual to Kasteen's vivid red fringe and Broklaw's midnight-coloured mop.

'And why us?' Broklaw added, which wasn't quite as odd a question as you might think. Valhallans are the finest cold weather troopers in the galaxy, without a doubt, but that doesn't mean much to the Munitorum when it comes to deploying them. Although the tacticians and strategists do their best to make use of any special skills a regiment possesses, all too often the never-ending requirement to prop up a faltering front somewhere or other means just sending in whoever's available. Which meant that in my time with the 597th I'd been baked as often as I'd frozen, although their habit of air conditioning their quarters to temperatures better suited to the storage of perishable provisions had made me grateful for my Commissarial greatcoat even in environments where I'd discarded it hastily as soon as I'd stepped outside.

'Nusquam Fundumentibus,' I began, answering the colonel's question first, and she nodded as though the name meant something to her. I suppose that shouldn't have surprised me, as iceworlds with a substantial human population aren't as common as all that, and bound to be of interest to someone who grew up thinking whiteout blizzards are the perfect weather for a postprandial stroll.

'We were there when the greenskins invaded,' she said, before glancing at Broklaw again, a spark of mischief animating the green eyes below her striking auburn fringe. 'The women, anyway.'

Broklaw shrugged, accepting the mild joke at his expense. The 597th had been cobbled together from the battered remnants of the 296th and the 301st after the tyranids had reduced both to well below fighting strength, and the initial amalgamation had not been a happy one. These days, however, it was hard to believe that any animosity had ever existed between the women who'd made up the 296th and the men of the former 301st. (Which caused enough problems of its own for me to fully appreciate why mixed gender regiments were the exception rather than the rule in the Imperial Guard, but I'd long since discovered that a judicious blind eye and a well-meaning chaplain were enough to let me sidestep most of them.) 'There were plenty left for us when we arrived,' he rejoined, a fleeting half-smile drawing any implication of criticism from the remark.

'I think we'll find enough orks to go round when we get there,' I put in, and the major's slate-grey eyes met my own, all trace of levity vanishing as suddenly as an unattended sandwich in the presence of my aide.

'Another invasion?' he asked hopefully, 'or a secondary outbreak?'

'An outbreak,' I confirmed, and Kasteen nodded judiciously.

'About time for one[1],' she agreed. 'Where's it centred?'

'Hard to tell,' I said, with a surreptitious look at the data-slate Zyvan had given me, and which I hadn't read with nearly as much attention as it deserved. 'They've hit a number of isolated settlements in the Leeward Barrens, but they've been staying well clear of the main cavern cities.'

'So far,' Kasteen said, a faintly cynical edge colouring her tone. By the time we arrived, the information we had would be so out of date as to be all but worthless, and we were seasoned enough campaigners to be well aware of the fact. 'What's the local garrison doing about it?'

---

1. *The difficulty of completely eradicating an orkish infestation once they've gained a foothold is proverbial; on world after world fresh warbands continue to appear years, or even decades, after the most comprehensive of greenskin defeats. The Magos Biologis have their own theories about why this should be the case; if they're correct, the only remarkable thing is the length of time which sometimes elapses before a fresh generation becomes numerous enough to cause trouble.*

'There isn't one,' I told her. 'It was withdrawn when the tau started expanding into the Halcyon Drift.' The Imperium had responded to the provocation by fortifying every system vulnerable to annexation, stripping far too many second-line worlds of their protection for comfort, in the hope that the notoriously opportunist xenos would back down in the face of a show of force. So far, to everyone's surprise, it seemed to have worked; although, knowing them, they'd probably already turned their attention to another target, probably one which had suddenly been left undefended as a result of the recent redeployment.

'So the PDF's taking up the slack,' Broklaw said, in tones which left me in no doubt what he thought about that. Like most Guard officers, he had a dim view of the martial prowess of the average planetary defence force; a view which, in many cases, was well merited, although now and again I'd fought alongside PDF troopers any Guard regiment would have been proud to call their own.

'Yes and no,' I told him, unable to suppress a certain degree of amusement as I spoke. 'There is one Imperial Guard regiment already engaged with the enemy, apparently.'

'And that would be?' Kasteen asked, happy enough to indulge my taste for the dramatic.

'The Nusquan First,' I told them. Neither officer seemed particularly happy to hear this, which I could hardly blame them for, as I'd been less than thrilled myself when Zyvan gave me the good news. 'Newly founded, but yet to ship out.'

'How many companies?' Broklaw asked, with the air of a man determined to get all the bad news out of the way as quickly as possible.

'Three so far,' I said, 'out of a mooted six.'

'Wonderful,' Kasteen said heavily. 'Half a regiment of new troopers to babysit, while every PDF trooper on the planet goes berserker trying to make the cut.'

'On the plus side,' Broklaw added, after a thoughtful pause, 'there's a planet full of orks to kill.' Which cheered Kasteen up, anyway, even if it didn't do a lot for me.

Editorial Note:

As Cain typically ignores most of the background to the conflict in which he was shortly to become embroiled, the following extract may prove illuminating for any of my readers prepared to face the ordeal of wading through it.

From *Like a Phoenix on the Wing: the Early Campaigns and Glorious Victories of the Valhallan 597th* by General Jenit Sulla (retired), 101 M42.

NOT A HEART among us failed to soar at the news we were to return to Nusquam Fundumentibus[1], a world whose pristine snowfields, majestic glaciers and towering snow-capped mountains were still recalled fondly by those of us privileged to have served there when last the greenskins dared to sully its face with their presence[2]. That the orkish horde had returned was hardly unexpected, as the long and bitter struggle to finally cleanse their taint from our Emperor-blessed home world had taught us, but I was far from alone in

---

1. *Apart from Cain's, presumably.*

2. *A select group of veterans which didn't include Sulla, who joined the 296th a few years after the Nusquan campaign. Kasteen and Broklaw had both been present, however, as recently-inducted recruits to their respective regiments.*

thinking that their renewed onslaught could hardly have been more propitiously timed. What better warriors of the Imperium to punish them for their temerity than the daughters and sons of Valhalla, and what better regiment from among their ranks than the 597th? For, in addition to the prowess in battle shared by all fortunate enough to have started life among the snows of Valhalla, and privileged enough to have been accepted by the Imperial Guard, we alone had the inspirational guidance of Commissar Cain to ensure our victory against whatever foes the galaxy chose to throw at us.

Knowing of the part he played in bringing the greenskins to heel some two decades before, I took my place among the company commanders for the tactical briefing with a thrill of anticipation, eager to see what words of encouragement he had for us, and I must admit to being far from disappointed. In accordance with protocol the briefing was given by Colonel Kasteen, but she was as aware as the rest of us of Commissar Cain's previous experience of the battlefield we were so soon to test ourselves on, and had invited him to attend, as had become something of a regimental custom. When the commissar spoke it was with his habitual modesty, of course – his advice concise, cogent, and to the point, with never so much as a single superfluous word wasted[1].

It seemed that, in the perfidious manner of their kind, a few greenskins had survived the campaign against them, fleeing like the cowards they were to seek refuge in the harshest and most inaccessible parts of Nusquam Fundumentibus. Since then they'd been biding their time, building up their numbers and preparing themselves for a fresh onslaught against the faithful servants of the Emperor. Now, it seemed, the time was right, a sufficiently brutal and ruthless leader having emerged among them to unite the factions, and lead them out of the caverns and passes of the Great Spinal Range to despoil the relatively sheltered regions which that awe-inspiring line of mountains protects from the worst of the prevailing blizzards, and which accordingly supports an appreciable

---

1. *A lesson apparently lost on at least one member of his audience.*

proportion of the total human population[1]. As yet they'd confined their depredations to small, poorly defended habitations, lacking the courage to face the Emperor's warriors in open combat, but that was sure to change as their easy victories engendered an arrogant and unmerited confidence, bringing fresh resolve and reinforcements to the banner of their leader, until even Primadelving[2] itself would be under threat.

That such a state of affairs would be intolerable to all devout followers of the Golden Throne need scarce be said, though none of us hearing the measured tones of Commissar Cain feared such an outcome for a moment. Inspired as always by his quiet confidence, I vowed on the spot that no greenskin would ever set foot in the very seat of Imperial power on Nusquam Fundumentibus, and I'm certain I was not alone in doing so.

Our spirits thus buoyed, we embarked on the ship assigned to us for the voyage with stout hearts and firm resolve, as yet unaware of the catastrophic fashion in which the voyage was to end, and the heroism which Commissar Cain was yet again to display in the face of so unexpected a reversal.

---

1. *Though Sulla clearly couldn't be bothered to look up the appropriate statistics, approximately thirty-five per cent of the Nusquan population live in the Leeward Barrens and surrounding provinces, which included the planetary capital and its satellite cavern cities.*

2. *The planetary capital.*

TWO

'DOESN'T LOOK LIKE much,' Jurgen said, punctuating his words with a blast of halitosis as he craned his neck for a better view of the vessel we were approaching. He'd maintained his usual taciturn silence as our overburdened shuttle battered its way through the atmosphere on its way to orbit, but now we were coasting smoothly through vacuum his stomach appeared to have settled sufficiently for him to attempt conversation again.

I turned my head to see through the viewport more clearly, and move my nose as far from my aide's vicinity as possible, feeling a faint flickering of apprehension as I got my first clear look at the hastily-requisitioned cargo ship which was to be our home for the next few weeks[1]. It loomed over our shuttle as majestically as any other starfaring vessel I'd ever seen, but my immediate impression was one of shabbiness rather than the awe-struck wonder I generally felt at such moments. Chimera-sized patches had been crudely welded over several of the hull plates, whose runes of protection looked faded and worn, while thickets of antennae and auspex

---

1. *Given that Cain is writing with hindsight, this is almost certainly a piece of hyperbole for dramatic effect.*

arrays hung at odd angles, clearly later additions to the super-structure. It didn't look anything like as decayed as the derelicts making up the space hulk I'd been foolish enough to board with the Reclaimers, of course, but, by and large, I'd seen orkish vessels which seemed barely less spaceworthy. As we drifted closer, I was able to make out several parties of servitors and void-suited artificers carrying out their arcane rituals on the hull itself, and felt far from reassured.

'Neither did the *Pure of Heart*,' I reminded him, more for my own benefit than his, 'and that got us to Simia Orichalcae and back.'

'She had her own tech-priest aboard, though,' Jurgen said. 'If this scow's got one, he's been slacking off.' Which seemed a fair assessment, and it was certainly true that fully ordained disciples of the Omnissiah were hardly common on a vessel of this size.

I shrugged, attempting to appear unconcerned for the benefit of the troopers surrounding us. 'I'm sure it'll be up to the job,' I said.

My first sight of the docking bay was sufficient to raise my spirits however, the purposeful bustle of troopers disembarking and stowing equipment almost soothing in its familiarity, and even the sight of Captain Sulla hectoring her platoon commanders about some discrepancy or other in their manifests wasn't enough to dispel the sudden improvement in my mood. As ever, she seemed determined that First Company would get stowed away first, and more efficiently than anyone else, and her undeniable expertise in logistics made her just the woman to get the job done[1]. There had even been some debate once her promotion to Captain was confirmed as to whether she should be given Third Company[2], where her skills could be best put to use, but by that time she'd settled in comfortably as acting commander of First, and Kasteen, Broklaw and I had eventually decided to leave well enough alone. Whether her tendency to impulsive action would be tempered by her greater responsibilities had yet to be answered, though, and I

---

1. *Sulla had served as the 296th's quartermaster sergeant, until the tyranids opened the way for her elevation to a commission by eating most of their existing officers.*

2. *Which included the 597th's logistical support units.*

made a mental note to stay well out of the way if there was even the remotest likelihood of her going into combat until the question had been settled.

'Commissar!' Inevitably she hailed me, despite my best efforts to sneak past while she was distracted, her face breaking into the familiar toothy grin which always put me in mind of something equine. 'Captain Mires here was wanting to speak to someone in authority.'

The name meant nothing to me, as we had no one of that name and rank in the 597th, and for a moment I wondered if we were going to be sharing our voyage with another regiment after all; then the coin dropped, and I found myself extending a hand to a short, bearded man in a white robe cinched with an over-stretched vermillion cummerbund. Like many of the civilian freighter captains[1] I'd met before, he seemed eager to show his appreciation at the honour being done his vessel by our presence, while underlining the fact that it was his ship and he wasn't about to change the way things were done aboard it for our benefit.'

Are you in charge, then?' he asked, taking my proffered hand for a single perfunctory shake, before dropping it again hastily as it dawned on him that not all the fingers inside my glove were the ones I'd been issued with at birth. Explaining my position outside the chain of command in terms a civilian could grasp was too tedious to contemplate, and I was sure Kasteen had better things to do than be bothered by self-important voiders in any case, so I simply nodded.

'Commissar Ciaphas Cain,' I said, 'at your service.'

I'd got used to a wide variety of responses to my name over the years, as my reputation continued to grow beyond all reason, especially once the wildly exaggerated tales of my exploits began to be circulated among the civilian population[2], but Mires's reaction took me completely by surprise. Instead of the faintly glazed

---

1. *As opposed to those of fleet auxiliaries, which, despite being cargo vessels, were Imperial Navy ships aboard which the appropriate military dress codes were to be expected.*

2. *The Commissariat being quick to see the advantages of one of their number appearing popular with the troops he led for once.*

expression of someone struggling to comprehend that I was real and standing in the same room, or slack-jawed awe, or the studied nonchalance of those refusing to appear impressed by me with which I had become familiar, he guffawed loudly, and slapped me on the back. 'Course you are,' he said. 'Nice one. Bet the fems fall for that all the time, eh?'

To my own surprise I laughed too, not least at Sulla's expression of disbelieving outrage; she was usually so full of herself that it was a refreshing novelty to see her taken aback for once. 'They have been known to,' I admitted, truthfully enough, although my days of carefree dalliance were pretty much behind me by that point¹. 'What's the problem?'

'Too many bits of cargo ending up in the wrong place,' he told me, with a pointed glance in Sulla's direction. 'My deckhands are responsible for stowage. They know how to optimise the space properly, and none of your lot will let them do their jobs.'

'I'm sure they're the best crew in the sector,' I lied shamelessly, 'when it comes to handling regular portage, but military equipment needs special skills to move safely.' I raised my voice a little above the noise of several crates of grenades cascading from their pallet, and the ensuing heated argument about whose fault it had been. 'The explosives need regular checking, so they need to be kept accessible. And away from anything liable to cause an accidental detonation.' Seeing Sergeant Jinxie Penlan, whose nickname was well earned, wading into her squabbling squad to restore order, I began to move away, Mires ambling after me.

'See your point,' he admitted, rubbing his nose thoughtfully. 'Best not to upset your system, eh? Don't want any holes in my deckplates.'

'I think we're in agreement on that,' I conceded. 'Was there anything else?'

'As it happens.' He jerked a dismissive thumb in Sulla's direction. 'The stroppy mare I was talking to says you want a hold left empty. Is that right?'

---

1. *So I would hope.*

'It is,' I confirmed, trying not to smile at his description of her, however much I might agree with it. 'We'll need a training area where our people can practise their combat drills in transit.'

Mires shrugged. 'So long as you pay for any damage to the bulkheads.'

We'd reached the corridor beyond the cargo bay by now, the door grinding closed behind us to cut off the hubbub of disembarkation, and I took in our new surroundings with no little surprise. If anything, the interior of the vessel seemed even less prepossessing than my initial sight of its exterior had led me to expect.

Several of the luminator panels in the ceiling were flickering fitfully, a couple of them completely dark, and an inspection panel in the wall hung askew, revealing a little of the wiring inside. Judging by the degree of yellowing on the prayer slip sealed to its lip by a dust-encrusted blob of wax bearing the cogwheel imprint of the Adeptus Mechanicus, the tech-priest it had last been removed for was probably in his dotage by now, if not reduced to dust and rust. 'I doubt we'll leave anything in a worse state than it already is,' I said.

Mires bristled. 'Nothing wrong with my ship,' he said, as affronted as though I'd just accused him of an unnatural affection for gretchin. 'She's a bit patched, I grant you, but as sound as your faith in the Emperor.' Which was far less encouraging than I imagine he intended it to be.

'No doubt,' I said, as diplomatically as I could. The last thing we needed was to hack off our skipper before we'd even broken orbit.

Mires nodded, accepting the implied apology. 'She could do with a bit of work,' he conceded. 'Here and there.'

'If you're lucky,' I said, unable to resist teasing him a little, 'you'll take a bit of combat damage. Then the Munitorum will stand you a refit.'

'You think that's likely?' Mires asked, trying not to sound apprehensive, and failing dismally.

'Not really,' I said, to his visible relief. 'The orks don't have spacecraft this time around. Unless they've called in reinforcements, of course.' Which hardly seemed likely, as orkish freebooter crews tended to be more interested in going after lootable cargoes, or warships capable of giving them a good scrap, than getting involved in anything to do with ground actions. Unless the fighting on Nusquam Fundumentibus escalated to a full-blown *Waaaaagh!* of course, in which case it would attract every greenskin in the sector; which made nipping this outbreak in the bud even more of a priority.

Had I known it at the time, the orks were going to be the least of our worries, even before the voyage came to its catastrophic conclusion; but in all honesty I don't see how anyone could have predicted the unfortunate outcome of the decades of neglect the *Fires of Faith's* most vital systems had been subject to.

Editorial Note:

Though Cain devotes a considerable number of pages to the conclusion of the Fires of Faith's final voyage, he seems to assume that any readers of his memoirs would be as familiar as he was with the mechanics of warp travel, which I suppose is hardly surprising given the amount of time he spent in transit from one war zone to another in the course of his career.

In order to fill this gap I consulted some of the less deranged members of the Ordo Malleus among my colleagues in the Concilium Ravus and, although helpful, the information they gave me seemed far beyond the comprehension of the casual reader, not to mention myself. Accordingly, I fell back on a rather more rudimentary source, which at least covers the essentials.

From *The Society for the Assistance of Travellers Handbook*, 212th edition, 778.M41.

Travel between the stars is not without hazard, since to do so is to pass through the realm of Chaos itself. Society members are accordingly urged in the strongest possible terms to seek the blessing of a priest before commencing any voyage, however short, and to ensure that every item of luggage to be stowed in the hold is protected by charms of warding, easily obtainable from duly

sanctified vendors at the point of embarkation. Prayers of thanks
for a safe deliverance are also customary as soon as practicable
upon arrival; many chapels and temples are generally to be found
in the vicinity of starports for such benisons.

  While under way, starfaring vessels are protected from the warp
by powerful wards applied to their hulls, and the Geller field, which
creates a bubble of reality around them, impervious to daemons
and the other foul denizens of that dire and cursed realm. The most
hazardous part of any journey is the transition into and out of the
immaterium, and travellers are advised to spend these portions of
the voyage in earnest prayer, seeking the Emperor's protection.

THREE

NOTWITHSTANDING THE DILAPIDATED state of the *Fires of Faith*, the voyage to Nusquam Fundumentibus passed tolerably enough. Mires and his crew kept to themselves as much as possible[1], which suited us fine, as we were able to concentrate on the upcoming campaign against the orks without any distracting friction between the Guard and the voiders. Even Corporal Magot failed to find someone to start a fight with, to her evident disappointment, and my unspoken relief. The pervading air of shabbiness aboard the *Fires of Faith* continued to nag at my overworked sense of unease, so any further cause for concern would have been distinctly unwelcome. I knew Kasteen and Broklaw well enough to realise that they were far from happy too, so when the message finally came down from the bridge that we were about to emerge from the warp, the air of relief among the senior command staff was palpable.

'About time,' Kasteen said, putting everyone's feelings into words. She glanced at me. 'You'll be on the first shuttle down, I take it?'

---

1. *Clearly successfully enough to avoid irritating Cain, since he fails to mention any of the dozens of crew members he would have encountered every day simply by walking down a corridor on a vessel that size.*

I nodded, as though considering the matter carefully. My leaving the transport ship as early as possible had become something of a regimental tradition, at least when there was little prospect of arriving in a hot LZ[1]. It consolidated my reputation for leading from the front, and it gave me a running start in securing the most comfortable quarters wherever we were being billeted. On the other hand, given her eagerness and organisational ability, the first shuttle down was almost certain to contain Sulla's command platoon, and the prospect of being subjected to her vacuous prattle all the way down was somewhat less appealing.

'I thought perhaps, under the circumstances, ladies first?' I suggested. Kasteen's impatience to get down to the desolate iceball we were destined to be stuck on for the next few months and start bagging orks as quickly as possible was more than evident, and it would have been churlish not to make the offer. She didn't exactly do handsprings, as that would have been beneath the dignity of her uniform, but she did smile at me with considerably more warmth than I expected to find on the surface of Nusquam Fundumentibus.

'Thanks,' she said. 'It's been a while since I took point.'

Broklaw looked considerably less happy than she did, but then he'd be stuck waiting for the last run now,[2] dealing with all the problems you'd expect to crop up while trying to get almost a thousand men and women, along with all their kit, vehicles, and supplies, offloaded, with only enough shuttles available to handle roughly a third of that number. He was too good a soldier to argue about it, though, so he just nodded. 'Save a couple of greenskins for me,' he said, with slightly forced levity.

'I'd better go and observe the transit, then,' I said. Protocol demanded someone senior on the bridge when we shifted into or out of the warp, although, like many traditions associated with taking passage on civilian ships, the origin of the practice was long

---

1. *A Landing Zone already under enemy fire.*

2. *The colonel and second-in-command would never travel in the same shuttle, as if it were downed by accident or a lucky enemy shot, the regiment they led would be effectively decapitated.*

since lost in the mists of time[1], and they'd both have their hands full from now on preparing for our deployment.

'Rather you than me,' Broklaw agreed. The last time we'd approached an iceworld on a civilian vessel we'd all crowded round the hololith on the bridge, eager to see what we were getting into, but Simia Orichalcae had turned out to be tainted in ways no one had expected, and I suppose we all wanted to make our arrival on Nusquam Fundumentibus as different as possible from the outset. (Something we definitely managed, as things turned out, but hardly in a manner any of us could have envisaged.)

The other main difference on this occasion was that the captain of the *Pure of Heart* had been so augmetically enhanced that he was practically an item of equipment; the only way Kasteen, Broklaw and I could talk to him was by visiting the bridge in person, so we'd spent rather more time there than we normally would during a voyage, and got to know him and his crew quite well. Mires, by contrast, had maintained his distance along with the rest of his matelots, so I hadn't even set foot in the place yet. Broklaw had observed our departure from Coronus, and had been made decidedly unwelcome; but one thing you get used to very quickly in the Commissariat is an air of sullen hostility radiating from most of the people in your vicinity, so a bit of snottiness wasn't going to bother me in the slightest.

Our deliberations were interrupted at that point by the welcome odour of fresh tanna, and the rather less welcome one of well marinaded socks, as Jurgen slouched in with a tray of refreshments. 'Will there be anything else, sir?' he asked, as he finished handing round the tea bowls, and I nodded, struck by a sudden idea.

'Yes, there would,' I said. 'I'm going to be paying a diplomatic call on the ship's captain, and I think it would be appropriate for my aide to accompany me.'

Jurgen nodded soberly, oblivious to the barely-suppressed grins

---

1. *It seems to date back to the Horus Heresy, when the loyalty of the crew couldn't be taken entirely for granted, and the presence on the bridge at every crucial juncture of someone with a gun was an essential guarantor of good faith.*

on the faces of Kasteen and Broklaw. Though, at the time, I had nothing more in mind than rewarding Mires as he deserved for his discourtesy to the major, I was to be more grateful than I could have guessed for the mischievous impulse to take my aide with me. 'I'd better get tidied up, then,' he said, with considerable understatement.

WELL, HE MADE an effort, even if I was the only man aboard who knew Jurgen well enough to realise the fact. By the time he joined me in the corridor leading to the bridge, his hair had been flattened by the hopeful application of a comb with a reasonable complement of teeth left in it, and his uniform hung less askew than usual, the arms and legs of his fatigues more or less aligned with the limbs inside them for once. He still carried the usual motley collection of pouches and kit which accompanied him everywhere, slung from his torso armour on a tangle of webbing that defied conventional geometry, but for once it was hidden, beneath the traditional Valhallan greatcoat most outsiders associate with the regiments from that world, and which in actual fact they hardly ever wear[1].

'Are you sure you'll need both of those?' I asked, with a nod at the weapons he carried. His lasgun was slung, as it always was, where he could grab the grip and squeeze the trigger in a heartbeat, while the melta he'd acquired on Gravalax hung across his back, to minimise the amount of time he'd spend getting the clumsy weapon hung up on low ceiling fixtures and the kind of narrow doorways which tended to be all too common on vessels of this type.

Jurgen shrugged. 'Our kit's packed up ready for loading,' he pointed out reasonably. 'I didn't have anywhere else to put it.' Meaning the melta, of course; like any Guardsman, or Guardswoman for that matter, he'd as soon be parted from his right arm as from his lasgun.

---

1. *The natives of iceworlds seem relatively immune to degrees of cold most other Imperial citizens would consider unbearable, and only bother bundling up when conditions become harsh enough to remind them of home.*

'Fair enough,' I agreed. After all, I was carrying a pair of weapons myself, although rather more discreetly; my chainsword and laspistol were as much a part of my uniform as my sash and my cap, and I'd have felt distinctly undressed without either.

Perhaps because of the amount of firepower we were carrying, the crew members we passed in the corridors seemed reluctant to engage us in conversation, even after we'd gone some considerable distance from the areas of the ship in which we'd been billeted. I'd been aboard enough starships to have some idea of where the bridge was, however, so we had no need to ask directions; which was probably just as well, as most of the people we encountered seemed too engrossed in keeping the *Fires of Faith*'s ramshackle systems functioning to be distracted. If any of them seemed unduly apprehensive, I put that down to the weapons my aide and I carried so openly: only with hindsight did I begin to wonder if that had indeed been the reason.

Shipboard security was apparently as lackadaisical as the maintenance schedule, and I was just beginning to think we would get all the way to the bridge unchallenged, before our way was finally barred.

'Crew only,' an officious woman snapped at us, popping out of a nearby doorway, presumably in response to the clattering of our boot-heels on the misaligned deckplates beneath our feet. Her jacket had a bit of fraying braid on one sleeve, so she may have been an officer or somesuch in the vessel's internal hierarchy, or perhaps it had just been there when she acquired it. In either event, she regarded us in a supercilious fashion, as though our instant deferral to whatever authority she imagined she had was a foregone conclusion.

'Transit observation detail,' I replied, in a tone which remained just on the right side of politeness, even if it was lobbing rocks across the gap. 'Captain Mires should be expecting us.'

'He never said nothing to me,' the woman said, scowling. My aide smiled, in what he fondly imagined was a reassuring manner, and our would-be obstructor blenched. 'Down there,' she said, pointing. 'Big door, with "Frak off, this means you" on it.'

'Thank you, miss,' Jurgen said, determined to be on his best behaviour.

'You're welcome,' the woman said reflexively, clearly astonished at the discovery he could speak, and now even more disconcerted if that were possible. 'Just got to go and...' she made an indeterminate hand gesture, 'you know, adjust the um, whatsits.' She beat a hasty retreat back to her lair, leaving Jurgen and I to continue our progress unmolested.

'Well done, Jurgen,' I said. 'Very diplomatic.'

'THIS MUST BE it,' my aide said, as we came to a halt before a stark metal doorway, on which the welcoming message we'd been told to expect had been daubed in red paint, and in something of a hurry judging by the irregularity of the brush strokes. There was a fairly graphic picture too, presumably intended to forestall interruption by the illiterate, which looked both painful and anatomically improbable.

I nodded, and pushed open the door, announcing our presence with a squeal of ungreased hinges.

'Can't you read?' Mires greeted us, rising from his control throne, his beard bristling belligerently. For a moment I thought he was alone, the crew members I'd expected to see bustling about the place apparently absent, but a moment later I was able to pick out a number of hunched figures poring over the instrumentation mounted in a line of control lecterns behind him. A good many of the posts were dark and unmanned, and a couple more attended by servitors, which looked as decrepit as everything else I'd seen since we boarded. The chamber itself was as highly vaulted and echoing as most ship's bridges I'd visited over the years, but the degree of illumination was considerably lower; like the corridors, several of the overhead luminators were broken, while others flickered in a manner which clearly indicated that their own failure was merely a matter of time.

'It's been a few minutes since the last time I did,' I said, 'but I don't think I've lost the knack in the meantime.' I stood aside to let

Mires get the full benefit of Jurgen, noting his startled flinch with a well masked sense of satisfaction. The low light levels set off my aide's unusual appearance to perfection, imparting a sinister aspect to the expression he fondly imagined was one of sober dignity, while the flickering glow from the large pict screen depending from the ceiling struck highlights from the weapons he carried, making them the immediate focus of everyone's attention. 'My aide, Gunner Jurgen. We're here to observe the transition.'

'Oh.' Mires looked from one of us to the other. 'Right.' He tried to seize the initiative again, with a nervous glance in Jurgen's direction, his fulsome facial hair not quite managing to conceal his growing discomfort at the realisation my aide was standing between him and the recirculators, wafting a steady draught of his unique bouquet in the direction of the control throne. 'I'd forgotten about that.'

'Then I'd advise you to refamiliarise yourself with the appropriate Munitorum protocols,' I said. I hadn't a clue what they were, any more than he did, but Mires didn't need to know that, of course. Throne alone knew why he'd been entrusted with conveying a Guard unit into a war zone in the first place[1].

'Good point,' he said, trying to sound conciliatory. He reseated himself with a fine show of brisk efficiency, breathing a little more shallowly through his nose. 'Preparing for transit in... How long to transit, Kolyn?'

'Throne knows,' one of the bridge crew said, screwing up his eyes against the smoke rising from his lho-stick, not bothering to raise his head from the instrumentation to reply. He banged the control lectern irritably with the heel of his hand. 'Told you we should have paid extra to have the unguents blessed.'

'Is there a problem?' I asked, feeling the palms of my hands beginning to tingle, in the manner they always did when my paranoia started kicking in ahead of any visible threat.

---

1. *Probably because his ship just happened to be in the Coronus system at the time, and was the first with sufficient cargo space for the 597th and their equipment to come up on someone's list of available vessels.*

'Course not. Everything's fine,' Mires assured me, a little too loudly and forcefully to be as reassuring as he'd obviously hoped.

I shot another glance at the crewman, who thumped the console again, and looked at the flickering dials with a palpable air of relief.

'That's got it,' he said, working the smoking stick to the corner of his mouth, and thumbing his palm for luck[1]. Seeing the gesture, I tapped the comm-bead in my ear.

'About to transit,' I voxed on the general command channel. 'Better brace, it's liable to be rough.'

Well, I wasn't wrong about that. Hardly had I finished speaking than the familiar sensation of nausea which always accompanied moving between the warp and the materium swept over me, leaving me gasping. Over the years, and innumerable journeys between worlds, I'd got reasonably accustomed to the discomfort, but on this occasion it felt very different; as though something had wrapped itself suffocatingly around me for a timeless instant, then suddenly torn, allowing me to breathe again. The closest comparison I could think of was the moment the *Hand of Vengeance* had been ripped out of the warp in the Perlia system by a cabal of orkish psykers, but at least on this occasion I'd been spared the crippling headache which had accompanied the sensation.

'What the hell do you call that?' Mires demanded, rising wrathfully to his feet, and taking a couple of steps towards the luckless Kolyn. 'You want the cargo to think we can't run our own reaming ship properly?' Suddenly aware of what he'd just said, he glanced in my direction with a faintly apologetic air. 'No offence meant.'

'None taken,' I assured him untruthfully. The tingling in my palms was intensifying, although at first I could see nothing to account for the unease which refused to loosen its grip on me. The pict screen was showing the stars again, instead of scrolling runes, so we'd emerged from the warp, at least; I presumed one of the pinpricks of light was the sun we were now orbiting, far out on the

---

1. *A gesture common throughout the region, in which the thumb is folded into the palm of the hand, so that the fingers resemble an Imperial aquila wing. Cain mentions doing so himself, at least figuratively, at several points in his memoirs.*

fringes of its gravitational influence, but at this distance it would appear no different to any of the others. Struck by the obvious thought, I searched the projected image for a sign that something inimical had followed us through, but if anything had done it was smart enough to keep out of sight of the hull mounted imagifiers.

Failing to spot any traces of an external threat, I began to study our surroundings more closely, beginning with Mires, who was continuing to chew out his luckless subordinate with a vehemence and imaginative use of profanity which drew a nod of admiration from my aide. Entertaining as I might otherwise have found his diatribe, however, this was hardly the time to stop and appreciate his verbal dexterity. Unbidden, my hands dropped to the weapons at my belt.

'It wasn't my fault,' Kolyn protested, finally managing to squeeze a word in as Mires paused for breath. 'The Geller field fritzed as we came through.'

'Did it fail?' I asked urgently. I'd faced daemons before, and had no desire to do so again; the Adumbria incident was far too fresh in my memory for that.

To my relief, Kolyn shook his head. 'Just wobbled a bit.' An edge of anger entered his own voice, echoing that of his captain. 'I've been telling you the wards need reconsecrating for months.'

'Fine.' A thin beading of sweat had become visible on Mires's forehead, as it started to sink in just how close his fecklessness had come to damning us all. 'I'll get an ecclesiarch on it as soon as we dock.'

'You'd better,' Kolyn said, in the tone of a loyal subordinate finally pushed to a decision he has no intention of being argued out of, 'but I'm still jumping ship as soon as we dock.' A few of his shipmates nodded, clearly bent on going with him. 'You don't rut around with the warp.'

'You're sure nothing could have followed us through?' I persisted, my own instinct that something was terribly wrong refusing to accept his assurances, and the brief hesitation before he nodded did little to calm my fears.

'Full status report,' Mires said, making a belated attempt to look like a captain at last, and after a fractional pause the officers around him began to comply, some grudgingly, a few with the brittle eagerness of subordinates noting a sudden unexpected vacancy in the command chain.

'There,' Mires said, as the last of them finished their litanies of gibberish, 'nothing to worry about. Everything's fine.'

'What about the rest of the stations?' I asked. 'No one's watching those.'

'Because they're not important,' Mires said, gesturing irritably at the nearest servitor, which had continued to twiddle knobs and poke levers with single-minded diligence throughout the little drama unfolding on the bridge. 'Do you think I'd leave those things in charge if they were?' He could clearly read the answer to that in my face, because he went on as though the question had been purely rhetorical, addressing the thing directly. 'Sigma seven, report.'

'All systems functioning within acceptable parameters,' the thing droned through its built-in vox-coder, and Mires turned back to me with a 'told you so' smirk.

'What about the other one?' I asked, giving it my full attention for the first time. Like its fellow, it was as decrepit as one might have expected, metalwork tarnished, and the fleshly components exhibiting a distinctly unhealthy pallor. Instead of staring dumbly at the lectern in front of it, however, it seemed to be quivering, as though in the grip of an ague. I drew my weapons in an instant, and Jurgen, following my lead as always, levelled his lasgun at it.

'Stop!' Mires shouted, horrified, before either of us could pull the trigger. 'It does that all the time. Jaren, give it a whack.'

The nearest crewman, one of the faction with an obvious eye on Kolyn's current job, strolled over and complied, fetching the thing a heavy blow against its reinforced cranium with a dented spanner evidently kept there for the purpose. The shuddering ceased, although the half-living construct showed no sign of returning to work. It simply stood there, its misshapen head turning slowly to scan the bridge, while Jaren hovered at its shoulder, clearly debating whether or not to repeat the operation.

'Resume designated duties,' Mires said, in the loud, slow manner required to instruct most servitors to do pretty much anything.

'Input initiated,' the vox-coder droned, while its head, having turned to the right as far as it could go, began a slow traverse in the opposite direction. I've never been particularly spooked by servitors, unlike some who find them deeply disturbing, but the measured, deliberate movement seemed watchful, somehow, as though the shambling assemblage of flesh and technotheology was assessing us.

'What input?' Mires demanded. He rounded on Kolyn. 'Have you been retasking the bloody things behind my back again?'

'Why would I do that?' Kolyn snapped turning to look at the servitor with irritated bafflement. 'Specify input.'

'Input continuing,' the machine-thing said, and Throne strike me down if I'm exaggerating, but I could swear I heard a glimmer of expression in that flat mechanical voice. An echo of contempt and spiteful amusement. Ignoring Mires, and heedless of whatever he might have to say about it, I squeezed the trigger of my laspistol.

I can't say I've had to take potshots at servitors all that often in the course of my long and inglorious career, most of the things wanting to kill me having been composed of flesh and blood (or something not too dissimilar: unless you count the necrons, of course, or some of the bizzare denizens of the warp, which aren't exactly living in any conventional sense), but I'd been faced with combat models programmed to make a mess of my uniform on more than one occasion. That experience came in handy now, guiding my aim to one of the more vulnerable points, where the neural modulator was plugged in to the base of its skull. (A system which would have been armoured on a combat model, of course, but which civilian ones left easily accessible for routine maintenance; although I doubted that those aboard the *Fires of Faith* would have benefited much from the arrangement.) The las-bolt hit it square on, with a satisfying shower of sparks, and a spatter of blood and lubricants.

'What the hell do you think you're doing?' Mires bellowed, while Jaren squealed like a startled gretchin and jumped back, gazing down in slack-jawed astonishment at the mess on his shirt.

Instead of falling, the servitor turned to face me, its eyes alight with malign intelligence, the ruined mechanism seeming to liquefy and meld with its necrotic flesh. Power cables tore free from the lectern it manned, wrapping themselves around its limbs, while cancerous growths sprouted around and between them, absorbing the crackling flails into its body. 'Input complete,' it announced smugly. 'I've arrived.'

'Look out!' I shouted, but it was too late: the cables snaked towards the fleeing Jaren, who jerked for a moment as the current coursed through his body, before falling insensible to the deck. Unsure whether he was still living, or merely twitching by galvanic reflex, I put my next las-bolt through his head before returning my aim to the abomination taking form in front of me: it was too late to save his life, but I might still have been in time to preserve his soul.

Jurgen, of course, had needed no urging to open fire himself, and was directing burst after burst of las-bolts at the deformed monstrosity. Jaren's body was being dragged towards it, still surrounded by a nimbus of crackling energy, as much witch-fire as electricity if I was any judge[1]; before my horrified gaze, it too began to flow, like melting wax, blood, flesh and bone going to redouble the size of the biomechanical horror in front of us.

'Daemon on the bridge,' I voxed, my voice cracking with panic. 'We need backup. Lasguns won't stop it!'

'What can we do?' Mires asked, all bluster gone, staring at the thing in slack-jawed horror.

'Run,' I said, preparing to do the same, and wondering if I'd need to use my chainsword to get through the little knot of panic-stricken crewmen blocking the door. 'Unless you want to be next on the menu.'

---

1. *And a reliable one, having encountered rogue psykers on several occasions prior to this.*

Unsurprisingly, he didn't, and joined the general exodus, while Jurgen and I kept peppering the abomination before us with ineffectual las-rounds to cover the civilians' retreat. Which, as I've already admitted, was hardly my first choice of action; but I had a pretty good idea that the more the daemon fed, the stronger it would become, and saving Mires and his rabble from becoming warp spawn munchies would make an appreciable difference to my own chances of getting off the *Fires of Faith* with skin and soul intact. Besides, under the circumstances, the closer I could stick to Jurgen the better, and by great ill fortune we'd ended up furthest from the door.

'Frak this,' Jurgen said, with what seemed to me at the time to be commendable understatement, and unslung the melta. Hardly the most suitable thing to be using on the bridge of a starship, surrounded by arcane mechanisms of all kinds, but any collateral damage we might do would be a problem for later; whereas the daemon was most definitely a problem for now. I'd faced such things before, though not often, thank the Emperor[1], so I knew we couldn't kill it; but if we could inflict enough damage on the ghastly thing it would be drawn back into the warp. I closed my eyes by reflex as Jurgen pulled the trigger, and felt the backwash of heat as the glare of the discharge punched through the thin layer of skin to leave pinpricks of light dancing on my retina. Blinking them clear, I could see a few scorch marks on the metal components of the writhing abomination, but no sign of damage to its flesh, which was continuing to flow like congealing fat, twisting itself into ever more bizarre forms.

'Chaplain's on his way,' Kasteen voxed, as the last of the panicking civilians cleared the room. 'Can you keep it pinned until he gets there?'

'We can try,' I said, with an eye on the door, careful not to say anything which sounded like a promise. So far as I was concerned

---

1. *Most people outside the Ordo Malleus only do so once, and most of those not for very long, which makes Cain's survival of these multiple encounters remarkable to say the least.*

we could pin it down just as well from the corridor, or, better still, from one of the shuttle bays.

'It's still growing,' Jurgen said, and with a thrill of horror I realised he was right. The metal floor was softening around the daemon, lapping against its bulging calves like the swell on a beach, the very fabric of the ship itself becoming fodder for the warp-spawned monstrosity. He fired the melta again, and this time I saw the flesh bubble and spit, like over-cooked stew, before scabbing over an instant later with a carapace of metal.

The daemon laughed, an ugly sound, all the more sinister for being filtered through the mechanical larynx which had once belonged to the mindless servitor now entombed at the heart of the living cancer swelling before my eyes.

'Take out the cables!' I shouted, seeing a new, more insidious threat. The waving mechanical tendrils which had snared and electrocuted Jaren were now snaking their way towards the control lecterns: even as I watched, the nearest began burrowing into the station Kolyn had manned. I had no idea what the monstrosity before us would do if it gained control of the ship, and had even less desire to find out.

Powering up my chainsword to its maximum speed, I sheared through the cable in a shower of sparks, feeling a jolt in my arm like a kick from a Space Marine as the current it carried discharged itself through the weapon. Fortunately the hilt was insulated for just such a contingency, and most of what sparked across the gap was taken care of by my glove. I can't pretend it was an enjoyable sensation, but I had no doubt that I'd be feeling a good deal worse if the daemon managed to carry out whatever plan it had in mind.

'The cables. Right you are, sir,' Jurgen agreed, as imperturbable as ever, and set about reducing the ones he could see to slag with a series of well-placed melta blasts, while I gritted my teeth and sliced through another one, with results as uncomfortable as before.

Disconcertingly, the daemon continued to laugh the whole time, as though it was finding the whole thing a tremendous joke; a moment later I discovered why. The cable ends I'd severed were still moving, instead of having the common decency to lie still on the deck the way they should have done.

My first intimation of the unexpected danger was the sudden strike of the metallic serpents, which coiled themselves around me while my attention was on the swelling mound of flesh and metal that had spawned them. I fought for breath as the tentacles contracted, my ribs creaking, expecting to feel them crack at any moment, while I struggled fruitlessly to free the arm holding my chainsword. At least the daemon could no longer discharge electricity down the wires, apparently needing a physical connection for that, but as the grey mist hovered in front of my eyes, that was scant comfort. Dimly, I felt myself drawn towards the hideous entity, inchoate terror pounding at my temples, as it prepared to devour my very soul.

Then, abruptly, I felt the constricting bands of metal falling away, and discovered I could breathe again; a mixed blessing, as my gasps brought with them a strong and familiar odour.

'It's all right sir,' Jurgen said, pulling the last coil away, and dropping it on the floor, where it lay reassuringly inert. 'They come off easy enough.' Which indeed they had, although I doubted whether anyone else could have managed it, devoid as they were of his peculiar talent[1]. Just to make sure, he reduced them to a puddle of slag with a quick melta blast, before turning to face the ghastly mound of flesh and metal again.

'Fall back,' I said, seeing our path to the door clear at last, and cracking off a couple of shots as I made for it. The daemon moved swiftly to cut us off then, as I'd hoped, flinched back at the last moment as it came within range of whatever it was about Jurgen so many denizens of the Cursed Realm found so disturbing. As it did so, he fired the melta again, and this time the damage he did remained, an ugly cauterised scar across its flesh, the softened metal licked by the beam glowing red in the dimly-lit bridge. For

---

1. *Jurgen was a blank, one of the incredibly rare individuals with a degree of natural immunity to all forms of warpcraft; which in no small measure accounts for Cain having, as previously noted, faced daemons on multiple occasions while surviving to tell the tale.*

the first time it stopped laughing, and a roar of anger and revulsion echoed around the chamber.

'Stick close to it,' I said, seeing the tiny pockmarks left by my laspistol bolts remaining on the distended skin, instead of fading as they had done before. The same thing had happened when we'd fought the daemon on Adumbria, I recalled, with a faint flicker of hope; but then we'd had the massed firepower of an entire company concentrated on the abomination, with Jurgen somehow nullifying its ability to heal itself, and even then it had been a close run thing.

I hesitated, wondering whether we should make the best of the tiny advantage we had, and hope to the Throne we could find a way to exploit it, or simply make a run for it while we still had the chance. Before I could make up my mind, however, the clatter of boots in the corridor and a resonant voice chanting arcane gibberish in High Gothic did it for me; I could hardly let the troopers see the legendary Ciaphas Cain heading for the saviour pods, and expect them to watch my back in the future, so as the chaplain and whichever squad had been unlucky enough to be found by him on the way up burst into the bridge I turned back to face the looming pile of flesh and mechanica, flourishing my chainsword in an appropriately heroic manner. By great good fortune I happened to catch a lump of flesh protruding from between two chunks of metal, and severed it in a suitably dramatic spray of ichor.

'Commissar! Get down!' Chaplain Tope bellowed, in a voice accustomed to carrying to the far corners of a chapel without the benefit of a magnavox, and I complied at once, Jurgen following my lead as always. Several small objects arced over my head, bursting against the daemon, which shrieked in a most satisfying fashion; as I rose to my feet, I could see great swathes of it hissing and bubbling, the flesh liquefying, and the metal subliming into froth.

'Acid?' I asked, perplexed, wondering where he could have found so much of the stuff, and Tope laughed, in what sounded like honest amusement.

'Holy water,' he said. 'Blessed it myself. Good, eh?'

Well, I could hardly argue with that; I've little enough time for Emperor-botherers in the normal course of events, but I can't deny they have their uses at moments like this. Before I could thank him, the screaming daemon lashed out in our direction, ripping a couple of the lecterns from the floor, and battering a handful of the newly-arrived troopers against the wall with them.

'Look out!' I warned, ducking again in the nick of time as a flailing tendril of melting flesh hurtled in our direction. I caught it a good one with the chainsword on the way past, but the whirling blade simply tore a gash along the length of it; despite my best efforts it struck Tope full on, with enough force to dent a Chimera, and sent him skidding away across the deck.

'It can't do that to a man of the Emperor!' Jurgen said, in tones of outraged piety, letting fly with the melta again, this time managing to punch a hole the size of his head deep into the daemon's guts. I don't know how much of the damage was due to his own ability, and how much to the chaplain's spiritual assault on the thing[1], but in any event it looked like the *coup de grace*; the towering abomination staggered, and crashed to the deck, assisted on its way by a volley of lasgun fire from the assembled troopers.

'Flamers!' Tope bellowed, scrambling to his feet with the aid of the nearest lectern, and adjusting the Guard-issue helmet he'd adorned with his rosarius to an incongruously jaunty angle[2]. Not for the first time, it seemed, his badge of office had protected him where lesser, or less pious, men would not have been so fortunate. 'Finish it!'

Since I couldn't argue with that, I stood aside, while a trio of troopers with incendiary weapons hosed the fallen giant down with blazing promethium, blistering the air in the suddenly smaller seeming chamber. The flames roared up, burning with an unhealthy bluish tinge, which reminded me once again of witchfire.

---

1. *In all probability it was a little of both.*

2. *Though many members of the Ecclesiarchy attached to Imperial Guard regiments retain their priestly vestments, a substantial number, which apparently included Tope, prefer to adopt the uniform of their hosts, with appropriate modification.*

The daemon's bellows were growing weaker, and it thrashed about futilely, making even more of a mess of the bridge controls if that were possible.

'It's shrinking!' I said, hardly daring to believe it, and shot a couple more pistol rounds into the spasming inferno, more for the sake of appearances than because I expected it to do any good.

'Losing its grip on the material plane,' Tope said, advancing, and beginning to recite the Rite of Exorcism. So far as I know he'd never had to perform one before, but he threw himself into it with rather more relish than I would have expected. Jurgen helped it along with a final melta blast, and the hideous thing suddenly vanished, with a sharp *crack!* of imploding air.

I looked around at the wreckage of the bridge, which had suddenly fallen silent, except for the groans of the wounded, and the faint crackle of the small fires scattered here and there, where spilled promethium from the flamers was slowly burning itself out. Hardly a control station seemed left intact.

'I'd better perform a full cleansing ritual before we let the crew back in,' Tope said after a moment, and I nodded, still trying to take in the extent of the devastation.

'If you think there's any point,' I said. 'They can hardly fly the ship from here now.'

A cold knot of fear began winding itself tightly around my stomach as I finished speaking, and the full import of my own words sank in. Barring a miracle, the *Fires of Faith* had just become a coffin for us all.

FOUR

'NOTHING ELSE FOR it. We'll have to evacuate the ship,' I said decisively. The weeks I'd spent aboard a saviour pod in the Perlia
system hadn't exactly been comfortable, but were infinitely more
so than the attempt to breathe vacuum which had immediately
preceded them. On the other hand, the saviour pods aboard the
Fires of Faith were probably just as decrepit as the rest of the vessel: trusting ourselves to them would be an act of desperation, but
right now I couldn't see any alternative.

'Can't be done,' Mires said, looking from me, to Kasteen, to Broklaw, and back, like a gretchin ordered to rustle up a snack for a
trio of hungry orks and having to admit that the larder was empty.
'We've got enough saviour pods for the crew, but–'

'Barely a tenth of what we need for the regiment,' Kasteen cut in,
sounding perfectly happy to leave Mires and his people aboard the
crippled hulk to suffocate or starve. Maybe she was: it was their
incompetence which had landed us in this mess, after all. But that
would still leave most of our own people flapping in the breeze,
and the Guard didn't abandon its own; we'd find a way out of
this for everyone, or go down together. Or at least the Valhallans

would; I've always found 'every man for himself' more to my taste. 'What about the shuttles?'

'Still standing by to take us off,' Broklaw said, which sounded a little more encouraging. 'The problem is, they were expecting us to make a stable orbit first.' He turned back to Mires, who squirmed visibly. 'And our chances of that are...?'

'Not good,' the captain admitted, with another horrified glance at the devastated bridge surrounding us. It was swarming with crewmen and artificers, conversing with one another in the clipped and incomprehensible dialect of the specialist, but they were completely out of their depth and they knew it. 'We're trying to get the manoeuvring system reconsecrated, but that's really a job for a tech-priest.'

'There's a Mechanicus shrine in Primadelving,' Broklaw said, having waded through the briefing documents like a good executive officer should, so Kasteen and I could get away with skimming them as cursorily as possible. 'If they could get a party of tech-priests up here, could they restore the damage in time?'

'They might,' Mires said, looking a lot more hopeful all of a sudden. He pulled out a data-slate, and rattled through a series of calculations. Then his face fell again. 'Couldn't make the rendezvous,' he said, holding out the tiny screen for us to read. Then, realising we couldn't all see it, he transferred the data to the big pict screen, which, by some miracle, had survived the mayhem wreaked all around it.

'What is this?' Kasteen asked, frowning at the complex diagram.

'Orbital mechanics,' Mires said, a measure of his old cockiness beginning to return, until I let my hand rest lightly on the hilt of my chainsword. 'This is us, see?' A stylised silhouette of a starship marked our position, its projected course indicated by a green line, which intersected with the circle marking Nusquam Fundumentibus somewhere towards the corner of the screen. Another line showed the motion of the planet, forward and back, like a bead on an abacus[1]. 'Anything coming out from the planet would have

---

1. *Presumably at this scale the curvature of the planet's orbit wasn't obvious, or, if it was, Cain doesn't bother to mention it.*

to shoot past us, turn around, and catch up. Can't dock without matching velocities.'

'We know that much,' I said, trying not to sound too impatient with him. 'We've spent enough time on shuttles transferring to starships. What's the problem?'

'Our speed,' Mires said, looking distinctly uncomfortable again. 'Even at full burn, a shuttle could never catch up with us.'

'Then we need to slow down,' Broklaw said, never afraid of stating the obvious. 'How do we do that?'

'Get the engines going again,' Mires said. 'Then use the manoeuvring thrusters to flip ourselves over. Burn the main engine along the course we're following.' He did something to the slate in his hand, and the starship icon (which looked a great deal more sleek and efficiently handled than its real life counterpart) dutifully did a backflip. He attempted a hopeful smile, which flickered and died again, in the face of our refusal to be mollified. 'We can fire them up again from the enginarium, so we won't have to wait for the control linkages to be reestablished from the bridge.'

'Which leaves the thrusters,' I said. 'How long until they're back in commission?' I watched Mires's face contort, as he tried to find an answer which didn't immediately translate as 'we're frakked.' 'Never mind,' I added, before he could speak. 'Too long, obviously.'

'What about the on-board shuttles?' Kasteen asked. 'You must have some, right?' We'd arrived aboard heavy cargo lifters operated by the Munitorum on Coronus, and expected to be taken off again by whatever was available at our destination. But every civilian vessel I'd ever travelled on carried auxiliary craft of some kind. Surely even the *Fires of Faith* wouldn't be an exception to that.

Mires shrugged. 'We've got two,' he said at last. 'Utility boats. We could maybe cram ten or twelve people into them.'

'That's ten or twelve fewer,' I pointed out, already determined to find a good reason to be among them if necessary. 'If there's time to make enough runs...'

Mires smirked openly at my ignorance. 'They could get off all right. But they couldn't get back, any more than the ones you were expecting.'

'I suppose not,' I said, my attention drawn back, despite itself, to the pict screen hanging over our heads. It may just have been my imagination, but the little starship icon seemed incrementally nearer to the bulk of the planet already.

I CAN'T PRETEND the next couple of weeks passed at all easily; the *Fires of Faith* continued to hurtle like a bullet towards Nusquam Fundumentibus, despite the best efforts of Mires and his crew to restore the damage done to the ship by the manifesting daemon. Their diligence was impressive, particularly after Kasteen had taken the precaution of posting armed guards outside the saviour pods and the shuttle bay, but futile for all that; every time they got one of the systems restored, it simply revealed another malfunction somewhere else.

The team working on the engines had the best results, probably because we'd let our own cogboys[1] loose down there, but it was a Pyrrhic victory; until we were able to turn round, and use them to slow our headlong rush towards the surface of the planet, firing them up would simply make us crash faster.

'Or would it?' Mires asked, when I voiced the thought, becoming unexpectedly animated as he considered it. He pulled out his data-slate, and started fiddling with it again. 'We'd be cutting it a bit fine, but...'

'But what?' I demanded.

'I should have seen it.' The captain handed me the slate, as much of his expression as I could see behind his beard appropriately rueful. 'But we've been so fixated on finding a way to slow down I never realised. We can speed up instead.'

'And ram the planet tomorrow instead of the day after?' I asked sarcastically, trying to make sense of his diagram. It looked almost identical to the one he'd displayed on the bridge screen a fortnight before, except that the ship and the planet were unmistakably much closer than they had been. Involuntarily, I glanced up at the big

---

1. *The Adeptus Mechanicus enginseers attached to the regiment, generally responsible for maintaining the 597th's vehicles and equipment.*

pict, which was showing the view from outside again; by now the sun was a visible disc, and although I knew it was still impossible to make out from this distance, I somehow managed to convince myself that one of the pinpricks of light nearby was the world we were so close to colliding with.

'Not quite.' Mires did something to the slate. 'If we accelerate enough, we might just reach that volume of space before the planet does.' The green line denoting the *Fires of Faith*'s future course seemed to move a little, then broke free of the globe, grazing the edge of it.

'And go sailing off into the void even more quickly than the rescue craft can get to us,' I said.

Mires shrugged. 'We'd have more time for repairs, at least. But if we juggle the thrust right we'll graze the upper atmosphere.'

'And incinerate ourselves,' I said sarcastically. 'Better and better.'

'Ship's tougher than that,' Mires said. 'You wouldn't want to be in any of the outer decks. But the middle ones ought to be survivable.' The green line bent, while I tried not to think too hard about the implications of *ought to be*. 'It'll take good timing, and even better luck. But look.' The line had begun to curl back on itself, which ought to mean...'

'We'd be in orbit,' I said.

Mires nodded. 'A long, elliptical one. Take us months to get back. Supplies would be low, and the air pretty thick. But we should have got control again by then.'

'And if we haven't, we'll have slowed enough for the shuttles to take us off,' I finished.

'Exactly,' Mires said, looking cheerful for the first time since our initial meeting in the docking bay. He glanced at me, anxiously seeking approval, clearly not wanting to sign off on such an insanely risky course of action alone. 'You want to run this by your people before we get started?'

I shook my head. I already knew what Kasteen and Broklaw would say; a slender chance of survival would be better than none as I'd proven for myself on far too many occasions. I sighed, trying not to wonder if this time would turn out to be the exception. 'Just do it,' I said, hoping I hadn't killed us all a day early.

FIVE

THE BRIDGE WAS still looking more like a collection of scrap than a functioning command centre, but a few more of the lecterns had been patched together and hastily manned by the time I took my seat as close to Mires's control throne as I could. My chair seemed solid enough, welded to the deck behind one of the shattered crew stations which hadn't been brought back into operation yet, and which would give me something to cling on to if the worst happened, which I was morbidly convinced it would. From where I sat I had a clear view of the pict screen, which at the moment was showing rather too much of the rapidly-approaching planet for my peace of mind, and, more importantly, a clear view of Mires: though it would be scant consolation, I'd privately determined that if things did go terminally ploin-shaped, he'd get to the Golden Throne a few minutes ahead of the rest of us.

'How are we doing?' I asked him, gripping the arms of my seat as I spoke, sure my augmetic fingers were leaving dents in the metal-work[1]. I kept my voice light, though, and I was careful to slump a

---

1. *Most unlikely; they may have been a little stronger than his natural ones, but hardly to that extent.*

little against the worn and lumpy padding, so I'd look more at ease than I actually was.

'Ready as we'll ever be,' he responded, sounding a lot more like how I really felt than I did.

'Best get to it, then,' I said, reflecting that as last words went, they sounded remarkably prosaic. Perhaps I should have made a run for the saviour pods, now the guards had been withdrawn in antici-pation of the outer decks becoming hotter than a baker's oven, while I'd had the chance; but if this ridiculous stratagem succeeded despite the odds, the Commissariat would have me packed off to a penal legion for desertion almost as soon as I hit the ground. At least if I died today my reputation would remain intact, much good it would do me.

By this time, the mottled white mass of the planet had grown to fill almost the entire screen: a second later the horizon line dis-appeared altogether, leaving nothing but the face of the planet towards which we were plummeting. Even in my most pessimistic imaginings, I'd had no idea we were as close to annihilation as that.

'Give it everything you've got!' Mires barked down the speaking tube to the enginarium, and, in spite of the on-board gravity field fluctuating to compensate, I could swear I'd felt a sudden surge of extra acceleration. Highly unlikely, of course, as the engines had been flat out ever since he'd suggested this insane manoeuvre, but perhaps his sweating subordinates had managed to wring a little more out of them by sheer willpower.

'Ciaphas,' Kasteen voxed, an undercurrent of tension in her voice which, under the circumstances, I could hardly blame her for. 'What's happening?'

'We're about to hit the atmosphere,' I said. 'Is everyone secure?' Even *in extremis*, I remembered to sound as though I cared about the welfare of the troopers; in the unlikely event of us getting out of this mess, we'd be going into action against the orks before too long, and I wanted to be sure they'd watch my back for me when we did.

'As secure as we can manage,' Kasteen said. 'We've welded the Chimeras to the deck, and padded them inside with as much bedding and other stuff as we can find. We're packed in like preserved rations, but we should survive the worst of the buffeting.'

'Glad to hear it,' I replied, hoping that an outward show of confidence would keep morale as high as possible under the circumstances. Gradually, to my inexpressible relief, the curve of the horizon reappeared in the pict screen, a faint sliver of black drifting up from the bottom left hand corner.

'Come on! Come on!' Mires urged, as if the *Fires of Faith* were a recalcitrant pack mule needing to be cajoled.

'It seems to be working,' I told Kasteen after a few more minutes of tense anticipation, the huge sense of relief I felt no doubt evident in my tone.

Confident that our headlong plunge to oblivion had been arrested, I began studying the face of the world we were approaching, hoping to pick out some landmark I recognised, but by now our ventral hull plating was beginning to glow a dull ackenberry red, the haze of ionising air rising all round the external imagifers, and all I could discern on the planet below us were a few patches of grey murk, which were probably just clouds dropping a fresh load of snow onto the already frigid landscape beneath them.

'Hang on,' Mires cautioned, 'it's going to get rough.' Something I'd already deduced for myself; despite the best efforts of whoever was trying to keep the internal gravity stable, the ship was beginning to judder around us as the tenuous upper atmosphere clawed at her keel.

My grip tightened on the armrests again. 'How much longer?' I asked, trying not sound as worried as I felt.

'Just a few minutes,' Mires said, his voice betraying the euphoria of a gambler who has just bet the pot on a low scoring hand, and is beginning to realise everyone else's is even worse. 'We're about to bounce back into space.'

At that moment, a darker speck appeared against the face of the iceball. I leaned forward in my borrowed seat, trying to get a clearer view of it. 'What's that?' I asked.

Mires began to look as though one of the other players had just drawn a pair of inquisitors. His face, or at least the portion of it I could see beneath his beard, paled. 'The orbital docks,' he said.

'They're not that big, are they?' I asked, as the horizon line continued to crawl across the pict screen. The dot moved with it, passing into the blackness of space, where it immediately began to shine like a bright star, smack in the middle of the screen.

'Big enough,' Mires said grimly.

I STARED AT the swelling image of the docks in the pict screen as we approached. The vast structure seemed to be growing with every passing heartbeat, and a quick glance at the auspex on the lectern next to mine was enough to confirm that we were hurtling towards it at a speed which would reduce both it and us to a cloud of scrap if we collided. The blip marking the void station was dead ahead of us, a couple of smaller, moving echoes nearby probably vessels casting off hastily in an attempt to scurry out of our way while they still could. They were even visible on the pict, or so I managed to convince myself, the faint glow of their engines moving slowly against the starfield.

'Are we going to hit it or not?' I demanded, my horrified gaze fixed on the orbital station, which now all but filled the screen. I was able to make out individual spires and docking arms by now, and a handful of ships like our own, which for whatever reason had apparently elected to remain despite the danger[1].

'I've no idea,' Mires said, chewing his lip nervously. I felt my fingers closing around the arms of my chair again, as though I had hold of his neck. 'It's going to be close.'

Fat lot of help that was. 'Can we use the utility boats' engines to nudge us off course?' I asked.

'If we could we'd already have done it,' Mires said dismissively, but right then I was too terrified to take offence. 'It'd do about as much good as climbing out an airlock and farting.'

---

1. *Or been unable to disengage in time, the procedure for doing so being both long and complex.*

'If the hatches haven't been welded shut by our skip through the atmosphere,' Kolyn added, glaring at his captain from behind the auspex station.

'Academic anyway,' Mires said, his gaze fixed on the station ahead of us. As the image grew, I began to appreciate just how vast and complex the city-sized structure we were hurtling towards was. The larger features I'd noticed before, the great central mass and the docking arms protruding from it, making the whole thing resemble nothing so much as a huge metallic starfish, took on texture, each blemish the size of a hab block. Auspex and vox arrays depended from them, like vines on a ruined citadel, and I began to discern innumerable smaller craft scurrying between them, like insects round a nest. If our own vox antennae hadn't been sheared off by our recent dive through the atmosphere, I'd no doubt a barrage of panic-stricken messages would be echoing through the bridge by now.

'Cut power to three, five and seven,' Mires barked, and I felt a sudden vertiginous lurch, as the unseen toilers in the enginarium complied with with his order. 'And sort that damned gravity out!'

The huge bulk of the void station began to drift away from the centre of the screen now, and I felt a sudden flare of renewed hope. 'Whatever you've just done, it seems to be working[1],' I said, although he seemed to have cut it a bit fine for my liking[2].

'We're not clear yet,' Mires said, gripping his arm rests as tightly as I was clenching mine. I held my breath, as one of the docking arms swept in from the corner of the screen, edge on to our bow. 'We're not going to make it!'

'Brace!' I voxed, an instant before we struck it a glancing blow, which made the old ship clang like a cathedral bell. The deck juddered beneath me, and half the luminators in the ceiling blew, showering us with broken glass; a second later harsh red emergency

---

1. *With power cut to the engines in one part of the array, the asymmetric thrust would nudge the ship a little to one side.*

2. *Mires would have to have waited until he was sure of his angle of approach to the void station before issuing the order; otherwise it could simply have made matters worse.*

lighting replaced them, bathing us all in blood.

A glittering cloud of venting atmosphere burst from the docking arm as we tore a great gash along it, and debris began haemorrhaging into space from the wound we'd inflicted. Chunks of metal, cargo containers, and what looked uncomfortably like bodies, blizzarded past the imagifer, then we were clear.

'What was that?' Kasteen voxed, too disciplined to add to the babble of profanity echoing round the bridge, although I doubt that I'd have been so restrained myself in her place.

'We hit the orbital,' I said. 'But we seem to be in one piece.'

Hull breached in sections Gamma two and Beta three,' Kolyn reported a moment later. 'Emergency bulkheads holding.'

'We've still got air, anyway,' Mires said, his eyes fixed on the pict screen. The stars had become a whirling kaleidoscope, and the ominous bulk of the planet rolled regularly across the screen. I'd seen the same thing in the saviour pod I'd left the *Hand of Vengeance* in so precipitately, so I didn't have to ask what was going on; we were tumbling, unable to correct our course or steady ourselves without the manoeuvring thrusters. 'Any casualties?'

'Not so far,' Kolyn said. 'The outer decks were still too hot for anyone to be there.' He shrugged, and gestured at the planet looming over us all. The hull was already beginning to glow red again, and the same faint wisps of ionising atmosphere I'd seen before were beginning to curl around it. 'Not that it matters. We'll all die together when we hit.'

SIX

IT WASN'T THE first time I'd arrived on a planet the hard way, of course. Our saviour pod had reached Perlia with most of its braking systems inoperative, after an orkish fighter pilot had used it for a spot of target practice as we'd entered the atmosphere, and the last time I'd set foot on an iceworld, the shuttle I'd been on had fallen victim to a lucky bit of speculative anti-aircraft fire on the way down, but I'd never crashed in anything even a tenth as massive as a starship. I'd like to be able to claim that the experience was less traumatic, but in truth it was just as terrifying as the previous occasions on which I'd first greeted a new world by knocking a dent in it.

Once again, the saviour pod I'd earmarked crossed my mind as a potential alternative to remaining aboard, but by now we were well within the upper levels of the atmosphere, which would render launching it risky at best; not to mention the fact that I'd probably fry before I got close enough to board the thing anyway.

I rose from my seat for a moment, unbuckled my belt, and refastened it around the back of the chair to fashion a makeshift restraint. No point in falling out if I could help it. No sooner had I finished the operation than I felt a tremor run through the entire hull. 'What was that?' I asked, trying to keep a note of alarm from my voice.

'Thermal shock,' Kolyn said brusquely. 'The outer hull's heating up faster than the core, so it's expanding unevenly. We'll be getting some stress failures before long.'

'You mean we're falling apart?' I asked, feeling a flare of panic. My chest felt constricted, the air harder to breathe, and after a moment I realised with some relief that this was because the temperature on the bridge was beginning to rise, not merely a response to the stress.

'I hope not,' Mires said grimly. 'Just minor stuff.'

'That's reassuring,' I said sarcastically as the buffeting increased, despite the best efforts of the beleaguered enginseers to keep the gravity constant. If it failed, our tumbling progress through the atmosphere would fling us about like grox steaks in a blender, and with much the same result. No doubt Jurgen's tender stomach was considerably put out by now; reminded by association of the thousand or so troopers accompanying him, I vox-cast a few appropriate platitudes, along with a suitably redacted report of our current position. 'We're still in one piece,' I told them, 'and descending slowly. If we all keep our heads we'll be fine.' Which was a bit of a stretch, even for me.

With the crimson glare of the emergency luminators, and the steadily rising temperature, the bridge was beginning to resemble the inside of a bake oven by now. I blinked a few drops of sweat from my eyes, and tried to focus on the pict screen, although the picture it was relaying from the outside was far from reassuring; the vessel's superstructure was flowing like candle wax, the spires and turrets protruding from the main hull softening under the incredible heat of atmospheric friction, or simply ablating away to join the comet tail of debris spiralling in our wake. I found myself blessing the foresight of whichever naval architect had seen fit to site the bridge and enginarium so close to the middle of the hull[1].

---

1. *A common precaution, particularly on merchant vessels and the lighter classes of warship, as the intervening layers of hull provide extra protection from incoming fire.*

Our tumbling progress through the atmosphere, and the nimbus of plasma surrounding us, made it hard to distinguish anything much beyond the hull, but it seemed to me that the horizon line on the pict screen was no longer curved. In fact it was looking positively jagged, and my bowels clenched as I divined the reason. 'Those are mountains!' I said. 'Can we get over them?'

'Throne knows,' Mires replied, gripping an aquila medallion so tightly I could see blood oozing from his fist. The vast bulk of the ship groaned, and we lurched violently, throwing me against my makeshift restraint.

'What the hell was that?' I asked without thinking, only becoming aware that I'd voiced the thought when Kolyn replied.

'Primary power relays just shorted out,' he reported. 'Everything's being channelled to gravitics.' Which was the only reason we weren't all dead already.

I took another glance at the screen, too terrified to tear my gaze away. We were low enough by now to be whipping up a hypersonic blizzard in our wake, ripping a gash though metres of ice and permafrost, while the atmospheric bow wave ahead of us pulverised the landscape. A few scrawny conifers clinging hopefully to the snow-encrusted slopes were whirled aside in an instant, mashed to kindling, and then, with a thunderclap like the wrath of the Emperor Himself, the hammerblow of air slammed against the wall of rock facing us.

The whole mountain seemed to stagger from the impact, the slopes in our immediate vicinity scoured of their covering of ice and snow in a heartbeat, boulders smashed to gravel an instant after that. Flung into the air, the largest pieces of debris clanged against our hull in an ominous carillon.

'We're almost down,' I voxed to the sweating troopers below decks, all too aware of how alarming it would sound to them, 'and running into a few pebbles being thrown up by our slipstream. Hang on, and brace for impact.'

The looming peaks were towering over us on both sides now, although it was hard to make out any details of the topography we were so comprehensively rearranging. At least we weren't likely to hit anyone; from what I remembered, most Nusquans remained comfortably tucked up in their cavern cities as much as they could, only venturing onto the surface when they absolutely had to. There might be orks around, of course, if the mountains we were skimming over were the Great Spinal Range, where the majority of the greenskins had gone to ground, but if we were doing them any harm it just served them right for being on somebody else's planet in the first place so far as I could see.

We ricocheted off a low-lying ridge, ripping another gash in our battered hull, then mercifully there were no more peaks barring our way. The pict screen was blinded by flying debris and whirling snow, our altitude no more than a few tens of metres, and, praise the Emperor, a huge expanse of clear ice fields suddenly opened out ahead of us through the murk. I just had time to vox a final warning to the troopers, getting as far as 'Everyone brace! We're about to–' when we did, with an impact which jarred up my spine like a kick from a Dreadnought, rattling the fillings in my teeth.

A second or two later I felt a second impact, then a third and a fourth, each gouging out a canyon a score or more kilometres long in the permafrost; how many times we bounced I couldn't have said, but each dissipated a little more of our momentum, and after a while the succession of hammerblows to my sacrum was replaced by a continuous juddering, which would undoubtedly have been a great deal more disconcerting had I not become accustomed to riding in a Salamander being driven by Jurgen over the years. It was hard to make out much on the snow-blinded pict screen, but so far as I could tell we were sliding in a cloud of steam, melting a channel in the ice about three quarters the depth of our hull, the temperature of which was visibly falling by the moment, the searing heat of atmospheric entry being leached away by the chill surrounding us. We'd finally reached a stable orientation too, more or less the right way up, for which I was more than grateful when our much abused gravity systems finally failed, hurling those crewmen who hadn't had the sense to lash themselves down the way I had into the corners of the bridge like so many sacks of meat.

Eventually the shaking subsided, until I finally realised that the residual tremors I could feel were just in my much abused muscles, and I fought my way free of my improvised seat restraint. The floor was canted at an angle, which unbalanced me for a moment, and I hung on to my chair for support.

'We're down,' I voxed, although I assumed that would be obvious. 'Many casualties?'

'Enough,' Kasteen said brusquely, so I didn't press her for details, content just to bask in the unexpected glory of my own survival.

'Medicae to the bridge,' Kolyn ordered, through some internal vox-system, and Throne knows they needed it; although I'd have laid pretty low odds on any surviving medicae among the crew having the time to respond. His face was pale, and he seemed to be nursing a broken arm; which put him among the healthiest of the civilian survivors that I could see.

'Lucky you resigned while the going was good,' I said, with a glance at the devastation surrounding us. Mires was still slumped in his control throne, and I tottered towards him across the sloping deck; to this day I couldn't tell you whether I was minded to congratulate him or finish him off for getting us into this mess in the first place. But in the event I was spared having to choose; his eyes were wide and sightless. Somewhere in the jarring succession of impacts he'd broken his worthless neck.

The deck shifted abruptly, and I turned my attention to the pict screen, trying to get a sense of wherever we'd ended up. The image which met my eyes was hard to interpret, everything shrouded in mist, but instead of the jagged icefields and drifting snow I remembered from my last visit to this benighted world, we seemed to be surrounded by a low, flat surface, which undulated gently about us in all directions. Now we'd stopped moving, the heat from our hull was leaching out into the ice, melting it.

Despite my initial incredulity, there could be absolutely no doubt – we were in the middle of a lake. And that meant...

'Emperor's bones!' I expostulated. 'We're sinking!'

SEVEN

'NOT RIGHT AWAY,' Kolyn assured me. 'Most of the pressure doors are holding.'

'But the hull's got more holes in it than a heretic's sermon,' I rejoined. It would be flooding in through the gashes left by our collisions with the orbital station and the peak we'd bounced off, let alone all the innumerable minor ruptures where rivets had sheared and plates bent as we'd skittered across the icefields like a stone on a pond. Not to mention the stress fractures and buckled buttresses inside where the structure had been fatally weakened by the furnace heat of our fiery plunge through the atmosphere. As if to confirm my darkest fears, the battered hulk lurched beneath my feet even as I spoke, a sudden shift in the angle of the deck playing momentary havoc with my inner ear.

'Make for the ventral docking bay,' Kasteen voxed on the general command channel, 'and assemble by platoon.'

'Good call,' I told her, already making for the door, leaving the crew to shift for themselves. Those who still could, anyway. 'The higher we are, the more time we buy.'

'And it's big enough to hold everyone without any shuttles docked,'

Broklaw added, which was also true; it would be a bit of a squeeze, with a thousand troopers packed in there, but we'd manage.

'What about the vehicles?' Sulla cut in. 'They're still welded down.'

'We'll recover them later,' I assured her, hoping we'd get the chance. 'People come first, then the kit.' With me as the person I most had in mind.

I found my way up through the maze of twisted corridors easily enough, my instinctive affinity for confined spaces proving as reliable as ever, making good time despite the buckled deckplates and collapsed ceilings which periodically blocked my path. Nevertheless, my sense of unease grew steadily, as the faint oscillation of the deckplates beneath my boots, caused by the shattered starship continuing to wallow in the lake it had created, became ever more pronounced. The periodic lurches became stronger, the intervals between them ever shorter, and I could picture the cause all too easily: the accumulated pressure of the water forcing its way past barriers which had held it temporarily in check, bursting through them in unstoppable torrents, to flood another series of compartments, as it had done in our stricken submersible beneath the waves of Kosnar.

Well, I hadn't drowned then, and I wasn't about to now, at least if I could help it. Clearing a path with my chainsword whenever the detritus impeding my progress became too irksome to squeeze through, I forged ahead, the audible trickle of water in the distance spurring me on.

'How are you doing?' I voxed, turning away from a dead end of tangled debris too large to break through. Perhaps I should have stuck with the civilians, I thought belatedly – they might have known a faster route.

'We've reached the docking bay,' Kasteen replied at once, 'but the loading doors won't open.'

'Welded shut by the heat of entry,' I said, recalling Kolyn's words on the bridge.

'Looks like it,' she said, clearly more concerned with the effect than with its cause. 'But Federer thinks he can blast our way out.'

Which didn't surprise me. Captain Federer, the officer command-
ing our contingent of sappers, had an enthusiasm for all things
explosive which bordered on the unhealthy; but he was undeni-
ably an expert where demo charges were concerned. 'He'd know,'
I agreed, feeling rather more confident that we'd be able to get out
of the slowly sinking tomb we were trapped in. If only I could find
my way up to join them. I took another passageway, which seemed
to be running in the right direction, and found my feet sloshing in
a few centimetres of icy-cold water. 'Better tell him to get a move
on. The water's rising fast down here.'

I spotted a ladder, giving access to a ceiling hatch halfway along
the corridor, and jogged towards it, the water already level with my
ankles. As I began to clamber up, a hollow booming noise echoed
along the passageway, and the whole ship shuddered. I knew at
once what that meant; the bulkhead through which the water had
been trickling had abruptly given way.

Galvanised by an adrenaline rush of pure terror, I scrambled
to the top and heaved at the hatchway above me, yanking at the
release handle with all my strength, but the blasted thing refused
to budge. A wall of water appeared at the end of the passageway,
hurtling towards me like a charging krootox; I reached for my
chainsword with some half-formed notion of attempting to hack
my way through, already aware that it was too late, and that in a
heartbeat I was going to be swept to my death.

Then the hatchway abruptly gave, and burst open. Welcome
hands, accompanied by a no less welcome odour, reached down
to haul me out.

'Up you come, sir,' Jurgen said, as I popped out of the hole, pro-
pelled by a piston of melt-water. Between us we wrestled the hatch
closed against the pressure of the fountain which had followed me
through, and I blinked at my deliverance in astonishment.

'Why aren't you with the others?' I asked him, energetically plying the
towel he'd produced from among his collection of pouches. We must
have been somewhere near the outer hull by now; the air temperature
was more than humid, and my drying clothes left me wreathed in a

cloud of steam as I followed him back towards the docking bay.

'I came to look for you,' Jurgen said, as though it should have been obvious. 'Heard you banging on that lid thing.'

'Thank the Throne you did,' I said, as we entered the vast echoing chamber, full of Valhallans grouped into their platoons as Kasteen had ordered. The medicae were busy in one corner, treating those who'd come off worst when we hit the ground; clearly not all were expected to make it, as Tope was there too, making the sign of the aquila. There were no body bags to be seen, so either someone had been tactful enough to keep them out of sight, or the fatalities had simply been left behind in the rush.

'We've not got long,' I told Kasteen, as the ship lurched again. 'The water's only a couple of levels below us.'

She nodded, and tapped her comm-bead. 'Federer. Now would be good.'

'Just setting the last of the charges,' the sapper told us, a disquieting note of eagerness discernible in his voice, even through the miniature vox-unit.

'How many have you used?' I asked, trying to sound as though the enquiry was merely a casual one.

'Enough,' Federer said, his attention no doubt entirely absorbed by the strip of det tape he was carefully peeling off the reel.

'You made it,' Broklaw said, emerging from the crowd at my elbow, and I nodded, trying to look as relaxed as I could under the circumstances, which was probably not all that much, come to think of it[1].

Before I could answer him, Federer bellowed 'Fire in the hole!' with what I can only describe as unseemly enthusiasm.

Broklaw and I flinched, along with pretty much every other trooper present, and ducked back, pressing our hands to our ears. Instead of the blast we'd expected, however, there was simply a loud *crack!*, like a lascannon popping off a single round, and a faint smell of burned fyceline.

---

1. *Sulla's description of these events dwell on his 'noble bearing' and 'manifest fortitude' at inordinate length, so he must have fooled at least one of those present; but as her account adds nothing of note to Cain's, I've been spared the necessity of inflicting any more of it on my readers at this juncture.*

'It hasn't worked,' I started to say, and took a couple of steps towards Federer, intending to offer a few words of encouragement. But before I could reach him, there was an agonised squeal of overstressed metal, and most of the outer wall of the docking bay simply fell away, remaining attached along the bottom lip, which bent and tore like an envelope Jurgen had taken it upon himself to open. While I continued to watch in open-mouthed astonishment, the far end of the makeshift ramp plunged into the frigid water surrounding us, raising a fountain of spray, and a wave which sent the whole vessel wallowing under our feet again.

'That went about as well as could be expected,' he said, with an unmistakable air of smugness.

'You were only supposed to blow the frakking doors off!' I said, astonishment and admiration at his resourcefulness mingling in my voice.

Federer shrugged. 'That wouldn't have helped us to get out any faster,' he pointed out, reasonably enough. 'At least this saves us a climb.'

'If you want to swim for it,' I rejoined, conscious that very few of the people on board could do that at all[1], and that none of us would survive more than a handful of minutes if we were incautious enough to enter the freezing water in any case.

'No need,' Broklaw said, staring out at the panorama of bone-chilling desolation before us as though it was the most beautiful sight he'd seen in a very long time (which, to be fair, so far as he was concerned, it probably was). The far distant mountains were wreathed in cloud, fresh snow already falling to erase the scars of our passage, while closer at hand flurries of it were being driven by the wind to heap up in hummocks against the cracked and broken surface of the ice fields. 'It'll be firm enough to walk on before long.'

Well, he'd know, I supposed, he was an iceworlder after all, so I edged a little closer to the gap, pulling my greatcoat more tightly

1. *Swimming being a skill which very few Valhallans acquire, given that water exists naturally on their home world only as a solid.*

around myself as I did so. There was still a little residual heat in the hull plating, but the wind was biting and rapidly dissipated the last traces of mist rising from the water surrounding us. I glanced down, noting with some surprise that a scum of ice was already beginning to form across the choppy surface, breaking up and reforming as the wavelets rippled beneath it, the open patches diminishing in size even as I stared in dumbstruck fascination.

It was then that I fancied I saw some flicker of motion in the murky waters, a dark shadow moving with sinuous purpose some distance beneath the surface. 'Did you see that?' I asked, and the major frowned.

'See what?' he replied, his eyes narrowing. We'd served together too long for him to dismiss anything I said out of hand, however outlandish it may have sounded to him, and of course I'd take anything he or Kasteen said equally seriously.

'I thought I saw something moving in the water,' I said, the palms of my hands tingling again, although given the freezing temperatures that could just have been impeded circulation. 'Like a big fish.'

'Probably just a bit of debris breaking off below the waterline,' Broklaw said, not quite managing to suppress a smile. Obscurely cheered by his manifest scepticism, I found myself returning it, although if I'd had any inkling of what we were later to discover, you can be sure my reaction would have been very different.

'Probably was,' I agreed, in blissful ignorance, and turned away, attracted by the familiar odour of my aide, mingled with the rather more appetising scent of tanna.

'Thought you could do with this, sir,' he said, proffering a steaming flask. 'Warm you up a bit after getting so wet.'

'Thank you,' I said, warming my flesh and blood fingers around it gratefully. The bitter cold was insinuating itself through the weave of my greatcoat, even though we were still sheltered from the worst of the wind by the enclosing metal walls; remembering the way it would cut through to the bone almost as soon as I set foot on the icefields, I resolved to make the most of the hot beverage while I could. 'Much appreciated.' Although if the ship kept settling, we'd all be getting wet again before long, Broklaw's optimism notwithstanding.

'You're welcome, sir,' my aide replied, staring past my left shoulder to get his first good look at the desolate snowscape beyond the gaping hole in the hull. The major's casual prediction of a few moments before seemed to be coming true already, a pristine sheet of ice now stretching from our battered hull to the drifts and ice boulders in the distance, a steady crepitation tickling the ear with an audible counterpoint to the visible freeze. My spirits began to rise. If there was enough air still trapped to keep us buoyant a little while longer, the solidifying ice would begin to hold us up, trapping the half-sunken vessel where it was instead of sending us to the bottom. 'How soon before we can get out there?'

'Not long,' I said, appreciating his impatience, which was no doubt shared by everyone aboard except me. As I narrowed my eyes against the chill wind, I thought I caught sight of a flicker of movement in the distance. 'Have you got an amplivisor with you?'

He did, of course, producing one from his collection of utility pouches after a few seconds of rummaging. I raised it to my eyes, and swept the distant snowfields, registering nothing but the entirely natural flow of the light, powdery surface under the impetus of the wind.

'Seeing things again?' Broklaw jested, and I shrugged, lowering the amplivisor a little sheepishly.

'Can't be too careful,' I began, just as my aide pointed into the middle distance, about ninety degrees from where I'd been looking.

'Orks,' he said, unslinging his precious melta with every sign of relish.

I spun round, lifting the amplivisor again, and nodded grimly in confirmation. 'Trucks and warbikes,' I said. 'Closing fast.' It was hard to be certain of their numbers, their progress churning up so great a quantity of snow around them that they seemed to be advancing in a blizzard of their own making, but it was certainly a considerably sized warband. Hardly surprising, given the spectacular nature of our arrival and the instinctive aggression of their kind;

we must have accounted for a good many of their number in our
cataclysmic progress through the mountains they'd infested, and
the survivors would be incensed and vengeful enough to be out for
blood even more than usual.

'Get the ramp barricaded!' Broklaw ordered, hurrying off to
organise our defence, and a fresh chill ran down my spine, completely unconnected with the harsh wind screaming across the ice
fields like the vanguard of the greenskin horde. Federer's stroke
of ingenuity had been intended to let us disembark quickly and
safely, but now it afforded the onrushing orks all but unimpeded
access to the downed starship instead. There could be no question
of getting everyone off now, and even if we did, anyone on foot on
the smooth plain of hardening ice around us would be easy targets
without a vestige of cover. The orks would fall on them like Fellon-
ian raptors[1] on a herd of grox.

It seemed that, even on the ground, the *Fires of Faith* was still a
deathtrap from which none of us could reasonably expect to escape
alive.

---

1. *An agile, fast-moving sauropod used as mounts by the rough riders of the Imperial
Guard regiments from that singularly unpleasant world. The undomesticated ones are
vicious, quarrelsome, and inclined to savage any living creature in their immediate
vicinity, which remains more or less true for the ones broken to the saddle. And their
riders too, come to think of it.*

EIGHT

MY PESSIMISTIC MUSINGS seemed not to be shared by my companions, however, which, given the circumstances, I suppose was probably just as well. If anything, the prospect of a stand-up fight with their ancestral enemies seemed to perk them up no end, affording a much-needed boost to their morale after the long and terrifying descent we'd so recently gone through. After being bounced around like so many tubers in a sack they were all eager to feel they were in control of their destinies again, and for a Valhallan there are few more enjoyable ways of working off a strop than killing a few orks. So, to that extent, the greenskins' appearance could hardly have been better timed.

Unfortunately there were considerably more than a few of them. As I continued to observe their approach, refining the focus of the amplivisor as best I could, given the clouds of snow crystals being thrown up all around them, and the even denser clouds of noxious vapours thrown out by their ill-tuned engines, it seemed to me that the greenskins still had us outnumbered. Add to that the position we were occupying, stuck in a vast metal box with an open side, things didn't look too good; huge as the rent Federer had blasted in

71

the hull was, fewer than a quarter of our people would be able to bring a weapon to bear, the others left milling about behind them, unable to get a clear shot past the press of their comrades.

'What do you suggest?' Kasteen asked, having more than enough experience in the field to notice this problem for herself long before I got the chance to stick my oar in. 'Charge down the ramp so we can get a few shots off before they run us down?'

I shook my head at the bleak jest, moving aside hastily as Captain Shambas, the commander of our Sentinel troop, clanked past us, a cargo container the size of a groundcar gripped casually in the handling claws of a power loader he'd managed to find. Emperor alone knew how he'd managed to get it running, considering it had been banging around the hold unsecured, but it would certainly make the business of getting some cover in place before the orks got close enough to start shooting a whole lot easier.

'Wouldn't work,' I said, smiling wryly. There are commissars who'd think that was a brilliant idea, of course, and want to lead the charge themselves to boot (probably finding out a little late that they were further ahead of the rest than they'd bargained for, too), but I've never been that stupid, or unconcerned with casualties. Losses are inevitable on the battlefield, of course, but in my view, no one's expendable apart from the enemy; angry, resentful troopers aren't going to cover my back when the las-bolts start flying, and if they think I've got no qualms about putting them in harm's way it won't just be the enemy's I have to worry about dodging. So I've always gone to a good deal of trouble to give the impression that I'm as concerned for their welfare as for my own. 'Too much to trip over.'

Which was true, as it happened. The metal hadn't sheered quite cleanly, and there were cracks and fissures in even the smoothest part which could trap a boot and twist an ankle; and that wasn't taking the multitude of protruding structural beams and torn-off utility conduits into account either. Not a problem in an orderly and organised disembarkation, of course, but under fire, bordering on the suicidal.

'What do you have in mind, then?' Broklaw asked, raising his voice a little as Penlan's squad doubled past, and began to set up a tripod-mounted autocannon in the lee of the crate Shambas had just dropped deftly to the deck.

'Fortify in depth,' I said. The faintly alarming shifts in my balance had almost ceased, so it seemed as though we were in little danger of sinking now, the gradually hardening ice beginning to support even the colossal weight of the downed starship. Reassured that we weren't about to drown after all, my mind had turned once again to the warren of passages I had navigated to get here. I had little doubt that I could evade the greenskins with relative ease in an environment I knew so well how to take advantage of, but bolting for them like a weasel for its burrow would hardly fit the image of resolute courage I generally took such pains to foster. On the other hand, if I made it sound like a carefully reasoned strategy... 'If we spread out through the passageways behind the docking bay, we can set up choke points and ambushes. Then if the greenskins get past the first line, we can pick them off piecemeal as they get split up.' It was a sound enough suggestion, I'd done it often enough downhive and in undercities, but I have to admit the notion of applying those lessons to the corridors of a derelict starship was something of a novel one.

Broklaw nodded thoughtfully. 'Might work, if we had time to organise it. But without a command unit to coordinate, we'd lose as many casualties to friendly fire as to the orks.'

'Good point,' I admitted, which it was; I'd only been thinking of going to ground in the warren of passageways myself. If we had properly functioning comms, and an auspex, and a pict screen to track the signals from everyone's comm-beads, not to mention a command Chimera to pack it all in, we'd have been able to turn the derelict craft into a highly efficient orkmeat factory. But under the circumstances, jamming several hundred stressed and jittery troopers into a confined space with instructions to shoot at the first hostile they came across would simply be doing the orks' job for them. I resigned myself to seeing this out in the bitter cold after all. 'Any other ideas?'

'Set up a crossfire,' Kasteen said, gesturing towards the tangle of galleries and catwalks clinging to the walls of the cathedral-high chamber[1]. 'Pack as many on the defensive line as we can, and space the others round the periphery, with overlapping fire lanes. Any orks get in, the reserves can pick them off from up there, while the rest of the line holds.' I could tell from her expression that she wasn't exactly happy at the prospect, but it was the best plan anyone had been able to come up with, so it would just have to do.

'Excellent,' I said, while Sulla's company scrambled to follow the Colonel's order, and, despite my natural caution, moved up to the barricades for a better look. Which might strike you as uncharacteristically reckless, but at the moment the risk seemed minimal; the orks were too far away to hit us with their crude weapons (which didn't stop them firing them anyway, of course, just for the pleasure of making a loud noise), and it certainly wouldn't hurt morale, or my fraudulent reputation, to be seen up at the sharp end. Besides, so far I'd only seen our position from some way back in the docking bay, and I have to confess to an almost childlike eagerness to view the outside of our much-abused vessel for myself. I'd seen the exteriors of starships from the viewports of shuttles on innumerable occasions, of course, but the prospect of being able to do so without an intervening expanse of vacuum seemed a fascinating novelty.

Accordingly, I slipped through one of the gaps which had yet to be plugged, and clambered awkwardly up the knee-high tangle of ripped and folded metal where the great metre-thick portal and the hull surrounding it had fallen away to the now solid sheet of ice a dozen metres below us. As I did so I gasped involuntarily, and shivered inside my heavy coat, the bone-clawing cold I remembered so well slicing through me like the malice of an eldar reiver[2].

---

1. *Something of an exaggeration, but less so than it may seem; the heavy cargo shuttles the bay was designed to serve would take up a considerable amount of room even at rest, and would also require space to manoeuvre, particularly when several were arriving and departing at once.*

2. *Though Cain encountered both craftworld eldar and their Chaos-touched kin on several occasions during his eventful career, whenever he refers to them in passing he seems unaware of, or, more likely, indifferent to, the distinction.*

Conscious of the number of eyes upon me, I drew my chainsword, determined to at least look the part, and make it perfectly plain that the only trembling the troopers could see was the result of the cold. (At least, if it wasn't, there was no harm in letting them think so.)

The view was certainly spectacular, although under the circumstances I didn't have much time to enjoy it. Unable to resist the temptation any longer, I glanced briefly back at the metallic escarpment behind me, lost for a moment in wonder that anything so huge had ever taken to the skies; even with the majority of it below the surface, it still seemed impossibly big, looming above me like a hab block or a manufactorum, seared and cindered by its passage through the atmosphere. Parts of it were rippled, where the metal had softened and flowed in the incredible heat, and, not for the first time, I found myself marvelling at the narrowness of our escape from certain death.

An escape which looked uncomfortably like being merely temporary. The rumbling of the approaching ork horde could be heard on the wind by now, and I turned to face them, an ominous sense of foreboding settling over me as if the darkening clouds above had descended to envelop my very soul.

'Looks like snow,' Jurgen observed, glancing in their direction as though that was the most pressing matter we had to deal with. He'd scrambled up the metallic slope downwind of me, so for once I didn't notice his approach until he spoke; then, not for the first time, his phlegmatic demeanour in the face of overwhelming odds heartened me, and I responded as casually as he had.

'Much of it?' I asked. A blizzard or two wouldn't disconcert the Valhallans, might even work to our advantage, given their ability to operate effectively in extreme weather conditions, but it wouldn't do a lot for me, and anything which reduced visibility would undoubtedly help the orks just as much. They knew precisely where we were, and not being able to see what they were shooting at wasn't going to degrade their usual lamentable standard of marksmanship to any great degree anyway; but we needed to be able to pick off as many as we could before they closed.

Jurgen shook his head. 'Fair to middling,' he said, unhelpfully, and turned to face the onrushing horde, which by now was approaching the shores of the lake, and showing no signs of slowing down. 'Nice we've got enough to go round for once.'

'I suppose it is,' I said, trying to recall the last time I'd seen him perturbed by the odds facing us, and, as ever, failing. 'Best get back under cover.' Greenskins were hardly the most observant of creatures, and we might yet retain some element of surprise if they weren't expecting to find any survivors.

'Right you are, sir,' he agreed, trailing me back behind the barricade with visible reluctance, no doubt disappointed that he wasn't going to get the first shot in as he'd clearly been hoping.

'Everyone hold their fire,' I counselled[1], taking up position behind the biggest and most solid-looking crate I could find, and drawing my laspistol. 'Let them get close enough to make every shot count.'

'We'll do that,' a familiar voice assured me, and I turned, to find a short, red-headed woman grinning at me with cheerful bloodlust. If she hadn't found her way into the ranks of the Guard, by means I felt it best not to enquire about, but which I was fairly certain had something to do with the magistratum of her home world, Magot's sociopathic tendencies would undoubtedly have found far less productive outlets; as it was, she'd tempered them into a useful tool, keeping them under control most of the time, and accepting the consequences of the occasional exception with unruffled good humour. We'd passed through a necron tomb together a few years ago, emerging from the experience reasonably intact and no less sane than before, and there were few troopers in the regiment I'd rather have with me when things looked really grim, so I returned the smile with a faint sense of relief.

'I'm sure you will, corporal,' I said.

Unfortunately the greenskins had other ideas. I'd been hoping our massed firepower would disrupt their headlong rush across the

---

1. *A general instruction over the vox-net, presumably, though he doesn't bother to mention that specifically.*

ice, doing enough damage to the front ranks to bring the whole mob of them to a shuddering halt, or, more realistically, break them up into smaller groups as they worked their way around the obstructions created by the fallen, which we could pick off a little more easily. It was a tactic that had worked well enough on Perlia, and on most of the other occasions I'd been unlucky enough to find myself in the path of a rampaging orkish warband; but on this occasion the vanguard of their advance was heralded by a sudden clattering roar, as a handful of crude flying machines burst out of the murk surrounding the charging horde and swooped towards us, the downdraft from their whirring rotors flinging up whorls and eddies in the snow beneath them.

Ignoring the great mass of vehicles behind them, which were still beyond effective range in any case, though not for much longer travelling at that speed, we concentrated our fire on the airborne scouts, hoping to bring them down before they were able to report back anything of use.

'Keep firing!' Kasteen bellowed over the clattering roar of the greenskin gyros, which were jinking all over the sky, trying to avoid a sudden storm front of ground to air fire. Most of what we were able to bring to bear were only small arms, of course, which wouldn't discommode them much, the las-bolts plinking harmlessly from the metalwork of their fuselages, and the extraneous armour plate hung all over the airframes, apparently at random. Their one weak point was the open cockpit, which left the pilots exposed, no doubt to savour to the greatest possible extent the experience of travelling at speed so many of the creatures seem to crave; a fatal flaw, which soon saw a couple of them spiralling to destruction on the fringes of the icefield, the orks crewing them dead before they even hit the ground.

I flinched as one of the ramshackle flying machines thundered towards us, the crude bolter welded beneath it chattering vindictively as it chewed a line of craters in the ice beside the ramp, and to my surprise I heard Magot chuckling as she slowly traversed the lasgun in her hands. 'Always knew the greenies couldn't hit the broad side of a starship,' she said, 'but I never expected to see it for myself.'

'He's finding the range,' I cautioned, as the line of explosive-tipped bolts began moving up the ramp towards us, although I'm bound to admit that the amount of damage it did was negligible compared to what we'd already done to the vessel ourselves. It would be a different story in a second or two, though, when the deadly rain began to find targets among the bodies of the troopers. I swung my arm, tracking the fast-moving target as best I could, but the chances of finding a weak spot or incapacitating the pilot with a relatively low-powered las-bolt from the handgun at this range were negligible.

'He doesn't have the head for it,' Magot told me, squeezing the trigger, and reducing the pilot's brains to a greasy mist, which the whirring rotors above him scattered in all directions. The suddenly pilotless gyro lurched wildly to the left, missing the open entrance to the docking bay by no more than a couple of metres, before crunching into the cliff face of metal, where it hung motionless for a moment before plummeting to the ice below, disintegrating as it fell.

'Nice shot,' I complimented her, and Magot nodded, before returning her attention to the advancing orkish ground force, which, displaying all the caution one might have expected from their kind, had just surged on to the ice without a second's hesitation, charging towards us intent on bloody slaughter.

'Take that frakker out!' Penlan urged her heavy weapon team, as the last surviving aircraft wheeled around, and began to pull away. It was moving relatively sluggishly, and after a moment I realised why; in place of the guns the others had carried, the ominous, rounded bulk of a large bomb was nestled under its belly, painted with the features of a snarling squig.

'Let him go,' I said. 'He's no threat if he's retreating. Concentrate on the trucks and buggies.'

'Sir.' She clearly wasn't happy about it, but relayed the order to her team with alacrity nonetheless. 'Retarget. Take out the ground vehicles.'

'Sarge.' The gunner acknowledged her with a nod, and depressed the barrel of his weapon a fraction. 'Nads, it's seized up again.'

'Let me.' Penlan gave the recalcitrant tripod a resounding whack with the butt of her lasgun. With a *crack!* of ionised air it discharged, and she flinched, glancing guiltily in my direction. 'I thought I'd left the safety on.'

'Good shot, sergeant,' I said dryly. The stray las-round had taken the fleeing pilot clean in the back of the neck; as I watched, fascinated, the uncontrolled gyro dipped, wallowed, and plunged straight into the middle of the onrushing mob of orks. As I got my first good look at them, my mouth went dry; there were far more than even my most pessimistic imaginings, turning the ice black, roaring forward in their collections of mobile scrap, or bailing out of them to charge us on foot, every last one of them intent on being the first to make it up the ramp and get stuck in hand to hand. We could never hold off so many, I thought.

Then a plume of smoke, pulverised ice and shredded ork rose into the air from the site of the gyro crash, and I distinctly saw the ice around the bottom of the ramp shift and flex. A moment later a thin dribble of water seeped out, freezing solid again almost instantly. Dropping my weapons for a moment I raised the amplivisor, which, by great good fortune, I hadn't got around to returning to Jurgen yet, and which still hung around my neck.

Something odd seemed to be happening at the site of the explosion, the greenskins milling around in disarray, breaking away from it in all directions. Only when one of the buggies lurched, and abruptly vanished, did I finally divine the cause. Before I could pass on my discovery, however, the onrushing horde finally found the range of their weapons, and the air around me became thick with bolter and stubber rounds.

'Heavy weapons, target the ice!' I voxed, before grabbing my laspistol and chainsword again, safe once more behind the sheltering crate. The lake we'd created might be freezing over, but it was still a huge volume of water: as yet, only a thin crust of ice had formed, just barely strong enough to support the weight of the orks and their vehicles. The bomb from the downed autogyro had been enough to rupture it; if we could only repeat the trick, on a larger scale, it might still be enough to save our necks.

'What I wouldn't give for some air support about now,' Broklaw grumbled, and I nodded in agreement; a Valkyrie or two would do the job in a single bombing run.

'Or some artillery,' I agreed, with a hopeful glance at the regimental vox op, still hunkered down with her backpack transmitter, trying to raise the local command net. But we weren't going to get any fire support, that much was plain; surviving our fall from orbit had been miracle enough for one day.

We opened fire with a will, our lascannons, autocannons, and heavy bolters scything into the massed ranks of the enemy below us, but for every greenskin that fell another flowed in to take their place; we might just as well have been punching holes in water.

'This isn't working,' Broklaw said, and I was forced to agree. The gunners were doing their best to comply with the instructions I'd given them, but the sheer press of orkish bodies in the way was dissipating the energy of the shots I'd hoped would begin to break up the ice. He tapped the comm-bead in his ear. 'Heavy weapons engage the vehicles, small arms the greenskins on foot.' He glanced at me, and shrugged. 'Maybe if we can cook off a few more ammo loads, that might do it.'

'Might do at that,' I agreed, more in hope than expectation, then my eye fell on Federer, popping off rounds from a grenade launcher with every sign of enthusiasm. Leaving Broklaw to coordinate the almost impossible task of stemming the tide of greenskins now lapping around the foot of our makeshift ramp, I hurried off to talk to its architect.

'Should be easy enough,' he assured me, once he'd grasped what I was after. 'Couple of satchel charges ought to do it. The thing is, they need to be below the surface for maximum effect.'

'And how do we do that, exactly?' I asked, with rather more asperity than I'd intended.

Federer shrugged. 'Haven't a clue,' he admitted cheerfully. 'But I can rig the charges for you at least.'

'Well, it's a start,' I conceded. There was an obvious answer to my own question, but it wasn't anything I wanted to do. Fighting our way down the ramp to the surface, hoping our comrades could provide enough covering fire to keep the orks from gunning us down on the way, wasn't exactly an appealing prospect.

Then I noticed the power loader, still idling where Shambas had parked it, and another option occurred to me; it was hardly any better than my first idea, but at least it offered a minuscule possibility of success.

NINE

THOUGH IT ONLY took a few moments to organise, every second was crucial, and I had good reason to fear that we'd be overrun before our preparations were complete. The heavy weapons on the orkish vehicles were pouring an incredible volume of fire into our refuge, and, despite the sturdiness of the defences we'd managed to erect, our casualties were mounting. Fortunately, there were still plenty of troopers in the rear ranks ready and willing to take their places on the line, and administer aid to the fallen, but our reserves weren't inexhaustible, and neither was our ammunition.

'Keep the ramp clear!' Broklaw commanded, and a fresh hailstorm of las-bolts swept it clean of the orkish vanguard, which, true to the instincts of the breed, seemed to have forgotten they had small arms of their own, and was simply intent on getting close enough to make use of the crude axes they were wielding. It was uncannily like watching the waves lapping against a beach, each surge of greenskins flowing a little further up the slope before falling back, gathering the strength to rush forward again.

'At least they seem to be concentrating on the foot of the ramp,' Shambas said, manoeuvring the power lifter as close to the edge of the drop as he dared. A few orkish rounds struck the heavy metal frame, and whined off into the distance, but he seemed unperturbed by the ricochets, no doubt used to that sort of thing in his usual mount.

'For the time being,' I agreed, peering down at the ice directly below us, which seemed mercifully free of ululating greenskins, and trying to ignore the spasm of dread which gripped me at the prospect of what I was about to do. Despite the impression most people have of me, I've never been the kind of man who laughs in the face of danger, much preferring to snigger behind its back and make vulgar hand gestures while it isn't looking. Nevertheless, I'd come up with this ridiculous plan, and, as usual, everyone had simply assumed that meant I intended to carry it out myself. Disabusing them would have unfortunate consequences, to say the least, undermining my leadership and the confidence of the troopers at a point when our very survival meant keeping everyone focused and up to the mark; so, once again, my undeserved reputation for derring-do had backed me into a corner.

'Try to plant the charges close to the hull,' Federer said, with the calm assurance of an expert, secure in the knowledge that someone else was about to do the dirty work. 'The shockwaves'll bounce off it, intensifying the effect.'

'I'll bear that in mind,' I said, having no intention of straying any further from safety than I could help in any case. While the greenskins continued to jostle for a foothold on the ramp, the patch of ice in its lee would remain shadowed, escaping their notice altogether with a bit of luck. The rich odour of fermenting socks informed me that the other half of our forlorn hope[1] had arrived, and I turned to meet him, trying to project an air of quiet confidence for the benefit of everyone around us. 'Ready, Jurgen?'

'Right you are, sir,' my aide responded, from somewhere within the folds of his thick Valhallan greatcoat. With the flaps of his fur

---

1. *An Imperial Guard term for a rear guard, or similarly exposed detachment, detailed to cover a retreat or otherwise protect the main body of troops; the low chance of survival contingent on such a task being reflected in the name.*

hat pulled down, and the collar pulled up, hardly any of his face was visible at all, which no doubt struck most of those present as a considerable improvement. There had been no question of his failing to accompany me; he simply took it for granted that his place on the battlefield was at my side, and that, short of a direct order to the contrary, where I went, so did he. An order I must confess it crossed my mind to give; but under the circumstances there was no one I'd rather have watching my back. Besides, if I left him behind, and by some miracle failed to get killed, I'd never hear the last of it; and an affronted Jurgen was never something to take lightly.

'We'll concentrate all our fire on the foot of the ramp while you're descending,' Broklaw said, and I nodded, grateful for the suggestion. Given the single-mindedness of the average ork intent on getting into melee, two men cautiously descending the face of the hull in the shadows it cast might well escape their notice altogether, but an additional diversion could hardly hurt.

'Good idea,' I agreed, shrugging into the harness one of Federer's people had rigged up, by the simple expedient of knotting some lasgun slings into loops and attaching them as securely as possible to the towing line bolted onto the chassis of the power loader. Normally it would be used to drag pallets across the holds, or to lift them into place after the improvised crane had scrambled into position on the narrow catwalks above them, but I would have laid a considerable sum of money that whoever had designed the thing had never envisaged the use I had in mind for it. I tugged at the tangle of webbing, experimentally, and to my relief it seemed solid enough. 'Will it take the weight?'

'And about five tonnes on top,' Shambas assured me, assuming I meant the line rather than the fragile-seeming slings tied to them, and taking up the slack by winding the winch about a quarter of a turn. The improvised harness dug uncomfortably into my armpits, hoisting me onto my toes, a sensation I found remarkably unpleasant, not least because it brought me bumping into my identically accoutred aide, at an angle calculated to give me the full benefit of his unique aroma.

'Then let's get on with it,' I said, aware that the bone-chilling cold outside would at least deaden my sense of smell. 'Are the charges secure?'

'They're fine,' Federer told me, slipping a pair of large, heavy satchels across my shoulders, one on each side 'for balance,' before kitting Jurgen out in a similar fashion. 'Primed and ready.'

'I'll try not to drop them,' I said, trying to ignore the vague sense of panic his words had stirred in me. 'And if you could keep your finger off the firing button until we're clear, I'd be very much obliged.' Under the circumstances we'd elected to detonate the things by vox-relay, in case Jurgen and I were both gunned down or hacked to bits before we had a chance to activate any timers, although no one had been tactless enough to put it quite like that; which also accounted for the fact that, against all the usual safety procedures, the fuses had already been set.

'I'll listen out for your order,' Federer assured me, tactfully failing to add 'or death rattle,' which seemed an equally probable cue for him to detonate from where I was standing; but there was nothing to be gained from thinking about that, so I teetered to the edge of the drop, and watched Jurgen swing himself outwards. Somewhat reassured by his failure to plummet to his death, I stepped over the brink myself, feeling the improvised harness digging a little more deeply into my abused armpits.

'Ground floor, please,' I jested feebly, and Shambas grinned, prodding the winch carefully into life.

I've experienced my fair share of apprehension and dismay in the course of my career, Emperor alone knows, but the sensation of dangling helplessly at the end of a cable less than fifty metres from a warband of blood-maddened orks was among the most suspenseful[1] few moments of my life. If any one of them had looked up in our direction, we would have been dead in an instant, our corpses so riddled with bullets and bolter rounds we'd have arrived on the ice in bite-sized chunks. I held the butt of my laspistol tightly, scanning our surroundings as best I could for any

---

1. *Cain seems oblivious to the unintended pun here.*

sign of a threat; but the diversion Broklaw had promised us arrived on cue, a barrage of fire so intense that the ork host actually gave ground for a moment, which diverted their attention nicely. For an instant I even dared to hope that their will had been broken, but of course it wasn't, the setback merely increasing their resolve to close with us and settle accounts hand to hand. With a collective bellow of *WAAAAAAAGHHHH!* they surged forward again, reaching the highest point yet on the bitterly contested ramp, before being beaten back to its foot once more.

With all that noise, the relatively faint chugging and squeaking of the winch went unheard, and before long I felt my boots crunch against the ice. It was rougher than I'd expected, frozen ripples and a light dusting of powdery crystals giving my bootsoles enough of a grip to be able to walk without slipping if I placed my feet cautiously enough; which, under the circumstances, was pretty much a given.

I shrugged the harness off with a great sense of relief; the wind had made us oscillate gently as we descended, and this, together with being so close to Jurgen, had left my stomach feeling a little unsettled. 'Be ready to pull us back up,' I instructed, not wanting to leave anything to chance, and the pair of us slunk gratefully into the shadows cast by the looming metal wall.

From the ground, the half-buried starship looked bigger than ever, an impression strengthened as we scuttled into the lee of its overhang. If there was one thing an old hive hand like me was good at it was lurking in shadows, and I must confess that my confidence rose a little as we gained the refuge they offered; my black greatcoat would blend in with the relative darkness very nicely, and Jurgen's dark grey one[1] would do the same. A quick glance in the direction of the orks was enough to reassure me that they were still happily occupied with being decimated, and I swung the first of the demo packs off my shoulder. 'Best get to it,' I said.

---

1. *Generally favoured by Valhallan regiments fighting in urban environments, or on garrison duty; out in the snowfields, they tend to adopt winter camouflage patterns, for obvious reasons.*

In the event, it was surprisingly easy to place the bulky charges; a quick blast from Jurgen's melta was enough to provide a hole suitable for our needs, and all I had to do was drop the satchel inside, with a quick glance to confirm that the standby rune was still glowing on the detonator. We worked our way along the hull, pausing at intervals of about fifty metres as Federer had directed, so that by the time we came to place the final charge we were close to the point where the lowering metal cliff began to curve away, affording us a little more cover from the bulk of the orkish army than we'd previously been able to enjoy.

Perhaps that made us careless, attracting the attention of a scouting party, or perhaps we were simply unlucky enough to be in the path of a late-arriving group eager to join the fray[1], but just as I was on the point of placing the final charge the bellowing of a badly-tuned engine assaulted my ears, followed almost at once by the rattle of a heavy-calibre weapon. Fortunately the gunner was no better a shot than the majority of his kind, the surface of the ice exploding into sharp-edged splinters three or four metres from where I was standing. I dropped reflexively into a crouch, fumbling the bag full of explosives down the hole, where it was less likely to be detonated by a lucky round, reducing Jurgen and I to an unpleasant stain in the process, and brought my laspistol up, searching for a target.

Unfortunately, there were several in sight, bearing down on us with frightening speed, led by one of the curious tracked cycle hybrids I'd seen so often on Perlia. The unmistakable cylindrical turret of a crude flamethrower filled the rear cargo compartment, and a trailered fuel tank bounced precariously in its wake, a couple of gretchin riggers clinging to the flexible fuel pipe between the two with the unbreakable grip of pure terror. Behind it, a couple of buggies rattled and bounced, the bellowing gunners clinging to their pintle mounts the source of the incoming fire which had first alerted us to their presence.

---

1. *Almost certainly the latter, as orks are seldom disciplined enough to stay out of a fight if there's one in the vicinity, however prudent it would be to guard their flanks.*

I cracked off a few shots, not really expecting much of a result at this range, and the ragtag convoy continued to bear down on us, as indifferently as if I'd done no more than sneeze in their general direction. Jurgen had better luck, however, simply raising the melta in his hands and squeezing off a shot at the closest target.

By great good fortune this happened to be the self-propelled flamethrower, which detonated spectacularly from the sudden thermal shock, its payload igniting with a roar and a blast of heat I'd probably have been grateful for if I hadn't lost all feeling in my extremities by this time. As it was, I felt the shockwave against my cold-numbed face, and flinched instinctively as pieces of scrap and barbecued greenskin clattered to the ice around me. 'Run!' I yelled, suiting the action to the word, and taking to my heels as a blazing slick of combusting promethium spread across the ice between us and the orks, flowing in our direction with unnerving rapidity.

'Commissar. Is something wrong?' Kasteen's voice rang in my comm-bead, as I realised we were now cut off from the winch we'd been counting on to haul us back to safety.

'Orks,' I snapped briefly, as I glanced back over my shoulder. 'What else?'

I was just in time to see the blazing slick envelop one of the buggies, which had failed to turn in time, the driver evidently caught by surprise at the lack of traction his tyres had on the smooth ice of the newly formed lake; he still had the clumsy steering yoke hard over, as, waltzing elegantly in a slow circle, the buggy slid gently into the heart of the inferno. The gunner just had time for a final defiant burst in our direction before the flames swallowed them, and their fuel and ammunition began to cook off in a small series of secondary explosions.

Of course a sideshow like that was bound to attract attention, and although the majority of the greenskins besieging the ramp continued trying to climb it with single-minded belligerence, all too many of those on the periphery of the pushing and shouting mob began turning their heads in our direction, pointing and gesticulating angrily. Though I couldn't hear a word of the ensuing conversation, I had little need to; before long, a score or more of the hulking figures broke away from the main group, and began racing towards us across the ice with deceptive speed. I'd fought orks too often before to be fooled by their ungainly appearance; lumbering they may well have been, but they could move fast when they had to, and I had little doubt that they would run us down quickly if we let them get close enough.

Worse, a few of the vehicles accompanying them seemed to be losing interest in pouring suppressive fire into the exposed docking bay, wheeling about to follow the breakaway faction.

Then the roar of a powerful engine reminded me that we still had an even more pressing matter to deal with, as the second buggy emerged from the plume of greasy smoke drifting from the site of the flamethrower's immolation. The driver of this one seemed a little more cautious, or had learned the lesson of his compatriot's demise, and advanced at little more than walking pace, hunched over the controls of his lurching, slithering vehicle in an attitude of intense concentration[1]. The gunner grinned down at us, exposing far too many teeth and tusks, and pulled the trigger of his autocannon, swinging the stream of lethal projectiles towards us with lazy deliberation.

There was only one way to go, and I took it, charging the idling vehicle head-on, wrongfooting the greenskins nicely: the gunner tried to depress the barrel of his weapon to follow me, responding to the discovery that I was now inside its range with a bellow of rage and disappointment. 'Take out the driver!' I shouted to Jurgen, confident that he would be dogging my heels as always, and cracked off a fusillade of laspistol rounds at the standing gunner. Several of the las-bolts hit the mark, but instead of putting him down, they simply maddened the brute; I just had time to draw my trusty chainsword before he launched himself at me, roaring like an angry cudbear. Forewarned, I pivoted, evading a blow from fists which could shatter rockcrete, and cut at him as he hurtled

---

1. *Evidently brighter than most of his kind, who, under most circumstances, will drive flat out whatever the probable consequences.*

past. The whirling blades bit deep, eliciting another howl of anger, before he was on me again in a frenzy of blows, any one of which would have killed me if it connected. Fortunately none did, and by the time I finished parrying them, his hands and forearms were seamed with ichor-oozing wounds.

Cursing the greenskins' preternatural resilience, I drove in again, taking one arm off just above the elbow, and thrust deep into his chest. It was a killing blow, which would have accounted for a human in an instant, but the ork merely staggered, driving the spinning adamantium teeth deeper into his own body as he tried to reach me with his remaining hand by forcing his way up the blade. To no avail: I sliced the sword free, severing his spinal column, and the greenskin collapsed, abruptly losing control of everything below the waist.

A bright flash and the stench of charring meat informed me that Jurgen had taken my order as literally as he usually did, and I turned in time to see the driver's headless body toppling from his seat. The buggy continued to roll forward, its engine grumbling, and as I turned to watch its progress, I caught sight once again of the breakaway mob bearing down on us. It was too close for us to attempt to return to the *Fires of Faith*, even if it were possible to find a way round the pool of burning promethium, the newcomers angling to cut us off from the downed ship and whatever refuge we might find there.

'There's a lot of 'em,' Jurgen said, raising his melta with the air of a man determined to do his best, despite being faced with a task he strongly suspects to be beyond his ability to complete.

I nodded, my mouth dry. If we tried to fight, we'd be cut down in seconds by the sheer weight of numbers, and there was no cover to be seen anywhere on the wind-blasted ice sheet. Then my eye fell again on the slowly-moving vehicle.

'Jurgen,' I said, 'can you still drive one of those?' He'd had plenty of practice with the buggy we'd captured on Perlia, and although no two greenskin vehicles are ever exactly the same, they looked similar enough.

Divining my purpose, he lowered his weapon at once, and began sprinting towards the errant vehicle; it was almost impossible to make out his expression, given the small amount of his face I was able to see, but I was fairly sure it was more cheerful than it had been a moment before. 'Been a while,' he called back over his shoulder, 'but I don't suppose I've lost the knack.'

I was about to follow, when something clamped itself painfully and immobilisingly around my ankle, and I looked down to see my erstwhile opponent glaring up at me with hate-filled eyes, his sole remaining hand clasping my boot, and his fang-filled mouth agape, ready to bite. In no mood to prolong our duel, I slashed down with my chainsword, severing his other arm, and kicked my way free of the suddenly relaxing fingers. I kept going, clambering into the passenger compartment of the abandoned buggy, and grabbed the pintle mount.

'Well?' I asked, and by way of reply my aide gunned the engine, handling the crude controls with every sign of confidence. Remembering the lessons I'd learned on Perlia, I clung as tightly as I could to the solid metal post, just as he smacked the accelerator open to its fullest extreme. The crude vehicle lurched forward, violently enough to loosen the fillings in my teeth, and I almost lost my footing despite my grip; as I'd expected, refinements like springing and shock absorbers had been unknown to the builder of the thing[1]. Nevertheless, despite the discomfort, we were moving away from the pursuing orks, at a rate sufficient to outstrip the ones on foot at least.

Stubber and bolter rounds began to chew up the ice around us, and occasionally pock the thick metal of the bodywork, but I could live with that: having more sense than to try using the crude heavy weapon the buggy was equipped with, which would be all but impossible to hold on aim unaided, and could well break my shoulder with the recoil, I hunkered low, and popped off a few rounds with my laspistol, although under the circumstances I had no great expectation of actually hitting anything.

---

1. *Or disdained as insufficiently orky.*

'What's happening?' Broklaw voxed. 'Some of the greenskins are moving off.'

'They're after us,' I told him, 'but we've commandeered one of their buggies, so we can keep ahead of them. I hope. Federer, detonate...' I'd been intending to add 'as soon as we're clear,' but the sapper captain must have had his thumb poised over the firing button, because no sooner had the words left my mouth than a quartet of fountains erupted right where we'd buried the charges. A low rumble followed, audible even over the racket of our untuned engine, and a filament of cracks began to radiate out across the ice.

'It's working!' Broklaw told me, unnecessarily, a note of concern belatedly entering his voice. 'Get off the ice!'

'That's the idea,' I said, fumbling the amplivisor back up, and trying to make sense of the bouncing image it relayed to me. The ice was breaking up all around the crippled starship, just as I'd hoped, fragmenting into floes and bergs which began to collide with one another, rising and falling on the swell created by the backwash of the explosions.

It took a moment or two for the majority of the orks to realise what was happening, and by the time they did it was far too late. Those on foot redoubled their efforts to gain a foothold on the ramp, turning on one another in their desperation, but much good it did them; most were engulfed by the freezing water in a matter of seconds, the tiny islands of ice they found themselves on tilting and sliding in the turbulence, responding to the frantic movement of those atop them. Many a greenskin plunged into the depths with his hands or jaws locked round the throat of another, while those that managed to gain the solid footing of the ramp were swiftly dispatched by the disciplined fire of the Valhallans, which had never faltered, however desperate the situation.

The vehicles fared no better than those on foot: by the time the drivers realised what was going on, and attempted to flee, the ice was already breaking up under them. Those nearest the site of the explosion sank almost at once, while those furthest away, and with most time to react, were quickly caught and overtaken by the widening network of cracks, which seemed to be spreading with blinding speed.

'How long until we hit the shoreline?' I asked, reluctant to disturb Jurgen's concentration at a time like this, but desperate to know if we were going to make it.

'Almost there,' he assured me, his voice a little attenuated by the comm-beads; I could almost have tapped him on the shoulder from where I was crouched, if I'd been willing to take my life in my hands and try moving about in the bouncing, rattling contraption we rode, but the noise from its engine drowned out any attempt at normal conversation. Then he added 'Seems I was right.'

It was only as the first few flakes of snow drifted into my face, accelerated to stinging velocity by our breakneck progress, that I recalled our earlier conversation about the looming clouds. With an abruptness which took me completely by surprise, the air became filled with whirling white flakes, which began to obscure my view of the debacle behind me. Giving up on the amplivisor, I narrowed my eyes, trying to make out what was going on as best I could unaided. The knot of orks which had broken away from the main mob to come after us was well behind, running in our wake with undiminished vigour, although whether to continue trying to engage us or to save their own skins it was impossible to tell[1]. At any event, it was academic now, the rapidly-expanding network of cracks easily outpacing their running feet.

Then, abruptly, they were gone; the ice lifting for a moment, as though some huge aquatic beast was surfacing beneath it, before subsiding again, to leave nothing but a pool of open water, which swiftly began to scab over with a fresh froth of ice.

'What the hell was that?' I asked involuntarily, wondering if I'd imagined the whole thing, but there was no time to consider the matter further, as a fresh rain of stubber rounds clattered against the armour plate protecting me. I turned my head, squinting through the thickening blizzard, to see a truck loaded with roaring green-skins coming up fast on our right hand side. It was flanked by a

---

1. *Knowing orks, probably both.*

couple of half-tracks, with a buggy bringing up the rear; a moment later this too upended abruptly, disappearing in its turn through the disintegrating ice.

'More orks,' Jurgen informed me, apparently under the impression that the sudden burst of incoming fire had prompted my rhetorical question. How he managed to stay ahead of the spreading pattern of cracks I'll never know; he was an iceworlder, of course, with an innate affinity for environments like this, and no doubt was able to steer us wherever the ice was strongest, instead of making a headlong rush in a straight line and hoping for the best, as most of the greenskins seemed to be doing with a conspicuous lack of success, but that would have been no mean feat under ideal conditions. Aboard a ramshackle, barely controllable ork machine, with thick snow obscuring his surroundings, it was little short of a miracle.

I returned fire again, with the same lack of success as before, achieving nothing beyond provoking another storm of inaccurate rounds from the orkish gunners. With a thrill of horror I noticed that the ice between us was breaking up now, which at least had the positive effect of forcing our paths to diverge.

'Hang on, sir!' Jurgen called, as if any other course of action was remotely feasible, and to my inexpressible relief I felt the first of a series of bone-jarring jolts, which my previous experience of riding in vehicles like this told me could only be the result of us finally travelling over solid ground. I tried to keep our greenskin escort in sight, but the blizzard was descending in earnest now, and a series of jagged ice ridges and snowdrifts intervened, so within seconds they'd vanished completely.

Jurgen cut the engine and we rolled to a halt, my spine finally beginning to unkink itself. My ears were still ringing from the deafening racket, so it took a moment for me to begin to distinguish ambient sounds; when I could, I frowned, in some perplexity. The faint rattle of orkish firearms was drifting towards us on the wind.

'Sounds like they're arguing about whose fault it was they lost us,' Jurgen said, an unmistakable tone of satisfaction in his voice. If there's one thing a Valhallan relishes almost as much as killing greenskins, it's the notion of greenskins killing one another.

'Maybe,' I said. My palms were too numb to tingle, but I was pretty certain that they should have been. Even orks would have taken a little longer than that to find something to squabble about after seeing an entire warband annihilated in front of their eyes. 'But perhaps we should check it out.'

All my instincts were urging me to find somewhere comfortably warm to hole up in until the ice froze hard enough to rejoin our companions, but the prospect of being ambushed by belligerent greenskins was hardly an inducement to relax; I'd long ago learned that knowing precisely where your enemies are is the only way to be sure of avoiding them, and that meant scouting our immediate surroundings as quickly as possible.

WE TOOK A few moments to secure the buggy, in case we needed it again, routines which had become second nature nearly two decades ago on Perlia coming back to me as though it had only been yesterday. I even felt a pang of nostalgia for the scorching desert we'd battled through in the early stages of our long and terrifying journey to safety, but a faceful of snow flung by a sudden gust of wind brought me back rapidly to the present, and we set out in the direction of the gunfire without further ado. The intense cold was beginning to make itself felt in earnest now, and it was all I could do to keep my frozen limbs moving though the knee-high drifts and the almost solid wall of wind-driven flakes which battered away at us.

If it hadn't been for Jurgen I'd have been irretrievably lost almost as soon as I'd set out, but his sense of direction in this desolate terrain seemed as reliable as my own inside a tunnel system, so I plodded in his wake, marvelling at his sure-footedness. He placed his feet carefully, maintaining his balance apparently without effort on the treacherous surface, and I felt certain that had he not felt obliged to keep pace with my own floundering progress, he would have been halfway to the horizon by now. Though visibility was remarkably poor we could still hear sporadic outbreaks of gunfire, and proceeded with all due caution in their general direction, having no desire to walk into an ambush, or the middle of whatever internecine squabble the orks had found to amuse themselves with.

'Good news,' Kasteen voxed me, as I slogged through a particularly deep patch, which Jurgen had negotiated with far less effort. 'We've managed to get through to one of the PDF patrols in the area. They're inbound to assist, and they're relaying our vox messages.'

'Good,' I said, stumbling in something which could have been a rodent burrow, and adding something profane under my breath.

The vox circuit must still have been open, because I was answered by an unmistakably feminine chuckle. 'Any luck with the ork hunt?'

'We can still hear gunfire,' I said, not entirely accurately, as the shooting had ceased while we'd been talking, 'and Jurgen's pretty sure he can locate where it's coming from.'

'Don't take too many chances,' she cautioned. 'You must have used up most of your luck ration by now.' Which was certainly true, and had been for a long time by that point: but despite the odds, here I still am, decades later. I had no idea of that at the time, of course, so I simply shrugged.

'You can count on that,' I agreed, wiping a thin veil of melted slush from my eyebrows, and trying to focus on Jurgen in the distance. He was climbing easily up a jagged outcrop of ice, as though it were no more slippery than a grassy knoll, and I sighed inwardly at the prospect of having to follow him. He'd take an easier route if I told him too, of course, but he knew this landscape far better than I ever would, and if he felt that was the way to avoid contact with the orks, it was fine by me. At which point I turned, attracted by a flicker of movement in the corner of my eye, but when I looked at it directly, all I could see was a whorl of wind-driven snow.

In retrospect, of course, the thought of how close I was to death at that point is a horrifying one, but by luck or the Emperor's grace I must have been hidden equally effectively by the blizzard, and was to remain in blissful ignorance for a little while longer.

'I can see something,' Jurgen said, his voice in my comm-bead hushed and urgent. 'Looks like they've abandoned the vehicles.'

Thanking the Emperor for the thin crust of snow now clinging to my greatcoat, the most effective possible camouflage in this desolate landscape, I scrambled and slithered my way up to join him, expecting some hulking greenskin to come bellowing out of the murk brandishing a combat blade at any moment. But none did, and I hunkered down next to Jurgen, fumbling the amplivisor into place once more.

Fortunately my augmetic fingers were immune to the numbing effects of the cold, enabling me to hold the device in place without blurring the image by shaking too much, and I studied the vista below with some bafflement. My aide had been right, the truck and the two half-tracks had clearly been abandoned, something I knew their drivers would never contemplate under normal circumstances. I studied them carefully, taking particular note of any pitting which marred the armour plate, but all the marks of combat damage I could see were old, a patina of rust masking the telltale brightness of fresh hits.

'If they were shooting at each other, they'd left the vehicles first,' I concluded, which made no sense at all, even for orks, which were hardly the most rational of creatures to begin with.

After a few more minutes of watching nothing happen, and losing the last vestiges of feeling in my feet while we did so, I decided we might as well make a closer examination of the abandoned transports. There was no obvious sign of damage on any of them, or at least no more than you'd expect, although we did find traces of orkish blood in a few places.

'That's odd,' Jurgen remarked, looking at a pool of disquietingly dark ice in one corner of the truck's passenger compartment. 'If one of 'em got shot here, you'd expect to find near misses all over the tailgate.'

I nodded, equally familiar with the vagaries of greenskin marksmanship. 'Must have been taken out hand to hand,' I concluded.

'That's what I thought,' Jurgen said. 'But if he was the one doing the shooting...'

I nodded again, my jaw cramping painfully from the effort of preventing my teeth from chattering. Orks are resilient, as I knew only too well from personal experience, but very few of them can stand up to a burst of heavy-calibre fire at point-blank range. It was hard to envisage an assailant getting close enough to get stuck in; or, for that matter, the ork being charged not to just drop his weapon to meet the challenge head-on.

'It wasn't just him,' I reminded my aide. 'It sounded like most of them. At least to begin with.'

'I suppose they'd have whittled each other down quickly enough,' Jurgen mused, and I glanced around us, at the shifting white blanket of wind-driven snow flowing across the relatively open space. It was beginning to drift against the abandoned vehicles, but as yet had got no higher than the rims of the tyres.

'If they'd done that, the ground would be littered with corpses,' I pointed out. The drifting snow would bury any cadavers in the area quickly enough, but there had hardly been sufficient time to cover a dozen or more without the slightest trace in the handful of minutes it had taken Jurgen and I to get here (even though it had felt a great deal longer to me, you can be sure). And even if it had, I knew Jurgen's feeling for snow was reliable enough for him to have noticed the telltale signs of their presence beneath the surface. 'Can you see any tracks?'

'I'm afraid not, sir,' he told me, shaking his head regretfully. 'Wind's too strong. They'd have been gone in no time.' To emphasise the point, he gestured back the way we'd come, the bootprints we'd made on the way here already erased by the scudding snow.

After a few more moments of desultory, and increasingly uncomfortable, poking about failed to uncover any further traces of the greenskins, or clues to their fate, we began our return to the dubious refuge of the *Fires of Faith*, spurred on, at least in my case, by the thought of fresh tanna in the largest mug imaginable. No doubt if that particular image hadn't been so insistently uppermost in my mind as we trudged across the rapidly refreezing lake, I would have been brooding on the mystery with a considerable sense of disquiet; but as it was, I barely gave the matter another thought until it was far too late.

Since, at this point, Cain's narrative makes one of the chronological jumps charac-
teristic of his account of events when he deems little of interest to have occurred in
the interim, this seems as good a point as any to insert the following extract, which
may make some of what follows a little clearer.

From *Interesting Places and Tedious People: A Wanderer's Waybook,* by
Jerval Sekara, 145 M39.

NUSQUAM FUNDUMENTIBUS IS well named, being both some distance
from the main warp routes, and as desolate as iceworlds generally
tend to be. Nevertheless, it has a good deal to recommend it for
those discriminating wayfarers prepared to look beyond its most
obvious characteristics.

For one thing, it has a surprisingly high population for such a
superficially unattractive world, who, for the most part, are to be
found in the dozen or so cavern cities scattered around the globe.
The largest, and by far the most comfortable, of these is Primadelving. The planetary capital boasts theatres, opera houses and duelling
pits equal, both in the opulence of their decoration and the qual-
ity of the diversions they offer, to those of many a better favoured

world. Its parks and gardens are plentiful, some occupying entire galleries of the vast underground complex, each devoted to the flora, and in a few cases fauna, of a different neighbouring star system.

Despite their troglodytic existence, the citizens of Primadelving enjoy a good deal of light, warmth and space. The first of these is provided by a complex arrangement of shafts and mirrors, through which the ambient light of the sun is directed to every corner of their subterranean habitat, preserving the diurnal round; when night falls on the surface, luminators and waylights are kindled, just as they would be in any open air metropolis, enabling life to continue in a properly civilised fashion. Though the average Nusquan prefers a degree of chill in the air, as one would expect, they are cosmopolitan enough not to assume similar tastes in their off-world visitors, and every establishment catering to them contains heaters which can be adjusted to levels bordering on the tropical, if so desired. It's advisable not to increase the temperature to quite this extent, however, if patronising a hotel on one of the upper levels of the city, as it may well be hollowed out of the ice itself, rather than the bedrock beneath it, with consequences which can be all too readily imagined.

Such apparent profligacy with the energy reserves such harsh worlds normally husband more carefully is less foolhardy than it might seem, since Primadelving, and the string of smaller towns and outhabs which surround it in the province known as the Leeward Barrens, are literally sitting on an inexhaustible supply. An asteroidal impact long before humanity first set foot on the world fractured the planetary crust, creating a ring of fissures, through which magma continues to seep not far below the surface, and into which the Adeptus Mechanicus has been able to tap by great ingenuity and the blessing of the Omnissiah. The towns and cities of the lesser provinces, being less well favoured, are forced to rely on fusion generators and fossil fuel furnaces instead, which, though effective enough, leave them less attractive to the discriminating wanderer; although the far-famed Ice Cathedral of Frigea is worth taking a shuttle flight to visit, if only to see one of the few permanent surface features erected by the Nusquans.

TEN

After all the excitement of our arrival, it was almost a relief to get stuck into the war, which we did with alacrity. Or, to be more accurate, the regiment did: I found it far more congenial to hang around in the relative warmth and comfort of Primadelving, while the Valhallans made the most of what they seemed to regard as the next best thing to a holiday resort[1].

Despite the damage our precipitous arrival had done to the orkish warbands lurking in the Spinal Range, there were still more than enough of them infesting the Barrens to keep everyone happy, and the 597th spent the first couple of months happily reducing their numbers even further. If anything, we seemed to be running out of greenskins to kill remarkably quickly, which should have been good news all round; but instead I was left feeling pensive and uneasy.

'The number of raids on outlying settlements and installations has dropped by nearly fifty per cent in the nine weeks since our

---

1. *Any readers wanting further details of this stage of the campaign are referred to Sulla's memoirs, where it's dealt with at inordinate length, if they feel the relatively minor clarification such reading would offer is really worth the effort.*

arrival,' I said, projecting a series of graphs and graphics on the ornately gilded hololith which dominated the middle of the operations room. Strictly speaking, I needn't have bothered with such an elaborate presentation, and if I'd only been discussing the matter with Kasteen and Broklaw I wouldn't have done, but we'd been either blessed or cursed (I had yet to make my mind up either way) with a planetary governor who took a lively interest in the progress of the campaign, and who insisted on remaining fully informed. Kasteen seemed to have hit it off with her at once, which meant that Her Excellency Milady Clothilde Striebgriebling had an unnerving tendency to wander into strategy meetings with little or no warning, and it would have been discourteous to present things in a manner she'd find difficult to follow. Besides, I'd never been averse to a bit of makework which would keep me away from the fighting, and the bitter cold up on the surface.

'Then you're clearly doing an excellent job,' Clothilde[1] congratulated us, with a particularly warm smile at Kasteen. Blonde and high cheekboned, she carried herself with confidence, but lacked the hauteur which so often went with it, and which generally made the aristocracy such tedious company. She looked as though she was in her early forties, which probably meant she was at least double that, if not heading into her second century, given the fondness of the nobility for the occasional juvenat treatment; but if that were so, at least she'd had the common sense not to arrest her age at a ridiculously low one out of misguided vanity, electing instead to reflect the maturity she'd acquired along with her responsibilities. Her gown was simple, pale grey and white, offset with a minimum of carefully selected jewellery, an understated simplicity which somehow made her the focus of the room, however many other people were crowding it.

Which in this case were rather too many, in my opinion. In addition to Her Excellency, and Kasteen and Broklaw, there was the colonel in

---

1. *Although Cain appears to have been on first name terms with the governor, which implies some degree of social contact, he gives little indication of how often, and under what circumstances, they met one another during his sojourn in Primadelving.*

command of the nascent Nusquan 1st, now up to four companies, her second-in-command, and a scattering of senior people from the PDF, who looked at them both with a mixture of respect and resentment, no doubt wishing they were still junior enough to have some chance of selection for the two companies which were still in the process of formation. Clothilde, of course, was surrounded by a coterie of advisors and hangers-on, who all seemed erroneously convinced that their opinions were of interest to someone other than themselves, and would therefore express them at every conceivable opportunity. The local Arbitrator's office[1] had sent a representative, the only man in the room apart from Broklaw and myself, who made no secret of his complete lack of interest in the entire proceeding; but at least we'd been spared the presence of anyone from the Ecclesiarchy or the Adeptus Mechanicus, whose members tended to a prolixly which would have slowed proceedings to a crawl.

And then there was the commissar attached to the Nusquan 1st, fresh out of the schola progenium if I was any judge, and a damn sight too eager by half for my peace of mind. She leaned forward now, thin-lipped, her dark eyes narrow with disapproval.

'The regiment from this world has performed extremely well too,' she reminded the governor prissily, 'not to mention the PDF.' She turned an appraising eye in the direction of Kasteen, Broklaw and myself. 'Though I'm sure we're all grateful for the assistance of these new arrivals, perhaps we should also remember the sacrifices your own citizens have made.' The Nusquan officers present puffed themselves up appreciatively, exchanging smug little half-nods with one another.

'Sacrifices which, in many cases, were completely unnecessary,' Kasteen responded tartly, provoking a raised eyebrow from the tyro commissar, who was clearly unused to the idea of troopers who talked back.

---

1. *The Adeptus Arbites had a theoretical presence on Nusquam Fundumentibus, overseeing the local law enforcement agencies, but, like many backwater worlds, this amounted to a single Arbitrator and a small administrative staff, who would be more than happy to palm off the responsibility for any civil emergencies they conceivably could to the PDF and any Imperial Guard units which happened to be in the vicinity.*

'Would you care to explain that remark?' the young woman asked coldly, in a manner she no doubt intended to sound intimidating. Knowing Kasteen rather better than she did, I settled back in my excessively padded chair, my concerns about the anomalous intelligence reports put on one side for the moment, in favour of the entertainment to come.

'I wouldn't have thought I'd have to,' Kasteen snapped back. 'Just because the greenskins make head-on attacks at every opportunity, that doesn't mean we should respond in the same way. Your casualty figures are three times ours, and the PDF's are even worse.'

'Only cowards avoid combat,' the young woman said, 'and they have no place in the Imperial Guard.'

I saw Kasteen's hand twitch towards her sidearm, and stepped in quickly before matters got too out of hand. I knew she had more sense than to draw the weapon, let alone use it, but the insult was a grievous one, and her self-control far from infinite. The governor had been kind enough to make one of the ballrooms of her palace available to us as a command centre, and I was certain that whatever alternative arrangements we'd be able to make if we wore out our welcome by an unseemly display of bad temper, particularly if it left bloodstains on the polished wooden floor, would be far less comfortable. So why take chances?

'Commissar Forres,' I said evenly, 'I suggest you withdraw that remark. I've served with Colonel Kasteen for the last ten years, and found her courage and devotion to duty beyond question.' Kasteen and Broklaw exchanged a look which I can only describe as quietly smug.

'Then perhaps your standards are lower than my own,' Forres shot back, her hackles visibly rising.

'I'm sure they are,' I replied, wrongfooting her nicely with an indulgent smile. 'But mine have been tempered with a little more experience of the real galaxy. You may also note that the number of confirmed kills by the 597th is a little more than double that recorded by your own regiment, and three times that of the PDF, which would hardly have been the case if they had indeed been avoiding contact with the enemy.'

'It's called using tactics,' Kasteen added. 'You might find it worth a try.'

Forres tightened her jaw, glaring at her with open dislike. 'I can see your standards have been tempered a great deal,' she told me, in what she no doubt fondly imagined was a withering tone. 'Rather more than I would have expected from a man of your reputation.'

Jurgen's remarkable odour materialised at my shoulder, the collection of data-slates he'd been minding for me cascading to the floor as he leaned in to speak quietly to me. 'If you'll be requiring a second, again, sir,' he said, in a confidential undertone which carried to every corner of the table, 'I'll get on with the arrangements.'

'What's he talking about?' Clothilde asked, with a faint frown of bafflement.

'The last time a commissar from another regiment accused Colonel Kasteen of being unfit for command,' Broklaw told her, clearly speaking more for Forres's benefit than for the governor's, 'Commissar Cain called him out.'

'You fought a duel for your lady's honour?' The governor looked at me in manifest surprise, and then at Kasteen with a hint of a conspiratorial smile. 'How very gallant.'

'Colonel Kasteen and I are merely comrades in arms,' I assured her hastily, not wanting to give the wrong impression, and all too aware of how rapidly gossip can spread. 'Any more personal relationship between us would be highly improper. The challenge was merely a matter of principle.' And because Tomas Beije was an infuriating little Emperor-botherer who'd been trying to get me shot for cowardice at the time, and I'd finally run out of patience with him.

'I'm sure it was,' the governor said insincerely, inclining her head in Kasteen's direction. 'And I'll look forward to hearing all about it the next time Regina is free to take tea.'

Forres looked at me, then at the worn and battered chainsword at my waist, no doubt contrasting it with the almost forge-fresh condition of her own. 'I withdraw the remark,' she said tightly.

'We're here to kill greenskins, not one another.' Which was the first sensible thing I'd heard her say since we'd sat down.

I leaned back lazily in my chair, sure that an appearance of complete unconcern would be the most likely way to get under her skin, and damned if I was going to let such a callow whelp get the last word in. 'Good,' I said. 'But I had no intention of killing you.' Or even challenging her to a duel in the first place, but she didn't need to know that. 'Just knocking a few of the rough edges off.'

Her face flushed, and the colonel of the Nusquan 1st exchanged a brief, startled glance with her second in command, which was followed almost at once by two hastily-suppressed grins. It seemed that young Forres had wasted no time in making a strong impression on her new regiment.

'So what's happening to the orks?' Kasteen asked, bringing us all back to the point with rather more tact than most of the people around the table seemed capable of mustering.

'A good question,' I said, switching my attention smoothly back to the matter at hand. 'If they're not attacking us, they must either be gathering for a really big raid against a strongly defended target somewhere, or they're migrating to another region, hoping the pickings will be easier.'

'And which of those would be your guess, commissar?' the Nusquan colonel asked, clearly addressing the question to me. Which, given that I'd seen more action against the greenskins than anyone else in the room by a considerable margin, should have been obvious. But before I could reply, Forres cut in, no doubt assuming that as the question had come from the commander of the regiment she'd been attached to, she was the one whose advice had been sought.

'They're obviously running away,' she said, as though there couldn't be the slightest doubt in the matter. 'Greenskins never have the stomach for a protracted fight against a well-armed foe.'

'On the contrary,' I interjected, more amused by her precocity than annoyed at the interruption, 'orks live for combat. They will retreat if they take sufficient casualties, but only in order to regroup;

which, given the nature of the species, can often take some time, while they sort out the new pecking order. If they're avoiding our patrols instead of engaging them, and harrying fewer outposts, they're almost certainly gathering somewhere in the Spinal Range, getting ready for a full-scale invasion of the Barrens.'

'Then we must strengthen our defences in readiness,' Clothilde said decisively, which was to save countless lives in the weeks ahead, although hardly in the manner which she envisaged at the time.

I nodded my agreement. 'That would be prudent,' I concurred, 'particularly around the foothills, and the approaches to Primadelving. That's the biggest prize on the planet, and if the greenskins are massing in sufficient numbers, they'll make for it like a ripper scenting blood.'

'They'd never dare attack us here,' Forres scoffed. 'We're far too well defended.'

'That didn't stop them during the invasion,' I said, remembering the desperate defence we'd had to mount against a seemingly unstoppable tide of the creatures, and how hideously close they'd come to overrunning the city before being beaten back at the very last minute.

'There are nothing like the same number of greenskins on the planet as there were then,' Clothilde said, and I realised for the first time that she'd probably been sitting right here while the barbaric creatures besieged her capital[1], keeping an anxious eye on the state of the war.

'For which we must all thank the Emperor,' I agreed.

'I hate to labour the obvious,' Forres put in again, 'but if they are pulling back because the resistance in the Leeward Barrens is too strong, where are they likely to go instead?'

'A very good question,' I said, to her manifest surprise, and called up a detailed image of the mountain range. 'The largest concentrations we were able to detect by orbital reconnaissance before the weather closed in were here, here, and here.' Green icons flared,

---

1. *Or somewhere in the same building, anyway.*

marking their positions, as Jurgen tweaked the controls on the elaborately inlaid control lectern. 'If they've returned to their old encampments, the most likely path of migration over the mountains is through these passes, which would place the western fringes of the Bifrost Marches most at risk. Particularly the townships along the Twilight Crevasse, and the manufactoria in Frozen Gorge.'

'A couple of companies ought to be enough to keep them bottled up in the mountains if they try to break out that way,' Kasteen said speculatively. 'At least until reinforcements arrive. I suggest the Nusquans deploy there, as they know the local terrain far better than we do.'

'We've got no intention of being sidelined,' the Nusquan colonel objected. 'My troopers would consider it a slur on their fighting ability.'

'For Throne's sake,' Kasteen riposted irritably, 'no one's implying anything of the sort. But it probably wouldn't hurt to redeploy them while you've still got a few left.' Which may have been true, but was hardly tactful.

Eventually, a compromise was arrived at, which basically boiled down to palming the job off on the PDF, and the meeting broke up in an atmosphere of simmering acrimony.

'Where do you think the greenskins are hiding themselves?' Kasteen asked afterwards, as we made our way along the corridor towards the elegant dining room which was now doing duty as the officers' mess.

I shrugged, feeling far from reassured, despite the measures we'd put in place to contain them in the event of an attack. In my experience, they were a foe it was easy to underestimate, and invariably fatal to do so. 'I suppose we'll find out before long,' I said, little guessing how horrifying the answer would turn out to be.

ELEVEN

AFTER THAT SOMEWHAT strained introduction, it was hardly surprising that the two regiments had as little to do with one another as possible, sticking strictly to their own areas of operation. The Valhallans went on applying the lessons learned in their centuries-long vendetta against the orks, while the Nusquans, urged on by Forres no doubt, persisted in squandering lives and materiel in head-on attacks at every opportunity. The PDF were, if anything, even more reckless, every trooper determined to win a place in the Guard, and apparently convinced that acts of desperate bravado were the way to attract favourable attention, although what they mostly seemed to attract was copious amounts of incoming fire.

'We'll be running out of both at this rate,' I commented sourly to Kasteen one evening. 'Orks and Nusquans.'

'Would that be so bad?' she joked, surveying the regicide board between us through the cloud of steam rising from her tanna bowl. 'Zyvan could leave us here to garrison the planet for a bit.' Which would undoubtedly be a very appealing prospect to a Valhallan. I could live with it, too, come to that, especially if the governor continued to be as hospitable as she had been, and I could avoid setting foot on the snowfields too often.

'Just in time for the rest of the greenskins to come out of hiding and invade the province,' I riposted, failing to find a move which wouldn't hand her victory on a platter.

Kasteen grinned. 'You're definitely talking me into it,' she said, staring at me expectantly, until I bowed to the inevitable and conceded the game. Accepting my surrender with a courteous nod, she began to set up the board for a rematch.

Before we could make the first move, however, we were interrupted by a familar phlegm-laden cough from the doorway. 'Sorry to disturb you, sir, ma'am,' Jurgen said, 'but Major Broklaw would like you to join him in the command centre. The greenskins are up to something.'

'We'll be right there,' I told him, wondering what could be serious enough to warrant our attention as well as the major's.

I began to understand why he'd felt the need for reinforcements as we approached the command post, however, as several female voices were echoing down the corridor to meet us. The thick drapes and lavish carpeting would have muffled them at a normal conversational level, but most were raised and forceful, carrying easily to our ears. 'Does that sound like the governor to you?' I asked, and Kasteen nodded.

'It does,' she said grimly, as conscious as I was that anything serious enough to get Her Excellency out of bed was hardly likely to be a minor skirmish.

I glanced round the high-ceilinged room as we entered, picking out the centre of the disturbance easily from among the bustle of troopers hurrying to and fro about their business beneath the glittering chandeliers. To my complete lack of surprise it was centred around the hololith, from where Broklaw glanced up as we entered, with a distinct air of relief. Clothilde was talking to him, her usual constellation of hangers-on supplemented by the unexpected presence of a man (so far as I could tell under the hood of his robe, and the usual encrustation of augmetics) in the russet robes of a senior member of the Adeptus Mechanicus[1].

Before I could take in any further details of his appearance my eye skipped past him, caught instead by the unmistakable black greatcoat of a fellow commissar. 'What's Forres doing here?' I wondered aloud.

'Holding Brecca's hand in case she starts showing a bit of common sense, probably,' Kasteen replied, which at least told me the name of the Nusquan colonel, who seemed to be conferring animatedly with Broklaw and the governor, a conversation which involved a great deal of gesticulation in the direction of the hololith. Wondering what could be so fascinating, I tried to catch a glimpse of the display, only to find my view blocked by the milling crowd of courtiers and a selection of Nusquan uniforms; the PDF had turned out in force as well, which, given the hour of the night, could hardly be a good sign either. 'What worries me is what he wants.' She nodded in the direction of the tech-priest

Before I could hazard a guess, Clothilde had swooped across the room like an expensively-coutured eldar pirate vessel, grappling my arm and steering me towards the hololith. 'Thank the Throne you're here, Ciaphas,' she said, oblivious to the black look that Forres aimed in our direction, no doubt inferring something scandalous from her use of my given name.

'It's no more than my duty,' I assured her, which happened to be true, although I'd probably have been there in any case; whatever was going on seemed pretty dire, and if I was going to get out of it with life and reputation intact, the more I knew the better. 'What's going on, exactly?'

'The orks have attacked two installations well behind our front line,' the governor told me, leading me across to the hololith, and pointing dramatically to the three-dimensional map being projected in the air above it. Two contact icons flared, worryingly close to Primadelving, and even more worryingly far from the fuzzy

1. *Being an Imperial institution, the Adeptus Mechanicus remained free of the cultural gender bias which made men in positions of authority on Nusquam Fundumentibus a comparative rarity.*

blobs marking the areas known to be infested. 'How could they have got through our defences without being detected?'

'A very good question,' Forres interjected, directing a withering look at Kasteen from beneath the brim of her cap. 'The Valhallans are supposed to be patrolling that area, are they not?'

'There's nothing supposed about it!' Kasteen snapped. 'Our people are all in place and doing their jobs.' She strode to the control lectern, and punched a few keys, bringing up the locations of our forward outposts. The line seemed firm enough to me, a reassuring bulwark against the massing warbands in the foothills.

'Then someone has clearly been negligent,' Forres shot back. 'Unless you seriously expect us to believe that the greenskins just slipped past your sentries without anyone noticing?' Brecca and a couple of the senior PDF officers laughed humourlessly, underlining the point, and no doubt hoping to curry favour.

'They're not exactly subtle most of the time,' I said, with the quiet authority of experience, 'but orks can and do use guile if it suits them. They have specialists highly skilled in the art of infiltration, and quite capable of getting through even a heavily patrolled area unnoticed.' Not that I believed that in this case, any more than Kasteen clearly did; in my experience any infiltrators in the horde we were facing would be more interested in eliminating one or two of our front line units, opening up a hole for the rest of the warband to pour through. If they'd penetrated deeply enough behind our lines to mount the attacks highlighted on the hololith, they'd almost certainly have been distracted by targets of opportunity on the way in, and forgotten all about the mission objective. Unless there was something here I was missing...

Forres's face was a mask of scepticism, but the governor was nodding in agreement with me. 'They took us by surprise several times during the invasion,' she recalled, 'so it's certainly possible.' The young commissar scowled, but had enough sense not to contradict her.

'No doubt the truth of how they got there will emerge once the shrine is retaken,' the tech-priest put in, which at least explained his interest in the matter; one of the sites must belong to the Adeptus

Mechanicus, who, lacking skitarii of their own in this desolate backwater, would naturally want the Guard to sort out the problem on their behalf.

'Quite so,' I agreed, eager to prevent matters from getting bogged down in fruitless discussion. 'The important thing now is to retake both objectives as soon as possible.' I glanced at the hololith again. 'What exactly are we dealing with here? Major?'

Broklaw cleared his throat, addressing Kasteen and I directly, but pitching his voice so that it carried to the rest of the group around the flickering insubstantial image. 'Around two hours ago,' he said, 'the civic authorities lost contact with the agricultural caverns in South Rising.' He indicated one of the icons, pulsing a deep, ominous red. 'Garbled vox messages were received, leading them to believe that the cavern complex was being overrun with orks, but before anything else could be determined the link went dead.'

'So we've no reliable estimate of numbers,' Kasteen said, in even tones; only Broklaw and I knew her well enough to be aware of how very much that idea disturbed her.

'None at all,' Broklaw confirmed, 'but there were a couple of PDF squads on site, who seem to have been overwhelmed almost at once. And given the size and extent of the cavern system, I reckon we'll need at least a platoon to be sure of retaking it.'

'Get Lustig in here,' Kasteen said, and I nodded my agreement.

'Good choice,' I concurred. Sulla's former platoon sergeant had inherited her old command when she'd been given First Company to look after, and was one of the most reliable and experienced warriors in the 597th. Though he'd accepted the concomitant promotion to lieutenant with some reluctance, he'd proven to be just as capable an officer as he'd been a non-com, and I couldn't think of a safer pair of hands in which to leave the matter.

'Our Second Company are closer,' Brecca pointed out, indicating a small rash of Imperial icons between South Rising and the Lower Barrens[1]. 'If I order Fifth Platoon in right away they should catch the greenskins before they're ready for a counter-attack.'

---

1. *The area around Primadelving.*

In my experience greenskins were always ready for a counter-attack, but I cut off the thought before it could reach my tongue. If the Nusquans were willing to get stuck in, leaving an extra platoon of our troopers standing between me and the bulk of the warband, I had no objections at all. Noticing Kasteen bristle, and almost certainly on the verge of disputing the point, I nodded quickly. 'That makes sense,' I agreed, to the poorly concealed surprise of most of those present.

'Then we'll leave you to it,' Kasteen said, as wrongfooted as anyone else, but willing to follow my lead after all those years of campaigning together. We didn't always see eye to eye, but we trusted each other's judgement, and the matter didn't seem important enough to argue over. 'If your people need backup, we'll be standing by to assist.'

'That won't be necessary,' Forres assured us. 'I'll accompany the first wave myself to ensure everything goes smoothly.'

'I'd have expected nothing else,' I said, accurately, although she seemed to take it as a sign of approval, and nodded at me in reply.

'Then by your leave, milady, we'll return to our regiment and commence operations at once,' Brecca said, inclining her head to Clothilde.

'By all means.' Clothilde gave an airy wave of dismissal, and Brecca, Forres, and about half the PDF staffers swept out at once, surrounded by the aura of their own good opinion of themselves.

'What the frak was all that about?' Broklaw demanded as soon as they were out of earshot. 'Those bluefeet[1] are going to get their heads handed to them.'

'So no change there, then,' I said, earning a swiftly-suppressed smile from each of them. 'But if they insist on sticking their hands in the grinder to see how sharp the blades are, at least they'll blunt them for whoever goes in afterwards to clean up the mess.'

'Good point,' Kasteen said, nodding. She turned to Broklaw. 'Get Lustig briefed, and his people ready to move. If the Nusquans

---

1. *A Valhallan expression for someone naive and inexperienced, too foolish even to take elementary precautions against frostbite.*

manage to handle it on their own, fine, but if they don't, I'm not giving the greenskins the chance to scatter.'

'They'd cause havoc this far behind our lines,' Broklaw agreed. He turned to one of the PDF rankers, a middle-aged woman with greying hair and a prominent facial scar. 'Can your people lay on a few Valkyries for transport?'

They wandered off to discuss the details in a quieter corner, leaving Kasteen and I to talk to Clothilde and the tech-priest, who finally introduced himself as Magos Izembard, one of the senior Adeptus Mechanicus on the planet. Which meant that the second installation the orks had attacked was probably the one we should really be worrying about. I looked at the hololith again, where the contact rune was still glowing an ominous red, then back to the Magos.

'What's so important about this shrine?' I asked, trying to conceal my puzzlement. It didn't seem to be sited anywhere strategic; just smack in the middle of a great deal of snow.

'All the blessings of the Omnissiah are important,' Izembard chided me, through a droning vox-coder uncomfortably reminiscent of the possessed servitor, 'but on a world such as this, the genetoria particularly so.'

'Indeed,' I said, understanding at once. The power stations were probably the most vital installations on the entire planet: without the energy they provided, the habs would freeze, condemning everyone to a slow and uncomfortable death. 'Are we in imminent danger from this one failing?'

Izembard shook his head, to my great relief. 'There is a considerable degree of redundancy built into the system,' he assured me. 'We wouldn't notice much difference if the supply of energy it provides were curtailed.'

'It's still running, then?' Kasteen interjected, in some surprise.

The colonel and I exchanged puzzled glances. Greenskins would hardly have bothered to keep the systems intact; in our experience they were more likely to have smashed anything left functioning after they took the place for the sheer joy of wanton destruction, or begun ripping out anything that looked vaguely useful in the hope of selling it to one of their mechanics[1].

'For the moment,' Izembard said, in a manner which, in someone whose voice was capable of emotional resonance, I would have to describe as evasive. 'But that may not continue for long.'

Although I couldn't have said why, I felt a deep disquiet stirring in me at those words, and it was plain that Kasteen shared my misgivings.

'And why would that be?' Clothilde asked, abruptly reminding me that she was still attached to my arm, apparently for the foreseeable future.

'Because of the nature of the generators,' Izembard explained; if he was at all put out by having attracted the governor's attention, he gave no sign of it, just droning on in the same mechanical monotone. 'Like almost all in the province they use geothermal energy to create power.'

'That was in the briefing slates we got with the assignment,' I said, omitting to add that I hadn't bothered reading any of them. No harm in at least appearing to be on top of the situation.

'I doubt that they will have gone into the details of the process,' Izembard said evenly, about as willing to be deflected from his prepared lecture as a charging Khorne cultist from thoughts of massacre. 'Essentially simple, it requires stringent monitoring to remain safe.'

'What do you mean, "remain safe?"' Kasteen asked, in tones which made it abundantly clear that she liked the sound of the phrase no more than I did.

'Without entering into the subtle complexities of the technotheology,' Izembard droned, showing no sign of irritation at having been so cavalierly interrupted, 'water is pumped down to the lava flow, which is quite close to the surface at that point. The intense heat converts it instantly into steam, which powers the turbines.'

---

1. *Though much of what passes for commerce among the orks falls somewhere between barter and theft, they do have a rudimentary monetary system, based around the use of their own teeth (or preferably someone else's) as a form of currency.*

'Are we getting to the "but" any time soon?' Kasteen asked, not bothering to conceal her impatience. 'Because we need to get the orks contained before they do any more damage, and I'm not sending my people in blind if I can help it.'

'The "but," as you put it, is that unless the flow of incoming water is kept to a constant rate, excess steam can build up, creating extreme pressure in the magma chamber,' Izembard explained, as imperturbable as ever. 'Unless relieved by the proper rituals, it will eventually vent itself uncontrollably.'

'You mean it'll blow up?' I interjected, unable to keep the consternation out of my voice.

'Blow up would be something of a misnomer,' Izembard said, after a moment's cogitation. 'Erupt would be a more accurate description.'

'How big a bang are we talking about?' I demanded, hardly in the mood to split hairs.

'It's hard to be precise, ' Izembard said, 'without accurate figures for the rate of flow, temperature fluctuations, and the porosity of the rock, but somewhere in the low kilotonne range seems the most likely.'

'And how soon?' Kasteen asked, looking as shocked as I felt.

'Again, it's hard to be accurate.' Izembard mused for a moment. 'But I would estimate somewhere in the region of four to five hours.'

'Plenty of time to get in there,' I said. 'Can the process be stopped?' Because if it couldn't, going in to tackle the orks would be a huge waste of time. Better to just cordon off the area, keep them penned in, and mop up any survivors after the bang.

'Indeed it can,' Izembard assured me, with a smile I found deeply disturbing. 'A man of your intellect should find the instructions for stablising the geothermal reaction perfectly easy to follow.' He and Clothilde looked at me expectantly, and, with an all-too-familiar sinking feeling, I realised they were expecting me to take care of the matter myself. 'It would, of course, be preferable to send a tech-priest with the requisite knowledge, but their chances of survival would not be high under the circumstances. Far better to restaff the shrine once the orks are out of the way.'

'Can't fault the logic of that,' I agreed, wishing that I could. Once again, it seemed, my unwanted reputation was about to frogmarch me into harm's way, and there didn't seem to be a thing I could do to avoid it.

TWELVE

WHICH DIDN'T STOP me from trying, of course, but every reason I could come up with to palm the job off on somebody else sounded hollow even to me; and besides, Forres had been seen to be leading her contingent from the front, so I could hardly appear reluctant to do the same. I'd just have to go through with it, and hope the troopers with me would keep the greenskins off my back.

Accordingly, I found myself in the passenger compartment of the antiquated-looking Valkyrie Broklaw's friend in the PDF had found for us, battling our way through another of the blizzards so common on the surface of Nusquam Fundumentibus. The airframe groaned audibly as the seat beneath me lurched, and I checked my chronograph anxiously, hoping that Izembard had erred on the side of caution in his estimate of the time left until the power plant vaporised. Assuming we arrived at all.

'Are we nearly there yet?' Jurgen asked, his face beneath its habitual patina of grime a little paler than usual, and I nodded grimly.

'We are,' I reassured him, gripping the arms of my seat a little more tightly as the Valkyrie hit another crosswind. If the Leeward Barrens were supposed to be the sheltered part of the hemisphere, I shuddered to think what conditions would have been like on the far side of the mountain range. No wonder the Nusquans had so few aircraft.

'Good,' Jurgen said, busying himself with the tenth unnecessary inspection of his melta since we'd taken off. Reassured that the powerpack was fully charged, and the emitters properly aligned, he began mumbling something under his breath that might have been the Litany of Accuracy, but which, knowing him as I did, I strongly suspected to be an inventively unfounded slander of our pilot's abilities and antecedents.

'We have a visual,' the pilot informed me, his voice echoing tinnily in my comm-bead, and I glanced out of the viewport, grateful that the movement took my nose as far away as possible from my aide.

'Take us round,' I said, 'wide and slow.' I wanted a good look at the objective before we set foot in it, in so far as it was possible to get a good look at anything with visibility so drastically obscured by the flurrying snow. 'And be prepared to suppress any sign of resistance.' Given their indifference to physical hardship, it was more than likely that there were orks on the surface, and if there were they were bound to start taking potshots at us. Then, struck by another thought, I added, 'Don't use the Hellstrikes unless you have to. Stick to the multi-laser.'

'Roger that,' the pilot responded, not quite managing to conceal his irritation at being told how to do his job. To be honest, I didn't think the heavy missiles slung under the wings were all that likely to spark off the explosion we were here to prevent, but you never could tell. Even if it didn't, I was pretty sure the Adeptus Mechanicus would take a dim view of their precious shrine being knocked about even more badly than the orks had already managed to do.

But, as we continued to circle, no enemy fire rose to challenge us.

'They must be inside, out of the cold,' Jurgen said, his airsickness apparently forgotten with the prospect of action so close, craning his head for a better look, and coming too close to my nose for comfort.

'We'll warm 'em up,' Magot said from the seat behind me, and snapped a fresh powercell into her lasgun with every sign of relish. 'Right, sarge?'

'Right.' Sergeant Grifen nodded, her clipped tones calmly professional. 'When we hit the deck, secure the ramp. Team one with me and the commissar. Team two follow us inside as soon as the Valkyrie lifts, while we cover you. OK?'

'You've got it,' Magot assured her, visibly pleased to have the first chance to take a crack at the orks. She and Grifen were close, personally as well as professionally, and could be relied on to anticipate one another's moves in the heat of battle without any discussion, an easy rapport which had made them my first choice of squad leaders for this assignment.

As we spiralled in, however, it looked as though Magot was going to be disappointed. There were no traces of occupying orks that we could see, just the communication and distribution towers[1], and the squat bulk of the turbine sanctuary looming out of the flurrying snow like an image on a badly-tuned pict-caster. A snow-choked landing pad drew our attention to its presence with a ring of flashing lights, a small blockhouse on the periphery providing access to the bulk of the complex, which, like almost everything else on Nusquam Fundumentibus, had been hollowed out underground, away from the ferocious conditions on the surface.

'No obvious signs of damage,' I reported, the vox-unit in the cockpit relaying my words to Izembard, listening in from the warmth and comfort of Primadelving, and the other squads in the platoon, who were supposed to be in position around the installation by now to intercept any greenskins making a break for it. (And come to our aid as fast as their transports could carry them if the barbaric xenos turned out to be there in greater numbers than we'd anticipated.) The palms of my hands tingled briefly as I spoke; if the orks had indeed invaded the complex, there should have been clear traces of their presence: scarring on the walls from the stray

---

1. *The power generated was transmitted to centres of habitation and industry by focused beams of energy, since conditions on the surface would make distribution by wire too vulnerable to climactic disruption. Given the relatively low volume of air traffic on Nusquam Fundumentibus this was less of a hazard to navigation than one might expect, although one or two cases of concussion from being struck by barbecued avians were recorded annually by the Nusquan medicae.*

stubber and bolter rounds, which would have been shot off with their usual abandon, at the very least.

'No vehicles parked, either,' Jurgen added. His face contorted for a moment with the effort of ratiocination. 'Could they have come on foot?'

'It's a long way to walk if they did,' I said, although, given the hardiness of the average ork, that didn't necessarily rule out the possibility. 'And if they didn't have vehicles, that would have made it a lot easier to slip through our lines undetected.'

'So we'll only have a small group to worry about,' Grifen said, with the assurance only a Valhallan could bring to a discussion of orkish strategy and tactics. 'Bad news is that if they made it this far undetected, we're up against infiltrators, and good ones at that. We'll need to keep an eye out for ambushes and booby traps every step of the way.'

I nodded in agreement. 'So we go in cautiously, checking for tripwires.' I took another look at my chronograph, and wished I hadn't; the time to Izembard's earliest estimate was far shorter than I would have liked, and if we had to waste time pussyfooting around instead of heading straight for the objective, our margin for error was going to be gobbled up rapidly. There was no help for it, though, so I voxed the pilot again. 'Take us in,' I said, hoping for the best, but bracing myself for the worst as usual.

WE GROUNDED IN the middle of the pad, the rear loading ramp dropping with a clang on the retro-blackened 'crete, and the cramped passenger compartment suddenly became full of flurrying snow. Gritting my teeth against the razor-edged wind which billowed in with it, I took my place behind Grifen, and followed her hurrying form out into the blizzard. Magot's team had fanned out around the ramp, peering over their lasguns at the snow-shrouded hummocks which surrounded the pad, and which for a moment my imagination insisted were greenskins lying in ambush. Then reason reasserted itself, and I realised they were nothing more threatening than fuelling points, their hoses retracted, waiting for shuttles to arrive with supplies and rotating staff.

Which reminded me... 'Weren't we told there were seventeen people here when the orks attacked?' I asked.

'We were,' Grifen confirmed.

'And not one of them got to a vox.'

Which was disturbing, to say the least. However stealthily the orks had approached it, the installation itself was too big to have been taken in a concerted rush, and most of the cogboys working there would have had several minutes to raise the alarm before falling to the barbarous invaders.

'The greenskins must have moved fast, then,' the sergeant said in response to my vocalised musings. 'Or there were more than we thought.'

'There are always more than you think,' Magot said cheerfully, her enthusiasm for a target-rich environment as keen as ever.

Grifen, a quartet of troopers, Jurgen and I double-timed it across the bare rockcrete, our bootsoles splashing in the refreezing slush where the covering of snow had been blown clear or melted by the Valkyrie's landing jets, and made it into the lee of the block-house without attracting any incoming fire. Which wasn't all that surprising, as any orks on the surface would have announced their presence by blazing away at the Valkyrie on its final approach, but by that point in my career I'd found it safest not to take anything for granted.

'The door's locked,' Grifen reported, with an air of surprise.

It was true, as a couple of experimental tugs was enough to confirm, and I felt a shiver of unease displacing the one engendered by the bitter cold. The rune pad was intact, with no sign of the blast damage I'd have expected if the orks had succeeded in forcing an entry.

While I was pondering the implications of that, the shriek of the Valkyrie's engine rose to a pitch which threatened to strip the enamel from my teeth. I glanced back to see it rising from the ground, Magot and her troopers hunkering down against the scorching backwash, their eyes narrowed.

'We'll keep circling,' the pilot voxed, 'in case the greenskins show themselves.'

'Don't go too far,' I cautioned, and the pilot chuckled.

'We'll be there when you need us,' he promised, and disappeared into the murk above our heads, the sound of his engine slowly blending in to the unending wind.

'So how do we open it?' Grifen asked, looking at me with a puzzled expression on her face, no doubt as uneasy as I felt.

'I can get us in,' Jurgen said confidently, raising his melta, and sighting on the lock.

'Wait.' I raised a hand to forestall him. 'They might have rigged charges to it.' Not a problem if the melta vaporised them before they went off, of course, but very bad news if the thermal shock of a near-miss made them detonate. I fumbled in a pocket for my data-slate, with clumsy, cold-numbed fingers. 'The magos gave me a schematic. Maybe the codes are in the map keys.'

Fortunately they were; I tapped in the numerals, and to my relieved surprise the runes on the pad suddenly changed colour from red to green, before being replaced by the words 'access authorised'.

'It worked,' I said, replacing the slate, along with an overly-generous portion of melting slush, in my greatcoat pocket, leaning against the door as I did so. To my surprise it suddenly moved, squealing aside on poorly-greased runners, sending me staggering into the corridor beyond.

'Commissar?' Grifen said, almost as taken aback as I was. I held up a cautioning hand as I recovered my balance. Nothing had blown me up or shot at me, and no axe-wielding greenskin berserkers had come howling out of the darkness, so I might as well look as though I'd taken point on purpose.

'Wait a moment,' I said, fumbling a luminator out of my pocket, and flashing it around. 'Let's just make sure it's safe before anyone else comes in.' I seemed to be in a tunnel, which was no surprise, angling gently downwards, wide enough for a pallet loader to trundle along, or for four people to walk in line abreast.

'Luminator controls are usually next to the door,' Magot put in helpfully, and, directing the beam back towards the rectangle of daylight fringed with curious faces, I was able to pick them out with little difficulty.

'There you go, sir,' Jurgen said, slapping the activation plate with the heel of his hand, and a line of overhead luminators began to flicker on ahead of us, lighting the way down into the heart of the complex.

'Want me to close it again?' Magot asked, as she passed through the portal with the four troopers under her command.

'Better not,' I said. We were as sure as we could be that there were no orks on the surface ready to follow us down, and my paranoia was always a little less acute for knowing we had a fast line of retreat open behind us; especially on this occasion, when, if something went wrong, we'd need to get out before the plant blew up. 'The flyboys'll pick off any greenskins who get near it anyway.'

'Works for me,' Magot agreed, trotting past to take point, with her team at her heels.

The rest of us followed, ever wary, our bootsoles ringing on the rockcrete floor despite our efforts to make as little noise as possible. We kept our eyes open for ambush or booby traps, checking every shadow, but seeing nothing, the absence of any concrete threat somehow even more disquieting than a charge of bellowing orks would have been. At least then we'd have known what we were dealing with. (Although, of course, if I'd really known what we were dealing with, I'd have been halfway back to the Valkyrie by now.)

At length we came to another door blocking the end of the passage; I was about to consult the data-slate again when it slid smoothly aside, revealing a neatly whitewashed wall beyond, embellished with a frieze of miscellaneous machine parts, which no doubt meant something in the iconography of the Adeptus Mechanicus. We instantly raised our weapons[1], seeking a target, but no one came through, and after a moment we relaxed again,

---

1. *Cain presumably having drawn his laspistol at some point, although he doesn't bother to mention the fact.*

seeing the unmistakable hand of the Omnissiah at work. Clearly the machine-spirits of the power plant recognised us as friends, and were working to aid us, a realisation which heartened us all.

'Clear left,' Trooper Vorhees reported, levelling his lasgun down the corridor, while Drere, his inseparable companion, aimed in the opposite direction, the faint *click! hiss!* of her augmetic lungs echoing eerily in the stillness.

'Clear right,' Drere echoed a heartbeat later, and the rest of us followed, the map on the screen in my hand leading us ever deeper into the heart of the complex.

'Still no sign of any damage,' Grifen murmured, clearly as perturbed by that as I was.

'Or of any of the cogboys,' I agreed.

'Then the greenskins must have killed 'em all,' Magot said, as though that were a foregone conclusion.

'Unless they took the survivors prisoner, so they could keep the plant operating,' I suggested. Orks commonly enslaved humans who seemed to possess skills they could use, although the unfortunate captives seldom lasted long.

'Why would they do that?' Grifen asked, and I shrugged, unable to find an answer.

'Found something,' Vorhees reported from further up the tunnel, holding up a hand to check our progress, and glancing down at the floor a few metres ahead of where he stood. 'Looks like blood.'

'A lot of it,' Drere agreed, trotting up to join him.

They were right, a large splash of it staining the grey rockcrete floor a rusty brown, around a still tacky centre, which shone with a sickly crimson sheen in the light of the overhead luminators. I scanned the walls, seeing no sign of any pockmarks or cratering; if someone had been shot here, it had been with a precision and accuracy completely foreign to the greenskins.

'Must have taken them down hand to hand,' Grifen said, having come to the same conclusion.

'Then where's the body?' I asked rhetorically. Orks would have looted the corpse of their victim and left it where it fell, unless they were hungry, and in that case we'd have found a lot more mess than just a pool of blood.

'Dragged it away?' Jurgen suggested, and I shook my head.

'Then there'd be a trail of blood on the floor,' I pointed out. The stain was clear-edged, unelongated.

'Carried it, then,' my aide said, unperturbed.

That was possible, I supposed; an ork would certainly be strong enough to carry a cadaver, but what would be the point? 'That seems remarkably tidy for an ork,' I said, but Jurgen just nodded, his constitutional immunity to sarcasm serving him as well as it always did.

'There are scratches on the floor here,' Drere reported, another handful of metres down the tunnel. The hairs on the back of my neck began to prickle, for reasons I couldn't quite articulate, as I squatted down to examine them. 'Some sort of cart, you reckon?'

'Could be,' I said, my old underhiver's survival skills letting me read the faint pattern of blemishes on the floor as easily as a sheet of print. Innumerable trolleys or carts had been wheeled along the corridor, as you'd have expected in a complex like this. But something about the marks Drere had found looked familiar, and different from the rest. Faint parallel scratches, as though something large, with clawed feet, had strolled through here not too long ago.

Vorhees spread his fingers, spanning the inner and outer scratches, finding his splayed hand fit comfortably between them. He flexed his fingers thoughtfully, and glanced at Drere, the two of them evidently coming to the same conclusion.

'Do they have ambulls on Nusquam Fundumentibus?' he asked, which seemed like a perfectly reasonable question to me. The last time we'd been on an iceworld we'd come across a whole colony of the creatures, which definitely shouldn't have been there[1], and if it happened once it could probably happen again. Drere and Vorhees looked at one another, no doubt remembering that it was an

---

1. *The creatures apparently having arrived on Simia Orichalcae through the necron warp portal, from some other world infested by both.*

ambull which had torn half her chest away on Simia Orichalcae, and that she'd been damn lucky to get back to the mining hab's sanitorium fast enough to get the damaged organs replaced.

'Could be an ambull track,' I agreed. It hardly seemed likely, but if they wanted to look out for ambulls as well as orks that was fine by me.

As we moved on, I took a final glance at the faint parallel scratches, and found Jurgen doing the same, his brow furrowed. 'Reminds me of something,' he said, coughing raucously, and marking the spot with a generous deposit of mucus, 'but I can't think what.'

'No, me neither,' I said, taking a firmer hold of my chainsword and laspistol. In the years we'd served together we'd faced so much that it was hardly surprising some of the details had got blurred along the way[1]. Nevertheless, we both kept our weapons readily to hand, and our progress, when it resumed, was even more cautious than it had been.

WE WERE TO find about a dozen more of the disquieting blood-stains before we reached the heart of the complex, but no other signs of the tech-priests who were supposed to be manning the place. In a couple of instances the spilled blood had been adulterated by lubricants and hydraulic fluid, indicating that this was where some of the larger servitors had met the same fate as their masters; which sparked another echo of memory. Since it stubbornly refused to come into focus, however, I merely shrugged and let it go, knowing from experience that the more I tried to force it, the more elusive the thought would become.

From time to time we came across more of the scratches in the floor, too, and ever since Vorhees had raised the matter, I'd found myself wondering if we ought to be looking for some kind of beast on the loose as well as the orks. Perhaps, in retrospect, this was why I didn't recognise the true nature of the threat we were facing

---

1. *In spite of which, Cain's powers of recall seem remarkably acute in his memoirs; either stimulated by the recollection of events in relative tranquillity, or being judiciously supplemented by a fair amount of artistic licence.*

until it was almost too late; my mind running along predetermined pathways, instead of remaining open to the evidence around me.

'This must be it,' I said at last, pausing outside a door which, unlike the others we'd passed through, refused to open at our approach. The temperature had risen steadily as we descended, so that by now I felt quite comfortable, and my Valhallan companions had opened their greatcoats to reveal the body armour beneath them, clearly wishing we were back on the surface where it was a nice comfortable thirty below.

'Looks like it,' Grifen agreed, scowling at another runeplated locking mechanism.

'Hang on,' I said, squinting at the data-slate again. But before I could find the codes I needed, Jurgen simply pushed the door open with his grubby fingertips, and poked the barrel of his melta through in search of a target.

'It's unlocked,' he said.

'Well it shouldn't be,' I said, recalling the instructions Izembard had given me. 'The power core and the control chapel are the most sanctified areas of the entire shrine. Access is supposed to be restricted to the most devout acolytes.'

The squad of troopers around me began to look at one another uneasily. It was one thing to be making a recon sweep through the main body of the complex, especially with the prospect of an ork or two to bag, but quite another to be trespassing on its most hallowed ground.

'And us,' I added cheerfully, raising a few nervous smiles in response.

'Then let's get in there, and get on with it,' Magot said, looking a great deal happier.

'Quite,' I said, with another glance at my chronograph. We had only a handful of minutes remaining before the short end of Izembard's estimate expired, and I wanted to be in the control chapel well before it did. I have to confess to finding our slow progress to this point irksome in the extreme, but, under the circumstances, proceeding with caution had been the only sensible option; and now was hardly the time to abandon it. The enemy we'd failed to contact on the way in would almost certainly be in or around our objective: I could think of no other reason for them not to have engaged us in combat before now.

We edged our way warily inside, me hanging back as much as I decently could, and looked around, orientating ourselves. I'd visited the inner sanctums of Mechanicus shrines on several occasions before now, almost invariably with equal reluctance, so I had some idea of what to expect; the burnished metal surfaces of control lecterns, reflecting the lights and dials which were supposed to tell their operators Emperor alone knew what, were all in place, but instead of the gleaming steel or brass walls embossed with the sacred cogwheel I'd expected, the chamber was bounded with naked rock, which had been hewn into a high-ceilinged cavern. (And into which the devotional icons of the tech-priests had been duly chiselled.)

Magot grimaced. 'Who let that one rip?' she asked, with a pointed glance in Jurgen's direction.

'The inner sanctum connects directly with the volcanic vents,' I told her.

Jurgen sniffed the sulphur-reeking air. 'Smells like Hell's Edge,' he said, and I nodded, reminded all too strongly of the settlement beside the magma lake on Periremunda, and the unpleasant surprise which had awaited us there.

'Secure the section,' Grifen ordered, and the troopers fanned out, one team to each of the tunnel mouths leading off from opposite sides of the chamber.

'Good idea,' I agreed, shoving the door closed behind us. There was a lot of the complex we hadn't covered on our way in, and the last thing we needed was to be taken by surprise by an ork or two sneaking up on us while we were engrossed in carrying out Izembard's instructions. The thin slab of metal wouldn't delay them for more than a couple of seconds, but the noise they made forcing it open would be all the warning we needed. 'Jurgen, keep the exit covered.'

'Very good, sir,' he replied, dragging a chair from behind the nearest of the lecterns. He subsided onto it, his melta aimed squarely at the door, resting comfortably on top of the abandoned control station.

I handed him the data-slate, after paging down to the directions the tech-priest had given me. 'I'll need both hands for this,' I told him, looking around at the instrumentation surrounding us. There were a lot of flashing lights and flickering dials, rather too many of them red or with the needles bouncing back and forth against their stops for my liking. 'Where do I start?'

'Three lecterns on a dais, it says here,' Jurgen told me, his forehead furrowing. 'What's a dais?'

'This is.' I mounted the circular platform, around the circumference of which three lecterns were equidistantly spaced, so that their operators would be facing outwards across the room. They'd all remained at their posts with single-minded dedication or been taken by surprise at exactly the same time, judging by the amount of blood which had been spilled here, and I moved gingerly, the soles of my boots adhering unpleasantly to the still tacky floor.

'The one facing the door should have a dial on it,' my aide continued, 'saying "Flow Chamber Pressure". Is the needle anywhere near the red bit?'

I looked down at the dial in question. 'If it was any deeper into it,' I said, 'it would be about to go round again.' The indicator was hard against the stop at the limit of its display, and I didn't need a tech-priest to tell me that things were looking grim. 'Which buttons do I press?'

'None of 'em,' Jurgen said. 'It says here you need the emergency pressure vent, on the pumps themselves. Down the left-hand corridor.'

'Left as I'm facing, or as we came in?' I asked, already on the move.

'As you're facing,' Jurgen said, and I abruptly reversed direction, heading for the opposite tunnel mouth. He rose to his feet as I sprinted past. 'Should I come too?' he asked, and I shook my head.

'Keep covering our backs,' I told him, glancing back as I did so.

'If this doesn't work we'll have to get out of here fast, and we won't want any greenskins getting in the way.' He was already out of sight by the time I finished, but our comm-beads relayed the rest of my words comfortably enough.

Despite the urgency of my errand, I found my pace slowing as I entered the chamber, unable to prevent myself from glancing around in awestruck astonishment. I was in a huge natural cavern, the walls fissured and cracked, many of them leaking foul-smelling vapours; no doubt the removal of a sense of smell was high on the list of augmetic enhancements for the tech-priests who worked here. In the centre of it the pumps rose, three or four times the height of a man, pipes a metre or more in diameter driven deep into the rock beneath my feet, or cutting horizontally across the cavern to disappear into the wall. Several of them pointed in the direction of the turbine hall we'd seen on our way in, while others presumably carried the water from wherever it was collected, ready to be forced down into the bowels of the planet.

'Commissar!' Sergeant Grifen waved to me from beneath the shadow of the nearest of the pumps. 'I think you should see this.'

'So long as it's quick,' I said, acutely aware of every tick of the clock. But Grifen was a veteran, and as cognisant of the danger as I was; she wouldn't divert my attention at so critical a juncture without excellent reason.

'We've found the bodies,' she said, sounding oddly uncertain. 'Bits of them, anyway. I think.'

As I rounded the huge metal tree trunk, I could see the reason for her reticence. A tangle of blood-slick metal and glass was piled up against the cavern wall, glittering eerily in the light from the overhead luminators.

'Janni recognised them,' Vorhees said, with a glance at Drere, who nodded.

'Augmetics. Believe me, I'd know.' Her mechanical lungs punctuated her words with an even *hiss! click!* 'Looks like someone ripped them clean out of the cogboys.'

'Or spat them out,' I said, a peculiar crawling sensation moving up and down my spine as the memories of Hell's Edge grew more vivid. The very notion was ridiculous, but I'd seen something almost identical then, and once planted the thought refused to go away. 'Keep away from the fissures!'

'Commissar?' Grifen looked at me quizzically, no doubt wondering if I'd taken leave of my senses.

'The fissures!' I gestured to the cracks in the surface of the rock. The mound of grisly trophies was right beneath the largest, which certainly looked big enough to take a human cadaver; especially if it had been filleted of its non-organic components first.

'Have you pulled the lever yet, sir?' Jurgen voxed.

'Just about to.' Recalled to the matter of the moment I turned back to the bulkiest of the metal structures. As Izembard had assured me, a large control lectern was set into it, almost completely obscured by the number of prayer slips and wax seals adhering to its surface.

Before I had taken more than a couple of strides, however, my attention was arrested by a faint echo of movement, almost inaudible over the steady rumbling of the mechanisms around us and the chugging of the pumps. I froze, listening intently, half convinced I'd imagined it.

Then I heard it again, an unmistakable scuttling. 'Pull back!' I called, gesticulating wildly. 'Get away from the walls!'

Clearly still puzzled, Grifen and her troopers scurried to comply; she, Vorhees and Drere no doubt remembering our expedition through the ambull tunnels beneath Simia Orichalcae all too vividly. One of the troopers with them, a recent replacement we'd picked up on Coronus, was a little slower, aiming his lasgun down the dark cleft in the rock beside him from what he undoubtedly imagined was a safe distance.

'I can hear some...' he began, before his voice choked off in a panic-stricken scream, as something dark and fast with too many limbs erupted from the fissure. He managed to get off about three shots before going down, torn to shreds in a flurry of blows from the creature's razor-edged talons.

'What's going on?' Jurgen voxed urgently, alerted by the noise. 'Are the orks attacking?'

'There never were any orks!' I shouted, as the four-armed monstrosity rose from the corpse of the eviscerated trooper, absently licking his blood from its face with a tongue that seemed far too long, to stare speculatively in our direction. 'The place is swarming with tyranids!'

THIRTEEN

'Tyranids?' Jurgen echoed, taking the news as phlegmatically as he always did. 'No one told us about them.'

The scuttling noise was all around us now, and even as the 'gaunt launched itself at me with its powerful hind legs, more of the creatures began to emerge from the rents in the rocks. 'Pull back!' I yelled, clipping it with a round from my laspistol, but the hideous creature barely slowed, its slavering maw gaping as it bounded in my direction with single-minded ferocity.

The troopers opened up with their lasguns, dropping several of the newcomers, but the swarm had been well and truly roused by now, and for every one that fell another came skittering out of the shadows with murderous intent, while reinforcements continued to pour through the clefts in the walls as though the rock itself was sweating tyranids. I parried the first slash of the oncoming 'gaunt's scything claws with my chainsword, biting deep into its chitin-armoured thorax, and shot it through the brain as it opened its mouth to either scream defiance or attempt to bite my face off.[1]

'Can you still get to the lever?' Jurgen asked, ever mindful of our

---

1. *Or possibly both.*

mission. I looked again at the largest pump, with its prominent control lectern; a dozen 'gaunts were bounding across the intervening space, and more movement flickered in the shadows at the base of the great metal column, almost as if they were guarding it[1].

'Not a chance,' I told him, as a volley of lasgun fire took out the three leading 'nids, just as they began angling to cut us off from the tunnel we'd entered by. I'd be torn to pieces before I even got halfway to the controls, let alone begun the intricate rituals required to override whatever instructions the machine-spirits within them currently had. I put a las-bolt through the thorax of another 'gaunt, which had hurled itself at me in the wake of the first, and turned back to the tunnel.

'Team two coming to assist,' Magot voxed, to my heartfelt relief.

'Stay in the control chapel and be ready to cover us,' Grifen responded. 'We're coming in with a swarm on our arses.'

'And get that Valkyrie back on the ground,' I voxed the pilot. If we managed to make it as far as the surface, I didn't want to go up with the power plant just because our ride was late.

'We'll be waiting,' the pilot promised, 'with the ramp down.'

Then my attention was completely taken up with the urgent matter of survival. The creatures clustered around the pumps had ranged weapon symbiotes fused to their forelimbs, the sinister hiss of their discharges almost lost in the general cacophony.

'Take out the gunners!' I bellowed. The close combat bioforms were only a danger if they got within reach of us, but the living ammunition of the fleshborers would devour us alive from the inside out if their bearers managed to get off a lucky shot. Fortunately for us, the superior range of the troopers' lasguns kept the 'nid gunners too far distant for accurate shooting, the deadly hail of tiny beetles they spat in our direction either falling short or going wide. But still they came, closing the distance every time we were forced to switch our aim to pick off a charging hormagaunt.

---

1. *Or possibly the reverse. Termagants, which by Cain's account made up a high proportion of the swarm, will instinctively retreat to cover in the absence of any overriding directive from the hive mind.*

'We can't hold 'em off for long,' Vorhees commented, firing short bursts in an attempt to conserve ammunition, but which we both knew would drain the powerpack frighteningly fast in any case.

'Then don't try!' I urged, already running for the tunnel mouth. 'We need to stay ahead of them!' Lacking the powerful hind legs of their compatriots, which were bred by the hive mind to get into close combat as fast as possible, the termagants should be easy enough to outpace; or at least keep from getting into fleshborer range too quickly.

I squeezed off a couple of shots at an outflanking hormagaunt, which was using its superior speed to try and cut us off from the tunnel we'd entered by, but the las-bolts ricocheted harmlessly from its exoskeleton; already committed to the attack, I ducked under a strike from its scything claws, felt the talon of one of its middle limbs catch for a moment in the fabric of my greatcoat, and rammed the tip of my chainsword up under its chin, tearing through throat and skull alike as I struggled to free the blade. A gout of vile-smelling ichor soaked my sleeve, and then I was clear, hurdling the carcass of another of the vile creatures, which had just been brought down by the lasgun fire of one of my companions.

'Grenades!' Grifen called, as we broke through the tightening noose to gain the dubious sanctuary of the tunnel.

'Good plan,' I agreed, turning to loose a couple of pistol shots at whatever was directly behind us, and finding that the entire width of the passageway was choked with bounding predators. I hit one in the leg, purely by luck, and it stumbled, impeding those behind it; which reacted by removing the obstruction in the most straightforward manner possible, slashing it to pieces in an instant. The only positive thing I could see in our situation was that at least the 'gaunts about to tear us apart were blocking the fire of their weaker broodmates with the ranged weapons.

Grifen yanked a frag grenade out from beneath her coat, and lobbed it over her shoulder without breaking stride[1]. The troopers did the same, and, although it was probably my imagination, I

---

1. *Other than to prime it, presumably.*

could swear I heard the clatter of the canisters hitting the rockcrete over the scuttling and hissing of the brood behind us. Then the onrushing tide of chitinous death rolled over them.

Just as I'd begun to convince myself that the fuses had been too long, and my shoulder-blades tensed in anticipation of a bone-shattering blow from behind, a quartet of overlapping explosions shook the corridor, jarring the floor beneath my feet. Unable to resist glancing back, I saw that the pursuing swarm had all but vanished, the walls and ceiling decorated with shreds of flesh and gouts of ichor; but before I had time to take in any more, the second wave surged into the passageway, flowing towards us with undiminished purpose. Once again the fleshborers hissed, and a clump of the deadly beetles they used as ammunition hit the floor a metre from where I was standing. The tiny creatures scurried around frantically for a second or two, in search of a host to burrow into, then mercifully expired.

'Termagants incoming!' I voxed, then turned and sprinted for the relative sanctuary of the control chapel.

'We're ready for 'em,' Magot assured me, to my inexpressible relief; then we were clear of the tunnel, flinging ourselves aside to allow our companions a clear shot.

The results were devastating. Magot had flicked her lasgun to full auto, and the troopers under her command had either followed her lead or been instructed to do so: a hail of fire scoured the tunnel, supplemented by a blast or two from Jurgen's melta for good measure. When the noise ceased, the passageway resembled nothing so much as a butcher's slab, the deadly organisms which had pursued us so relentlessly ripped apart by the merciless barrage as effectively as they'd threatened to do to us.

'That's seen 'em off,' Magot said, with a fair dose of optimism, considering she'd seen for herself just how implacable the tyranids could be during their abortive invasion of Periremunda.

'I wouldn't count on it,' I cautioned, and, sure enough, the unmistakable skittering sound of claws on rock were already forcing their way through the dying echoes of Magot's massacre. 'They'll come after us again as soon as they realise we're not defending the choke point.'

'Then let's not hang around till they work it out,' Grifen said, a sentiment I heartily agreed with.

'Why didn't they attack us as soon as we arrived?' Jurgen asked, falling into place at my shoulder, his melta reassuringly ready for use. 'They'd have taken us completely by surprise.'

'I don't think they realised we were here,' I said. 'They'd already killed everyone in the shrine.' That much was a given; a swarm the size of the one we'd just encountered would have scoured the place before anyone had time to react.

Jurgen nodded. 'So they were sleeping it off when we arrived,' he said, his brow furrowed with the effort of joining the dots.

'Essentially,' I agreed, although some of the details of what we'd found continued to nag at me. It made sense that the swarm would make for the deepest part of the complex to digest its meal, the instinctive behaviour of its constituent organisms would ensure that, but how had so many of the creatures got inside in the first place? The main entrance had definitely been sealed when we arrived.

'At least we won't have to worry about tripping any greenskin booby traps on the way out,' Grifen commented, as we double-timed our way back towards the pad.

'That's something,' I agreed, straining my ears for the scrabbling of talons against the rockcrete floor behind us. I was just beginning to hope, against all reason and experience of the hideous creatures, that we'd succeeded in intimidating them so thoroughly that they'd given up the pursuit, when, faintly at first, almost drowned by the clattering of our bootsoles, I heard it.

'What is it?' Grifen asked, seeing me tilt my head in an attempt to isolate the elusive echo.

'They're coming,' I said. 'Behind us.'

No sooner were the words out of my mouth than an agonised scream echoed down the corridor. Our point woman was down, a massive hole chewed through her torso by a fleshborer shot. As she flailed on the grubby rockcrete, innumerable tiny parasites continued to writhe inside the hideous wound, enlarging it, and burrowing ever deeper in an attempt to feed on the luckless squaddie's vital organs.

'And ahead,' Magot said, pausing only to grant the Emperor's peace[1] to her unfortunate subordinate, who was clearly beyond all hope of medical aid.

'How did they get ahead of us?' I asked, opening fire on the small knot of 'gaunts which had appeared round a bend in the corridor. Then my own question was answered by the sight of an air vent further down the corridor, its metal mesh cover ripped and shredded by powerful claws. If they'd got into the utility conduits they could be anywhere.

A storm of lasgun fire followed my lead, reaping bloody revenge for our loss. The leading tyranid lost its weapon and a large chunk of its carapace to Jurgen's melta, but the survivors regrouped almost at once, bolstered by another group of new arrivals. I glanced back down the corridor behind us, seeing a flicker of movement in the distance, which could only be the main bulk of the swarm in hot pursuit.

'We're blocked in,' I told Grifen, hoping I didn't sound as panicky as I felt. 'We need another way out.'

Spotting a door in the wall a couple of metres away I flung it open, finding a small workshop behind it, which, judging by the scattering of tools, lubricants and lumps of flesh floating in jars of some foul-smelling liquid, had probably been used for the repair and maintenance of servitors.

As refuges went, it wasn't much, but everyone piled in after me gratefully enough, and began to barricade the door. A final glance before we slammed it was enough to underline the seriousness of our predicament: the 'nids were closing in for the kill from both directions, blocking the corridor ahead and behind. Attempting to force our way through either group would be suicidal. Jurgen glanced up from the data-slate I'd given him to hold what felt like a

---

1. *An Imperial Guard euphemism for the mercy killing of critically injured comrades.*

lifetime ago. 'The nearest parallel corridor's that way, sir.' He indicated the direction with a grubby thumb. 'Through eight metres of rock.'

'Never an ambull around when you need one,' Drere remarked, the feeble jest raising flickering smiles from those of us who'd encountered the creatures on Simia Orichalcae, and remembered their remarkable tunnelling ability.

'I'd settle for a flamer or two,' Magot said.

'Well, we've got what we've got,' I replied, looking around the workshop for anything which looked potentially combustible, explosive, or at least sharp, and finding little of any immediate apparent value. Most of the tools looked as though they'd be equally at home in a medicae facility, and I was loath to try activating any of the pieces of equipment racked around the walls; the machine-spirits residing in them might wake up as cranky as I generally did, and there was no telling what they were supposed to do anyway. 'Let's get that bench wedged against the door.'

We manhandled it into position, finding it reassuringly heavy, and not before time; almost as soon as we got it into position, the scrabbling of talons against the thin sheet of metal started echoing round the room. Genestealers would have torn through it like Jurgen with a sandwich wrapping, but, fortunately for us, the scything claws of the 'gaunts were meant for close combat and little else.

'That won't hold them for long,' Grifen said, ripping the power cable from one of the strange devices and jamming the bare ends against the metal door. There was a fizzle of sparks, an eerie ululation from the corridor, then the lights went out. After a moment's silence the scrabbling began again, its enthusiasm undiminished.

'Worth a try,' I said encouragingly, as everyone except Jurgen and I snapped on their luminators and began attaching their bayonets to the barrels of their lasguns. A moment later the lights flickered back on, a little dimmer than before, the presiding machine-spirit of the complex apparently continuing to take an interest in our welfare after all. 'How close are we to the surface?'

'Pretty close,' Jurgen told me, after a moment's hesitation while he worked it out. He pointed at the ceiling. 'I think we must be under one of the shuttle refuelling points.'

'Let me see that,' I said, taking the slate. If I was reading it correctly, the pump control chamber was only a ceiling's thickness above our heads. Using the melta so close to a fuel tank the size of a swimming pool would be an insane risk, but if we stayed where we were we'd be vaporised anyway; the only moot question was whether we'd end up as tyranid indigestion first. I pointed upwards at the whitewashed ceiling. 'If you wouldn't mind?'

'Of course not, sir,' my aide replied, aiming the melta upwards and pulling the trigger, while the rest of our party took cover beneath the workbenches. The actinic glare I'd become so familiar with since he'd acquired his favourite toy punched through my tightly closed eyelids, the backwash of heat singed the hair in my nostrils, and charred debris clattered and pinged off the gleaming metal surfaces above our heads. 'Almost there.' He fired again, then coughed, in evident satisfaction. 'That ought to do it.'

'Indeed it should,' I agreed, looking up at the hole above our heads. The edges were still almost molten, but cooling fast, hastened by a blast of frigid air which could only be coming from the surface. The Valhallans looked at one another, visibly cheered by the chill, then turned to the door as something large and heavy rammed into it from the other side. The workbench quivered. 'Time we were leaving, I think.'

Despite the cooling effect of the breeze from the surface, the edges of the hole were almost too hot to touch, but that was the least of my worries. If we didn't move fast, we were going to get a great deal hotter before long, and no one hesitated before jumping off from the much-abused benches, trusting to our gloves and heavy greatcoats to keep us from burning as we swarmed up through the hole.

We found ourselves in a high-ceilinged chamber, most of which was taken up with a peculiar assemblage of piping, connected to a hose the thickness of my arm, which disappeared through a hole in the opposite wall. The whole contraption was mounted on a hydraulic platform, clearly intended to raise it to the level of the surface.

After a moment I identified a faint whining sound as the engines of our Valkyrie, muffled by the layer of rockcrete still sealing us in, and exhaled with relief; the pilot, it seemed, had been as good as his word.

'Target the main entrance,' I voxed him, nightmare visions of being outflanked by the 'nids again rising up to plague me, 'and take out anything that moves.'

'Sir?' The pilot sounded confused, and I couldn't say I blamed him. 'Won't that put you and your squad in the firing line?'

'We're leaving another way,' I told him, clambering onto the platform. A small control lectern stood near the welded metal steps, and I studied the controls as Jurgen and the others scrambled up behind me, crowding the narrow operating station far more than its builders had ever envisaged. Its most prominent feature was a large red button, so I prodded it hopefully.

For a moment nothing seemed to happen, then, with a loud *clunk!*, a narrow band of daylight appeared above our heads, followed almost at once by a pattering of disturbed snow cover falling through the gap. As it continued to widen, the wind reached in to claw through my coat, and even a few of the Valhallans refastened theirs.

'We're rising!' Drere shouted as the platform beneath our feet shuddered into motion and began cranking itself up towards the surface.

'And not before time,' I added, spotting a flicker of movement through the still-steaming hole in the floor. The 'nids had finally succeeded in forcing the door of the workshop; a moment later the first termagant scrambled up through it, raising its fleshborer as it came. Before it could fire, a volley of lasgun rounds tore it to pieces, but within seconds the riddled corpse had been shoved aside by another, and another after that as the newcomer met the same fate.

Before the third could fire, the rising platform reached the surface, sealing our pursuers into a rockcrete tomb their weapons could never penetrate.

A flurry of snowflakes battered into my face, driven with even more force than usual by the backwash from the engines of the Valkyrie hovering just above the pad. I sprinted for its boarding ramp, my eyes narrowed against the blizzard, which seemed to be blowing with undiminished enthusiasm.

'I've got movement by the bunker,' the pilot voxed, and I turned to look, a sudden flare of panic urging me to even greater speed. A swarm of close combat organisms was boiling from the entrance, their distinctive long, curved claws marking them out as hormagaunts, and I cursed my earlier decision to leave it open for a quick evacuation; although, to be fair, I could hardly have foreseen the situation we now found ourselves in. I cracked off a couple of laspistol shots, although if I actually hit any of the fast-moving targets through the obscuring snow at such extreme range I have no idea, trying to gauge if they'd reach the hovering Valkyrie before we did. So far as I could tell, it looked like being a dead heat: which would still be bad news for us, as we'd never be able to scramble aboard if we were too busy fighting for our lives.

Then the pilot vectored his jets, scooting straight backwards, the open ramp raising a constellation of sparks as it skittered towards us across the pad.

'In!' I yelled, leaping aboard just before the thick metal plate ploughed through my ankles. The forward-mounted multi-laser triggered, scything through the onrushing 'nids with a sound like the sky being ripped in two, and I found myself gaping in astonishment at the pilot's audacity. 'Nice flying.'

'Needed to open the range a bit,' he responded. 'Everyone aboard?'

'All accounted for,' Grifen assured me, and I smacked the closing mechanism with the butt of my chainsword, reluctant to let go of either of the weapons I held until I was convinced we were safe.

'Go!' I told the pilot, and was immediately obliged to grab hold of the nearest stanchion[1] to prevent myself from being pitched straight back out of the closing hatch, as he put the nose up and kicked the main engines to maximum thrust.

With the aid of Jurgen's outstretched hand, I hauled myself over

---

1. *Evidently dropping at least one of the weapons, then...*

to the nearest viewport, looking down at the rapidly-shrinking huddle of buildings below. I strained my eyes for any further signs of the swarm, but if there was any movement on the surface other than the wind-blown snow, the blizzard obscured it.

Abruptly, without warning, the aircraft shook, buffeted by a shockwave which threatened to tear it from the sky. A dense column of smoke and ash burst from where the Mechanicus shrine had stood an instant before, to be followed almost at once by a geyser of bright orange magma, its vivid colour even more shocking against the monochrome landscape. We lurched, our engine faltering as the dust from the explosion was sucked into the turbines, then began to claw our way back into the sky as the pilot brought us round upwind of the livid wound in the planet's crust.

I breathed a sigh of relief, and settled into my seat as our course steadied. The presence of the tyranids had been an unpleasant surprise, to say the least, but no doubt we'd get to the bottom of their sudden appearance soon enough. And, in the meantime, there were still the orks to be taken care of.

'Commissar,' Kasteen said, her voice unexpectedly cutting into my comm-bead. 'Can you confirm a tyranid infestation at objective two?'

'We can,' I said. 'Termagants and hormagaunts for certain; if there were any other bioforms present we didn't encounter them.' I took another look at the ash plume, diminishing in the distance. 'Luckily there only seemed to be a small nest, and the explosion should have taken care of them nicely.'

'I wouldn't count on that,' Kasteen said, her voice grim. 'We've lost contact with Commissar Forres and the platoon she took in with her at objective one.'

'Are Lustig's people inbound yet?' I asked, remembering the contingency plans we'd discussed before I'd set out on this unexpectedly perilous reconnaissance sweep.

'They are,' Kasteen said, 'but you're closer, and if objective one's infested as well...'

'They'll need all the recon data we can give them,' I agreed. Even though I was outside the chain of command, she could still ask for my assistance, and I was in no position to refuse it: my standing with the common troopers would be cut off at the knees if I let an entire platoon walk into the maw of a tyranid swarm blind. I sighed, and tried not to grit my teeth. 'Diverting to assist,' I told her. 'Vox the coordinates to the pilot.'

Meanwhile, the campaign against the orks continued. As Cain rather loses sight of this, a failing for which, under the circumstances, he can hardly be blamed, the following, mercifully brief, extract is appended in the interests of presenting a slightly more rounded picture.

From *Like a Phoenix on the Wing: the Early Campaigns and Glorious Victories of the Valhallan 597th* by General Jenit Sulla (retired), 101 M42.

THEIR FULL MIGHT unleashed against the greenskin foe, the daughters and sons of Valhalla fell on the barbaric interlopers like the wrath of the Emperor incarnate, hewing their way to victory like the true heroes they were. First Company were, I'm proud to say, at the forefront of the campaign, striking the greenskins hard, and harrying their inevitable retreat, until they'd been driven back to the foothills in a series of hard-fought engagements which brought our forces to the brink of ultimate victory.

Indeed, at the time, I thought we must truly have been blessed by the hand of Him on Earth, as our advance proceeded at a pace far beyond the most wildly optimistic forecast. Divine intervention appeared to be the only rational explanation for our success, and the manner in which the enemy seemed to melt away in front of us, notwithstanding the undoubted martial prowess of all those fortunate enough to have been called to the ranks of the 597th; chief amongst them, of course, Colonel Kasteen, a tactician without peer, and whose early lessons were far from lost on my younger self. Indeed, I may go so far as to say that the successful defence of Diogenes Gap[1] was only made possible by the diligent application of the principles I observed her apply on innumerable occasions.

If credit for our victories in the Nusquan campaign belongs to anyone, however, it must surely be Commissar Cain, whose inspirational leadership and unfailing dedication to the path of duty did so much to bolster the resolve of all. Though more pressing matters kept him from the front line for much of our campaign, I for one continued to let the simple question 'What would the commissar do now?'[2] guide my actions at every point I felt the burden of command beginning to weigh heavily upon me, and on every occasion the path of duty became instantly clear.

It was while I was in my command Chimera, studying the maps of the foothills, and charting the route of our planned advance to minimise the risk of attack from ambush, that the order came to hold our positions. Commissar Cain had typically reserved the most hazardous assignment for himself, and while leading a recon team into the heart of an enemy-held area, discovered a threat beside which the surviving greenskins seemed but a minor irritation. Inspired by his selfless heroism, I too prepared to meet a new and terrifying foe, my faltering resolve bolstered as always by his shining and inspirational example.

---

1. *A notable Imperial victory, won under Sulla's generalship some fifty years later.*
2. *Fortunately without having the faintest idea of the actual answer.*

FOURTEEN

IN VIEW OF what we'd discovered at the power plant, you can be
sure that the prospect of facing another tyranid swarm so soon (or,
to be honest, ever again) was far from welcome. 'How certain are
we that the 'nids are responsible this time?' I asked, trying not to
sound too hopeful.

A hope Kasteen dashed almost at once. 'We can't be sure of anything,' she told me, her voice attenuated by the comm-bead's tiny
vox-receiver, and the muffled roar of the Valkyrie's engine. 'Forres
and the Nusquans went in, and split up to search the caverns by
squad. We picked up a bit of vox traffic at first, all routine, then
someone reported a contact and everything went dead.'

'It could still be the orks,' I said, not really believing it myself.
'The chances of two nests of tyranids going undetected for years
must be vanishingly small.'

'True,' Kasteen said. 'But given the sudden loss of contact, and their
distance from the greenskins' lines, my money's on the 'nids again.'

A cold hand seemed to take hold of my bowels, and squeeze
slowly. 'If there are two nests,' I said, reluctant to verbalise the
thought, 'there could be more.'

'So we need as much information as we can get,' Kasteen added. 'Movement, numbers, types of organism. It could just be an isolated outbreak, but if it isn't, Throne help us all.'

'I'll keep my eyes open,' I promised, not bothering to add 'and run like frak if I see anything', as that wouldn't exactly be helpful under the circumstances. 'Maybe there's a hive ship somewhere in system, licking its wounds after the battle for Periremunda.' Several of the living starships had fled, grievously wounded, as the Imperial Navy broke the siege of that beleaguered world, and it was possible one such survivor had drifted into the orbit of Nusquam Fundumentibus[1] undetected. I couldn't think of any other explanation for the presence of so many 'gaunts, instead of the scout organisms which usually made up the vanguard of a tyranid invasion.

'Objective in sight,' the pilot voxed, cutting into my anxious speculation not a moment too soon.

'Good,' I replied, trying to sound as if I meant it. I switched frequencies. 'Lustig, where are you?'

'On final approach,' the platoon leader assured me. 'About twenty minutes behind you. If this head wind doesn't ease off.'

'We'll be waiting,' I assured him. Twenty minutes would be a long time if the worst happened and we needed reinforcing in a hurry, but it could be worse. At least that's what I thought at the time: in the event, it turned out to be worse than I could possibly have imagined.

As we circled the objective, I must confess to a strong sense of *deja vu*, not unmixed with apprehension. We seemed to be repeating the sequence of events which had preceded our ill-starred investigation of the power plant, and I couldn't shake a formless feeling of dread that this time we wouldn't be so lucky. The only positive thing that I could see was that the snowfall had eased again, so I was able to make out our destination in a fair amount of detail.

---

1. *Presumably Cain means the system as a whole rather than the planet which shares its name; a common source of confusion in Imperial nomenclature.*

Like the power plant, there were a number of low structures studding the snow-shrouded surface, affording sheltered access to the caverns beneath; but in this case, instead of clustering together, they were widely separated, spread out across an area roughly a kilometre across. Wanting to know as much as possible about the environment I'd be entering in a few moments time I'd requested a map of the cave system, which Kasteen had transmitted to my data-slate, and after studying it for a minute or two my knack for remaining orientated in complex tunnel systems kicked in as reliably as ever, leaving me sure I'd be able to find my way around with little difficulty. Now, looking down, I was able to match each surface feature to the underground passageway or cavern connected to it with complete confidence.

'Where are their Chimeras?' Jurgen asked, his curiosity giving me the full benefit of his halitosis as he leaned towards the viewport for a better look.

'They must have taken them inside,' I said. Several of the blockhouses on the surface were designed to admit the heavy cargo crawlers[1] which carried the foodstuffs grown here to Primadelving and the other nearby settlements, so getting the much smaller Chimeras under cover would have presented little difficulty. 'Keep the engines from freezing in the cold.'

Jurgen nodded. 'You'd want them to start again quick if you needed 'em,' he agreed. 'Especially if the shooting started.' The Nusquan Chimeras were fitted with multi-lasers in their turrets, rather than the heavy bolters favoured by the Valhallans, and their powercells would swiftly become depleted without the engines running to recharge them.

'Well, we'll soon know,' I said as the pilot began his descent.

'Same orders as last time?' he asked as we hovered over the flat roof of one of the blockhouses, which we'd selected as a landing point in the absence of any purpose-built shuttle pad.

---

1. *Tracked vehicles with wide treads, particularly suited to the kind of conditions prevailing on an iceworld. In the absence of a road network, which would have been impossible to keep clear in any case, they were the primary means of transport on Nusquam Fundimentibus.*

'Almost,' I replied. 'Keep circling, and report any sign of movement. There are supposed to be fifty or so Nusquans around[1], so don't shoot unless you're sure they're 'nids or greenskins.'

'Will do,' the pilot confirmed. 'Multi-laser only.'

'Or the Hellstrikes, if you feel they're warranted,' I said. 'I doubt the crops are going to explode.'

'Unless they're growing those pod things Sergeant Penlan tripped over on Seigal,' Jurgen added. 'Took days to get the last of the goo out.' He shuddered at the memory, or another spasm of airsickness, it was hard to be sure which.

'The demiurg got the worst of it,' I reminded him. 'They'd have overrun us if they hadn't got mired in the stuff.'

'Can't see it slowing the 'nids down,' my aide said, shaking his head.

'Neither can I,' I agreed, wondering, not for the first time, how conversations with Jurgen tended to become quite so tangential to the original topic.

'Nothing moving on the auspex,' the pilot told us, although that was only of limited reassurance where tyranids were concerned, their ability to evade detection almost second to none. 'No visible signs of life either.'

'Then let's get to it,' I said, unable to think of any reason to delay further, despite my best efforts. 'Any vox traffic?' Which was a pretty pointless question really, as if the crew had detected any they would certainly have mentioned the fact by now.

'None, sir,' the navigator confirmed[2], speaking directly to me for the first time. 'Still scanning on all frequencies.'

'They could be too deep to get a signal out,' Grifen suggested, clearly no more convinced of that than I was. The vox gear in the command Chimera should be able to punch a signal through the intervening rock with no difficulty at all, allowing us to monitor the comm-beads of everyone in the cavern complex.

---

1. *Which implies four full squads, plus the command element, Forres, any aides she had with her, and the Chimera crews. Rather a small platoon: clearly Cain wasn't exaggerating about their combat losses earlier.*

2. *The second crewman would be in charge of monitoring the on-board equipment, leaving the pilot free to fly the aircraft without distraction.*

'Maybe,' I said, not wanting to consider the alternatives too closely. Before I could say anything else the Valkyrie lurched, its landing skids hitting the rockcrete of the roof, and came to rest a comfortable distance from the vertiginous drop to the snow below. We'd chosen the largest and most central of the blocky structures to set down on, not least because of the extra margin for error the scrumball pitch-sized area allowed the pilot, and because according to the data provided by Kasteen there was an access hatch to the building, which would allow us ingress with a minimum of difficulty.

I was also fairly sure that this would have been the entrance to the agricaves the Nusquans would have chosen, as they could have fanned out from here most efficiently, and if we followed in their footsteps we were most likely to find out what happened to them; preferably in time to avoid sharing their fate. At least if there were tyranids here we'd know what to expect: the Nusquans would have gone in as blissfully ignorant of the true threat as we had at the Mechanicus shrine, and, lacking our experience of fighting the 'nids, they'd have had no idea of how to prevail against them.

Once again the somewhat battered boarding ramp clanged outwards, allowing full access to the razor-edged wind, which howled across the bleak wilderness surrounding us. This time we disembarked more slowly, partly because we had no fear of being shot at, and partly, in my case at least, because none of us were keen to encounter whatever flesh-sculpted horrors might be lying in wait beneath our feet. I shielded my eyes as the Valkyrie took to the skies again, and began to circle the point at which we stood, feeling as reassured as possible under the circumstances.

'We're down,' I reported, as Magot's team crunched across the snow which lay beyond the roughly circular zone cleared by the Valkyrie's landing jets. After a short search of the roof they unfolded their trenching tools, and began scraping the area around the trapdoor free of the ice and snow hiding it from view. 'Second wave ETA?'

'Still twenty minutes, commissar,' Lustig voxed almost at once.

'We're proceeding inside,' I told him. 'If you follow the same route, you should catch up with us soon enough.' At least I hoped so. If the entire cave system was indeed riddled with tyranids, I'd need a lot more troopers to hide behind than a single squad, already depleted to almost three quarters of its original strength.

By the time I'd finished speaking, the troopers under Magot's command had managed to lever the heavy metal slab open, no mean feat considering how firmly it had been frozen in place, and a telling testament to how at home the Valhallans were in this hideous environment. Despite the reservations I might normally have had about moving into harm's way, I was down the ladder after our vanguard with almost indecent haste, my eagerness to get out of the bone-biting cold no doubt being misinterpreted as impatience to enter the fray by those around me.

The ladder descended to a narrow catwalk, some two and a half metres below the ceiling, apparently for the convenience of those artisans charged with the maintenance of the luminators; which left sufficient headroom to walk upright, although doing so encumbered with our weapons and equipment over a drop of ten metres or more was somewhat disturbing. The net result, in my case at least, was a curious combination of vertigo and claustrophobia, all the more unsettling for experiencing either so seldom[1]. Fortunately the catwalk terminated in a wider platform, from which a rickety staircase descended, affording us a clear look at the floor of the warehouse as we made our way down.

'We've found the Chimeras,' I voxed. 'Three of them, anyway.' The vehicles were parked close together, near the middle of the huge structure, the rest of the space it enclosed empty and echoing.

'The others must have gone to different entrances,' Grifen said, 'to sweep the tunnels from the other end.'

'More than likely,' I agreed. It was a tactic which would have worked well against the orks the Nusquans expected to find here, trapping them between squads advancing from both directions,

---

1. *Another natural consequence of growing up in an underhive, where confined spaces and abyssal shafts are simply part of the environment.*

and cutting off their lines of escape. It was fatally flawed against tyranids, though, simply allowing the swarm to pick off the intruders piecemeal, instead of being able to combine their firepower against it.

'Something's not right,' Jurgen said, as our bootsoles hit the rockcrete, and we glanced round orientating ourselves. His voice echoed in the wide, high space, unimpeded by anything other than the ominous metal shapes of the abandoned Chimeras. 'Where's all the food waiting to be loaded?'

A good question. A line of empty pallets stood against one wall, their contents gone.

'Maybe the crawler just left,' Vorhees suggested, 'and they haven't started stacking the next load up yet.'

'Not according to this.' Grifen bent to pick up an abandoned data-slate, which had drawn her attention to itself by skittering across the floor in response to an accidental nudge from her boot. 'Crawler's not due for another three days.'

I glanced at the manifest still displayed on the cracked and flickering screen. According to that, there should have been about two hundred tonnes of miscellaneous foodstuffs stacked up around us, awaiting dispatch to various destinations. The implications were disturbing, to say the least, although not as much as the smear of blood still visible on the keypad of the device.

'The 'nids must have eaten it all,' Jurgen said, no mean trencherman himself, and clearly impressed. I tried to picture a swarm large enough to consume two hundred tonnes of food, and immediately wished I hadn't; it would be orders of magnitude larger than the one we'd already faced and escaped today.

'The food stores in the warehouse have been cleaned out,' I voxed for Kasteen's benefit, before adding 'so move carefully. There must be hundreds of organisms around here,' to the troopers around me.

'Let's check out the Chimeras,' Grifen said, beginning to walk towards them.

'Pity the command one isn't here,' I agreed, falling in at her shoulder. 'We'd be able to read everyone's positions on the auspex.' As we moved closer to the abandoned vehicles, it became increasingly obvious that something wasn't right. The thick armour plate was rent in several places, ripped apart by powerful claws, and Jurgen and I shared a look of grim understanding as we got our first clear view of the damage.

'Genestealers, you reckon?' he asked, and I nodded, the picture of their powerful talons tearing through the Reclaimers' Terminator armour aboard the *Spawn of Damnation* all too vivid in my mind's eye.

'Too precise for one of the big ones,' I agreed; the hulking monstrosities would have crushed and dented the hulls, tearing their way inside with far less finesse. As I studied the damage to the trio of vehicles more carefully my eye fell on the unit markings of the nearest, half obscured by a slash of parallel talon marks. 'That can't be right.'

'What can't?' Grifen asked, then her eyes narrowed as she made out the almost obliterated identification code. 'That's the command vehicle. But where are the vox and auspex antennae?' They should have been obvious and distinctive, marking it out instantly to the naked eye.

'Sheared off,' Drere reported, from the top of the crippled Chimera. She picked up a tangle of metal and threw it down for my inspection, raising a clangor of echoes in the vast space as it hit the rockcrete floor. A look of consternation crossed her face, as it dawned on all of us simultaneously that if there were any tyranids in the immediate vicinity she'd just announced our presence to them in no uncertain manner, and everyone tensed, readying their weapons; but, after an agonising wait of a minute or two, no tide of chitin came scurrying out of the depths to challenge us, and the tension began to ease.

'Sliced through cleanly,' I said, somewhat reassured by the failure of the 'nids to slaughter us all instantly where we stood, and returning my attention to the ravaged vox array. The edge was straight, the metal bright, and faint indentations further up the strut betrayed where the 'stealer responsible had gripped it with a couple of its other limbs to steady the assembly before hacking through it. 'They took out the comms on purpose.' The reason for which was obvious; with the relay in the command vehicle down, the comm-beads carried by the Nusquans would be blocked by the layers of rock between the caverns, isolating the squads from one another, and making it impossible to coordinate them.

Reminded, if I ever needed to be, that the hive mind was at least as cunning and capable of subtlety in its tactics as any other foe the Imperium faced, although it was all too easy to forget this when faced by the endless sea of bestial creatures it controlled, I looked at the solemn faces surrounding me. If Drere's moment of careless-ness had indeed attracted its attention, our only chance of survival was to be somewhere else when the genestealers returned; and hope our reinforcements arrived before they caught up with us.

'No signs of life,' Drere reported, after a cursory look through the top hatch of the ravaged Chimera. She grinned mirthlessly. 'Big surprise there.'

'The others are empty too,' Magot reported, trotting back from investigating them with a couple of her troopers. 'Unless you count a lot of bloodstains.'

'Then let's get moving,' I said. Well-lit ramps led off from each edge of the chamber, disappearing into the depths below, and I picked the nearest more or less at random. There was no telling which one Forres and her people had taken, so one tunnel was as good as another so far as I could see.

'Move out,' Grifen said, as happy to follow my lead as anyone would be under the circumstances, which was not a lot, and we set off.

To my initial surprise, my overriding impression as we made our way through the cavern system was one of space, although I suppose that shouldn't have been all that unexpected, given the purpose to which it had been put. The tunnel we took was wide and high, about four metres by three, and well-lit; the reason for which became obvious soon enough.

'Is that a truck?' Jurgen asked, in tones of surprise which quite accurately reflected my own.

'More or less,' I agreed. It would have looked pretty much at home on the city streets of any world with a more equitable climate, although the open cab would have been inconvenient when it rained. It had crashed into the tunnel wall, crumpling the bodywork and breaking an axle, which was a shame; commandeering the thing would have moved us all a lot faster. 'It must have been ferrying food up to the loading area.'

'Till the 'nids decided to eat here,' Vorhees added, with a grimace at the rust-coloured stains disfiguring the ripped-up driving seat.

I nodded thoughtfully. The driver had clearly been fleeing the swarm, losing control as it overwhelmed him; the suddenness and ferocity of the attack could have left no more eloquent a testimony. 'Stay sharp,' I admonished, quite unnecessarily I'm sure.

'I've got all the sharp I need,' Magot said, running a thumb along the edge of her bayonet.

'Let's hope you don't need,' I rejoined, eliciting grim smiles from most of the troopers around me.

THOUGH WE FOUND plenty of traces of the tyranids' passing as we penetrated deeper into the cavern system, the creatures themselves remained worryingly elusive. Shortly after stumbling across the abandoned truck, we found ourselves entering the first of the agricultural caverns, a cathedral-sized space still displaying the cracked and fissured walls of a natural rock formation. The floor had been smoothed, however, and powerful luminators mounted on pylons spaced at regular intervals around it; finding my boots splashing in a thin film of water, I resolved to give them as wide a berth as possible, since a loose cable on any of them would turn the shallow pool into an instant deathtrap.

There was no question of where the water was coming from; the whole cavern was filled with metal troughs, mounted on stanchions driven into the floor, and which had at one time no doubt contained it. Now they were bent and shattered, their contents spilling all over the cave.

'Hydroponics,' Kasteen explained, as I reported what I'd seen for the benefit of the approaching platoon, and the analysts back in Primadelving. 'We grow most of our food like that on Valhalla too[1].'

'No sign of any plants,' I said, my apprehension growing as the realisation sunk in of what that meant. I had no idea how much vegetation the cavern had contained yesterday, but if all these troughs had been full, it was a huge amount, and my already pessimistic estimate of the size of the swarm we were facing increased by another order of magnitude. If all the other caverns had been stripped too...

'Only one way to find out,' Grifen said when I verbalised the thought, and I nodded reluctant agreement.

My knack of remaining orientated in an underground environment proving as reliable as ever, we moved on, down another of the wide tunnels to the next cavern. This was considerably deeper, the subterranean road connecting them descending in a wide spiral, so that the open space was hidden from us until we were almost on top of it.

'At least our feet are dry,' Jurgen said, moving his head slowly as he scanned the open space in search of a target.

I nodded, taking in the panorama of ripped and shattered animal pens. I had no idea what manner of creature had been reared down here, but I was in no doubt of what had happened to them, butchered along with their keepers to feed the insatiable hunger of the hive mind. Even the dung had gone, the 'nids being fastidious when it came to garnering raw material for the creation of more of their kind.

'The animal pens in cavern twelve are empty,' I reported, hearing only the faint hiss of static in my earpiece by way of reply. Our rapid descent down the spiral way had evidently taken us too

---

1. *Water being a great deal easier to obtain on a world covered in ice than soil would have been.*

deep for our comm-beads to remain connected to the vox-unit of the Valkyrie[1], and I felt a brief surge of panic, which I fought down briskly. The important thing was to return to the higher levels as quickly as possible, where we could re-establish contact and join up with Lustig's platoon.

For a moment I debated going back the way we'd come, but as we'd fanned out across the open space we'd moved a fair way from the tunnel mouth we'd entered the cave by, and another pair in the far wall were almost as close. One led up upwards, I was sure, looping round through a couple of other nexus points, to bring us back to the entrance building we'd started from by another of the tunnel mouths leading off from it. Doing so would complete our recon sweep in a manner comprehensive enough to look as though we'd done our duty, and enable us to join up with Lustig's command squad, which I had no doubt a soldier of his experience would leave where it was least likely to make contact with the enemy. (Something Lustig was never averse to personally, but I knew he took his new-found responsibilities seriously enough not to risk compromising his ability to coordinate the squads under his command by having to fight off hordes of 'gaunts at the same time.) No doubt Forres had developed the same idea, parking the Chimeras well behind where she expected the battle lines to be: but unlike her we knew what we were up against, and, more importantly, how to fight it.

'This way,' I said, angling towards the tunnel mouth leading upwards.

Magot glanced down the other, the gently inclined floor of which led even further into the bowels of the planet, and wrinkled her nose. 'There's that smell again,' she said.

Turning my head in her direction, I was able to catch a faint whiff of sulphur on the air currents wafting up from the cavern below. 'This place connects to the volcanic vents too,' I explained, as though I hadn't just learned that myself from the information Kasteen had supplied. 'They use the heat to warm the place and help the plants grow.'

---

1. *Or the aircraft's patrol pattern had moved it temporarily out of range.*

'Should we check it out before we head back up?' she asked, and I shook my head, trying to seem casual about it.

'Better get back into contact as soon as we can,' I said, all too aware that if the 'nids followed the same pattern of instinctive behaviour as the ones at the power plant they'd be congregating in the lowest point of the cave system, and that our chances of survival if we disturbed a swarm as big as the one I'd inferred could be there would start at non-existent before growing rapidly worse.

'You won't hear any argument from me,' Grifen agreed, taking the path that led upwards, and we began our ascent as circumspectly as we'd descended, despite the urge to hurry that nagged at us with every footfall. I've often observed that fatal mistakes get made more often on the return leg of a recon mission than the outward one, no doubt because the simple fact of turning back creates the false impression that the worst is over; whereas the enemy is still as alert as ever. Most of the troopers with me were far too experienced in the ways of war to succumb to that fallacy, however, and we remained fully focused, a fact which was to save our lives before many more minutes were over.

We'd almost reached the next cavern when I became aware that the faint wash of static in my comm-bead was modulating slightly, and before I'd taken many more paces the vague fragments of sound began to coalesce into voices. I still couldn't make much sense of it, but I'd been in enough tight corners over the years to recognise the clipped urgency of orders being given and received in the middle of a pitched battle.

'What is it, sir?' Jurgen asked, raising his melta, attuned to my moods by our long years of campaigning together. Picking up their cue from him, Grifen and Magot looked expectantly in my direction.

'Sounds like Lustig's arrived,' I said grimly, 'and the 'nids have laid on a welcoming party.'

No sooner had the words left my mouth, however, than the voice of the lieutenant himself sounded clearly in my earpiece.

'Commissar, do you read?' Lustig asked, sounding remarkably calm for a man I'd presumed to be fighting for his life.

'Cain, go ahead,' I said, my surprise no doubt evident in my tone. 'What's your status?'

'Just disembarked,' Lustig said, sounding equally surprised, 'and securing our perimeter. You think 'stealers took out the Chimeras in here?'

'Positive,' I said, stopping abruptly. We'd almost reached the entrance to the next cavern, but I was damned if I was going to take another step. 'Because I'm looking right at them.'

FIFTEEN

My companions followed my lead, freezing in place instinctively, as the sinister shadows bounded across the cavern in front of us; there must have been a dozen at least, although under the circumstances I didn't feel particularly disposed to making an accurate head count. Long, lolling tongues curled from their fang-filled mouths, while sinister highlights flickered from the talons tipping the hands on each of their four arms. For a heart-stopping moment I thought they'd seen us, but fortunately their attention appeared to be elsewhere; in an instant, it seemed, they'd crossed the flooded floor of a hydroponic chamber in no better condition than the first we'd found, their taloned feet kicking up a mist of spray from the thin film of water, to vanish down another of the connecting tunnels.

'That was lucky,' Jurgen said, as though we'd just avoided nothing worse than a rain shower. 'Another minute and we'd have run right into them.'

'We would,' I agreed, hoping my voice wasn't as shaky as the rest of me. The tunnel they'd come from was the very one I'd been intending to take back to the chamber we'd arrived in. Which reminded me... 'Lustig. The 'stealers were in the passage between your position and chamber nine on the schematic. It's probably clear now, but advance with caution.'

'Acknowledged,' Lustig said, sounding even more surprised than before. 'Where did they go?'

'The exit for chamber sixteen,' Grifen said, consulting her own slate[1] with a frown of puzzlement. 'And fast. Maybe you spooked them.'

I shook my head. 'Genestealers don't panic. Not like that. They were running towards something, not away.' The faint echoes I'd noticed before were still in my comm-bead, and the realisation suddenly dawned. If it wasn't Lustig's platoon under siege, then... 'It must be the Nusquans. The hive mind's calling in reinforcements.'

'Say again, sir?' Lustig requested, evidently still too distant to hear the faint vox traffic for himself.

I gritted my teeth, already well aware of where this conversation was bound to lead. 'We're picking up faint vox signals,' I said, 'on Guard frequencies. If it isn't you, it has to be be the Nusquans, what's left of them. They must be holed up in sixteen, or whatever's beyond it.' Even as I spoke, my ever-reliable mental map filled in the answer; another exit to the surface. Presumably they were trying to fight their way through to their remaining Chimeras.

'Squads two, three and five are on their way to assist,' Lustig said, effectively sinking any hope I had of palming a heroic rescue attempt off on someone else for a change. 'Can you recce for them?'

'We're on it,' Grifen said, before I had a chance to come up with a good reason to refuse, or at least wait for another thirty troopers to catch up with us.

'Keep an eye out behind us as well,' I cautioned, all too aware that if any more tyranid reinforcements turned up, we'd be caught between them and the main army. Our only chance of surviving the next few minutes was to avoid the notice of the hive mind altogether, which was a chancy proposition at the best of times;

---

1. *Kasteen presumably having passed on the details Cain requested to the squad leader too, unless he did this himself.*

although I'd managed the trick on a few occasions before[1], so I knew it could be done.

Though still mindful of the need for caution, we picked up our pace as we began to follow the 'stealers, hoping that the swarm's attention would be directed at the Nusquans it was trying to consume, rather than behind it. A risk, true, but a calculated one, and unavoidable if we were to intervene while there was still someone left to rescue.

Before long the whispers in my ear had swelled to faint voices, growing steadily stronger, and I was not at all surprised to discern Forres's clipped and self-assured tones prominent among them. I couldn't tell how many survivors were left standing, but damned few by this time I'd wager, and if the voices I could hear were anything to go by they'd entered that strange state of mind where the certainty of imminent death brings complete clarity and a curious absence of fear. (A sensation I'd already experienced often enough in my own turbulent life to recognise at once.) Which is all very well in its way, the lack of any sense of self-preservation sometimes enabling desperate people to achieve extraordinary things, but if I was going to be forced to play the hero again I wanted there to be someone left to appreciate it.

'Commissar Cain to Nusquan unit,' I voxed, knowing that the realisation that help was on its way would infuse the beleaguered survivors with fresh purpose. 'We're approaching with reinforcements. I need a sitrep ASAP[2].' The last thing we needed at this stage was to blunder into the middle of a pitched battle and get annihilated before we got the chance to achieve anything.

To my complete lack of surprise, Forres answered, any astonishment she may have felt at this unexpected reprieve firmly suppressed. 'Completely surrounded,' she replied. 'We've taken refuge on the catwalk, but they keep on coming.'

---

1. *Generally while accompanied by Jurgen, whose ability to neutralise psychic phenomena apparently disrupted the synaptic link between the various organisms of a swarm equally effectively.*

2. *Situation report, as soon as possible, a particularly egregious example of the military mania for abbreviation.*

'You got as far as the blockhouse on the surface?' I asked, impressed by her tenacity if nothing else, the memory of the narrow walkway we'd traversed from the roof still fresh in my memory.

'The agricave,' Forres corrected, interrupting herself with the harsh bark of a bolt pistol, exactly the sidearm I'd have expected her to choose. Loud, ostentatious, and making a spectacular mess of its target, a lot of commissars favour them because they think they're more intimidating[1], although I've found the solidly reliable laspistol far better suited to service in the field. I've lost count of the number of times I've recharged it on the fly, when I'd have been long out of ammunition for a projectile weapon. 'There's a short one for maintaining the inlet pipes.'

'We'll spot it,' I assured her. In truth I hadn't noticed any such arrangement in the caverns we'd passed through before, my sole interest in the pipework above us being the absence of any lurking genestealers poised to pounce.

'That'll be where the 'stealers were off to in such a hurry,' Jurgen said, never slow to point out the obvious. 'Most tyranids can't climb.' Which wasn't entirely true, but they were clumsy at best, having only their feet and middle limbs to do the job with, the weapons fused to their forelimbs only getting in the way. Genestealers, on the other hand, were perfectly adapted to swarming up near vertical surfaces, and if Forres and her people had sought refuge by climbing, the hive mind would have called in as many as it could to drag them down.

As we got our first sight of the cavern, it was just as obvious where the Nusquans were as the junior commissar had promised. A huge, swaying pyramid of intertwined tyranids rose from the floor beneath a fragile-seeming catwalk, to which a dozen determined survivors clung grimly, pouring lasgun fire into the seething mass of flesh below. So far it was about three metres high, and growing inexorably, already well over halfway to its goal.

'Single shots!' Forres shouted. 'Pick your targets!' Suiting the

---

1. *Which is why so many orks find this kind of weapon appealing, of course, although I suspect few members of the Commissariat would thank you for the comparison.*

action to the word, she picked off a termagant teetering near the top of the pile, which was just bringing its fleshborer up on aim, with commendable accuracy. To be conserving ammunition in straits this dire they must be almost out, an impression reinforced a moment later by one of the Nusquan troopers, who gave up pointing his gun at the horde of horrors below, and began fixing his bayonet.

'I'm out,' his voice crackled over the vox, confirming my deduction.

'Look up there,' Jurgen said, and following the direction of his grime-encrusted finger, I was able to pick out a whisper of stealthy movement among the stalactites above our heads.

'Well spotted,' I commended him, and activated the vox. 'Forres, you've got 'stealers above you. Three groups, one, five, and nine o'clock.'

The Nusquans redirected their fire towards the new threat, and a couple of the taloned horrors fell, bursting like foul and over-ripe fruit as they hit the floor and the hydroponic troughs, the impact raising small fountains of water and viscera. The water frothed where they'd hit, as uncountable writhing serpentine forms swarmed to tear them apart, greedily devouring the still-twitching corpses with single-minded diligence.

'Rippers,' Vorhees said simply, in horror-struck tones, recognising the razor-fanged worms with a shudder of revulsion. The flooded floor was carpeted with the foul things, as far as the eye could see.

'We'll need flamers,' I voxed the approaching troopers. 'The more the better. The whole cavern's infested.' If we could advance behind those, and a solid barrage of lasgun fire, we might be able to force our way over to the Nusquans and get them out before the tyranids recovered the initiative. Possibly. So long as we maintained the element of surprise until we were ready.

'We can't target the genestealers from this angle,' Forres told us, matter-of-factly. 'The stalactites are in the way. You'll have to pick them off from the floor.'

'If we do that, the hive mind will know we're here,' I pointed out. 'As soon as we're ready to extract you we can...' Before I could finish the sentence the 'stealers swarmed forward, charging as quickly and easily as if they were running on solid ground; another second or two and they'd be on the swaying gantry, carving their way among the troopers like kroot through a meat locker. 'Frak it, fire!'

Our lasguns crackled, and Jurgen's melta added its sinister hiss, wreaking havoc among the brood clinging to the ceiling; more fell, riddled with las-bolts or baked by the melta, these last raising clouds of steam where they hit the floor, or crashed into the flooded troughs. Not all were killed outright by the fall: several stirred, trying to rise, while one in particular pulled itself to its feet with a grasping hand on one of the troughs, despite the loss of a limb and a deep crack in its carapace through which some noisome fluid seeped. It turned its head slowly, seeking the source of the unexpected interference, its eyes seeming to lock on mine; then it began a lumbering charge, managing two or three halting paces in our direction before the water frothed around it, and the serpentine scavengers closed in. Like the rest of its brood it was torn apart and consumed in seconds.

'Why did they do that instead of letting it attack us?' Jurgen asked, but within a heartbeat we had our answer; all round the cavern, 'gaunts and the hulking warrior forms which gave them volition were turning, as though suddenly made aware of our presence.

'Because the rest are about to,' I said, preparing to run. We'd done our best, but there was no point in allowing ourselves to be devoured along with the Nusquans. If we were fast enough, maybe we could get behind the protection afforded by the flamers the troopers behind us were bringing up. A few gouts of burning promethium would fill the corridor, holding the hideous creatures off long enough for us to make it back to the Valkyries uneaten. I hoped. 'Valhallans, where are you?'

'Chamber nine, commissar,' Jinxie Penlan told me, her voice overlaid with the unmistakable sounds of combat. 'There's a whole swarm of them coming up from the lower levels. We're holding them off with the flamers, but we can't get through to you.'

'Just keep them off our backs for as long as you can,' I said, cursing under my breath. No retreat that way.

I glanced up at the Nusquans on their precarious perch, where a desperate struggle was going on against the two or three 'stealers which had survived our intervention: Forres was engaging one with her chainsword, and looked like getting her face bitten off, until she jammed the muzzle of her miniature bolter under its chin and pulled the trigger, while a luckless trooper at the other end of the gantry was slashed almost in two, and fell, flailing, to be torn to pieces by the waiting swarm the moment he hit the ground. We'd get no help from up there, either.

'Pick your targets,' Grifen said, sounding oddly like Forres for a moment, before adding some rather more pertinent advice, 'and aim for the large ones every chance you get[1]. If we can disrupt the swarm we might have a chance.'

'If the little frakkers don't rip our toes off first,' Magot said, looking at the thrashing killer worms, her face contorted with revulsion. It was no idle comment; under the influence of the hive mind, they were abandoning the corpses and the remains of the crop which used to be here (some kind of root vegetable, judging by the few partially intact examples I could see), and were already swarming towards us, while the specialised combat forms began to untangle themselves from the ungainly circus act beneath the catwalk, and trot in our direction behind them. The leading warrior aimed its deathspitter at us, and a second later the water a metre or so in front of my boot began to bubble and hiss furiously as the ball of acid it had fired started eating its way into the cavern floor.

'Fire!' I commanded, abruptly reminded that our sole remaining advantage was the superior range of our weaponry, and that we'd almost squandered it already. 'Before it can get another one off!' The synapse creature was promptly riddled, and went down, but instead of pausing to feast on the corpse the rippers continued their remorseless advance, slithering towards us with malign intent. 'Two more over there!'

---

1. *It's not always true that the largest creatures in a tyranid swarm are the ones through which the hive mind focuses its control of those around it, but it's a good enough rule of thumb to be trusted by troopers who've fought tyranids before and managed to survive the encounter.*

'One,' Jurgen said, nailing the left-hand one neatly with the melta, reducing the devourer it carried to a mass of charred meat, but the hideous creature rallied, and came on, clearly intent on dicing us with its scything claws instead: in the unlikely event of the screen of smaller creatures it and its companion were lurking behind leaving anything larger than mincemeat, in any case.

'Full auto, take down the ones with the guns,' Grifen ordered. 'Before they get close enough to use them.' Our erstwhile companion's gruesome death fresh in our minds, we needed no further urging, unleashing a withering hail of fire as we retreated step by step up the tunnel, while the tide of slithering, ankle-high fangs continued to snap at our boots as we went, the bloated serpentine bodies behind them writhing over the wet footprints we left on the rockcrete floor.

At which point, belated inspiration suddenly struck, as I recalled my idle thought about the lighting pylons in the first of the flooded chambers we'd found. 'Jurgen!' I shouted. 'Can you bring down one of those luminator rigs?'

'No problem,' my aide assured me, scanning the narrowing view of the chamber in front of us, which each retreating step closed in a little further. 'Any one in particular?'

'The easiest to hit,' I said, wanting to leave as little to chance as possible. Jurgen's marksmanship may have been exceptional, but so was his ability to take whatever I said to him literally, and if I was any more specific he'd continue grimly plugging away at whichever one I'd designated even if that meant having to bring down half the swarm to get a clear shot at it.

'Right you are, sir,' he responded, as if I'd asked for nothing more troublesome than a fresh bowl of tanna, and I closed my eyes reflexively just as he pulled the trigger. 'Frak it, get out of the way! Sorry, sir, just winged that big one instead.'

He must have done more than just winged it, because the tide of squirming death at my feet checked its advance for a moment, the cohesiveness of the hive mind disrupted; then, with the inconvenient obstruction out of the way, he fired again.

As the supporting girder work flashed into incandescent vapour, the metal around it softening and buckling, the metal pylon lurched sideways, and began to sag. 'Again!' I began, but before I could complete the command, gravity overwhelmed the weakened structure and it toppled gracefully to the cavern floor.

The effect was immediate, the luminators shattering, and the thick electrical cables supplying them fizzling as they hit the water. The shallow pool began to froth, churned to foam by the agonised spasms of the countless organisms infesting it, and jagged lightning arced between the metal surfaces of the hydroponic troughs, electrocuting those tyranids which had the luck or quick-wittedness to be out of the water just as effectively as those caught in it. The surviving warrior form staggered, roaring and bellowing like a drunken ork, discharged its venom cannon in a final reflex (which fortunately failed to hit anything other than a couple of expiring hormagaunts), and collapsed into the boiling pool. Silence suddenly fell, broken only by the faint, sinister buzzing of the abused electrical system.

'They've stopped moving,' Magot said, prodding the nearest ripper cautiously with the tip of her bayonet. Those closest to us were too far from the water to have been electrocuted themselves, but deprived of the controlling influence of the hive mind, they'd simply become inert lumps of staggeringly ugly meat.

'Then we'd better collect the Nusquans and get out of here,' I said.

'Preferably without boiling us in the process,' Forres said, stowing her weapons, and looking down at us severely from her perch near the ceiling. 'Which is something of a flaw in your otherwise impressive stratagem.'

'No "thanks for saving us from being 'nid bait," then,' Magot muttered. 'Snotty femhound.'

'Corporal,' I reproved, but to be honest I pretty much shared her opinion, so stopped short of an outright reprimand; an omission which, judging by her smirk, had not gone unnoted, nor my reasons uninferred. Besides, Forres did have a point: so long as the cable was in the water, we couldn't re-enter the chamber, and the

Nusquans couldn't descend from their perch, without getting electrocuted just as thoroughly as the 'nids.

'We're being forced back here,' Penlan voxed, just to crank the pressure up a little more. 'We've laid down a flame barrier between the swarm and your tunnel mouth, but it's only going to burn for a few minutes.'

'Acknowledged,' I said, acutely aware that another tidal wave of scuttling malevolence would be bearing down on us as soon as the flames died, and that the only way forward was across the electrified pool. If I didn't think of something fast, we were going to be 'nid bait ourselves.

'There's a junction box on the north-west wall,' Forres cut in, pointing at something I couldn't quite see from her elevated perch. 'The cable from the luminator you downed seems to be plugged into it.'

I took the proffered amplivisor from Jurgen, and focused it. She was right. Taking it out should cut the power to all the luminators in that portion of the cavern.

I turned to the troopers as my aide shrugged his bulky melta aside and unslung his lasgun, in anticipation of my next order. If anyone among us was capable of hitting so small a mark, I was confident it would be him, but under the circumstances the sooner the power was cut the better, and we didn't have long to try. 'Double ale ration for whoever hits that box thing on the wall over there first,' I said, and stood back, ready to leave them to it.

'Allow me,' Forres interjected dryly, casually putting a bolt through the box from the swaying catwalk before anyone else could pull the trigger. The explosive bolt struck true, and detonated, ripping the target to shreds, and plunging the entire cavern into darkness, relieved only by the light leaking from the tunnel mouths on either side.

'Nice shot,' I said. 'But perhaps a slight flaw in your stratagem?'

Magot snickered quietly as we kindled our luminators again, and began sloshing though the water, picking our way as best we could through the innumerable dead horrors choking it. The larger creatures had to be dodged around, and I kept my laspistol trained on each one as I did so, particularly the warrior forms, having learned long ago that it took a great deal to kill a tyranid, and the jolt of high voltage electricity might merely have stunned some of them.

'We have to get moving,' I said as we reached the vicinity of the dangling catwalk. 'We're out of the hive mind's awareness at the moment, but it knows something's knocked a hole in its neural net, and right where it happened; it'll be sending more tyranids in after us as sure as the Emperor protects. Our only chance is to be gone by the time it does.'

'And how do you suggest we get down?' Forres asked, with a touch of asperity. 'We had to take out the ladder with a krak grenade. You'll need to get a rope from the Chimeras, bring it back, and...'

'End up in a digester pool like the rest of the poor frakwits you led in here,' I interrupted. 'When we get to the Chimeras we're firing them up and driving them out. Come along now if you don't want to get left for the 'nids.'

'They'll be here any minute,' Grifen added, with an apprehensive glance at the tunnel mouth we'd come in by.

'We can't jump from up here, we'll be killed!' one of the Nusquans objected.

'No you won't.' I swung my luminator round to spotlight the pile of tyranid corpses beneath the catwalk. It wasn't as high as it had been, but it would do. 'If you hang by your hands first, it's only a couple of metres to drop to the top of the heap, and you can climb down that fast enough.' The chitinous exoskeletons wouldn't exactly supply a soft landing, but they'd be a lot more comfortable than a five metre fall to solid rock, that was for sure.

I expected more argument, but the Nusquans had evidently learned the lesson that a slim chance is infinitely preferable to none as well as I had by this time, and followed my suggestion without further ado. Forres watched them for a moment, then tucked her weapons away and simply jumped, her black coat flapping like a gargoyle's wings as she reached out for a hold among the mound of monstrous corpses, and swarmed her way down them talon by tusk. 'Are you always that inventive?' she asked, and I shrugged.

'Sometimes you have to be,' I said. 'The manual doesn't cover everything.' I glanced at the tunnel we'd entered by, certain I'd heard the first faint scuttling of a new horde back in the throat of it. 'Now let's get out of here, before the rest of them arrive.'

SIXTEEN

'I CAN SEE them!' Magot reported, her team having taken point as we scurried up the tunnel as fast as our legs could carry us. Grifen's team had taken the rearguard, leaving the Nusquans in the middle, as by this point they'd expended so much ammo they had little to defend themselves with beyond withering sarcasm, which in my experience tyranids were seldom bothered by. 'Two Chimeras, still parked.'

Though my natural instinct was to run for the safety they represented as fast as I could, I'd dropped back a little to confer with Forres; partly because it would be expected of me, and it was vital to pass her report back in case we failed to make it out of here, but mainly because if the 'nids had managed to outflank us and were waiting in ambush I'd rather not be the first one to find out.

'They just came at us out of nowhere,' Forres said, her voice steady, but her eyes still numb with the shock of what she'd been through today. 'We deployed for a sweep through the caverns, but as we'd found no sign of the greenskins on the surface we assumed they must already have withdrawn. By the time those creatures appeared, we'd got sloppy.' Her jaw tightened. 'I should have kept a tighter rein, kept everyone up to the mark. But I got careless too.'

'A dozen of the troopers with you survived,' I said, partly because I'd got so used to boosting morale over the years that an encouraging word at times like these had become almost second nature to me, and partly because our conversation was being monitored and that was the sort of thing a Hero of the Imperium was supposed to say, instead of 'What the frak were you thinking, strolling around a war zone like you were on leave?' I had a reputation to consider after all, even if I didn't deserve it. 'Under the circumstances, I'd say that's a pretty strong testament to your leadership. Where did they come from?'

'Up from the lower levels,' Forres said, looking a little happier now that I'd thrown her a bone. I could still remember my first assignment as a newly-inducted commissar, one which had also been interrupted by the sudden appearance of a tyranid horde, so I suppose I may have felt rather more sympathetic towards her than I might otherwise have done; although I doubted that her first impulse had been to head for the horizon while the going was good, like mine had been. 'We were deep enough to smell the volcanic vents, but before we could descend any further they just started pouring out of the tunnels, and we could hear the other units screaming over the vox. Lieutenant Caromort ordered the survivors to link up with her command squad, but we couldn't get through to join them, and the main group was wiped out. I told Sergeant Lanks to pull back and return to the Chimeras, but the swarm caught up with us before we could make it, and cut us off. I spotted the gantry under the pipework, and got everyone who was left up onto it.'

'Which saved their lives,' I pointed out. 'Well done.'

'Not well enough,' Forres said grimly. Some people you just can't help, and now was hardly the time to try and talk some sense into her, so I simply nodded formally, and moved up to join Magot, whose fireteam had reached the floor of the blockhouse we'd been aiming for and begun to fan out across it.

'Doesn't look good,' she greeted me, with a baleful glare at the

Chimeras. I can't say I was surprised to find them in much the same condition as the ones we'd found on our arrival, but the disappointment was profound nonetheless; as so often when things looked really dire, I'd clung to the shred of hope that they might not have been quite as bad as they appeared.

I turned to look at Forres, who had moved up with the rest of the party and was staring at the wrecked vehicles as though someone had just shot her puppy. Concerned murmuring began among the Nusquans, incipient panic not far beneath the surface, and she rounded on them, her expression becoming severe and unemotional as abruptly as the flick of a switch. 'Stay focused,' she snapped. 'We're getting out of this.' It was a good performance, but I'd seen enough to realise she was as terrified as any of them. Me too, come to that, but I was even better at concealing how I felt than she was, having notched up many more years of practice.

'Did you know the crews were dead?' I asked quietly.

'I knew we'd lost contact,' she said, not quite answering the question. 'But I hoped we could get moving without them if necessary.'

'That's not the problem,' I said, pleased to note that Grifen and the sole surviving Nusquan NCO, Lanks I imagined, were already setting up to cover the tunnel mouth as effectively as possible with the limited resources at our disposal while we spoke. 'Jurgen and Magot can drive Chimeras.' After their own idiosyncratic fashion, admittedly, but under the circumstances I wouldn't quarrel with my aide's propensity to jam the throttle as wide open as possible, with a complete disregard for whatever else might be in the vicinity. I gestured at the ripped and battered metal in front of us. 'The problem is that these heaps of scrap aren't going anywhere, however many drivers we've got.'

'It might not be as bad as it looks,' Forres said crisply, before glancing into the driver's compartment of the nearest, the controls of which had been comprehensively mangled in the 'stealers' attempts to wrinkle out the morsels within. Her face fell. 'Oh.'

'"Oh" pretty much covers it,' I agreed, looking round at the rest of the cavernous space. It was smaller than the one we'd entered by, though not by much, and almost as empty. 'We'll have to get out through the main door, and hope our pilot can pick us up from the open ground before the 'nids get too close.' I was no keener to face the bone-chilling cold of the surface than I'd been before, but given the alternative it seemed positively inviting. Unfortunately, the Valkyrie which had brought us here was now providing air cover for the retreating Valhallans, if the transmissions I'd been monitoring in my comm-bead were anything to go by, and it would take several minutes to disengage, circle round, land, and embark us; minutes I was by no means sure we had. I glanced hopefully at the ceiling, but there was no sign of a trapdoor there, or anything by which we could have accessed one even if there had been.

'There's movement on the surface,' the pilot added, as I heard the first unmistakable scrabbling in the depths of the tunnel which meant the swarm beneath our feet was on the move again too. 'Closing on Blockhouse Four. Is that your position?'

'It is,' I confirmed, as the lasguns opened up again behind me. The external doors were solid, but they wouldn't hold an entire swarm back for long, and with another horde of drooling malevolence doing its best to swamp us through the corridor, we couldn't divert any of our rapidly-dwindling firepower to defend against an attack from the outside anyway.

I walked round the Chimeras, which had blocked my view of the far side of the entrance chamber, then stopped, staring, almost unable to believe the evidence of my own eyes. A cargo crawler was parked there, its loading doors open, and its bodywork miraculously unmarred by the furrowing of genestealer claws.

'Jurgen!' I called, sprinting towards it. 'Can you get this thing started?'

'Looks easy enough,' my aide said, clambering up to the cab with remarkable agility, given that he was still burdened with the bulky melta. 'Why isn't it ripped apart like the Chimeras?'

'Nobody hiding inside it, I suppose,' I said, not really caring. It was intact enough to run, and that was all that mattered to me. I hauled myself into the cab after him, finding it a little cramped competing for space with my aide, his body odour, and our mutual collection of weapons, but I'd take a little crowding in preference to ending up as regurgitated biomass in a digestion pool any day.

Jurgen began poking around on the dashboard and I popped my head back out, cracking off a couple of shots at the termagants in the shadows of the tunnel mouth. It seemed that the hive mind had learned to be wary of us, and, unsure of how we'd managed to eliminate so many of its meat puppets in one fell swoop, wasn't keen to commit them to a massed assault just yet. The Valhallans, Nusquans and Forres had hunkered down behind the wrecked Chimeras, and the two sides were exchanging largely ineffectual potshots. From my elevated position I was able to pick off one of the termagants with a, frankly, lucky head shot, before wondering belatedly if attracting their attention was such a good idea, but it raised morale and, more importantly, made it clear that I was getting stuck in along with everybody else. A second or so later, Forres, not wanting to be outdone, blew another apart with a shot from her toy bolter, which neatly established her as a higher priority target in any case.

'That's done it,' Jurgen said a moment later, and the crawler's engine rumbled into life. 'Just need to get the outer doors open.

'There should be a remote override somewhere in the cab,' Lanks put in helpfully over the vox[1].

'Come on, then,' I urged, cracking off another couple of covering shots as the Nusquans began running for the rear cargo doors. It was going to be pretty uncomfortable back there with nothing to sit on, but given the alternative I wasn't expecting anyone to complain.

'Pull back, by fire and movement,' Grifen ordered crisply, and Magot's team trotted after the Nusquans who'd begun scrambling up behind us, while Grifen's switched to full auto, laying down a

---

1. *Surface transportation on an iceworld rarely maintains a reliable schedule, and there isn't always someone available to admit a crawler when it arrives at its destination.*

barrage to cover their retreat. Confident that I'd done enough to be seen to be participating, I ducked back inside the cab and scanned the unfamiliar dashboard.

'This, you think?' I prodded a large button speculatively, and flinched as an ear-splitting klaxon rebounded from the walls around us.

'Try that one, sir,' Jurgen suggested, indicating another, helpfully annotated *ext. access*. Slamming the cab door behind me I pressed it, while Magot's team and the few Nusquans left with an effective fire-arm started laying into the encroaching swarm with commendable vigour from inside the cargo compartment, and Grifen's people ran for the crawler as if Abaddon himself was after them. After what seemed like an agonising wait, but was probably no more than a handful of seconds, the great doors at the end of the hall began to move slowly apart, with a grinding of frozen metal and a crackling of ice still dimly audible through the metal and armourcrys enclosing the cab.

'Here they come!' Grifen called, and a torrent of tyranids burst from the tunnel mouth, as the coin belatedly dropped that the prey they'd believed trapped was on the verge of getting away. A volley of sustained fire met them, ripping into the front rank, and several of the creatures fell. The rest charged on, their headlong rush barely checked as they trampled the fallen underfoot in their eagerness to get to us.

'Go!' I shouted, but Jurgen had already slammed the cumbersome vehicle into gear and was accelerating away, leaving the hor-magaunts which had broken free of the pack bounding fruitlessly in our wake. Howls and cheers of relief and derision echoed in my ear, until Forres restored vox discipline with a few choice words and some pious humbug about serving the Emperor to the best of our abilities. For a moment I feared we wouldn't make it through the still-widening gap, but Jurgen judged it to a nicety as always, and our spinning tracks barely grazed the thick metal slabs on either side before finally biting down in the thick snow for which they'd been designed. 'Hang on back there,' I voxed. 'It's going to be a rough ride.'

A prediction which, had I but known it, would turn out to be all too true.

'Incoming,' Jurgen said, pointing through flurries of wind-driven snow. A dark mass seemed to be moving towards us, flowing across the frigid surface, and with a shudder that had nothing to do with the ambient chill seeping through the insulation of the cab, I realised what it was. The swarm the pilot had warned us about had arrived.

'Can you avoid them?' I asked, and Jurgen shook his head, gunning the engine to a pitch which would have had our enginseers wincing in sympathy.

'They're moving too fast,' he said, and I swallowed, my mouth suddenly dry. The tide of chitin seemed endless, although as tyranid swarms went I suppose it was still on the small side, and it had already swept round to envelop us. 'I'll have to punch through.'

'Good luck,' I said grimly, all too aware of how slim our chances were. I wouldn't have fancied them much even in a well-armoured Chimera, which had forward and turret-mounted heavy weapons to clear the way and a reassuring amount of metal plate to hide behind; but the relatively fragile civilian vehicle had neither. The minute we butted heads with a carnifex we'd be torn apart, even if we hadn't been slowed to a halt by the sheer mass of lesser creatures facing us, clogging our tracks with their pulverised bodies. I'd seen Baneblades immobilised that way before now, so I didn't give much for our chances of forcing our way through in the lightly-built crawler.

'We'll keep the ticks off your back,' our pilot's voice assured us cheerily, and the Valkyrie abruptly appeared from behind us, roaring in over our heads and opening fire on the frenzied mass of tyranids scuttling towards us as it came. The multi-laser scythed through their ranks like a scalpel through flesh, creating a carpet of downed and flailing monstrosities, while those on either side of the line of destruction fell back, milling in confusion for a crucial few seconds as the surviving synapse creatures rearranged themselves to re-establish the neural net and regain control of the others.

'Hold on,' I voxed through to the rear compartment, 'it's about to get bumpy,' then the tracks were mashing chitin and flesh into the snow, staining it colours which made the gorge rise to look at too closely.

'Looks like someone threw up a seafood dinner,' Jurgen said, displaying an uncharacteristically poetic streak, and I nodded, not wanting to think about that too much under the circumstances. A hail of fleshborer rounds rattled against the bodywork and windows, and a few gobbets of acid hissed their way through the metalwork, but fortunately without appearing to damage anything vital.

'Anyone hurt back there?' I asked.

'A few holes in the side,' Grifen reported, 'but no casualties.'

'Stupid frakkers just gave us some firing points,' Magot added, no doubt itching to poke her lasgun through and start potting 'nids again.

'No need,' I assured her as the Vakyrie banked lazily in the distance, and came back for another strafing run. 'The flyboys are doing the job for us.'

'All part of the service,' the pilot assured us, a tone of amusement entering his voice. Then the nose-mounted weapon opened up again, carving another swathe through the swarm and throwing it into confusion once more. By the time he'd banked round for a third run the first of the Valkyries carrying Lustig's people to safety had joined in too, and the balance had tilted decisively in favour of the Imperium. With too few of the hulking warriors left to coordinate the swarm effectively, the entire formation began to disintegrate, the termagants scuttling off in search of a place to hide, while the hormagaunts began devouring the carrion which littered the gruesomely-stained ice.

'We're clear,' Jurgen said a moment later, slewing us round a little to bounce a fleeing termagant under the tracks, where it expired messily.

'I believe we are,' I said, sighing deeply with relief, and realising rather too late that I was going to be in a confined space with

Jurgen for several hours. 'Let's hope we get a clear run back to Primadelving.'

My aide nodded, in his usual phlegmatic manner, his attention almost entirely on the snowfield in front of us. 'Powercells are charged, and the weather looks fair,' he assured me. 'We should get there without too many problems.'

A prediction which was to prove a long way wide of the mark.

SEVENTEEN

I WAS NO stranger to iceworlds, and to this one in particular, but I must confess to finding the long journey back to Primadelving a rather enjoyable novelty. (At least until its premature and unfortunate termination.) On most of the previous occasions I'd been driven across the surface it had been aboard a Chimera, from which the view had been somewhat restricted to say the least; but the high, glazed cab of the crawler afforded an unimpeded view of the icefields and undulating snowdrifts, which enabled me to appreciate the rugged panorama in a manner which had previously eluded me. I'd been out there on foot, of course, rather more often than I would have liked, but on those occasions I'd been a bit too preoccupied with the immense discomfort of the cold, and the likelihood of something trying to kill me, to stop and admire the view.

About half an hour after we'd left the agricave behind, the snowclouds which seemed to have blanketed everything since our first arrival on the surface of Nusquam Fundumentibus finally parted, revealing a sky of bright, translucent blue, against which the snow and ice glittered, dazzling the eye.

'You don't want to be looking too long at that,' Jurgen said, manipulating one of the controls to polarise the windscreen. 'It'll send you snowblind.'

'At least I'm not the one driving,' I said, picking out the bright moving dot of one of the Valkyries in the distance; still searching for tyranids roaming about on the surface, although most of the remnants of the swarm had long since retreated back into the depths of the agricave, safe from aerial bombardment, and all but the most suicidal of attempts to dislodge them from their underground refuge. 'I'm sure Magot would take a turn if you needed a break.'

By way of reply he just snorted, and opened the throttle a little wider, sending us skimming across an open ice sheet, the plume of powdered snow flung up by our tracks dissipating slowly in the air behind us. 'Have you seen how she drives?'

'Good point,' I conceded, not wanting to wound his pride, and noticing that for once he seemed to be moderating our speed. Not only that, he was adjusting our course seemingly at random, turning to the left or right every few moments for no reason that I could see. 'Is there a problem?'

'Crevasse field,' he told me, as though it were only a minor matter, which I suppose for an iceworlder it may well have been. 'The snow covers most of 'em, but the ice is riddled.'

'Very deep?' I asked, trying to sound casual, and Jurgen nodded.

'Probably no more than twenty or thirty metres for a really big one,' he said. 'But there won't be many of those to worry about. It's the small ones that'll break our tracks if we hit 'em wrong.'

'I see,' I said, trying not to think about a thirty metre plunge any more than I could help, and glancing around us for some sign of a distraction. A flicker of movement near the crest of a nearby ice ridge caught my attention, and I fumbled the amplivisor into my hand for a closer look.

'More 'nids?' Jurgen asked, and I nodded, trying to focus the image despite the bouncing of the fast-moving vehicle.

'Close combat forms,' I said, finally getting a clear image. 'About half a dozen, looks like. And one of the larger warrior forms.'

'That's unusual,' Jurgen remarked, changing our course towards them, just as the last of the group disappeared behind the ridge. 'They don't normally bother herding so few.'

'No, they don't,' I agreed, uneasily. 'Perhaps I just saw the tail end of a larger group.'

'Do you think we should check it out?' Jurgen asked, and I nodded.

'I think we'd better,' I conceded reluctantly. In my experience, tyranids acting atypically never meant anything good. If they had another little surprise to spring on us, I'd rather they did so where there was plenty of room to see it coming, and from a vehicle which would allow me to outrun them easily. I voxed the Valkyrie. 'We've just sighted a small group of 'nids,' I said. 'Moving to intercept.'

'Acknowledged,' the pilot said, 'and on the way. They should be easy enough to spot from the air. Just got a few stragglers to mop up here first.'

'I'm not sure these are stragglers,' I confided to Jurgen. We'd seen several packs of 'gaunts wandering aimlessly through the desolate landscape, or attempting to take refuge from the shadows of the gunships[1], but none so far had been under the direction of a synapse creature; whereas the ones we'd seen were definitely moving with purpose. 'Can you get close enough for a reasonable view, without coming into range of their weapons?' The warrior I'd seen only seemed to be carrying the deathspitter common to such creatures, which made sense if it was leading a swarm of close combat organisms, but there could easily be another I'd missed, with something longer ranged, and capable of making a mess of our vehicle.

'Reckon so,' Jurgen agreed, starting up the side of the ridge, heedless of the profanity echoing from the cargo compartment behind us as the floor suddenly tilted without warning. 'If I stop just short of the crest, we can take a look over without them seeing us.'

He was as good as his word, as always, bringing the ungainly crawler to a halt in the lee of a cluster of ice boulders, which the

---

1. *Technically, the Valkyries were armed transports rather than dedicated weapon platforms, like the Vendetta variant, but more than capable of carrying out a seek and destroy mission against unarmoured infantry nevertheless.*

wind had sculpted into semi-transparent mirrors. Ignoring my bizarrely distorted reflection, I trained the amplivisor down to the floor of the defile beyond the line of the ridge.

'They're just hitting the ice with their scything claws,' I said, in some puzzlement. 'Breaking it up into small pieces.'

'Are they trying to dig in?' Kasteen asked, her voice buzzing in my comm-bead, and sounding almost as bewildered as I felt. Tyranids never built fortifications, or anything else come to that; manipulating their inanimate surroundings was as alien to their nature as horticulture to a necron. 'Or trying to tunnel back to the caves to get away from the aircraft?'

'I don't think so,' I said. They were spread out too widely to be pooling their efforts, although each one was making quite rapid progress in pulverising the ice in its immediate vicinity. 'They're not exactly designed for digging.' Though I had to concede that the long, curved claws seemed to make pretty effective pickaxes.

'Only one of the big ones I can see,' Jurgen put in helpfully, and I nodded, more puzzled than ever. The presence of the warrior implied a specific end in view, but what it might be continued to elude me.

'Not for long,' the Valkyrie pilot assured us, and began his attack run. Warned by the noise of the engine and the shadow which swooped across them, the 'gaunts raised their heads and shifted uncertainly, looking for something to charge, but their overseer kept their instinctive aggression in check, and they began moving towards an overhang of ice at a rapid trot.

Before they could make it, the Valkyrie opened fire, strafing the group with its multi-laser. A line of steam and pulverised ice swept across the scattered swarm, tearing several of them apart, and throwing the rest into momentary disarray, but the warrior remained unharmed and rallied them, turning to fire its deathspitter ineffectually at the harrying aircraft as it banked steeply and came round for another go. This time all the creatures had managed to reach the refuge of the overhang, but it did them little good: the whole ice face disappeared for a moment in a cloud of superheated steam, then, with a grinding roar audible even through the bodywork of the crawler's cab, it collapsed on top of them.

'Job done,' the pilot said, with every sign of satisfaction.

'Let's hope so,' I said, having considerably more experience of the resilience of tyranids than he did. Accordingly we remained where we were, the engine idling, while I kept the amplivisor trained on the pile of frozen rubble, alert for any sign of movement; but after some minutes passed without so much as a twitch, I began to breathe easier. (Or as easy as it was possible to do, sharing a small cab with Jurgen.)

'Shall we go, sir?' my aide asked, once it became clear that the 'nids weren't about to pop up again, and I nodded.

'Might as well,' I agreed, mindful of the pot of hot tanna waiting for me back in Primadelving, and raised the amplivisor for one last look. An impulse I regretted instantly. 'Do iceworlds have earthquakes?'

'Not really,' Jurgen said, craning his neck to look in the same direction. 'The ice shifts sometimes, or you might get an avalanche...' His voice trailed off, taking on an unmistakable tone of puzzlement. 'That's not an avalanche.'

The ice was beginning to crack and bulge, right where the 'gaunts had been hammering away at it, rising up and falling away, to reveal something vast and living beneath it. A roar of anger and frustration echoed across the icefield as something huge and animate fought to free itself from the imprisoning ice.

'Go!' I shouted, slapping Jurgen on the shoulder in my eagerness to be anywhere but here; a desire he evidently shared, judging by the speed with which he slammed the crawler into gear and took off, our spinning tracks throwing up a glittering arc of pulverised snow in our wake.

'What's that noise?' Forres voxed from the rear compartment, her voice overlapping with Grifen's somewhat calmer request for information.

'One of the huge ones,' I replied, glancing back to see a mountain of chitin rearing up to its full height, its bloated body dwarfing our crawler, as it shook the last of the broken ice from an impossibly spindly-seeming leg.

'Then we should stop and engage it,' Forres said, 'before it can join the main body of the swarm.'

'If we do that, we'll die,' I snapped back, in no mood for any more of her head-on approach to warfare. 'Our small arms can barely scratch its hide.'

'Nevertheless,' Forres said, audibly bristling, 'our duty demands...'

'Our duty demands we live to report this, so we can mount an effective defence and save this planet for the Emperor,' I said, in no mood for argument. I glanced back, seeing, to my horror, the vast bulk scrambling over the ridgeline behind us, blotting out the watery sunshine as it came, clearly in pursuit of our fleeing vehicle. 'If you want to take a crack at it anyway, just open the rear door.'

'I thought you'd never ask,' Magot chipped in happily, and a second or two later the rapid *crack* of lasguns became audible through the bulkhead separating the cab from the cargo compartment.

'Sir,' Grifen reported a moment later, 'it's started spawning. Just dropped a dozen or so of the gunners.'

'Keep down,' I advised unnecessarily. 'If they get close enough to use their fleshborers...'

'I know,' Grifen said. 'Can't we outrun them?'

'That's the idea,' I said, turning to Jurgen as I spoke. 'Can we speed up at all?'

'It's risky,' he replied, the thin furrows of grime on his forehead eloquent testament to the effort he was having to expend to keep up our pace on the treacherous terrain. 'The ground's very broken here, and there's no telling what's under the snow.'

'I can tell you what's behind us at the moment,' I said acidly, then regretted it at once. Jurgen had an almost preternatural ability to push a vehicle to its limits, which he exercised at every opportunity, and if it was at all possible to be travelling faster he undoubtedly would be. 'Just do your best. Under the circumstances, there's no one I'd rather have in the driving seat.'

'Thank you, sir,' he said, any offence he might have taken at my earlier offhand manner effectively neutralised, and returned his attention to picking his way through the treacherous landscape. Our engine roared as we lurched over innumerable cracks in the surface and metre-high ridges, every obstruction costing us a little more of our precious lead. 'If I can just get through this, we should be back in the clear at any...' Then the snow gave way beneath us, and the whole vehicle dropped.

For a heart-stopping instant I thought we were dead, about to plunge thirty metres to an icy grave, but we turned out to have hit nothing more than a shallow trench, little different to the ones which had impeded us before. This time, however, the angle had been bad, leaving us canted awkwardly; Jurgen gunned the engine, but nothing happened, beyond a howl of protest from the abused mechanism and a short burst of profanity from my aide.

'That's it,' he said shortly, 'the track's frakked,' and, sure enough, as I looked out of the side window, I could see that it had been sprung from its guide wheels by the impact.

'Can you ease it back on?' I asked, with an apprehensive glance at the looming bulk of the onrushing leviathan, bearing down on us like an ill-tempered storm front, its progeny skittering around its feet as it came.

'Not a chance,' Jurgen said gloomily. 'We're wedged in.' He grabbed the melta and flung open the cab door, replacing his aroma with air so cold I lost the ability to smell anything almost at once. 'Best get to it, then, I suppose.'

'I suppose we'd better,' I said, following him out onto the snowy surface after a quick scramble up a slope of broken ice. The Valhallans and Nusquans bailed out after us, still blazing away, as though it would make any difference to the behemoth.

'Place your feet carefully,' Jurgen advised. 'There are bound to be more crevasses about.

'I'll bear that in mind,' I said, looking around for something to take cover behind, and almost bumping into Forres, who was staring at the gargantuan creature bearing down on us as though still struggling to take it in. (Which I suppose, in all fairness, she might well have been.) I smiled at her, but without much amusement. 'Well, commissar, it looks as though we'll be trying it your way after all.'

'Aim for its head,' she told Lanks, pointedly ignoring me. 'That'll be where it's most vulnerable.'

'It's not vulnerable anywhere to lasgun rounds,' I said. 'Concentrate on the termagants. Leave the big one to Jurgen and the Valkyrie.' The melta had been designed to knock out tanks, so it should be able to get through the huge creature's exoskeleton, although whether it would hit anything vital once it did would be a matter for luck and the Emperor.

'Sounds good to me,' Grifen said decisively. Lanks looked at her, then me, then finally back to Forres.

After a moment the young Commissar shrugged. 'Follow their recommendations,' she said shortly. 'They've fought tyranids before.'

'And won,' Magot added cheerfully.

I nodded, as if I shared her confidence, although truth to tell I was far from doing so. The frozen ground was shaking beneath my feet, and the shadow of the oncoming leviathan seemed large enough to blot out the sun. The crack of lasgun fire opened up again, still disciplined, I was pleased to note, and the termagants scuttling round the feet of the gigantic creature flinched for a moment before the overriding will of their dam drove them on.

'Commencing attack run,' the Valkyrie pilot voxed, and a moment later twin streaks of fire struck the monster high on its flank, followed almost at once by a double explosion which tore open its carapace. Viscera and noisome fluids gushed and fountained, and the towering creature staggered, bellowing in anger and pain. It reared up on its back four legs, flailing at the swooping aircraft like a man bothered by a fly, then staggered as its forelimbs crashed back to the ice. Its retinue began to mill around uncertainly, failing to press the attack. 'Lucky I hung on to the Hellstrikes like you told me to.'

'It was indeed,' I agreed. The two warheads had inflicted a hideous wound, but the tervigon seemed far from out of the fight. It came on inexorably towards us, slipping occasionally in the spreading slick of its own ichor, exposed organs and musculature pulsing as it came. It had slowed, however, and that alone was reason enough to hope.

'Get down!' Grifen bellowed, having spotted the telltale quivering along its back an instant before I did. The Valhallans and I hit the snow, Forres and the Nusquans following suit a moment later, without stopping to argue or ask questions about it, which I suppose was progress of a sort. A salvo of cluster spines hissed through the air, shattering into a storm of razor-edged flechettes as they hit the ground, which pattered all around me like sinister rain, and felled a couple of the tardiest Nusquans.

'Target the wound!' I shouted, raising myself enough to crack off a few shots at the towering monstrosity with my laspistol, and the troopers followed suit, Valhallans and Nusquans alike.

'You said it was pointless firing lasguns at it,' Forres said, her tone challenging, 'and to concentrate on the termagants.'

'That was before. It's vulnerable now.' I continued to shoot steadily as I spoke. 'If we kill it, the spawn die too.'[1]

'If they don't kill us first,' Forres observed, as the first fleshborer fusillade fell a few metres short of our position, but she shifted her aim nonetheless, peppering the area around the gaping hole in the behemoth's armour with a flurry of bolts[2]; a couple detonated against the organs inside, and the flesh mountain staggered again. The constant rain of las-rounds against exposed viscera must have been agonising, which may have accounted for the loose control it appeared to have over its offspring; they skittered nervously, firing individually, then scurrying back into the cover afforded by their parent's legs, instead of forming a skirmish line ahead of it as I would have expected.

'Whenever you're ready, Jurgen,' I said, as my aide lined up a shot

---

1. *A frequently observed phenomenon, apparently the result of some form of psychic feedback.*

2. *Despite the size of the target, the range would still be extreme for a pistol shot, so it's hardly surprising she didn't hit the mark consistently.*

with the melta. 'Take your time.' The shot had to be a clean one: as soon as he fired, he'd mark himself out as the greatest threat among us, and the tervigon and its offspring would react accordingly.

'Almost there, sir,' he assured me, shifting the cumbersome weapon a millimetre or two, then pulled the trigger. I closed my eyes reflexively, seeing the bright flare through the lids, and blinked, afterimages continuing to dance on my retina. 'That ought to do it.'

'I think you're right,' I said, in mingled surprise and relief. The shot had been a clean one, as I'd had no doubt it would be, the ravening blast of energy penetrating deep into the monster's body. With a keen ululation it fell, legs scrabbling for traction, and crushing most of the termagants around it into the ice with the weight of its own body.

'Forward!' Forres yelled. 'Finish it off while it's down!' Brandishing her chainsword, she ran towards it, while the rest of us looked at one another in astonishment.

'Look out!' I shouted, seeing its head turn, jaws which could bite a Chimera in half snapping angrily. I had no objection to her getting herself killed – in fact it would probably save a lot of lives in the long run – but just standing aside and watching it happen wasn't the kind of behaviour expected of a Hero of the Imperium. If there was any chance of saving this miserable iceball, we needed the Nusquans to be fully committed to its defence, and convinced they could win, which unfortunately meant living up to my unmerited reputation yet again. Cursing all over-enthusiastic idiots, I charged forward, intending to drag her back; but she'd seen the danger, and her bolt pistol barked, just as the downed leviathan opened its jaws. The explosive round detonated against the back of its throat, and the entire monstrosity convulsed.

'That should put an end to it,' she said, in a self-congratulatory fashion, holstering her weapon as she turned to meet me.

'It was dying anyway!' I expostulated, catching a glimpse of movement behind her. It may have been down, but it was certainly not out, spawning a fresh brood of termagants to take revenge on its behalf. A small knot of them was moving out of the shadow of their parent, their carapaces still glistening with the fluids of the nutrient sac they'd been cocooned in during their dormancy, flesh-borers raised. I fired my laspistol, turning to flee, then the snow gave way beneath my boot.

I pitched forward, falling free for a moment, then slammed into a steep slope of ice, down which I slithered for a second or two, doing my much abused uniform no favours in the process. Above my head I could hear the crackle of lasgun fire, and the distinctive *hisssss crack!* of Forres's miniature bolter, then everything abruptly went silent.

'Commissar!' Grifen's voice echoed in my comm-bead. 'Are you all right?'

'I'm fine,' I replied, after a second or two to make sure of the fact. Dim blue daylight reflected off the ice all round me, so I was able to make out my surroundings with little difficulty. I was in an icy cleft, some three or four metres deep and of indeterminate length, roofed over for the most part by a thick layer of compacted snow. 'Just found one of those crevasses Jurgen warned me about. What's going on up there?'

'It just died,' Grifen said. 'And the termagants with it. Just rolled over in the middle of the firefight.'

'Any casualties?' I asked, because it never hurt to look as if I cared.

'No fresh ones,' Grifen assured me, 'although one of the Nus-quans is in a pretty bad way from the cluster spine barrage. Can you climb out the way you fell in?'

'Don't think so,' I said, taking out my luminator and shining it around in an attempt to get a better picture of where I was. The slope I'd slithered down was too sheer and slippery to even think about trying. 'There might be a cable or something in the crawler's toolkit.'

'Already on my way back to see, sir,' Jurgen cut in, as reliable as ever, and, reassured, I began to make my way along the crevasse. At least I was out of that damned wind, for once, and although it could hardly be described as warm, at least I felt more comfortable than I had on the surface.

'I'll see if it gets any easier further along,' I said, by no means certain that it would, but at least going to find out would give me something to do while I waited for rescue. The reflective nature of the ice surrounding me made the luminator appear much brighter than it would normally do, and I made good progress, in spite of the treacherous surface underfoot.

As I went on, I began to notice occasional patches of discolouration in the translucent ice, and, moved more by idle curiosity than anything else, I stopped by one which seemed clearer than most. There seemed to be something solid embedded in it, and I held up the luminator, rubbing the smooth surface with my glove as if trying to clear the condensation from a misty window. It achieved nothing, of course, beyond making my palm wet, but as I moved the hand holding the luminator a little more to one side, the angle of the beam shifted, throwing the entombed object into sharp relief.

'Emperor's bowels!' I expostulated, with an involuntary flinch backwards. The serpentine form of a tyranid ravener, twice my size, was coiled through the ice, seemingly poised to burst out and attack. A moment later, as the hammering of my heart died back to more normal levels, I began to breathe a little more easily. The foul creature was clearly inert, entombed like the tervigon had been. It might even have been dead, but after what I'd seen earlier, I doubted that; it only needed the presence of an active synapse creature to rouse and join the ever-swelling ranks of the tyranid invasion.

'Say again, commissar?' Grifen asked, with an air of puzzlement.

'There are 'nids down here,' I said, all too aware of the consternation my words would be causing back in Primadelving. 'Hibernating or dead, although my money would be on the first. If they all wake...' I let the thought trail off, unwilling to verbalise it.

Kasteen, however, had no such scruples. 'We won't stand a chance,' she finished for me.

EIGHTEEN

'WELL, AT LEAST we know where the greenskins went,' Broklaw said, with a typically sardonic grin. 'The 'nids have been eating them.'

I nodded, although none of the other faces ranged around the conference table in a room adjacent to the main command post seemed to find anything remotely amusing in the situation. Kasteen, Broklaw and I were seated along one side of the polished wooden slab, while Colonel Brecca, her second-in-command (whose name I still hadn't managed to catch), and Forres faced us, looking fidgety and uncomfortable, which I could hardly blame them for. At the rate things were going, they wouldn't have a regiment left to lead before too much longer[1]. Clothilde was at the head of the table, as protocol demanded, surrounded by a small clot of advisors, who, for the most part, seemed well aware of how out of their depth they were, and were sensible enough to stay quiet as a consequence. The PDF contingent was on the same side

---

1. *Something of an exaggeration, as recruiting among the PDF was continuing at more or less the same rate as before, although most of the newly-inducted troopers were going to replace combat losses in the existing companies rather than swell the ranks of those which still existed only on paper.*

of the table as the Nusquans, which seemed reasonable enough as it was their damn planet and they were used to working together, which left the Adeptus Mechanicus delegation (headed of course by Izembard), and the other Imperial institutions[1] on ours.

'Thus replacing one problem with another,' Clothilde remarked, with a glance towards the PDF general staffers, who for the most part looked as far out of their depth as she did.

'We should be able to turn this to our advantage,' Forres said, with the calm assurance of total ignorance. 'If we can manoeuvre the tyranids into directly confronting the orks, they'll eradicate the greenskins, and be weakened enough for us to pick off the survivors easily.'

'Except that every ork they consume makes the whole swarm stronger,' Kasteen pointed out[2], 'not to mention their own casualties. Trying to use the 'nids against the orks is about as sensible as trying to hide a scorch mark in the hearthrug by burning the house down.'

'A colourful analogy,' I said, to forestall any heated response from Forres, 'but the point is essentially correct. The orks are a sideshow now, and they'll keep. We need to turn every resource we possess against the tyranids, while we can still make a difference.' Kasteen and Broklaw were nodding in agreement, knowing all too well how big a threat the creatures posed compared to the one we'd been sent here to deal with. To my relief Clothilde was nodding too, evidently convinced by our argument.

'What I want to know is where the horrid things came from in the first place,' she said. 'Our auspexes haven't recorded any unusual activity in the system, have they?'

---

1. *Although he doesn't bother to specify which they were, the minutes of the meeting record the presence of a delegate from the Arbitrator's office, several members of the Administratum, a cardinal from the cathedral, presumably there to provide purely spiritual support as the Orders Militant of the Adepta Sororitas had no members currently active on Nusquam Fundumentibus, and a senior astropath from the Choir in Primadelving.*

2. *Which makes her considerably more far-sighted than Inquisitor Kryptmann, whose attempt to pull off the same trick on a galactic scale left an unholy mess for the Ordo Xenos to sort out.*

This last question was addressed to a woman with iron-grey hair, in the uniform of an admiral of the System Defence Fleet; judging by the strain her girth imposed on the fastenings, her days of active service in the cramped confines of a warship were long behind her.

'Nothing,' she responded at once, 'although that doesn't mean there's nothing there. Tyranid vessels are notoriously difficult to detect at long ranges. The SDF is mounting a reconnaissance sweep of the inner system, but that'll take some time to complete.'

'Especially as the entire fleet consists of two customs cutters and a courier boat,' Kasteen muttered, *sotto voce*[1].

'If there is a hive ship in system,' I said, 'it must be alone. Astropathic communication hasn't been disrupted by the shadow a fleet would cast in the warp.' Something I was completely certain about, having dispatched a brief summation of the situation to Amberley at the earliest opportunity, on the assumption that the sudden appearance of tyranids far in advance of the oncoming hive fleets was bound to be of interest to her particular branch of the Inquisition[2]. The chances of her turning up to sort out the matter in person were unfortunately minimal, however, which left us on our own to deal with it.

'That's something, anyway,' Clothilde said. 'At least we can call for help.'

'Already done,' Kasteen said crisply, with a nod at the grey-robed astropath sitting at the far end of the table. 'Reinforcements should be on their way from Coronus. How long they take to arrive, though...' She shrugged expressively, all too familiar with the vagaries of warp travel, not to mention the inertia of the Munitorum, and the pressing need for far more troopers in far more places than the Guard actually possessed.

'That's most encouraging,' Clothilde said, 'but it still hasn't answered my question. Why have the tyranids suddenly appeared out of nowhere?'

---

1. *Not entirely true; they also had three Aquila class shuttles on the roster, although one of these was undergoing a routine refit at the time and was unavailable for use.*

2. *An assumption which was most certainly correct.*

'Because they've always been here,' Izembard said, his flat mechanical drone adding to the drama of his announcement. 'Preliminary analysis of the specimens found by Commissar Cain, and the depth of the ice around them, would suggest that they were frozen approximately seven thousand years ago. Assuming a relatively even rate of ice formation, of course.'

'Long before the planet was colonised,' Brecca put in, for the benefit of those of us from offworld.

'They must have been stranded here,' Izembard went on, unperturbed by the interruption. 'Finding nothing to consume, they returned to the dormant state in which they'd travelled between the stars, becoming buried by the drifting snow.'

'But people have been living here for millennia,' Forres protested. 'How come nobody's stumbled across one before now?'

'Because it's an iceworld,' I said. 'People stick close to the cavern cities or one of the outposts, unless they absolutely have to. That's how the orks disappeared so thoroughly after the invasion.' Then, struck by an even more unsettling thought, I added: 'Besides, maybe someone has found a 'nid from time to time. If one got roused by the presence of prey, it'd go dormant again after feeding, wouldn't it?'

'Perhaps,' Izembard said, his artificial monotone failing to disguise his scepticism.

'That still doesn't explain why so many of them have woken up now,' Broklaw objected, 'right after we arrived...' His voice trailed off as a rather large coin suddenly dropped.

'It was us,' I said. 'When our ship crashed, it melted the ice all around the impact site, and there must have been a few tyranids close enough to be thawed out.' All of a sudden the movement I remembered spotting in the water, and in the snowstorm when Jurgen and I had found the abandoned ork vehicles, took on far greater and more sinister significance.

'Then why didn't they just attack you while you disembarked?' Forres asked, clearly impatient with so wild a flight of fancy.

'Because they've been biding their time,' I said. 'Picking off the orks for biomass, and digging out more of the buried ones.'

'So now we're facing an army of the things,' Kasteen concluded.

'I'm afraid we are,' I said. 'The only good news is that we'll be getting reinforcements and they won't.'

'We can't just sit back and wait for the troopships to arrive,' Forres said, making her first intelligent contribution of the day. 'The tyranids could have overrun us by then.'

'We're stretched pretty thin already,' Brecca put in, 'and there are hundreds of sites around the Leeward Barrens we need to protect. If we pull our picket lines back, that'll give us more units to redeploy, but the rest of the orks can just rampage across the province.'

'The orks are not the problem,' I reiterated, amazed that she hadn't seemed to grasp that yet. 'If they do advance, they'll just keep the 'nids busy while we evacuate as many of the outlying settlements as we can, and get on with reinforcing the garrisons in the main population centres.'

I exchanged an uneasy glance with Kasteen and Broklaw as I spoke. We all knew from experience that concentrating the population in larger groups was doing little more than setting up a smorgasbord so far as the tyranids were concerned, but at least it would mean fewer sites to defend.

'That still leaves us stretched damnably thin,' Brecca said, reasonably enough. 'What we really need is some way of predicting which sites are most at risk of attack.'

'Magos?' Clothilde asked, looking down the table at Izembard. 'Have you any suggestions?'

'We are working on a predictive algorithm,' the tech-priest assured her, 'but the variables involved are both numerous and difficult to calculate.'

'It might help if we knew why they attacked the sites they did,' Forres said, which made two sensible comments in a row, a record so far as I could see.

'And how,' I added. 'The external doors to the power plant were all sealed when we arrived.'

'Same with the agricaves,' Forres said.

'No mystery why they struck there,' Broklaw put in. 'All that bio-mass would seem like the motherlode to a 'nid swarm.'

'That doesn't explain how they detected it,' Brecca said. 'Or how so many of them were able to get inside without anyone noticing.'

'They do have some specialised organisms bred for infiltration,' Izembard put in helpfully.

'But we didn't see any of those,' I replied. 'Just 'gaunts and gene-stealers, with a few of the warrior forms to keep them focused.'

'That's all we saw too,' Forres confirmed. 'When we arrived, the place seemed abandoned, then they just started swarming up out of the lower levels.'

'Which is where we found them in the power plant,' I added, just as Jurgen leaned over my shoulder to place a mug of recaff on the table. Given the sensitivity of the matters we were discussing, few of the palace servants could be trusted to serve refreshments during the meeting, so Jurgen was standing in for them, his status as my aide putting both his probity and discretion beyond question. As I moved to pick up the steaming beverage, I caught a full strength whiff of his personal miasma, and a stray thought fell into place. 'Near the volcanic vents.'

'There were vents in the agricave too,' Forres added. 'We could smell the sulphur, even though we never got down to the deepest parts.

'You're surely not suggesting these creatures got in through the lava flow?' Clothilde asked, incredulity ringing in her voice. 'They'd be burned to a crisp.'

'They would,' I agreed, the memory of the swarm advancing across the narrow isthmus of rock surrounded by magma to attack Hell's Edge still uncomfortably vivid, 'if they fell in. But I've seen them withstand incredible temperatures. And some of them can squeeze through gaps far too narrow for a human.'

'Warriors can't,' Kasteen objected.

'It's an interesting hypothesis, nevertheless,' Izembard put in. 'Many of the tyranid forms are adapted for burrowing, and Com-missar Cain himself witnessed hormagaunts digging in a manner most unusual for their kind. With sufficient determination, the swarm might well be able to enlarge the natural fissures in the rock enough to squeeze through.'

'Then we're frakked,' Broklaw said flatly. 'This whole area's riddled with them, isn't it?'

'It is,' Izembard confirmed, his mechanical drone imbuing the words with an air of inescapable doom. 'However, the geological stresses would force any passages dug closed again in relatively short order.'

'So the entire swarm can't travel that way?' Kasteen asked, and the magos shook his head.

'Not in any great numbers, or for any appreciable distance. I would assume it to be a strategy for circumventing defences, or striking without warning.'

'That's something anyway,' Kasteen said, clearly determined to find something positive in the situation. 'We just need to keep a look out for the main body on the surface, and rig up seismographs to warn us if any are tunnelling in.'

'They may not be entirely reliable,' Izembard warned, 'given the unstable nature of the Leeward Barrens. Minor shocks and tremors are registering all the time.'

'It's got to be better than nothing,' Kasteen said, triggering nods of agreement around the table.

'Does any of this help your predictive algorithm?' I asked Izembard, trying to purge the question of any lingering trace of sarcasm, and he nodded thoughtfully.

'It narrows a few of the parameters down,' he said cautiously. 'But there's one target I can predict with complete confidence.'

'And that is?' Forres asked, as though itching to march off at once to defend it.

An expression as close to surprise as was possible on a visage with so high a proportion of metal to flesh flickered across the tech-priest's face. He raised an arm, sweeping it to take in our immediate surroundings. 'Primadelving,' he said, as though it was obvious.

I nodded, my mouth dry. 'Biggest concentration of biomass on the planet,' I agreed.

Editorial Note:

In the interest of giving a wider perspective on the campaign, I have once again been forced to turn to the most reliable and least readable of the eyewitness accounts. Those of my readers who feel that the additional clarification it affords is scant recompense for the labour of perusing it may rest assured that nothing essential will be lost by omitting to do so, although it does fill in a few gaps in Cain's account.

From *Like a Phoenix on the Wing: the Early Campaigns and Glorious Victories of the Valhallan 597th* by General Jenit Sulla (retired), 101 M42.

IF ANY AMONG us felt dismay or trepidation at the news of the tyranid presence here, among the pristine snows and cloud-capped mountains of fair Nusquam Fundumentibus, no sign of it was evident among the doughty warriors I was so privileged to lead. Instead, a spirit of grim determination suffused us all, our resolve bolstered as always by the shining example of Commissar Cain. Despite enduring so much to uncover this new and dreadful threat, Cain remained calm and resolute, his unfailing good humour and unshakable confidence in our ultimate victory doing so much to steady the nerves of any who might waver.

To my quiet pride, First Company was given the task of cleansing the cavern complex of the swarm which had infested it, and from which the noble Commissar had so heroically rescued the beleaguered survivors of the Nusquan First, his exceptional leadership and expertise in overcoming these loathsome creatures proving as inspiring to the women and men of the fledgling local regiment as to our own.

Having read and reread his characteristically self-effacing account of events, along with Sergent Grifen's after-action report and that of her Nusquan opposite number, I had determined our optimum strategy to be a steady advance, cavern by cavern, with the flamers of our special weapons squads in the vanguard, supported by the massed firepower of at least two infantry squads. This, I felt, would be sufficient to blunt any attempt to overwhelm us by sheer weight of numbers, the favoured tactic of the hive mind, but one which would be far less effective in the relatively confined spaces of the cavern system, where the passageways connecting them would create choke points, restricting the number of creatures able to engage us at any given time. In order to maximise this advantage, I proposed to block the passages tangential to our advance with demolition charges, thus preventing the foul xenos spawn from outflanking us.

In the event, however, the meticulously-planned operation proved something of an anti-climax; as our Chimeras parked around the periphery of the complex, where their heavy bolters could create overlapping fire lanes, either clearing the way for our advance, or, Emperor forfend, covering an orderly retreat should the enemy prove more formidable than expected, we could detect no sign of movement on the surface, beyond the picturesque swirling of the wind-driven snow. Our advance into the complex went almost completely unopposed, only a handful of the unnaturally twisted organisms remaining there, no doubt, to ensure that no speck of organic matter which might previously have escaped their notice went unconsumed; these were dispatched as quickly and enthusiastically as one might wish, and their cadavers incinerated to ensure that the tyranids would be permanently deprived of the resources they contained. Of the great mass of the swarm there was no sign to be seen, the vast majority of its members already having departed in search of fresh provender to consume.

In the days that followed, however, we were to see plenty of evidence of its further depredations, as outlying settlements and installations fell victim to its relentless advance. Though the planetary governor, following the sound advice of Colonel Kasteen and Commissar Cain, had ordered a general evacuation of all such vulnerable habitations, the work took time, and the tyranids exploited every delay. Almost as bad, in its way, was the advance of the orkish hordes, which took full advantage of the redeployment of the Imperial forces to meet the greater threat by surging unchecked across the icefields, looting and despoiling such luckless communities as fell into their hands before the tyranids could reach them.

Inevitably the two xenos breeds clashed, buying valuable time for the evacuation effort, but we were all aware that a battle for our very survival, and that of the whole planet, was imminent. When it came, of course, Commissar Cain was to be at the forefront, his contribution decisive, as so often in his illustrious career.

NINETEEN

As so often happens when facing the tyranids, we were thrown on the defensive, which is never a good place to be. Just to make matters worse the tyranids had split into several smaller groups, which ranged the Leeward Barrens more or less at will, striking small and undefended targets before they could be evacuated or defended[1]. The only positive thing was that, so far, the infestation was still confined to the Barrens; so the evacuated civilians were sent to other provinces, in the hope that we could contain the situation before it grew to the point where they'd be back on the menu wherever they were.

'We should be thinking about evacuating the capital too,' I said, seizing the chance for a relatively quiet talk with Clothilde which an invitation to dine in her private quarters had afforded. It was nothing unusual for a planetary governor to host some kind of reception for the senior officers of a newly-arrived regiment, which was generally extended to include the Commissar and any other

---

1. *Some sites, like the remaining power stations, were too vital to abandon completely, their skeleton staffs supplemented by no doubt terrified PDF troopers, whose Valkyries stood ready to pluck them to safety should their defences be breached.*

advisors attached to the command staff, but the guest list for such affairs normally ran into the low hundreds, all the local nobility and their hangers-on jockeying for a chance to be seen with the defenders of the Imperium. Given the swarms of inbred parasites which my inflated reputation seemed to attract, despite the presence of Jurgen at my elbow, I generally sent my excuses, but in this case the governor had made it quite clear that it was to be a small, informal affair; and given the culinary skills of the average palace chef, I'd felt it churlish to refuse.

Even so, I'd been surprised to find that Kasteen, Broklaw and I would be dining solely with her, and scarcely less so by the subsequent discovery that the reason was her desire to discuss the situation more openly than she'd be able to do surrounded by her usual coterie of advisors.

'Out of the question,' she said. 'Primadelving is the seat of government, and this palace the symbol of Imperial authority. Abandoning it would send entirely the wrong signals to the populace.'

'I'm not suggesting you go,' I said, slicing into some kind of roast mushroom which almost covered my plate[1], 'but there's a significant civilian population here, which remains at risk for as long as the tyranids are at large. They should be moved to a safer area as soon as possible.'

'All three million of them?' Clothilde asked, with a hint of amusement.

'As many of them as possible, anyway,' Kasteen said.

Broklaw nodded, chewing, and swallowed hastily before chiming in too. 'Three million civilians is three million pieces of 'nid bait,' he said. 'The hive mind will already have sensed such a large concentration of biomass, and be preparing to assimilate it. If it hasn't attacked yet, it's only because it can't marshal a big enough force to be sure of breaking through our defences.'

'Is that all my people are to you, major?' Clothilde asked coolly. 'Potential fodder for the tyranids?'

---

1. *Fungi of various sorts being a staple on many worlds where the bulk of the population live underground, for obvious reasons.*

Broklaw flushed. 'Of course not,' he said, 'but we have to remain aware of the strategic picture.'

'Spoken like a true soldier,' Clothilde said, with a smile, and Broklaw flushed again, realising for the first time that she was pulling his leg.

'Ruput has a point,' Kasteen said, loyally coming to the rescue of her subordinate, 'and so does Ciaphas. We've all fought the tyranids before, and the lessons we've learned were hard won.'

'I'm sure they were.' Clothilde took a delicate bite of her mushroom steak. 'But a mass evacuation on that scale would be impossible with the resources we have to hand. We're stretched to the limit as it is just clearing the non-combatants from the Barrens.' She paused to take a sip of wine. 'And the last thing we need at this stage is to spark a panic.'

I nodded, trying not to picture the effect an outbreak of civil unrest would have in the confines of a cavern city, and the dire consequences it would have on our state of readiness.

'Nonetheless,' I pointed out, 'the fewer innocent bystanders we have to protect when the las-bolts start flying, the better.' Izembard's dire prediction was still fresh in my memory, and I could think of no reason to doubt it. 'If we could persuade some to leave of their own volition, that would be something.'

'It's possible, I suppose,' Clothilde conceded, nodding thoughtfully, and leaning across to refresh Broklaw's wine glass. We were all here to speak frankly, and that meant doing without the servants who'd normally take care of such niceties. 'The newsprints and pictcasts are reporting the existence of the swarm, but playing down the danger. I'll suggest they start being a bit less restrained, emphasise that the other provinces are safe, and let the proles work the rest out for themselves.'

'That should persuade some to get out while the going's good,' Kasteen said. 'And it might help if the PDF start escorting the crawler convoys too. The last thing we need is the 'nids to massacre one while we're trying to convince the civilians to travel.'

'Good point,' I agreed.

'Any word on the reinforcements yet?' Clothilde asked, and Kasteen nodded.

'Another three regiments are on their way from Coronus. Two more Valhallan infantry ones, and some heavy armour to give the bigger beasties a hard time. If we can keep the outbreak confined to the Barrens until they get here, we might just have a chance.'

'There's a Space Marine strike cruiser inbound too,' I added, noticing the covert look which passed between Kasteen and Broklaw, who were well aware of my association with Amberley, and no doubt suspected I'd got her to pull some strings on our behalf; although on this occasion it appeared to be no more than a fortuitous coincidence[1]. 'From the Bone Knives Chapter. It seems they picked up our call for reinforcements, and are responding.'

'That's excellent news,' Clothilde said. 'How soon will they be here?'

Kasteen shrugged. 'In a month or so, Emperor willing.'

'I see.' The governor chewed another forkful of mushroom thoughtfully. 'Then let's hope we're still around to welcome them.'

AS THE FOLLOWING tension-filled days piled up to form a week, I began to hope that the governor would get her wish after all. The evacuation continued to run as smoothly as could be expected, snatching innumerable civilians, quite literally, from the jaws of death, while our forces fought a number of skirmishes which we hoped would prevent the disparate segments of the swarm from joining up into a single unified force. Our own troopers had fought the 'nids often enough to know the value of keeping the neural net stretched thinly enough to knock the occasional hole in, and to my surprise the Nusquans seemed to be learning the lesson too, having sufficient sense to copy the tactics the Valhallans were using to such positive effect, instead of just charging in to get butchered as they had done against the orks.

Even more surprisingly, it seemed, we had Forres to thank for their change in attitude; though she was still gung-ho to the point of

---

1. *If it suited him to believe that, far be it from me to take the credit.*

psychosis, at least from where I was standing, our little run-in with the 'nids in the agricave, and the scrap with the tervigon, seemed to have cured the delusion of immortality common to youngsters fresh out of the schola progenium, and her hard-won pragmatism was transmitting itself to the troopers under her care.

'Every life wasted on the battlefield is a victory to the Emperor's enemies,' I counselled, when we met one morning in the corridor leading to the conference room, in response to some fatuous platitude she'd just quoted about the nobility of sacrifice, and she looked at me a little strangely.

'I hadn't thought of it like that,' she said, then hesitated. 'May I speak frankly, commissar?'

'By all means, commissar,' I replied, amused by her formality.

'I believe I owe you an apology,' she said, taking me completely by surprise. 'In all honesty, when we first met, I thought your reputation must have been greatly exaggerated.'

'I knew we had to agree about something,' I said, inflecting the truth like a joke, and thereby reinforcing the impression of modesty that everyone seemed to have of me.

The corners of Forres's mouth quirked, before she hastily erased any sign of amusement. 'They used to tell us all about you at the schola progenium,' she said. 'Making you out to be some kind of ideal we should aspire to.'

'I wouldn't inflict that on anyone,' I said, equally truthfully.

'So when I met you in person,' Forres ploughed on, 'I suppose I was a bit disappointed. You just seemed a bit...'

'Human?' I suggested, and she nodded gravely. 'We all are,' I said. 'Guardsmen, PDF, civilians...' I broke off, to nod a courteous greeting to Izembard. 'Even him, although he wouldn't thank you for saying so. That's what makes us strong, and assures us of victory.'

'Yes. Well.' Forres shrugged. 'Just thought it needed saying, that's all.'

'I appreciate the thought,' I assured her. 'And your candour.' Which was all the more ironic, given the rote platitudes I'd just fobbed her off with. It seemed to work anyway; she gave me a tight little smile and went off to join the Nusquans in their corner of the room.

'Magos,' I said, as Izembard seemed to have interpreted my greeting as a desire for conversation, and lingered in my vicinity instead of taking his own seat at the table. 'Any developments that the rest of us should be aware of?'

'All in due time, commissar,' he chided. 'The Omnissiah reveals his secrets slowly. But one aspect of our work concerns you, in a way, so I suppose you may have an interest.'

'Me?' I asked, feeling as bewildered as you might expect. 'In what way?'

'The frozen tyranids you found,' Izembard buzzed. 'Our preliminary estimate of the time they've been entombed may have been in error.'

'Fascinating,' I said, trying to conceal my complete indifference to the topic, although had I realised the significance of what he was saying at the time I'm sure I'd have listened with a great deal more interest. 'How long have they been there then?'

'Considerably longer,' the tech-priest said. 'Although we are still attempting a more accurate determination, they could even pre-date the asteroidal impact which formed the geology of this region.'

'Bully for them,' I said. Rather more pressing from my point of view was the undeniable fact that the swarm was becoming more cohesive, and the tactics it employed more sophisticated, and I lost little time in saying as much as soon as the meeting started.

'We've seen this before,' Kasteen said confidently. 'The hive mind analyses the tactics being used against it, and modifies its own accordingly.'

'I would be inclined to agree,' Izembard said, 'were it not for the speed with which these changes are occurring. We're beginning to see separate sub-swarms coordinating their efforts, which would be far beyond the capabilities of the synapse creatures previously identified.'

'Then how are they doing it?' I asked, the familiar tingling sensation in the palms of my hands forewarning me of serious trouble to come.

'We hypothesise,' the magos said, after what seemed to me to be suspiciously like a pause for dramatic effect, 'that some major node of the hive mind survived whatever catastrophe overwhelmed the lesser creatures, and lapsed into dormancy along with them. Now the increased synaptic activity among the neural net is causing it to revive, rallying the other bioforms.'

'You mean the bioship which brought them is waking up?' I asked, my stomach knotting at the thought.

Izembard nodded thoughtfully. 'It's possible,' he said, 'although if such a vessel were anywhere in the vicinity of Nusquam Fundumentibus it would almost certainly have revealed its presence by now. It's more likely that some fragment of it accompanied the other organisms to the surface.'

'Then we have to find it and kill it,' Kasteen said, her face pale even for an iceworlder, 'before it wakes completely. If it's that strong, it could start to call the fleet it originally came from.'

'And if it does that,' I concluded, 'we'll be facing a full scale invasion.'

We stared at one another, the full horrific implications sinking in. We knew from bitter experience that even a small splinter fleet could annihilate a world in a matter of weeks. With its relatively low, highly concentrated population, just a single fully functional bioship would probably be enough to lay waste to Nusquam Fundumentibus before the reinforcements we were expecting had time to arrive.

'Could it be lying low in the halo?' Forres asked. 'It would be almost impossible to find among the cometary debris.'

Broklaw shook his head. 'It would need to be a lot closer to maintain reliable contact with the swarm on the ground,' he pointed out. 'Perhaps it's in orbit, concealing itself somehow?'

'Hive ships are notoriously difficult to detect on auspex,' Izembard said, 'but there are no records of any managing to evade notice entirely at so close a range. The controlling intellect is almost certainly somewhere on the surface of Nusquam Fundumentibus.'

'If all the active 'nids are in the Leeward Barrens, then the hive node must be too,' I speculated aloud.

Izembard inclined his head. 'A reasonable inference,' he agreed. 'Although that still leaves a considerable area to cover.'

'Too big,' Kasteen said. 'We're spread far too thin already to mount a search on the ground, even if we knew what we were looking for.'

'What about aerial reconnaissance?' Brecca asked, and the senior PDF officer present shook her head.

'All our aircraft are fully committed to the evacuation,' she said. 'We could redeploy them...'

'No,' Clothilde cut in, forcefully. 'Getting the civilians out of danger has to be our highest priority.'

'With respect, your Excellency,' Forres said, 'saving the planet should be our highest priority. Collateral damage is regrettable, of course, but...'

'Then I suggest you find a way to achieve that without feeding my citizens to the first tyranid organism that happens along,' Clothilde replied, in a voice which brooked no argument.

'Aerial reconnaissance probably won't help much in any case,' I said, in my most diplomatic manner; the last thing we needed now was to start bickering among ourselves. 'Whatever this hive node is, it's probably buried just as deeply as the rest of the 'nids.'

'Then we'll just have to hope someone spots them digging a hole,' Kasteen said dryly, 'in time to call in a bombing run.'

To my surprise, Izembard was nodding again. 'That would probably work,' he said. 'Killing the primary node would, at the very least, severely disrupt the swarm. If we were particularly fortunate, the resulting psychic shock would incapacitate the majority of the subordinate organisms into the bargain.'

'So how do we find it?' I asked.

To my surprise Izembard shrugged, with the air of a man who only vaguely remembered how the gesture was performed. 'Blind luck is somewhat beyond the scope of the Omnissiah,' he said.

'Luck works best if you make your own,' I replied, trying to sound confident, but in truth I was anything but. If Izembard was right about the existence of a higher coordinating intelligence, then the swarm was infinitely more dangerous than we'd believed.

Editorial Note:

While the Imperial Guard braced itself for further attacks from a foe which now appeared even more formidable than they'd believed, the efforts Governor Striebgrie-bling had initiated to persuade the civilian population of Primadelving that it would be better off away from the firing line continued. Though only a relatively small proportion of the total number heeded the carefully dropped hints, a steady trickle of refugees began to make their way to other cavern cities; which, though relieving the pressure a little in the capital, began to create administrative difficulties of its own in the other population centres.

This selection of extracts from the printsheets and other sources should give some-thing of the flavour of the efforts to influence the most footloose among the citizenry to leave.

From *The Nusquan Diurnal Journal,* 373 942 M41

XENOS INCURSIONS INCREASE

Governor calls for calm.

DESPITE THE BEST efforts of the planetary defence force and the recently arrived Imperial Guard units to defend them, reports are continuing to come in of outlying settlements throughout the Leeward Barrens falling victim to the depredations of the tyranids. Though efforts to evacuate the civilians most at risk continues, further casualties seem inevitable before the xenos interlopers can be dispatched.

Noting that the vast majority of those rescued are being taken, not to Primadelving, as would seem most reasonable under the circumstances, but to cities in other provinces, it is not hard to conclude that the planetary capital itself is considered vulnerable to the xenos horde, speculation which Governor Striebgriebling did little to play down in her most recent address.

'We must all remain steadfast and vigilant,' she told the Delegate Assembly, 'even where safety seems most assured. The tyranids undoubtedly pose a potent and terrible threat. We must not, however, allow blind panic to dictate our actions, but proceed in a calm and rational manner to ensure our safety.'

From *The Solar*, 373 942 M41

THOUSANDS FLEE RAVENING XENOS!

THE FULL HORROR faced by desperate snowsteaders[1] became clear this morning, with the arrival in Primadelving of the survivors of a tyranid attack on the village of Eastridge. Over half the population were slaughtered by the ravening beasts, before a detatchment from the 597th Valhallan could respond to their vox messages pleading for help.

'It was a nightmare,' ice filtration artisan Jezeba Cleff told us. 'They were ripping people to bits and eating them wherever you looked. All we could save of my gran was her specs.'

'The Barrens aren't a fit place to bring up kids in now,' her husband added. 'We're moving on to Polatropolis as soon as Jezeba can line up a job.'

(Exclusive picts, pages 3,5,6 and 8. Comment & cartoon, page 2.
'Don't panic,' says Governor, page 7.)

---

1. *A Nusquan slang term for those living in small, outlying communities; the faintly pejorative implication of the phrase being that the townships in question are so small and lacking in resources that they've only been dug out of the ice and snow, instead of the bedrock beneath.*

From *The Nusquan Diurnal Journal*, 376 942 M41

WESTERMINE BOOM BRINGS JOB OPPORTUNITIES

RAPID GROWTH IN the economy of Westermine, fuelled by the recent completion of new starport facilities second only to those of Primadelving, has led to a critical skills shortage in this burgeoning metropolis. Wages have risen sharply as a result, with some skilled artisans seeing as much as a thirty per cent increase in their incomes, making them noticeably better off than those doing the same job in Primadelving. Despite the greater costs involved, many businesses remain desperate to take on staff, and are pinning their hopes on a fresh influx of workers from the Leeward Barrens, where the tyranid and greenskin incursions are causing some disruption to traditional patterns of employment.

Extract from a pictcast by Governor Striebgriebling, 387 942 M41.

THE EVACUATION OF the Leeward Barrens has been a remarkable success, with uncounted numbers of innocent lives preserved from the tyranid menace. But let us not forget the heroic sacrifice of so many members of the Imperial Guard and the planetary defence force which has made this possible. Even now they are engaging ever-growing numbers of these obscene and deadly creatures, which, deprived of the easy prey they had hoped to consume, must surely be seeking fresh victims.

Primadelving remains a well-defended refuge, but this is no time for complacency. Many of the creatures among the swarm are skilled at infiltration, and must surely be testing our fortifications, hoping to find a way in. Remain vigilant, and report anything out of the ordinary to the appropriate authorities at once.

Remember, you are our first line of defence.

TWENTY

'I THINK THE troopers out on the ice might disagree with that,' I said. 'Surely they're our first line of defence?'

Clothilde had just made some remark in a pictcast which effectively told the civilians skulking in the warmth and comfort of Primadelving that they were just as much in the firing line as the men and women fighting for their lives in the frozen wilderness, and even allowing for the hyperbole I'd normally expect in such a speech, that had struck me as a trifle inconsiderate. The governor looked at me across the hololith in the command centre, as her projected image faded, a curious expression on her face.

'I take your point,' she said, 'and I don't mean to play down the heroism of anyone out there facing the tyranids. But you know as well as I do that it's only a matter of time before they attack the city.' We all glanced at the display, where a chain of contact icons formed an ever-tightening noose around our collective neck. 'It's getting harder and harder to keep the crawler routes open; the more citizens we can persuade to leave before they're severed the better, and a little judicious scaremongering should help to get a few more moving.'

'Besides, it's a fair point,' Kasteen conceded, much to my surprise. 'Sooner or later we're going to see a lictor or a genestealer brood sneaking past our defences, and when that happens we're going to need all the eyes we can get.'

'There might be such a thing as too many,' I said, turning back to Clothilde. 'If we're going to lose the crawler routes soon, then we need to get a proper evacuation under way as quickly as possible. I understand your reluctance, but...'

'No,' she said flatly, 'I don't believe you do. This may be an abstract tactical problem to you, but to me it's the lives and homes of millions of people who put their trust in the Emperor, and in me as His official representative. Abandoning the capital would be like turning our backs on all the Imperium stands for.'

'With all due respect, your Excellency,' Forres said, chiming in equally unexpectedly, 'we can defend all the Imperium stands for far more effectively without millions of civilians blocking our fire lanes, and being devoured wholesale so the tyranids can spawn Emperor knows how many reinforcements. Now the Barrens have been cleared, and we have the resources available, we should begin evacuating the city at once.'

'Well said, commissar,' I put in, happy to let someone else draw the ire of a hacked-off planetary governor (which in my experience could be quite formidable, especially if they turned out to be a genestealer hybrid, or a gibbering madman with a personal retinue of daemons, as had happened on a couple of memorable occasions in the past).

Clothilde looked at Brecca, and the PDF contingent, no doubt hoping to find some support for her position there, but found none; all were looking at Forres, clearly in complete agreement.

Kasteen coughed delicately. 'If you feel unable to give the order,' she said, 'perhaps it would be a good time to bring the province under the direct protection of His Divine Majesty's armed forces.'

Clothilde looked at her in open incredulity. 'Are you threatening me with some kind of *coup d'etat*?' she demanded.

'By no means,' I said, as diplomatically as I could, which was quite a lot given the practice I'd had over the years. 'Colonel Kasteen is simply pointing out that the most senior Imperial Guard officer present is entitled to declare martial law if a state of civil emergency exists, and if the planetary authorities are failing to respond in a timely and appropriate manner.' I inflected the phrase to sound as though I was quoting, although the actual wording of the appropriate regulation was far more syntactically mangled, and I couldn't recall it in that much detail anyway. 'Technically, that's subject to ratification by the most senior member of the Commissariat available[1],' I added as an afterthought, a requirement presumably intended to rein in any Guard officers fancying a career change to governor, 'but as the most senior commissar on Nusquam Fundumentibus is me, and I trust the colonel's judgement implicitly, we can take that as read.'

'But she isn't the most senior Imperial Guard officer,' Clothilde said, with the air of a regicide player unexpectedly taking the king. 'Colonel Brecca is of equal rank.'

'Colonel Kasteen has several years seniority, which makes her the ranking officer nevertheless,' I pointed out. 'And a gun. Both of which enable her to declare martial law right now, with, for the record, my full approval, should she see the need.'

Kasteen caught my eye, signalling her gratitude for my support with a barely perceptible nod. 'Are we all agreed on the necessity of an immediate evacuation, then?' she asked.

'We are,' Clothilde said tightly, after a fractional pause.

'Then I'd say the civil authorities are responding appropriately,' Kasteen said, looking distinctly relieved. 'For the time being, anyway.'

'I'M NOT SURE this is a good time to be making an enemy of the governor,' Broklaw said, when we filled him in on the events of

---

1. As the Commissariat doesn't have a hierarchical structure, like that of the Imperial Guard, seniority is determined purely by length of service and number of commendations. In the last century or so the convention of referring to the longest serving and most decorated veterans as Lord (or Lady) Commissars has gained some currency, although Cain, who would most certainly have qualified for such an honorific, disdained the practice, and always refused to be addressed in such a manner.

the last meeting. His face was still reddened from the driving sleet on the surface, where he'd been supervising the construction of a ring of new defences around the perimeter of the city, and he'd clearly been enjoying the jaunt among the snowdrifts the job had afforded him. 'But under the circumstances, it doesn't sound as though you had much choice.'

'I'm afraid we didn't,' I said. 'The last thing we need is... what was the phrase you used?'

'"Three million pieces of 'nid bait getting in the way,"' Kasteen supplied helpfully, while Broklaw grinned at the good-natured leg-pulling.

'Exactly,' I said. 'I'm sure she won't bear a grudge, once she's had a chance to think things through.'

'I hope not,' Kasteen said, flinching a little as Jurgen passed close enough to hand her a steaming tanna bowl. 'It'd be a pain in the arse having to shift our command post at this stage.' She glanced round my office, paying particular attention to the opulent drawing room furnishings I'd found on moving in, and which I'd promptly had pushed back to the walls to make room for my desk. Accepting the governor's hospitality had been convenient when we first arrived, but that could turn out to be highly problematic if we fell out with her.

Broklaw took his tanna gratefully, warming his hands around it, before sipping the fragrant liquid. 'I don't see the problem,' he said. 'If she gets difficult, declare martial law anyway, and let Ciaphas threaten to shoot her again.'

'I did nothing of the kind,' I said, accepting my inevitable share of the ribbing[1]. 'I just pointed out that Regina was carrying a gun.'

'Which could so easily have escaped her notice,' Kasteen said dryly. 'Anyway, we made our point. The evacuation order's been issued.' She spoke with some relief, which I must confess I shared. Putting Primadelving under martial law would have saddled us

---

1. *One of the many indications in the portion of his memoirs dealing with his time attached to the 597th of the unusual closeness he shared with the senior officers of that regiment. Very few commissars would be prepared to exchange friendly banter with the officers they served with, or feel comfortable doing so.*

with innumerable responsibilities connected with its governance, which in turn would have impeded our efforts to deal with the tyranid problem almost as much as leaving the civilians underfoot.

'Will that be all, sir?' Jurgen asked, handing me the last of the tanna bowls from the tray he carried.

After a moment's consideration, I nodded. 'It will,' I confirmed. The main reason for holding our meeting in my office was the near certainty that we wouldn't be interrupted once he resumed his post in its anteroom, deflecting all but the most urgent petitioners with his habitual mixture of obstructive politeness and near-lethal flatulence.

'The big question is how many of the civvies we can get out before the overland routes become too dangerous for the crawlers,' Kasteen said. 'Once we're restricted to aircraft, we're frakked.'

Broklaw and I nodded thoughtfully. The pitifully few aircraft the Nusquans had available would be wholly inadequate for the task of moving so many people, even if the atrocious weather on the surface didn't keep them grounded half the time[1].

'We'll need to requisition everything we can get our hands on,' I said. 'Cargo crawlers as well as passenger vehicles.' The memory of the steady stream of profanity which had accompanied our abortive journey back from the agricaves flashed across my mind. 'It won't be comfortable, but it'll be better than ending up as 'nid rations.'

'We'll need to protect the convoys too,' Broklaw pointed out. 'They're far too vulnerable on their own, and as soon as the 'nids realise there are large numbers of people moving across the ice they'll be down on them like eldar reivers.'

'I know.' Kasteen looked troubled. 'We can send a few squads along in Chimeras, but they'll find it heavy going in these conditions. If we're not careful the crawlers will outpace them.'

'The Sentinels might be better,' I suggested. 'They're fast and agile

---

1. *Something of an exaggeration, although, as noted before, flying conditions on Nusquam Fundumentibus were far from ideal; and there were indeed prolonged periods where nothing could take to the air.*

enough to keep the convoy together, and they've got enough fire-power to bring down one of the really big ones if the 'nids decide they're going to play rough.'

'They might,' Kasteen agreed, 'if we had enough walkers to do the job. But we'll need a couple of squadrons at least to protect just one convoy, let alone the number that'll be leaving.'

'I'll liaise with the PDF,' Broklaw promised. 'They've got a lot of Sentinels for hit and run raids against the orks. The Nusquans have a troop too, although how many of them are left by now is any-body's guess.'

Before I could formulate an adequate response to that, I became aware of raised voices from the anteroom where Jurgen was now lurking; although, to be more accurate, I was able to distinguish one raised voice in particular, unmistakably feminine, my aide no doubt responding in the same phlegmatic manner in which he dealt with most attempts to get past him. His doggedly polite obstructiveness had reduced generals to apoplexy before now, but this particular interloper was evidently made of sterner stuff. With a ringing declaration of 'Well, he'll see me!' the door to my office shivered on its hinges, revealing the not entirely unexpected sil-houette of a young woman in a Commissarial greatcoat.

'Commissar Forres,' I said, determined to appear unconcerned. 'An unexpected pleasure. Jurgen, could you find the commissar a tanna?'

'Of course, sir,' my aide said, hovering on the threshold, evi-dently relieved to find the problem somebody else's now, despite the glower he directed at Forres's oblivious back as she strode into the room. He dropped his voice. 'I'm sorry sir, she just barged right past me. Nothing I could do to stop her, short of opening fire.' An option he found distinctly appealing, judging by his expression as he glanced in the young woman's direction again.

'You weren't to blame,' I assured him. 'I doubt the Emperor Him-self could have slowed that one down.'

'Probably not, sir,' he agreed, somewhat mollified, and went off in search of refreshment for our unexpected guest.

'You need to see this,' Forres said, without any preamble, and dropped a data-slate on my desk. Kasteen picked it up and activated it, while Broklaw and I moved round to get a clearer view. 'It went out on all the pict channels about ten minutes ago.'

Clothilde's face appeared, in mid-speech, and I glanced questioningly at Forres. 'Shouldn't we have started at the beginning?'

The young commissar shook her head. 'It's just the usual platitudes,' she assured me. 'This is the important bit.'

'I have accordingly,' Clothilde said, with exaggerated gravitas, 'and with a heavy heart, decided to transfer responsibility for this great and grave undertaking to those most capable of shouldering it. Commissar Cain's renown as a staunch defender of the Imperial virtues is too great for his advice to be casually disregarded, however much it may go against my own inclinations. The evacuation effort will therefore be carried out under the jurisdiction of the Planetary Defence Force, and I urge all loyal citizens to cooperate fully with our gallant defenders.'

'And so on, and so forth, *ad* frakking *nauseum*,' Forres said, cutting off the recording, the first time I could recall hearing her swear, or seeing her angry enough to do so.

'She's outflanked us,' I said, torn between annoyance and amusement. 'Regina can't declare martial law if she's already done it herself.'

'The difference is, she's in charge of the PDF[1],' Forres pointed out. 'She can drag her heels and obstruct the evacuation all she likes now, and there's nothing we can do about it.'

'We may not have to,' I said. 'The PDF have been up at the sharp end enough to appreciate just how big a threat the tyranids are. My guess is they'll do the best job they can, whether the governor likes it or not.'

'Which begs the question of whether their best will be good enough,' Broklaw said, forthright as always. 'It'll be a logistical

---

1. *As on most worlds, the Planetary Governor of Nusquam Fundumentibus was also the Commander in Chief of its planetary and system defence forces, at least on paper; although only the governors of highly militarised societies, such as those of Cadia or Gulfsedge, tend to actively participate in their activities on a day to day basis.*

nightmare, and they're not exactly Guard calibre, are they?'

'We could offer to assist,' Kasteen said thoughtfully. 'Sulla would keep them up to the mark. But if the 'nids attack, we'll need her snowside more than we do shuffling data-slates.'

'Sounds like a job for a commissar,' I said, glancing meaningfully at Forres.

She nodded thoughtfully, beginning to calm down as she considered the implications. 'That's true,' she said, looking a good deal happier than when she'd come in. She even took the tanna bowl Jurgen somewhat sullenly offered her without flinching. 'And with you looking over their shoulders they shouldn't screw things up too much.'

'Me?' I said, surprised. 'I thought with your experience of working with Nusquans, you'd be the obvious choice.' And too busy to get in my way for the foreseeable future, more to the point.

'But you're a Hero of the Imperium,' Kasteen pointed out, not quite managing to hide her amusement. 'Hearing you're in charge will reassure the civvies far more than a commissar they've never heard of before, and that means they'll be a lot more inclined to do as they're told.'

'Good point,' I agreed, considering the matter. My inflated reputation had evidently preceded me here, as it tended to do pretty much anywhere I'd visited[1], particularly the part I was popularly supposed to have played in the first campaign against the orks; it wouldn't take much to turn that to my advantage in dealing with the locals. Not to mention the fact that as long as I was herding as many of them as possible on to the crawlers, no one could reasonably expect me to lead a do-or-die charge against the 'nids.

'You'll do it then?' Forres asked, not quite concealing her eagerness

---

1. *Though Cain spent most of his life in the Damocles Gulf and adjoining sectors, he did range further afield on occasion; there's some evidence that he visited Valhalla towards the end of his attachment to the 597th, for instance, and he makes reference on a few occasions to having set foot on Holy Terra itself, although the circumstances under which he may have done so are hard to imagine. The vast majority of the datafiles making up his memoirs have still to be examined in all but the most cursory fashion, however, so it's quite possible that these may shed a little more light on the subject.*

to leave the job in the hands of a dull old fogey like me, while she scampered off to save the galaxy from the terror of the hive mind. I found myself wondering for a moment if I'd ever been that young and impetuous, before deciding that no, I hadn't; which was more than a little ironic, given the way trouble had insisted on following me around regardless.

'I suppose I'd better,' I said, with as much reluctance as I could manage to feign. 'Someone has to, and, as you say, I seem to have something of a public profile already. We might as well make use of that if we can.'

'We're agreed, then,' Kasteen said. 'Ciaphas herds the proles, while the rest of us get back to the war.'

'Good luck with that,' I said, quietly enjoying the stunned expression which had flickered over Forres's face at the casual use of my given name. 'May the Emperor walk with you.'

'And with you,' Forres said, responding automatically, as though she was still in the schola chapel. At the time I took it as a mere reflexive pleasantry, but in retrospect I was to find I needed all the help the Golden Throne could give me.

TWENTY-ONE

AT FIRST, I must admit, my new responsibilities were far from onerous. My inflated reputation performed its usual trick of pre-disposing most of the people I had contact with to listen to me without arguing too much; particularly the civilians, who gener-ally swallowed the modest hero pose wholesale. The PDF were even more susceptible, if that were possible, since, even if they were unimpressed by my widely-credited triumphs, there were still my sash and greatcoat to consider, not to mention the side-arms that went with them; and, in my experience, being allowed to shoot anyone who disagrees with you tends to persuade them of the validity of your viewpoint with remarkably little difficulty[1]. Though the average citizen was as reluctant as you might expect to pack up her husband and children and abandon their home, the prospect of being consumed by tyranids was even less appeal-ing, so many more than I'd expected turned up at the crawler park

---

1. *Not an option which Cain generally favoured, incidentally, being both possessed of sufficient charm to sway opinion his way under most circumstances, and conscious that resorting to more direct methods of persuasion would generally result in bad feeling, often expressed in an equally straightforward fashion should the opportunity to do so arise.*

when directed to do so. There were the inevitable exceptions, however, which caused us a few headaches, even after I'd authorised
the release of some appropriately grisly picts of tyranid attacks to
the public news channels.

'The problem,' I said candidly, in one of my periodic meetings
with the governor, 'is you. Not in any personal way, of course, but
as long as you remain adamant about remaining in Primadelving,
there are always going to be civilians who insist on following your
example.'

'I'm sure there are,' Clothilde said, smiling graciously at me. She
didn't seem to be holding a grudge about losing control of the
evacuation effort, and the opportunity to disrupt it, if that had
really been her agenda[1]; but I'd spent long enough around politi-
cians not to let my guard down anyway, just in case. 'But I'm not
budging. You've been in enough war zones to know what happens
if the governor flees. Panic, disorder, looting and anarchy. While I
stay, the rule of the Imperium remains solid.'

We were meeting in one of the outer rooms of her personal quarters, which, though physically connected to the areas of the palace
complex given over to the 597th by broad, well-lit tunnels, might
just as well have been on another planet. (Where, incidentally,
most of the furnishings appeared to have originated.) Like most
of the palaces I'd visited over the years, opulence seemed to count
for more than good taste in the selection of decor, but at least this
example seemed relatively restrained in that regard; provided you
were able to ignore the gilded cherubs which leered at you from
every conceivable surface.

'Up to a point,' I said. 'But the big difference is that you've got a
personal shuttle standing by to get you out of here if the 'nids break
through. The civilians haven't.' As I spoke, the beginnings of an
idea began to stir, but before I could bring it into focus Clothilde
banged her tea bowl down on the table next to her, with scant
regard for either marquetry or porcelain.

---

1. *More likely she'd simply seen the opportunity to distance herself from a potentially
unpopular decision, and seized on it.*

'Then I suggest you prevent the tyranids from getting in,' she said peremptorily, as if that was simply a matter of bolting a couple of doors, or telling them firmly to go away. 'What are you doing about the citizens who refuse to leave?'

'There's not much we can do,' I admitted, 'other than try to persuade them.' Forres had suggested simply arresting the non-compliers, and marching them aboard a crawler at gunpoint, but appealing as the idea was in the abstract, I'd been forced to veto it on the grounds of practicality. The resulting resentment would, at best, make everyone's jobs considerably more difficult, and more than likely spark off precisely the kind of civil unrest we most feared, diverting troopers and resources from the urgent business of defending against the swarm.

'And how do you propose to do that?' Clothilde asked, as if the question were merely an academic one.

I shrugged. 'In all honesty,' I admitted, 'I haven't a clue.'

'Then you need to find out why they're not going,' the governor said. 'They can't all be staying put just because I am.'

'Not all,' I admitted. 'Some are reluctant to leave their homes because they're afraid of looters, and some don't believe the tyranids can be as dangerous as they are. Most of them are just afraid to make the journey, though, and in all honesty I can't blame them. We've only had three convoys attacked so far, and the escorts drove them off easily enough, but that's how the hive mind works; every failure will have taught it a little more about our weapons and tactics, and it'll refine its strategy until it comes up with one that succeeds. When it does...' I shrugged. 'There won't be any more convoys. Everyone still in Primadelving will be stuck here, waiting for the main attack.' Including me, which wasn't a comfortable prospect.

'I see.' Clothilde nodded thoughtfully, and reached for some sticky confection in a cut glass dish. 'Then it seems to me that you need to find a way of persuading people to follow your lead before it's too late.'

* * *

'IT'S A SIMPLE matter of psychology,' I said, huddling deeper into my greatcoat as the bone-chilling cold whistled in through the thick outer doors of the main crawler park. The cavern was close enough to the surface to be hewn from solid ice, rather than the bedrock beneath, and although it was a good deal warmer than the snowfields above, it seemed chilly enough to me. The iceworlders milling around the wide open space seemed to consider it almost tropical, though, their coats and jackets unfastened as they clambered aboard the promethium-spewing vehicles crowding the cavern, shepherded by grim-faced PDF troopers. 'If they see me going along, they'll think there's nothing to worry about.'

'I see.' Sulla nodded, her own greatcoat folded casually over one arm, her vaguely equine features alight with her manifest eagerness to be away from here, and preferably shooting at something. Just my luck that, in an attempt to make use of her logistical expertise without pulling her out of the front line entirely, Kasteen had assigned her company to oversee the security of the convoys; and that, in an excess of enthusiasm by no means unusual, she seemed to have decided to take command of this particular one herself[1]. 'You want to convince them it's safe.'

'Safer than staying here, anyway,' I agreed. The tyranid swarms were circling the city more tightly than ever, and we could only count on a few more convoys getting through before their cordon became impenetrable. So far we'd been damnably lucky, getting around a hundred thousand people away through the gaps in their envelopment, but those were narrowing all the time; and I had no doubt that if it hadn't been for the number of recon flights being flown by the pilots of the PDF, far fewer groups of refugees would have been able to avoid them.

'We'll get you through,' Sulla said, with complete conviction. 'And back in one piece.'

'I've no doubt you will,' I replied, although in all honesty the notion of returning to face an army of tyranids once I'd evaded

---

1. *Cain seems to be missing the point here; no doubt Sulla was taking personal charge of security for the convoy because of his presence.*

their clutches was far from appealing. I was pretty sure I could find some urgent reason to remain at our destination, however, at least until the worst of the fighting had died down. Admitting as much out loud would hardly fit the image of imperturbable courage I'd had foisted upon me, and which I was forced to work so hard to maintain, however, so I simply let my hands drift down to rest on my weapons for a moment, and adopted a look of quiet resolution, as though I couldn't wait to start using them again.

To my complete lack of surprise, Sulla bought it, simply gazing at me in the vaguely vacant fashion I was so familiar with, a faint smile on her face, before snapping a salute of parade-ground crispness and turning away to go and bother somebody else. The reason for her abrupt departure manifested itself a moment later, preceded by the odour of well-matured socks.

'Sorry to keep you waiting, sir,' Jurgen said, his voice emerging from the narrow strip of psoriasis visible between the pulled-down brim of his bulky fur hat and the turned-up collar of his greatcoat. 'I was just making a flask for the journey. Thought you might need it.'

'I probably will,' I agreed, suppressing another shiver as the keen wind found a hitherto unseen chink in my multiple layers of clothing. 'But not as much as that, if things turn ploin-shaped.' The reassuring bulk of his melta was slung across his back, next to the more slender silhouette of his lasgun, and my aide patted it almost affectionately.

'Then let's hope it doesn't,' he said, turning to clear a path for me through the small knot of pictcasters and printsheet scribes standing between me and the crawler which, according to plan anyway, was to be our home for the next thirty-two hours[1]. Remembering the purpose of the exercise, I paused to give them a platitude or two, and strike some suitably dramatic poses for the imagifiers, before escaping gratefully into the vehicle I'd selected; a venerable,

---

1. *Which implies, although he doesn't bother to mention their intended destination, that the convoy he joined was bound for the cavern city of Underice, the second largest settlement on Nusquam Fundumentibus.*

but comfortably appointed, snowliner, which, though crowded far beyond the imagination of its designer, still afforded a measure of luxury – at least compared to banging about in the back of a cargo hauler.

As well as comfortably padded seats, into which Jurgen and I sank gratefully, the passenger crawler had the inestimable advantage of large windows, affording an uninterrupted view of the surrounding landscape, which would at least enable me to see what was about to try to kill me before it did. Though I had no intention of letting anything get close enough to make the attempt, of course.

At length, the rumbling of engines rose to a level which drowned out all other ambient noise, and, with a lurch, we were underway, grinding up the ramp of compacted ice leading to the world outside.

Just as I had when we were escaping the agricave aboard the requisitioned crawler we'd so fortuitously discovered there, I found the sight of the frozen landscape around us a fascinating novelty. This time the sun was low on the horizon, painting the snows around us the colour of blood, and I found myself shuddering, not entirely from the residual chill forcing its way through the thick slab of glazing material. I can't deny, however, that it also possessed a disturbing beauty, the westering sun striking highlights from the hard edges of the partially buried structures which occasionally broke the surface of the snow[1], and scintillating through the larger blocks of ice which bordered the track we were traversing[2].

'Escorts forming up,' Sulla told me, her voice echoing faintly in my comm-bead; turning my head a little, I could see Shambas's Sentinels bounding among the larger vehicles, uncannily reminiscent of ovinehounds herding a flock, while a couple of our Chimeras kept pace along the flanks, at least for the time being. (Despite Broklaw's best efforts, there simply hadn't been enough

---

1. *Presumably the tops of the shafts which afforded natural illumination to the inhabitants of the cavern city.*

2. *Though roads as such were unknown on Nusquam Fundumentibus, the easiest routes between cities became well worn from frequent use, and could often be distinguished by the naked eye.*

Sentinels to go round, so we were just having to make the best of what we'd got: if the Chimeras had a problem keeping up with the broader-tracked crawlers, the whole convoy simply slowed down to accommodate them.) I was able to distinguish Sulla's command vehicle easily by the distinctive vox and auspex arrays sprouting from it; her head and shoulders were protruding from the turret, and she waved cheerfully at me, before moving up past a battered-looking cargo hauler festooned with towing chains and lashed-on barrels of promethium, its silhouette so obscured by the encrustation of stowage that it put me in mind of the orkish contraptions we'd seen after our precipitous arrival. The rickety vehicle looked like an accident in search of someone to happen to, and I breathed thanks to the Throne that I was able to make the trip in comparative comfort.

'I see you,' I responded calmly, while continuing to look all around us for the first sign of hostile movement. It was a bit early for that, of course, but under the circumstances, I felt, a little paranoia certainly couldn't hurt. 'Anything on the auspex?'

'Nothing but friendlies,' Sulla assured me, although if I hadn't been sure of that, I'd never have begun this trip in the first place. The Valkyries were continuing to fly sorties over the convoy routes and the major concentrations of tyranids, and their pilots hadn't seen anything close enough to our intended line of travel to afford any serious concern. Nevertheless, I remained ill at ease, obscurely convinced that I'd missed something; tyranids should never be underestimated, I'd learned that the hard way.

'Let's hope it stays that way,' I said, although of course it didn't.

Editorial Note:

Cain's casual mention of his mode of transport, and occasional details in the subsequent part of his narrative, don't make it entirely clear how much the passenger vehicles which plied between cities on Nusquam Fundumentibus differed from their more utilitarian, and generally smaller, cargo-carrying cousins.

Accordingly, the following extract has been inserted here, in the hope that it may prove illuminating.

From *Interesting Places and Tedious People: A Wanderer's Waybook*, by Jerval Sekara, 145 M39.

GIVEN THE ABOMINABLE climate, the only practical manner of visiting centres of population, other than the one at which the shuttle bearing the curious wayfarer may have landed, is by means of the snowliners which ply between them on a regular basis. These are large and comfortable enough to be tolerable for all but the longest of journeys, being typically arranged on three decks: the lowest devoted to the engine, promethium tanks, and stowage for the luggage of passengers; the middle to seating, of variable comfort depending on price, and the sleeping compartments which long distance travellers would do well to avail themselves of, despite their rudimentary nature; and the upper to an observation lounge, from which the landscape may be observed for as long as it remains of interest, along with dining areas offering basic sustenance of one sort or another.

Needless to say, a plentiful supply of reading matter is essential.

TWENTY-TWO

BY THE TIME darkness fell, I have to confess, the novelty of the landscape had begun to pall. No doubt my travelling companions, Valhallans and Nusquans alike, were able to distinguish subtle beauties in the endless vista of ice and snow which had escaped me, but I was finding it increasingly dull; and the slow encroachment of night brought its own worries. Every patch of deeper darkness could conceal a tyranid, and I kept an anxious vigil, despite the periodic bursts of conversation in my comm-bead which assured me that our escort remained alert, and that so far there was no sign of the ambush I dreaded.

By great good fortune, the clouds which obscured most of the sky for so much of the time had parted, allowing the faint bluish radiance of the stars to shimmer from the ice around us, every surface reflecting and refracting the glory of the heavens. This was supplemented by a more diffuse yellowish glow, which puzzled me for a while, Nusquam Fundumentibus being devoid of a moon, until I discerned a point of light in the sky far brighter than the stars surrounding it; then the coin dropped. The orbital docks we'd come so close to obliterating in our headlong plunge from the empyrean were large enough, and in a low enough orbit, to reflect a little of the sunlight they caught to the planet below.

Though this was sufficient to prevent the darkness around us from becoming entirely stygian, it left far too many patches of utter blackness, in which anything might lurk, for my peace of mind, and I was heartily glad to see the bright beams of the searchlights mounted on our Chimeras and Sentinels swinging constantly around us, ever alert for any threats.

None came, of course, and the weary, sleepless night dragged on. A few times I rose from my seat, hoping to restore some vestiges of circulation to my lower limbs, but movement was all but impossible; the snowliner had been built to carry around a hundred people in reasonable comfort, but was now jammed with nearly three times that number, so even a visit to the head involved negotiating an obstacle course of bodies and belongings which choked the aisles. Reaching the upper deck would have been completely impossible, even if there was anything to be gained by making the attempt, the refreshment facilities which would normally have been there having been ripped out to make room for more passengers. This left us reliant for sustenance on the supplies Jurgen had secreted about his person, with his usual diligence; Guard-issue ration bars, with their usual lingering flavour of nothing identifiable, washed down with a more than welcome flask of tanna.

At that, I suppose, we did better than many of the poor wretches surrounding us, who appeared to have brought nothing at all to keep them going. To my carefully concealed relief, none of the refugees made any attempt to engage us in conversation; no doubt due to Jurgen's miasma, which I'm bound to note became progressively less noticeable as the hours passed and the fetor of so many bodies in such close proximity began to grow, and to the weapons we both carried so openly[1].

At length, dawn began to break over the desolate landscape, the rising sun once again washing the snowfields in a vaguely sinister

---

1. *Perhaps typically, it doesn't seem to have occurred to him that most of the passengers were simply in awe of his reputation.*

crimson glow. As I yawned, regarding it balefully, one of the out-crops of ice in the middle distance suddenly crumbled, sliding gently to the ground beneath it in a cascade of glittering crystals.

'Did you see that?' I asked Jurgen, who for some time had been fully occupied in picking his nose.

'See what, sir?' he asked, raising his eyes from the porno slate he'd been reading in a faintly desultory fashion.

Before I could elaborate, Sulla's voice burst into my comm-bead. 'We've got ground shocks, incoming,' she told me, the shiver of excitement at the prospect of action I'd learned to dread not quite suppressed in her clipped, professional tones. 'Reads like a burrower.'

'What kind?' I asked, with an apprehensive look at the frozen landscape beyond the window. I rose to my feet, and craned my neck, hoping for a better view.

'Can't tell yet,' Sulla said, 'but it looks like it's alone at any rate.'

'Another probe,' I said, beginning to relax a little. We might still be in for a fight, most of the tyranid burrowers being huge and well armoured, but at least it wouldn't be an all out attack, and once our escorts were in a position to concentrate their fire it wouldn't last long. 'Testing our defences again.'

'That's how I read it,' Sulla agreed.

Before I could reply, the entire snowliner lurched beneath my feet, eliciting cries of alarm from the civilians surrounding us; a chorus of apprehension I'd have been happy to join in with if it hadn't been for my audience[1]. A moment later, something huge reared up beyond the window, thick plates of chitin encasing a serpentine body a couple of metres or more thick, before a head like a daemon's nightmare smashed into the glaze. I stumbled back, impeded by the chair behind me, as razor-sharp shards of the stuff fell all around where I was standing, and drew my laspistol reflexively.

'Frak off!' I shouted, the sudden influx of freezing air almost as

---

1. *It's unclear here whether he means the other passengers, or Sulla, who would of course be listening to him over the vox-net.*

keen as the fragments of the window, and cracked off a few futile shots, which impacted harmlessly on the armour of the monstrous creature before me as it reared back and prepared to strike again. 'It's just surfaced!' I added, over the vox-net.

'Acknowledged,' Sulla said crisply. 'Surround and engage,' and an encouraging number of Valhallan voices assured her of their intention to comply with the instruction as rapidly as possible.

'I can't get a shot, sir,' Jurgen said apologetically, 'you're in the way.' Which was where it looked as though I was staying, unless the ghastly thing ate me, as I couldn't get through the seats hemming me in on either side, or back past my aide to safety. A mouth wide enough to swallow me whole swooped in my direction, surrounded by far too many fangs and tusks, and impelled by instinct I jumped through the gaping hole in the ruined window, the only avenue of escape left open to me.

For a moment I thought I'd left it too late, dooming myself to a lingering and agonising demise as the giant worm's stomach acid slowly digested me[1], but I missed its strike by a hairsbreadth, or so it seemed to me, ending up winded and gasping in a snowbank some three metres below. A bright flash behind me, a roar of pain and frustration and the stench of charring flesh was enough to tell me that Jurgen had taken full advantage of the sudden clearing of his sight line, and the creature reared back again, shaking its head and bellowing.

'Commissar! Can you hear me?' my aide asked, sounding remarkably agitated, even for a man who's just potted a gigantic carnivorous worm at point-blank range, and it belatedly occurred to me that perhaps he attributed my sudden disappearance to having been eaten.

'Loud and clear,' I assured him. 'Just getting my breath back.' Not to mention my wits; a moment later I was forced to scuttle deeper

---

1. *A widespread belief among Imperial Guardsmen who've encountered these creatures, and who therefore regard them with particular horror, although the very notion is, of course, ridiculous: anyone swallowed whole would expire almost instantly from suffocation, and being crushed in the bioform's constricting gullet. Which isn't all that reassuring, come to think of it.*

under the belly of the snowliner to avoid being mashed into the snow by one of its track assemblies, which rumbled past on guide wheels taller than I was. 'Where's the 'nid?'

'Burrowing again,' Jurgen said. 'Maybe I scared it off.'

'Maybe,' I said. And maybe the Traitor Legions would come to their senses, renounce the Ruinous Powers, and return to the light of the Emperor, which seemed almost equally likely.

'They hunt by vibration,' Sulla reminded me, as though that were something liable to have slipped my mind under the circumstances. 'It'll be homing in on your footfalls.'

And it would have headed straight for the biggest source of noise and vibration in the convoy too, of course, which meant it would keep coming back to the snowliner until we somehow managed to get rid of it.

Unnecessary as Sulla's advice had been, it was sound enough. I needed to get off the snow, and fast. Seeing a step on the side of the track assembly which had so recently almost reduced me to an unpleasant stain, apparently there to facilitate maintenance while the huge vehicle was at rest, I broke into a sprint, managing to catch it up in a handful of strides; after which it was only a moment's work to scramble up to a narrow metal walkway, in uncomfortable proximity to far too much machinery capable of ripping me to shreds if I fell into it. Almost as soon as I'd reached the dubious sanctuary, I noticed a rippling in in the ice below, exactly where I'd been standing a few seconds before; then a huge fanged maw appeared, snapping disappointedly for a moment, before sinking again, once more lost to view. Abruptly reminded of the narrowness of my escape, I felt a shiver pass through me unconnected with the bone-chilling cold.

'It just broke surface under the snowliner,' I said, warning the escorts as best I could. The most disconcerting thing about this particular subspecies of tyranid was its ability to strike upwards from below without warning, and when it did so it could easily cripple a vehicle, tearing the tracks to pieces, and ripping through the relatively thin armour of the floor to get at the crew inside. Fortunately, the hulking passenger crawler seemed too big for it to try the trick on, its great bulk and low centre of mass making it almost impossible to turn over. Which didn't mean it wouldn't have better luck with one of the other crawlers in the convoy, of course; fortunately it was acting entirely on instinct, lacking the intelligence to work that out for itself. The only thing capable of diverting its attention would be the distinctive vibrations of potential prey on foot, as I'd just come so close to demonstrating.

Then something odd about the situation struck me. This would be a pretty pointless test of our defences if there wasn't a synapse creature somewhere around to relay the news of the burrower's success or failure back to the hive mind for evaluation. 'Captain,' I said, 'there must be something else close by, pulling this one's strings. Stay alert.'

'We will,' Sulla assured me, no doubt convinced that my wits had been addled by the fall[1], but before she could continue one of Shambas's Sentinel pilots cut in.

'Movement on the ridge line, looks like warriors. Five confirmed, but there may be more behind them.'

'Jek, Rowen, check it out,' Shambas ordered, before Sulla could get a word in edgeways for once[2]. The designated pilots went trotting off, and, so far as I could tell from the subsequent vox chatter, had a thoroughly enjoyable time using their superiority in both speed and the range of their weapons to carve up the warriors like sides of grox[3].

---

1. *In fact, her account of the incident goes on at some length about his keen intelligence and unrivalled insight, so clearly she was impressed by the accuracy of his deduction.*

2. *Though Sulla appears to have been in overall command throughout the engagement, the 597th's Sentinel troop was attached to 3rd Company, along with the other specialised units; so, on paper at least, wasn't under her direct authority. Even if it had been, Sentinel pilots have a well-deserved reputation in the Imperial Guard for acting on their own initiative without reference to the command structure, so Shambas's display of independent thought here is far from untypical.*

3. *An impression which Sulla's rather more long-winded description of their actions confirms; the detached squadron (she mentions a third Sentinel, so either Cain forgot the name of one of the pilots, or they were so used to working together it wasn't necessary to issue specific orders to him or her) were able to trap the approaching warrior forms in a withering crossfire, using their speed and manoeuvrability to remain beyond the effective range of the devourers most of the tyranids carried.*

Despite the advent of the warriors, the mawloc continued to circle the snowliner instead of making for easier prey[1], and I began to realise that my perilous refuge was even more precarious than I'd feared. The next time the huge creature surfaced, a mouth wider than I was tall snapped at the tracks, leaving deep, bright scores in the rusted metal; if I stayed where I was, clinging to the huge crawler's undercarriage, sooner or later it would manage to grab me by sheer blind luck. 'Can't someone get this bloody worm off my back?' I asked, hoping I didn't sound too petulant.

'We can't get a clear shot,' Sulla said, a trifle huffily, as though I was deliberately keeping all the fun to myself. 'Every time it surfaces, it's hidden beneath the crawler.'

'Then we'll have to get it out into the open,' I said, before once again realising that my mouth had betrayed me. There was one very obvious way of doing that, which I'm sure occurred to everyone on the vox-net at pretty much the same instant.

'Are you sure you want to do that?' Sulla asked, in the faintly awestruck tone of someone who not only expects the answer to be yes, but can't conceive of the possibility of a refusal. If I baulked now, it would be all round the regiment in a matter of hours that Cain was losing his touch, and the unearned respect I relied on so much to keep my back covered and my hide intact would begin to erode. Before I knew it, people would start to question my motives at every turn, and it wouldn't take long for the whole charade to come crashing down around my ears.

'Not in the least,' I admitted, secure in the knowledge that at least it would be taken as a joke, and tensed; if I didn't move fast, my body would lock up, to prevent me from doing anything so potentially suicidal. 'But if I stay here it'll have me for sure.' Just to emphasise the point, the giant worm chose that moment to surface again, the whole sinuous length of it rearing up against the underside of the snowliner. The huge vehicle shuddered, and I grabbed a convenient stanchion to prevent myself being pitched into the

---

1. Presumably because they were too busy being killed to act as an effective conduit for the hive mind.

grinding cogwheels mere centimetres from my face. Definitely time to go. 'Just make sure you're on target.'

'We'll be there,' Sulla assured me.

I could see no point in delaying any further, and jumped, landing as lightly as I could on the churned-up ice where the gigantic creature had come and gone. Something as big as that would take a moment or two to turn round and come after me once it had filtered the distinctive vibration of running footsteps from the interference provided by the convoy, and by the time it did, I hoped by all that was holy to have found another refuge. Luckily, I had the perfect one in mind.

No sooner had my boots hit the ground than I started running, angling towards the slowly brightening daylight on the other side of the grinding track assembly. As I rounded the back end of it, and emerged fully into the open air, I breathed a sigh of relief; the ramshackle transport crawler I'd noticed the evening before was still where I remembered, rumbling along close to the snowliner, which loomed over it like a Baneblade surrounded by Salamanders.

'Commissar!' a voice called, and I glanced up to see Jurgen's familiar and grime-encrusted face looking down through the broken window, his melta still ready for use. 'It's coming round again!' I followed the direction of his grubby finger, seeing a rapidly-approaching bow wave of snow and ice, and my breath seemed to freeze in my chest for a moment; it was bigger, and faster, and a lot nearer, than even my most pessimistic imaginings.

'Grenades!' I voxed, sprinting for the rust-encrusted cargo crawler. 'Do you have any?' Which wasn't such a strange question as you might imagine, given my aide's tendency to prepare for any contingency he could possibly foresee.

'Frag or krak?' he asked, as I leapt for one of the towing chains which had caught my eye before, and which looped low enough to be grabbed with a little effort.

'Krak,' I said, swarming up the rusted metal with some difficulty, despite having returned the useless laspistol to my holster by this point. Though the links were large enough to afford reasonable hand and footholds, the whole thing was swaying in a manner I can only describe as alarming, and I found myself even more grateful than usual for the firm grip afforded by the augmetic fingers on my right hand. 'I need something that'll make a dent in the bloody thing's armour.' A job my laspistol most decidedly wasn't up to.

Then the mawloc burst from the ground again, right where I'd been before my desperate leap for the dangling chain, and Jurgen nailed it with another blast from the melta; a deep score appeared in one of the plates of chitin protecting its back, but failed to penetrate the thick armour. He'd clearly had a little more success the first time, however, as a livid wound had been raked along the edge of its jaw, and it clearly flinched, despite being unharmed by the strike. As it put its head down and began to burrow again, a multi-laser burst caught it in the flank, vaporising more chitin, and biting deep into the flesh beneath before the ghastly creature vanished from view once more.

Gaining the slightly less precarious sanctuary of the cargo crawler's hull, I looked round to see that our Sentinels were beginning to join the convoy at last; the command one was jogging comfortably alongside the snowliner, and eliciting no end of excited gesticulation from the passengers aboard it.

'Nicely done, commissar,' Shambas said, waving cheerfully from the open cockpit of his mechanical steed. 'That flushed it out.'

'For a moment,' I said. 'But it'll be back after the snowliner now.'

'Grenades, sir,' Jurgen voxed, leaning out of the shattered window at what seemed to me a near suicidal angle. He had a webbing pouch in the hand he wasn't employing to hang on for dear life, and as I glanced up in his direction, he lobbed it at me. The package arced through the air, clanged against the grubby metal hull of the cargo hauler, and began to slide down the sloping metal, before coming to rest wedged against one of the promethium drums lashed to it. There were, at least, plenty of handholds in between, and I began to make my way from one piece of stowage to the next, heedless of the grime transferring itself to my already much-abused uniform, which by now was beginning to take on a distinctly russet hue, thanks to my passage up the oxidising chain. I can't pretend it was an altogether enjoyable experience, my movements slowed by the biting cold, and the metal rendered slippery by the encrustation of ice which had built up in every crevice, but I managed to cling on somehow, my resolve boosted no end by the realisation of what would happen if I fell to the ice below.

'Got them,' I confirmed at last, as my hand closed around the pouch, and cast around for something to lob them at. There was no obvious sign of the subterranean monster, but that didn't mean much in itself; I already knew it was bound to return to the snowliner.

So fixated, in fact, had I become with this idea, that I didn't notice the real danger until it was almost too late.

'Shambas,' I shouted, suddenly noticing the telltale wave in the snow a score or so metres away from where I'd expected to see it, 'look out!' The ice was rising at the Sentinel's mechanical heels, the huge bulk of the great worm bursting out of the ice, its obscenely wide jaws agape.

Shambas reacted instantly, directing power to the walker's legs, and it leapt clear, kicking back at the 'nid's malformed snout as it did so, in a spectacular display of piloting skill, the equal of which I've seldom seen before or since. The Sentinel landed a few metres away, and staggered, gyros whining hysterically as Shambas fought to regain its balance. The mawloc turned to follow, and with a blinding flash of insight, I suddenly realised what was happening: the hideous creature was unable to distinguish the mechanical footfalls of the walker from natural ones, and had mistaken it for prey.

All too aware of the scrutiny of hundreds of snowliner passengers expecting the Hero of the Imperium to save their hides, not to mention that of the beleaguered walker pilot, I cast around desperately for some kind of diversion which would at least give Shambas time to regain control, and allow the other pilots in the squadron to get a shot off too[1]. Fortunately, inspiration struck: priming one

---

1. *It's unclear where the rest of the Sentinels were at this point: although it's probable that they found their lines of fire blocked by the other vehicles in the convoy.*

of Jurgen's grenades was the work of a moment, as was wedging the pouch containing them into the strapping round the nearest cluster of fuel drums. A couple of swipes with my chainsword was sufficient to sever the lines securing them to the rattling crawler, and within seconds the whole bundle was bouncing across the ice.

The stratagem succeeded beyond my wildest expectations. At best, I'd hoped merely to confuse the beast, and possibly inflict some minor hurt from the detonation and the subsequent conflagration; but, no doubt confused by the pattern of movement, the creature apparently mistook the collection of objects for prey. Whipping its head around, it lunged for the promethium cannisters, and swallowed them in a single gulp.

A moment later the serpentine form convulsed, as the grenades detonated inside its gullet and the spilled promethium from the ruptured tanks ignited. A billow of fire erupted from its mouth, and it crashed to the ice, where it thrashed for a few moments, wreathed in the spreading flames, before gradually becoming still.

'Nicely done, sir,' Jurgen said, his voice in my comm-bead all but swamped by the hysterical cheering of the civilians around him.

'Thanks,' Shambas said, with another wave.

'You're welcome,' I told him, trying to sound as modest as possible. 'Now can somebody stop this bloody thing, so I can get warm?'

TWENTY-THREE

UNSURPRISINGLY, I FELT I'd had enough of the dubious comforts of the snowliner by now, and elected to continue our journey in the scarcely less cramped, but at least reassuringly familiar, confines of a Chimera. On the downside, protocol, and the fact that there was more room in it due to the smaller size of her command squad[1], meant travelling in Sulla's; but by now even the prospect of her company for the remainder of the trip seemed an acceptable trade-off for the extra security afforded by the heavy bolters the AFV carried. I wasn't really expecting another attack, after driving off the last one so decisively, but you never could tell with 'nids, and I was in no mood to take on another behemoth single-handed.

Fortunately, Sulla seemed fully occupied with coordinating the escort, especially given the Sentinel pilots' tendency to do whatever they saw fit without bothering to clear it with her first, so I was spared the worst of her excessive enthusiasm. Better still, even though the vox and auspex systems the command Chimera were fitted with gave

---

1. *Like most Imperial Guard units, the command squads of the 597th at both company and platoon level consisted of an officer and four specialists to assist them, occasionally supplemented by advisors of one sort or another; chief among which was Cain himself.*

her a thoroughly comprehensive overview of the tactical situation, she persisted in the habit she'd acquired in her days as a platoon commander of riding in the turret for much of the journey, half out of the hatch, where she could see the lay of the land directly, and act as a visible rallying point for her subordinates. (Though this may have had as much to do with the fact that Jurgen was accompanying me, and his presence in the confined space of the passenger compartment was somewhat hard to ignore.)

'Sounds like you're in for quite a reception when we get to Underice,' she said, on one of the occasions she favoured us with her presence, possibly attracted back inside by the smell of fresh tanna one of the troopers had just drawn from a samovar in the corner[1] next to the weapon rack.

'Does it?' I asked, wondering what in the name of the Throne she was driving at, and warming my hands (apart from the augmetic fingers) gratefully round the mug Jurgen had just handed to me. The jolting personnel carrier was a good deal warmer than the landscape outside, but internal heating was hardly a priority for Valhallans, and I still found it more than a little chilly for my tastes.

'Of course it does,' Sulla told me, wedging herself into a narrow gap between the auspex console and the ammunition locker, where she could sip at her own drink without having most of it spilled by the jolting of the tracks. 'Everyone on the snowliner with a portable vox has been talking non-stop about the way you killed that burrower single-handed.' She glanced at the vox operator, who nodded confirmation, and I felt a sudden sinking feeling in the pit of my stomach. My own comm-bead was only tuned to the command frequencies, of course, so the civilian chatter had passed me by, but it was his job to monitor everything, so he should know. 'The casters and printscribes will be all over the crawler park when we arrive.'

'Good,' I said decisively. 'Then we'll disengage from the convoy as soon as we get within the defence perimeter, and make directly for the PDF garrison.' I've no objection to being the centre of attention

---

1. *A common modification to Valhallan vehicles, although their use on the move is not without hazard.*

under most circumstances which don't involve incoming fire, but right now the last thing I felt like was being surrounded by a mob of gawping idiots asking imbecilic questions. A hearty meal and a large goblet of amasec seemed a far more appealing prospect. Sulla looked at me a little oddly, so I added 'we could all do with a little downtime before we head back.' No harm in appearing more concerned about the troopers than myself either; it all helped to keep them focused on watching my back when the need arose.

'We could,' she agreed, no doubt impatient to start in on the 'nids again at the earliest opportunity.

We reached Underice without further incident, just as dusk was beginning to fall across the endless snowfields[1]; a sight I was able to enjoy (in so far as it was possible to take pleasure in anything while losing all sensation in my extremities) from the command Chimera's turret hatch, Sulla having relinquished her favourite perch while she dealt with the formal handover to the local forces. Loath as I was to face the freezing temperatures again, I felt it wouldn't hurt to afford the local media the chance of a pict or two, as a form of consolation prize for the interviews I'd be denying them. (And which they'd probably just make up anyway.)

Musing thus, I was a little startled to see a thin plume of rising snow, which I assumed had been thrown up by the tracks of vehicles like our own, forming a thin streak of white against the bruise-coloured clouds lowering in the distance. This latter sight filled me with foreboding, as I'd spent enough time on iceworlds, including this one, to recognise the harbinger of the kind of ferocious whiteout which would make venturing out into the open almost suicidal; but the oncoming storm seemed reassuringly distant, and we'd certainly be under cover before it hit. More immediately disturbing was the approaching group of vehicles, which must have been quite sizeable judging by the height of the plume.

'It is,' Sulla's auspex op informed me cheerfully. 'I've got around twenty blips so far, and more coming on screen all the time. It looks like half the city's turned out to meet you.'

---

1. *Nusquam Fundumentibus having a roughly thirty-five hour day.*

'Emperor's teeth,' I said, taking Sulla's remarks seriously for the first time, and quietly congratulating myself on having already taken steps to avoid the worst of it.

The vanguard of the oncoming blips was, of course, composed of the local forces coming out to escort our charges to safety, which was just as well, all things considered. They managed to take up their positions just in time to keep the majority of the sightseers off our backs, but even so, we were soon surrounded by uncounted numbers of utility crawlers, light and heavy, along with a goodly proportion of tracked cycles, which reminded me a little too strongly of the peculiar hybrids favoured by orks; although I couldn't deny that these seemed fast and manoeuvrable enough for these icy conditions. Wherever I looked, someone seemed to be pointing an imagifer at me, and I even had to duck on a couple of occasions as lens-toting cyberskulls swooped at my head. Fortunately I managed to overcome the impulse to bring these down with a couple of bursts from the pintle mount, although my tiredness and irritation made it a close run thing.

At last we broke free of the crush, our Chimeras and Sentinels forming up in a protective cordon around the command vehicle, and went barrelling across the relatively open icefield surrounding the south-west quadrant of the city[1]. Like most urban areas on Nusquam Fundumentibus there was little to show the existence of a thriving subterranean community just beneath the snow, although a few low structures broke the surface from time to time, their purpose for the most part obscure.

Given the regularity of the landscape, it wasn't hard to pick out the occasional exception, and I was particularly intrigued by a line of much larger shapes, partially hidden by drifting snow, which loomed in the middle distance. Impelled by curiosity I raised the amplivisor I'd found in the turret, doubtless so Sulla could keep a more effective eye on her underlings, and brought the enigmatic structures into focus.

'Throne on Earth,' I said in astonishment. 'What are they doing there?'

---

1. *Housing, as it did, the main PDF base, this area was closed to civilian traffic.*

'Commissar?' Sulla asked, her voice in my earpiece sounding almost as puzzled as I felt. 'Is there a problem?'

'It's the cargo shuttles that were supposed to collect us from the *Fires of Faith*,' I said, as their hull markings gradually became clearer, partially obscured by the crust of snow adhering to their fuselages. 'They look like they've been abandoned here. But why would anyone do that?'

IT WAS SULLA who solved that particular little mystery, of course, her logistical expertise coming to the fore once more. Perhaps her sense of good order was affronted by the cavalier waste of so potentially useful a resource, or perhaps she was simply looking for something to do while we sat idly in the PDF garrison at Underice waiting for the storm I'd seen approaching to blow itself out. Throne alone knew, I was chafing at the enforced inactivity more than a little myself, and I was hardly the most eager among us to get back to Primadelving and meet the tyranid threat head-on again.

'Typical Administratum cock-up,' she assured me cheerfully, dropping uninvited into the chair on the opposite side of my table in the mess hall some three days after our arrival, where I'd been nursing a mug of recaff and a hot grox bun for some time, in the vague hope that something would happen to lift the tedium. The local PDF officers might not have been quite so effusive in their adulation as the civilians, but they were so in awe of my supposed heroism that it was almost impossible to hold a conversation of any kind with them anyway, let alone try to get a card game going. 'As the shuttles had been assigned to meet the *Fires of Faith* before we crashed, they've been written off as destroyed along with it.'

'I see,' I said, my head spinning as it so often did from the sheer idiocy of the bureaucratic mindset. 'So how did they end up here?'

'The pilots couldn't get clearance to leave the planet,' Sulla said, 'because they officially didn't exist. But the starport authorities in Primadelving ordered them to clear the pads in any case.'

'Right,' I said, trying to grasp it. 'They sent an official order to shuttles which they refused to acknowledge were there.'

Sulla nodded, her prominent teeth growing more visible than ever as she grinned at the absurdity of it. 'They did. But not in so many words, of course. Just a general order closing the pads for routine refurbishment, and requiring all traffic currently grounded to withdraw. Which they did.'

'But why here?' I persisted.

'It has relatively few incoming shuttle flights,' Sulla told me, 'so they never got round to building permanent landing pads. They just land on the icefield, and their cargoes are brought in by crawler.'

'So no one in Underice can tell them to frak off,' I concluded, and Sulla nodded.

'Which is lucky for us,' she added, in tones so cheerful I automatically began to fear the worst.

'How's that, exactly?' I asked, already sure I wasn't going to like the answer.

'They can take us back to Primadelving,' Sulla said, as though that should have been obvious. 'These are heavy duty cargo shuttles, remember, not aircraft. They've got enough power to punch though the weather regardless, or even take us out of the atmosphere entirely if that makes the job easier.'

'They have,' I agreed, nodding slowly. And drop us right back in the centre of the tightening tyranid noose, which was not a prospect I relished. On the other hand, try as I might, I couldn't think of a good reason to oppose the idea; which, given my reputation, would raise too many eyebrows in any case. 'How do you suggest we get our hands on the shuttles?' I asked at last, clutching at straws. 'If the Administratum's blocking access...'

'They can't,' Sulla told me, clearly carried away with her own cleverness. 'They've already recorded their deployment as part of a Guard operation. So we just tell them they were right all along, and the shuttles are part of our regimental assets.'

'They've also listed them as destroyed in the crash,' I pointed out, sure she'd have an answer for that one too, and intrigued enough in spite of myself to wonder what it might be. 'How do you account for them being back in operation?'

'Salvage,' she said, with a perfectly straight face. 'But we probably won't have to: military operational requirements automatically overrule Administratum protocols[1].'

'They do,' I agreed. 'What about the pilots? How do they feel about this?' Knowing Sulla she'd already tracked them down and twisted their arms, although under the circumstances I doubted that she'd have to apply much pressure. They had literally nowhere else to go.

'All for it,' she assured me, confirming my intuition. 'So long as they can get back on the flight deck, they're happy.'

'Well done, captain,' I said, with all the enthusiasm I could counterfeit. 'Your initiative does you credit.'

Sulla beamed at me, as though I'd just offered her a sugar lump.

'I do my best,' she said smugly.

---

1. *Much to the irritation of generations of scribes and codicers, who are thereby obliged to amend cherished inventories, often to something resembling objective reality.*

TWENTY-FOUR

I WAS RIGHT, the situation hadn't improved at all while I'd been away: quite the reverse, in fact. The hellish weather conditions hadn't bothered the 'nids in the slightest, and the first thing I saw when I arrived back in the command post was a ring of icons poised to choke the life out of Primadelving. The realisation that we had at least acquired the use of some spacegoing shuttles, which could loft me to the safe haven of the orbital docks, well out of reach of the tyranids if the worst came to the worst, was something of a comfort, of course, but on the whole I'd much rather have been somewhere else entirely.

'Welcome back,' Broklaw greeted me, without a trace of irony. 'I was beginning to think you'd miss all the fun.'

'I'm sure there are enough 'nids to go round,' I replied, reflecting that if this really was his idea of a good time then he desperately needed to get out more. 'What did I miss?' Not that I cared a jot, but it never hurt to look interested, and at least finding something else to concentrate on kept my mind from dwelling too much on all the worst case scenarios.

'The 'nids are still on the move,' Kasteen said, with a wave at the hololith, apparently in case I hadn't realised for myself just how badly we were frakked. 'And the whiteout's put paid to any more refugee convoys.' She shrugged expressively. 'Which were getting more and more chancy anyway, since the 'nids started closing in.'

'At least we've got the shuttles now,' I said. 'We can resume the evacuation at once.' I didn't envy the passengers at all, our relatively brief journey having been unpleasant in the extreme; for once I'd begun to appreciate how Jurgen usually felt on taking to the air. True to form, though, he'd kept his feelings to himself, enduring the buffeting with his habitual stoicism.

'Good thing too,' Broklaw said. 'We've still got about eighty per cent of the civilians to get out from underfoot.'

'Which means we can clear the lot in about five hundred flights per shuttle,' I said, 'if we modify the cargo holds with temporary flooring to create a couple of extra decks.' Catching his interrogative look, I added, 'Sulla's already dealing with that.'

'Five hundred flights?' Kasteen said, in tones of stark incredulity. 'We'll be overrun long before they've completed that many.'

'I know,' I said. 'But there are shuttles at the orbital docks too, dozens of them. Sulla's requisitioning those as well.'

'Shame nobody thought of that before,' Broklaw said sourly, and I shrugged in agreement.

'You can blame the Administratum for that,' I said, 'taking everything too literally as usual.' To give her her due, once getting her hands on the abandoned shuttles had planted the idea, Sulla had gone after the rest with the single-minded tenacity she usually reserved for tackling enemies of the Imperium; and although I'd been perfectly happy to weigh in with whatever support my position and reputation afforded, I'd ended up more or less spectating as she ploughed through the obstructing bureaucrats like a Baneblade through a rabble of gretchin. 'They were told to give the PDF a list of all the assets on Nusquam Fundumentibus capable of assisting in the evacuation effort, and the orbital docks are in space. So it fell outside what they thought was their remit[1].'

---

1. *An excuse I've heard a few times too, although once you've mentioned you want information on behalf of the Inquisition, even the most obdurate of bureaucrats generally becomes remarkably helpful.*

Kasteen made a sound deep in her throat, indicative of infinite disgust at the limitations of the bureaucratic mind, while Broklaw muttered something about 'both hands and a map.'

'So how many of the cattle can we get out from underfoot?' Kasteen asked, returning to the point. 'And how long will it take?'

'Hard to say,' I said, erring as always on the side of caution. 'Once the modifications are complete, on all the shuttles, we can maybe lift around a hundred thousand a day.'

'Four to five days,' Kasteen said, doing the arithmetic. 'Let's hope we've got that long.'

We all glanced at the hololith, thinking the same thing: barring a miracle, we almost certainly hadn't.

'What about the defensive perimeter?' I asked, hoping for better news.

'It's complete,' Broklaw told me, 'and as tight as we can make it. So long as they attack on the surface, we should be able to hold them. Long enough to complete the evacuation, anyway, Emperor willing.'

'Why wouldn't he be?' I asked, raising tight, tension-diffusing smiles from both of them. We all knew that throwing back the tyranid tide would be all but impossible, but with the right tactics, and a little luck, we might be able to delay them long enough to rob them of the huge prize of biomass they hoped to seize. Which was all anyone could reasonably hope for, especially as we were part of it. 'Any word on the reinforcements?'

'Still in the warp,' Kasteen said, which meant incommunicado; the first message we'd get would be when they emerged back into the materium, and, given the capricious nature of the warp currents, there was no telling when that was liable to be.

'Then let's try to whittle the 'nids down a bit for them before they get here,' I said, with as much resolution as I could muster.

'Our main problem is going to be securing the city,' Kasteen said, manipulating the controls of the hololith. The image changed, to show the network of trenches and weapon emplacements on the surface, and the vast, tangled skein of caverns and connecting tunnels beneath them. 'We know they've got burrowers, and even before they became active the smaller organisms managed to infiltrate the power station and the agricave through the fissures round the old impact crater.'

'Which we're sitting right in the centre of,' I added, to show I was, paying attention.

'Exactly,' the colonel said. 'So we should be prepared for a tunnelling strike.'

I stared at the flickering image in the hololith again, my old tunnel rat's instincts giving me as good a feel for the subterranean space as ever. The knowledge that our enemy could strike anywhere, from three dimensions, made it seem horrifyingly vulnerable, the surface fortifications pitifully inadequate.

'We can never hope to defend all this,' I said, my mouth dry.

'We can't,' Broklaw agreed. 'So we're not going to try. We're evacuating cavern by cavern, back to the surface, and sealing each one as we go. Just leaving a narrow corridor for the tech-priests ministering to the power plant on the lowest level to get out through.'

'If they can be persuaded to leave,' I said, having had far too much experience of trying to talk sense into acolytes of the Omnissiah in the face of almost certain destruction. (I still suspect Felicia never quite forgave me for blowing up her precious dam in the Valley of Daemons, and as for the Interitus Prime debacle, the only problem with being the sole survivor is having no one around to say 'I told you so,' to.)

'The 'nids'll do that for us when they start coming through the walls,' Broklaw said matter-of-factly, 'and until they do the generators need monitoring. We don't want them going up like the one in the Barrens.'

'Absolutely not,' I agreed fervently, all too aware that the explosion I'd so recently escaped by the skin of my teeth would pale into insignificance compared to the cataclysm waiting to be touched off if the mechanisms and warding charms protecting the far bigger installation which fed the city failed. 'How are you sealing the caverns?'

'Bringing the connecting tunnels down with demo charges,' Broklaw said. 'Federer's sappers are placing them now.'

'I bet the governor loved that,' I said, 'blowing most of her precious capital to rubble.'

'We reached a compromise,' Kasteen said dryly, and I found myself obscurely grateful for having been out of the city for a few days, ravening mawlocs notwithstanding. The negotiations had evidently been fraught; Kasteen, I knew, wouldn't give ground on operational necessity however much political pressure was applied, and though I didn't know Clothilde half as well, I'd seen enough of her to be aware of how firm her resolve could be too. 'The charges are being set, but won't be detonated unless the 'nids make it into the city itself.'

'So the Nusquans won't have to dig the passages out again if the 'nids get bored and go away,' Broklaw added, an edge of sarcasm creeping into his tone.

'The whole point of this operation is to save the city, isn't it?' a new voice asked, and Clothilde strode into the room, her usual rabble of advisors and sycophants yapping at her heels. She looked seriously hacked off about something.

'If at all possible,' I said, cutting in smoothly before Kasteen or Broklaw could say something inadvisable. Diplomacy wasn't exactly my strong suit, but I was definitely better at it than either of them, and with the 'nids almost certainly about to attack, the more unity I could promote the better. I glanced surreptitiously at my chronograph, finding, to my distinct lack of surprise, that it was nowhere near time for a regular scheduled briefing, and plastered a relaxed, welcoming smile on my face. 'What seems to be the problem, Excellency? Pleased as we always are to see you, I doubt that this is entirely a social visit.'

'You're right, it's not,' Clothilde snapped, turning to Kasteen, with an expression fit to melt ceramite. 'Are you aware that one of your subordinates has taken it upon herself to disrupt commerce across the entire planet?'

'If you're referring to Captain Sulla's requisitioning of every available shuttle, then Commissar Cain was just appraising us of the matter,' Kasteen said frostily. Whatever she may have thought of Sulla on a personal level, she was an officer under her command, and was therefore to be defended from criticism by outsiders whatever their status. 'I haven't had the opportunity of consulting the Captain yet, but I can only commend her initiative.'

'Then I take it you have no intention of rescinding this ridiculous edict?' Clothilde asked, affronted.

Kasteen shook her head. 'I have not,' she confirmed. 'It's the only way to save the lives of the civilians in this city, and it's no thanks to your administration that we stumbled across it. The shuttles remain in military hands until the evacuation's complete. After that, they can go back to making sure you've got enough caba nuts for your next cotillion.'

'Assuming all the debutantes haven't been eaten by then,' Broklaw added, while the governor's face went slowly puce.

'You'll have to forgive the colonel and the major for their lack of verbal finesse,' I cut in hastily, while the sycophants hissed and tutted. 'Soldiers are blunt by nature at the best of times, and this is hardly that.' I gave the two officers a warning glare. 'We're all suffering from lack of sleep.'

'Quite,' Clothilde said, swallowing her anger with manifest difficulty. 'But I'm sure you can keep those loathsome creatures at bay, without it having to affect the entire world. While you're dealing with this little local matter, life goes on perfectly normally in the rest of the provinces.'

'With respect,' I said, 'this is far from a local matter. The entire planet is under threat, and if it falls, worlds right across the sector will be at risk.' I couldn't believe how blinkered she was; nice enough, so long as she was getting her own way, or could be convinced of another viewpoint, but entirely lacking in the ability to see beyond the end of her nose. Which she wrinkled at me now, in a fashion I was evidently intended to find disarming.

'Surely you exaggerate,' she said.

'The Lord General has dispatched a task force,' I said patiently, 'and an Adeptus Astartes vessel deemed the matter sufficiently serious to divert here to assist as well. I can assure you that Space Marines would have a great many claims on their attention, and wouldn't take a decision like that at all lightly.

'I'm sure that's what they believe,' Clothilde said, 'and I'm sure that you're equally sincere. But these creatures are quite simply too few in number to pose much of a threat. As soon as the Space Marines arrive, they'll mop them up in no time.'

'Let's hope they do,' I said. 'But the tyranids grow stronger with every kill they make, and if they manage to consume everyone currently in the city they'll become unstoppable.' And, more to the point, I wouldn't be around to see anyone try. Then something else occurred to me, and I changed tack. 'If you really want to preserve Primadelving as a symbol of Imperial rule, supporting the evacuation would be the best way to do that. The tyranids are besieging us because of the vast reserve of biomass the population represents; on an iceworld they're not going to find a lot else to consume. If the population goes, then so does their reason for being here.' Which wasn't exactly true, of course, but I was pretty sure the governor would buy it; one of the problems with being surrounded by toadies all day is that you get used to only hearing the news you want. If I made it sound as though the 'nids would just give up and go away if we got on with what we were doing, there was an excellent chance that she'd leave us alone to do it.

'Are you sure about that?' She nibbled her lip thoughtfully, while I nodded, with every appearance of sincerity.

'It's got to be worth a try,' I said, perfectly truthfully.

'I suppose so.' She nodded once, decisively. 'But I want those shuttles back on their scheduled cargo runs as soon as the operation is concluded.'

'They will be,' I promised, although so far as I was concerned that would include hanging around to pull out as many troopers as managed to make it to the pad as well, and I firmly intended to be among the foremost.

'Then keep me informed,' she said, and swept out, with a final disdainful glare at Kasteen and Broklaw.

'"Your next cotillion?"' I asked. 'What were you thinking?'

'I wasn't,' Kasteen admitted, having the grace to look a little embarrassed, then we got back to the urgent business of saving the planet.

UNSURPRISINGLY, THE ATMOSPHERE at the next formal briefing session was more than a little frosty, Clothilde and her hangers-on sitting ostentatiously as far down the table from the Imperial Guard contingent as they could get. Being able to report that a remarkable number of civilians had been cleared out of the city already, thanks to Sulla's initiative, only seemed to make their mood worse, and they received the news with carefully moderated enthusiasm; but at least the governor had stopped short of evicting us, no doubt reflecting that protecting her planet was a little more important than exacting petty revenge for a few barbed comments[1].

'That's excellent,' Forres complimented us, unwittingly rubbing salt in the wound. The Nusquans and the Valhallans were grouped together round the hololith now, I noted, instead of remaining at arm's length from one another, compelling testament to the growing respect between them; by now the survivors of the Nusquan 1st were battle-hardened veterans, who the Valhallans were more inclined to accept as equals, while the fledgling regiment had learned the hard way that the Tactica Imperialis didn't cover every contingency, and that following the lead of troopers who'd seen off tyranids before was probably their best chance of coming out of the whole mess alive. In this, I'm bound to say, Forres had played a considerable part, developing a fair degree of common sense, which seemed to have filtered down to Brecca and her command staff[2]. 'The lower levels are completely clear, apart from the power

---

1. Not to mention the fact that, if she tried, Kasteen would simply declare martial law, leaving the erstwhile governor completely without influence.

2. Typically, it doesn't seem to have occurred to Cain that a considerable amount of Forres's change in attitude was due to her following his example; or at least what she fondly imagined that to be.

plant, and we're stationing units ready to hold back the 'nids if they break through along the fault lines.' She indicated the hololith, where a rash of unit icons marked the caverns the Nusquans had elected to garrison.

'Exemplary deployment,' I said, my affinity for three-dimensional spaces kicking in automatically. They'd put at least a company down there, the Nusquans securing the lower levels, while the Valhallans manned the surface defences (which was fine with me, as we'd be the first to the shuttle pads when it was time to pull out, even though we'd be expected to hold them while the Nusquans caught up), and the PDF milled around inbetween, trying not to get in the way too much. 'You might want to put another platoon over here, in the stalagmite glade[1], to bolster your flank.'

'We'll do that,' Colonel Brecca said, considering the display for a moment, and nodding. 'Good idea.' It was only an abstract tactical problem for me, of course, as I certainly had no intention of venturing into the lower levels; but as things were to turn out, I'd be grateful for that glimpse of the layout down there sooner than I thought.

Just as I began to turn away, a red rune suddenly flashed into existence, and my breath stilled. It might be a false alarm, of course, but I knew how unlikely that was; and a glance at Colonel Brecca, who was listening to her comm-bead, her expression grim, was enough to snuff out that last, faint hope.

'They've broken through,' she said. 'Burrowers, large and small, with Throne knows how many 'gaunts following up through the tunnels the big ones have left.' She turned, and beckoned to her aide. 'We're needed back in our ops room.'

'Target the burrowers,' I counselled. 'If they're still active, blocking the routes to the surface won't make any difference.'

Brecca acknowledged the advice with a brief nod, then the Nusquans hurried out, Forres trotting after them, her hands already falling to the weapons at her waist.

---

1. *A striking natural feature in one of the caverns, which had been preserved as a park.*

The PDF officers looked nervously at one another. After a moment's debate they left too, to bolster the second defensive line, leaving us alone with the governor.

'It seems you were right,' she said tightly.

'Apparently so,' I conceded, while Kasteen and Broklaw got on with the urgent business of ensuring the shuttle pads were adequately defended. At least the storm had blown itself out by now, so our troopers were able to man the trenches without being frozen to death within moments, and I could breathe a little more easily knowing that a couple of companies stood between me and the overland assault which was certain to accompany the underground one[1]. I coughed delicately. 'Perhaps it might be time to consider withdrawing to another city while you can. Purely in the interest of maintaining continuity of government, of course.'

'Of course.' Clothilde shot me an appraising glance. 'But I've no intention of leaving. My job is to inspire and rally the people, and I'm hardly going to do that if I run away at the first sign of trouble.'

'Then I'll wish you good luck,' I said.

'Thank you.' For the first time since we'd met, the governor looked a little unsure of herself. 'If I'm honest, I'd be on the first shuttle out I could, but my mother and grandmother never shirked their duty, and neither will I.'

I nodded gravely, as if I gave the proverbial flying one. 'Ten generations of forebears looking over your shoulder must be lot to live up to,' I said.

Clothilde looked surprised for a moment. 'No,' she said, 'the actual bloodline only goes back two generations. Granny took the throne after poisoning her aunt.' I must have looked surprised, because she coloured a little. 'Only because she had to,' she added hastily, and her entourage nodded vigorously in agreement. 'The aunt was quite insane. Completely paranoid.'

'I've met a few governors like that,' I assured her, straight faced,

---

1. *First and Fifth Companies undertook the surface defence of Primadelving, along with the Sentinel troop; the other line companies were still engaged in harrying the outlying swarms.*

marvelling inwardly yet again at the mentality of the aristocracy, and went to deal with the tyranid incursion, which at least was relatively easy to understand.

TWENTY-FIVE

THE NEXT FEW days fell into a predictable pattern of tyranid assaults above and below, which we repeatedly repulsed, although not without grave losses among the defenders. The Nusquans bore the brunt of it, retreating cavern by cavern from the lower levels, and sealing the tunnels behind them wherever they could; but the tyranids were relentless, boring new passageways as soon as the old ones were closed, and altering their tactics with every fresh assault.

We hardly had it easy on the surface, either; although for the most part, at least, the encircling swarm only came at us over the ice, the hive mind evidently having decided to reserve the majority of its burrowers for the assault on the caverns below. The few exceptions it threw at our fortifications in an attempt to outflank them were easy meat for the overlapping fire lanes of our heavy weapon emplacements: mindful of the lessons they'd learned so painfully on Corania, the 597th were well prepared for this particular tactic, and the 'nids soon went back to attempting to swamp us by sheer weight of numbers. We also had air support from the Valkyries of the PDF, which did sterling work in breaking up the main formations before they could throw themselves against our trench line, and for which we were truly thankful; but a continuous tide of malevolent chitin continued to batter against the breakwater of our defences with little respite.

'I'm surprised they're not using gargoyles against us,' I said, having seen for myself how effective the airborne horrors could be at circumventing fixed defences more often than I would have liked, but to my vague surprise this particular swarm seemed to be eschewing the use of winged bioforms.

'That would be because the crosswinds are too strong and unpredictable,' Magos Izembard remarked tonelessly, sweeping into our command centre without warning, and making his way over to the hololith through the horde of bustling troopers necessary to coordinate such a huge operation. He seemed unusually agitated, although his familiar monotone did nothing to betray it; his body language was another matter entirely, however, and I must confess I was a little surprised. It's an article of faith among the Mechanicus that strong emotions are a human weakness, and an unwelcome distraction on the path to understanding the Omnissiah, so whatever had the magos so worked up had to be grave indeed.

'A pleasant surprise,' I greeted him, although my suddenly itching palms were strongly intimating that his sudden advent was liable to be anything but good news. 'What can we do for you?'

'You can vox the commanders of the Nusquan 1st and the PDF,' Izembard said, 'and the governor, if you see much point in that. I have attempted to do so repeatedly, along with yourselves, but been unable to get a message through.'

'All the vox-channels are pretty clogged,' I said, reflecting that he'd probably taken their overloading as a sign of the Machine-God's displeasure. 'And operational messages get the highest priority.'

'As they should,' Izembard droned. 'But I have news of the utmost importance.'

'The last civilian shuttle's just cleared the pad,' Sulla voxed at that moment, from her command Chimera on the fringes of the starport[1], and a ragged cheer broke out across the operations room. I didn't suppose for one moment that we'd managed to clear every single civilian from the city; there were bound to be a few who'd stayed hidden with the idea of looting the deserted metropolis, or because they were just too stubborn or eccentric to leave, but, quite frankly, I felt that they deserved all they were going to get.

'Pass the word to the Nusquans,' Kasteen ordered, with some relief. 'Abandon the lower levels and pull back.' She glanced at the hovering tech-priest. 'And you'd better get your cogboys out of the power plant too. When the troops leave, their lifeline's going to be severed.'

'Begin withdrawal,' Broklaw transmitted to our people, almost simultaneously. 'Fall back to the pads, and keep them clear.'

'Commissar,' Izembard said, ignoring the frantic activity around us. 'You have to listen. We have a definite time at which the bio-forms you found were frozen.'

'Good for you,' I said, adopting an expression of polite interest, and waiting for him to come to the point, which even a tech-priest was bound to do eventually. 'You must be delighted to have finally worked it out.'

'It's not just a question of intellectual curiosity,' Izembard grated, 'it's a matter of life and death. For this entire world.'

To say I was surprised would be understating the matter considerably. In my experience, tech-priests were hardly given to exaggeration, and I looked at him again, more seriously, noting once more the signs of agitation he was obviously taking considerable pains to suppress. I furrowed my brow. 'I'm afraid I don't follow,' I said. 'Why should it matter so much when the 'nids arrived?'

'Because of the impact which formed the geology of this region,' Izembard said, striding to the hololith, and erasing the current tactical display with a flick of his mechadendrites. Broklaw took a step

---

1. *Rather a grandiose title for half a dozen rockcrete pads, standing next to tunnels giving directly to an underground staging area, which enabled passengers and cargo to embark or disembark with a minimum of exposure to the freezing temperatures on the surface.*

forward, a trenchant protest about this cavalier behaviour forming on his lips, which I forestalled with a gesture. Whatever this was about, I wanted to see it.

A stylised cometary fragment appeared in the display, on an intersecting orbit with the looming bulk of Nusquam Fundumentibus, and duly collided with it. A few mountain ranges fell over, an impact crater appeared, and gigatonnes of vaporised slush rose up to enshroud the whole globe. When it cleared, the geography was more or less as I remembered it from the picts in the briefing slate.

'The asteroid,' I said. 'You were trying to work out whether the 'nids got here before or after it hit.'

'That's the whole point,' Izembard said. 'So far as we can tell, they arrived at exactly the same time as the impact event.'

'They hitched a lift on a comet?' Broklaw asked, not bothering to hide his incredulity.

'There was no comet,' I said, the whole thing suddenly making sense to me. 'It was a bioship, which crashed here, just like we did. Only at a much steeper angle.'

'Exactly,' Izembard said, and a cold chill rippled down my spine.

'Which means we're sitting right on top of it,' I said.

'A fragment, at least,' Izembard said. 'And from the increasing cohesion of the swarm we've observed recently, it's safe to assume that it's regenerating.'

'The missing orks,' I said, with horrified understanding. 'The swarm's been feeding it all this time.' Which must mean that the whole of the Leeward Barrens was riddled with burrower tunnels, all the way out to the Spinal Range, and that for every 'nid we'd observed on the surface, untold numbers had been scuttling around undetected beneath our feet.

'My thoughts exactly,' Izembard said. 'Fortunately the city was too well defended for it to risk a direct assault before now, or it would have been fully reactivated by this point.'

'When it does, it'll re-establish a connection with the hive fleet that sent it,' Kasteen said, her expression of stark realisation no doubt mirroring my own. 'And there are over a dozen worlds in this sector which have been settled in the last few thousand years.'

'It'll be banging the dinner gong,' I said, 'with the entire sector on the menu.'

'Then we need to destroy it,' Kasteen said. 'I'll pass the word to the Nusquans to counter-attack, and we'll reinforce with as many units as we can.'

'That would be extremely inadvisable,' Izembard said, to my immense and well-concealed relief. 'The bioship fragment must be at least a kilometre beneath the lowest level of the city, and the only access to it would be along the tunnels bored by the tyranids themselves. We can infer that the system is extensive, but beyond that we have no way of telling which connect to the hive node, which to other destinations, and which have simply been left by a burrower moving from one place to another.'

'And the tunnels aren't going to be all that wide,' I added. We'd all seen termagants swarming out of them, in the wake of the huge serpentine burrowers, so we could picture the number of troopers they'd hold easily enough. 'We'd have to go in on foot.' Which would make any large body of troops terrifyingly vulnerable, clustered together in the dark, the majority unable to turn around or use their weapons; and there was no doubt about it, we'd need huge numbers on our side to have any chance at all of getting through to our objective, even if we had a clue where it was.

'Suicide to try,' Broklaw agreed, which at least saved me the bother of trying to weasel my way out of leading this ridiculous expedition, as everyone would undoubtedly expect a Hero of the Imperium to do.

I nodded, as though I'd been considering the matter carefully. 'Not much chance of a kill team getting through either,' I added, contriving to give the impression that I was reluctantly ruling that out as well; if the thought occurred to anyone else, it was carrots to credits who'd get stuck with the job of leading them in, so I'd better shoot it down now before someone started getting ideas. 'There must be thousands of 'nids down there.'

'Clearing the tunnels is a job for the Space Marines,' Kasteen agreed. 'We'll brief them as soon as they arrive.'

'Regrettably,' Izembard said, 'unless they do so within the next six to eight hours, it will be too late.'

'Too late why?' I asked, already dreading the answer.

'Because our analysis of the response time of the outlying elements of the swarm to changes in circumstance elsewhere is tending towards zero,' Izembard proclaimed dramatically. He glanced from one of us to another, seeing nothing but blank incomprehension on every face. 'It's woken up,' he explained, in plainer Gothic, 'and it's coordinating the swarm with almost complete efficiency. We calculate that it will be strong enough to begin reaching out to the fleet which spawned it before the end of the day.'

Kasteen, Broklaw and I looked at one another, shocked speechless. After a moment, I found my voice.

'That doesn't mean there are other bioships close enough to respond straight away,' I said, aware even as I spoke that I was clutching at straws. Even if that were true, it would just be a matter of time before an armada of the hideous creatures descended on the sector, dooming not just Nusquam Fundumentibus, but untold numbers of other worlds; which would leave me uncomfortably short of boltholes to run for.

'It doesn't mean there aren't, either,' Broklaw said.

'If we can't get to it, there's no point debating the matter,' Kasteen said decisively. 'We'll just have to pray that the task force or the Space Marines arrive before it can call in any reinforcements, and bombard the site from orbit.'

'That may not be enough,' Izembard said. 'Even a concentrated lance barrage would be unlikely to damage a target buried so deeply.'

'Then we're frakked,' I said, reflecting that at least we'd be spared having to break it to Clothilde that the Navy were about to start using her precious capital for a spot of target practice; news I felt sure she was unlikely to take well. 'All we can do now is pull out, before the 'nids overrun the place, or the power plant blows up.' My voice trailed away, as my brain finally caught up with my mouth. I turned to Izembard. 'How long is it likely to be before the power station goes critical once your people abandon it?'

'It shouldn't go critical at all,' Izembard said, looking as affronted as it was possible to with a face composed mainly of metal. 'We have protocols in place for an ordered shutdown before those ministering to the system pull out. The plant in the Leeward Barrens had been left unstaffed by the actions of the tyranids, preventing the safety precautions from taking effect.'

'How long would it take to go bang if they just ran for it, then?' I persisted. 'Without hanging around to shut things down properly and light the incense?'

Kasteen and Broklaw were nodding thoughtfully, seeing where I was going with this, but Izembard still seemed to be struggling with the idea. 'Pressure levels would begin to rise towards critical in about twelve hours,' he said. 'But an actual detonation would take considerably longer, depending on the strength of the welds, and how recently the prayer slips had been renewed.'

'We don't have twelve hours,' Broklaw said. 'Can your cogboys do anything to speed it up a bit?'

The few remaining areas of flesh on Izembard's face paled, then went a strange mottled purple, and when he spoke again his vox-coder seemed to buzz a little more than usual. 'That would be complete anathema to a faithful servant of the Omnissiah,' he said flatly.

'So would leaving an entire planet to be eaten by 'nids, I would imagine,' I replied.

Izembard's shoulders slumped, as much as was possible given their inhuman rigidity, and the heightened colour slowly drained from his face, returning the skin to the unwholesome pallor it normally displayed. He nodded slowly. 'Certain safety protocols could be circumvented,' he conceded. 'But that wouldn't accelerate the process enough to culminate before the hive node recovers fully.'

'Then we're still frakked,' Broklaw said.

'Not necessarily,' the magos said, startling us all; not least himself,

I suspected. 'I strongly disapprove of the wanton destruction of any mechanism, but the Omnissiah teaches us that dispassionate analysis is the surest way to the correct solution, and in this instance the dictates of pure reason would seem to admit of no other choice. A sufficient quantity of explosives, placed near the inlet filters, would release the pressure from the magma pocket beneath the power plant.'

'Causing a volcanic eruption,' I said, to show I'd caught on, although the object lesson I'd received in the Leeward Barrens was hard to forget.

'Precisely,' Izembard said. 'Although may the Omnissiah forgive me for suggesting it.'

'Under the circumstances, I'm sure He'll be prepared to stretch a point,' I said. 'Better to lose one power plant than have every machine on the planet shut down, surely?'

Izembard nodded slowly, looking somewhat reassured, and I turned to Kasteen again. 'We need Federer,' I said. 'The Nusquans don't have any sappers of their own.'

'He's too busy shoring up our defences on the surface,' Broklaw said, 'and he'll be busier than ever now we're pulling back. Slapping a couple of demo charges on a pipe and setting a timer isn't exactly advanced theology.'

I couldn't be entirely sure, but I thought I saw Izembard wince as he spoke.

'I'll vox the Nusquans and advise,' I said. 'They should still be holding the plant if the tech-priests haven't pulled out yet.'

'Thanks.' Kasteen was already turning away, to where a small group of aides were hovering anxiously, all carrying data-slates. 'That would help.'

My comm-bead was tuned to the 597th's operational frequencies, of course, but it wouldn't take much to find out which ones the Nusquans were using; but all our vox ops were busy, and, knowing that lives probably depended on leaving them to get on with their jobs, I was understandably reluctant to interrupt them. Then an alternative occurred to me, and I switched to the band reserved for the Commissariat.

'Forres, this is Cain,' I began, launching into the most condensed version of the crisis facing us that I could manage, without bothering to waste any time on the preliminary pleasantries. She listened carefully, asking a few questions when my desire for brevity overwhelmed the need for clarity, and waited for me to finish.

'Sounds like we're frakked,' she said. 'We're still hanging on at the objective, but we used the last of our demo charges to bring down a trygon tunnel the 'nids were using to try and cut us off from the Spiral[1]. You'll have to bring some more with you.'

'We'll get right on it,' I said, cursing under my breath. As you'll appreciate, I had no intention at all of putting myself in the firing line, being rather more concerned with how quickly I could bag a seat on one of the shuttles which were, even now, on their way to pluck us to safety. But Forres clearly expected me to undertake this fool's errand myself.

I glanced at the hololith, which by now had been restored to the tactical display Izembard had so cavalierly overridden, looking for a unit I could palm the job off on, but, try as I could, none of them seemed able to assist. The tyranids had redoubled their efforts in the face of our withdrawal, and every unit out on the ice was being hard pressed.

With a faint sigh, I bowed to the inevitable, knowing that if I didn't, the planet, the sector, and, most importantly, the undeserved reputation I relied on to make my life as trouble-free as possible, given the trouble-magnet nature of my job, would all vanish down the maw of the hive fleets.

'I'll be there ASAP[2], I assured her. After all, the Nusqans still seemed in control of the power station and its immediate surroundings, so I'd have plenty of troopers to hide behind: and with the scout Salamander I generally favoured as a personal conveyance, I should be able to outrun most of the trouble we were liable to encounter,

---

1. *A main highway connecting the industrial caverns to the residential units on the upper levels.*

2. *As Soon As Possible, one of the more exotic examples of the Imperial Guard's mania for abbreviation, in that it consists of four letters rather than the usual three. Somewhat disconcertingly pronounced 'ae-sap:' I ask you, what's wrong with plain Gothic?*

especially with Jurgen in the driving seat. Which ought to leave me arriving back just in time to board a shuttle, with another piece of relatively risk-free conspicuous gallantry to affect modesty about under my belt. Not to mention that, while I was running around the city like a glorified delivery boy, there was no chance of being dragged out onto the surface to freeze my nads off encouraging the troops.

All in all, I began to convince myself, things could be a good deal worse; little realising just how much so they were about to become.

TWENTY-SIX

JURGEN WAS WAITING for me as I left the governor's palace, by the side door next to the kitchens, the engine of the scout pattern Salamander he'd requisitioned from the vehicle pool growling quietly. Though I generally favoured the rugged little vehicles for personal transport, I'd been understandably reluctant to use one on Nusquam Fundumentibus; the sub-zero temperatures made the open passenger compartment far too uncomfortable to endure for long, so on the occasions when I really couldn't avoid venturing out onto the surface I'd made do with the relative warmth and comfort of a Chimera. The wide open spaces of the cavern city were all climate controlled, of course, feeling to me no cooler than a brisk spring morning on a temperate world, so I clambered up to my habitual perch next to the pintle mount without so much as a shiver, and a reassuring sense of familiarity. Not even grazing my shin on the crate of explosives I found waiting there was enough to distract me from a growing sense of optimism about the success of our mission.

'Sure you've brought enough demo charges?' I asked Jurgen light-heartedly, and he hitched himself up in the driver's seat to peer at me over the armour plate separating us with a frown of consternation.

'We can get some more if it's not enough,' he said, taking the pleasantry as literally as he took most other remarks.

'I'm sure it'll be fine,' I assured him. 'You've got enough here to bring down a gargant.'

'If the orks had one, and the 'nids hadn't eaten 'em all,' he agreed, nodding sagely, then resumed his seat and gunned the engine. Years of familiarity with his robust approach to driving had prepared me for what followed, and I grabbed the pintle mount reflexively as we jerked into rapid motion, keeping my feet with relative ease.

The governor's palace was halfway up the wall of the largest of the upper caverns, where the good citizens who lived in the streets below could get a good look at it towering over their heads[1], and as we passed the wrought iron gates enclosing the formal gardens which fronted it, I was able to appreciate the full scale of Primadelving for the first and last time; rattling about in a Chimera was hardly the best way to sightsee. Tiers of streets, houses and emporia fell away before us, in a vista as spacious as any fair sized town on the surface of more Emperor-favoured worlds, and it was an effort to remind myself that there were more than a score of similar bubbles in the rock, all painstakingly excavated over countless generations, of a similar size to this one. The thought was sobering, to say the least; if everything went well with my errand, all that hope and effort would come to naught, obliterated in an instant by a cataclysm so vast it was all but impossible to imagine.

As we descended towards the cavern floor at Jurgen's usual break-neck pace, I found the quiet, deserted streets uncomfortably eerie, imagining movement in every alley mouth and behind every shuttered window. All nonsense, of course, although that didn't stop me from checking that the heavy bolter on the pintle mount was loaded and ready to fire at a moment's notice; if the tyranids had sent a lictor or two to scout out the terrain ahead of their advance,

---

1. *Like many cities on worlds with inhospitable surfaces, many of the buildings were partially buried in the sides of the interconnecting caverns, so that a series of terraced structures and streets rose up the walls, making maximum use of the space. The gubernatorial palace would, of course, be sited where it was most prominent, reassuring the citizens of the Imperium's constant vigilance.*

I'd have no warning of an attack other than a flicker of movement in the corner of my eye.

Jurgen, of course, positively relished the emptiness of the streets, and opened the throttle to its fullest extent, sending the little vehicle howling down the boulevards as though all the daemons of Chaos were after us, which was fine by me; if anything was going to come bounding out of the shadows waving its scything claws it would have to be moving even faster than we were to have a hope of making an effective strike.

Now and again we caught sight of a Nusquan unit, or a squad or two of the PDF, pulling back from the lower levels on their way to the shuttle pads, although, disinclined as always to share the road with anything which might slow him down, Jurgen generally directed us along parallel carriageways to the retreating troopers. They were pulling back in good order, so far as I could see, although they'd clearly been in a hard fight, the weary trudge of those on foot, and the horizon-piercing stares of all, proclaiming their psychological as well as physical exhaustion.

'We're just leaving the palace district,' I voxed Forres, as we bulleted into one of the tunnels connecting it to the next cavern in the downward chain; although it was so wide and high that it hardly felt like a tunnel at all, with side roads and hab blocks surrounding the main highway on all sides (including the roof).

'Don't take too long,' she replied, the sound of gunfire audible over the vox-link. 'We're being pressed hard down here.'

'Hold as long as you can,' I said, trying to sound calm. With the bulk of the Nusquan forces withdrawing, the 'nids were advancing on all sides, and the geothermal power plant had become the tip of an increasingly precarious salient; into which I was now heading as fast as Jurgen could take me, which was very fast indeed. Positively the last place anyone with the remotest vestige of common sense would want to be, under the circumstances.

But there was no turning back now; practically every trooper on Nusquam Fundumentibus would know I was on my way, and believe me eager to enter the fray on their behalf. For many, the prospect of fighting alongside the hero I was popularly supposed to be, in the confident expectation that I would somehow be able to turn the tide, was undoubtedly the only thing keeping them in the fight, beset as they were on all sides by bloodcurdling horrors. If I let them down, morale would collapse, our orderly withdrawal would become a bloody rout, and the 'nids would be all over us like Jurgen's psoriasis. My chances of making it to a shuttle in one piece would be slender at best, and as soon as it started to get round that the celebrated Hero of the Imperium had cut and run like a panicked gretchin, I wouldn't be able to count on anyone to watch my back from now on.

'We're coming up on the Spiral,' my aide informed me a moment later, as we flashed through an intersection, and began descending fast enough to pop my ears. I swallowed, gaining some relief, and glanced around at the caverns we passed through[1]. The deeper we went the more the vista changed, from affluent residential areas to poorer ones; then the manufactoria took over, huddled in the lowest levels, where the inexhaustible supply of geothermal power could keep them running indefinitely. On the opposite carriageway the Nusquans were retreating in a steady stream, many of the Chimeras carrying additional troopers clinging to their upper surfaces, unable to hitch a ride inside; seeing us, they waved and cheered, each '*Huzzah!*' another coffin nail in my steadily dwindling hopes of just being able to offload the demo charges we were carrying and make a run for the surface ourselves, while Forres and her troopers got on with the job of planting them. By now everyone was probably expecting me to lead a charge down the burrower tunnels to butcher the bioship with my chainsword.

So musing, I gradually became aware of the sounds of combat: the rattling of lasguns, the harsher bark of autocannon, and the occasional dull thud of explosive detonation making themselves heard above the roar of the Salamander's engine. 'Looks like

---

1. *The Spiral wasn't a literal one, but was so named because the highway descended through half a dozen different caverns, each lower than the next.*

trouble ahead,' Jurgen remarked laconically, and with his habitual understatement.

Trouble just barely began to cover it, I thought, as we roared into a wide plaza, surrounded on all sides by the towering walls of fabrication mills and the loading bays from which whatever was produced here would be dispatched by lorry to the far corners of the city[1]. Guard troopers in Nusquan uniforms were taking what cover they could, while firing grimly at a solid wall of tyranids, advancing inexorably on their positions. Wave after wave of the ghastly creatures fell to the withering fire, but still they advanced undaunted, as indifferent to the deaths of hundreds of their kind as we would be to the expenditure of an equal number of las-bolts. Among them larger forms loomed, lumbering pyrovores gorging on the fallen, tyranid and human alike, while the weapon sym-biotes embedded in their backs vomited plumes of fire at the beleaguered defenders. A couple of the Chimeras were replying in kind, their forward-mounted flamers incinerating the scuttling mass of smaller creatures in front of them, while the multi-lasers in their turrets swept the ranks behind.

'Can you get us through?' I asked, ducking below the armour plate protecting the passenger compartment while fleshborer and devourer rounds rattled and splattered against it. The barrage abruptly ceased as Jurgen triggered our own flamers, and I popped back up again, grabbing the pintle-mounted heavy bolter and cracking off a few rounds myself just to show willing. I might just as well have been lobbing pebbles for all the difference it made to the horde charging down on us, but it looked suitably heroic, and it wouldn't hurt to boost the troopers' morale a bit. So far as I could see, the route deeper into the cavern city was about as com-prehensively blocked as it was possible to be, but it never hurt to sound fully committed to the mission; you never knew who might be listening on the vox-net.

'Not till we get the road clear,' Jurgen told me, as though that was

---

1. *And beyond, the broad highway of the Spiral terminating comfortably close to both the shuttle pads and the crawler park.*

simply a matter of time, although looking at the wave of chitin flowing into the square, I must confess to feeling considerably less optimistic than he evidently did.

As I scythed down a brood of 'gaunts which were balancing on a nearby rooftop, poised to pounce on an oblivious heavy weapon squad, one of the tracked cycles I'd noticed up on the surface came roaring towards us, apparently just as much at home on the paved surfaces of the city as among the snowfields above. Instead of the garish colours of the civilian machines I'd seen before, it had been painted in the arctic camo scheme the Chimeras were sporting, and a pennant waving from the vox antenna behind the driver carried a Nusquan unit patch. Evidently they had rough riders[1] somewhere in their SO&E[2], although no one had thought to mention the fact to me.

The cycle pulled alongside us, its rider tapping his comm-bead as he scanned the frequencies to synchronise with mine; before he could manage it, one of the smaller serpentine forms burst from the ground almost in front of him, slashing the air with its scything claws, which no doubt proved something of a distraction. He responded instantly, however, rearing the bike up on its tracks to put the bulk of the machine between himself and the barrage of spinefist needles spitting from the creature's thorax; the deadly slivers struck the roaring engine and the spinning treads, before the rapidly-moving vehicle collided heavily with the startled ravener, moving in swiftly beneath the reach of its flailing claws. The rider hit the carriageway hard, and rolled, unslinging his lasgun as he rose: but before he could fire I squeezed the trigger of the bolter, and reduced the slithering nightmare to a pile of shredded offal.

---

1. *The popular image of these units is of cavalry, and the vast majority of rough rider units do, of course, use horses or other riding beasts to great effect: horses are at home in terrain no vehicle can tackle, are self-fuelling in many environments instead of relying on the proximity of a promethium supply, and are able to replace their own losses to some extent. Some regiments do use light all-terrain vehicles instead, however, particularly those from iceworlds or other environments where the raising of livestock is less than practical.*

2. *Slate of Organisation and Equipment, a slightly archaic term referring to the inventory of regimental assets and their disposition.*

'Thanks,' the man said, jogging towards us as Jurgen coasted to a halt, and to my surprise I recognised the NCO who'd accompanied Forres into the agricave complex.

'Sergeant Lanks,' I said, returning his salute. 'An unexpected pleasure.'

'It's lieutenant, now,' he replied, looking faintly embarrassed. 'First man in the regiment to get a commission. Good to see you again too, sir.'

'Shame it wasn't under quieter conditions,' I said, ducking as one of the lumbering pyrovores belched flame in our direction and set fire to a warehouse a score or so metres away. The mass of the tyranid swarm was closing in around us, and the Nusquans were losing ground, despite their best efforts. 'What's going on?'

'They've cut off the commissar,' he said, baffling me for a moment, until I realised he meant Forres. 'Her group's still holding out at the power station, but we can't get through to reinforce or extract them.'

'We'll get through,' Jurgen said, with rather more determination than practicality, revving the engine as if eager to start. Forewarned, I grabbed the pintle mount for support as he spun us in place, triggered the flamer again, and barbecued another brood of hormagaunts.

'If there was a way, we'd have found it,' Lanks said, with vehemence, as though my aide's words implied criticism of the resolve of the troopers fighting and dying all around us.

'I don't doubt that for a second,' I said, with a surge of relief. If we couldn't get through an entire army of tyranids it was hardly our fault; we'd done our best, but we'd been beaten back by the sheer mass of the swarm facing us. Now I could withdraw with the Nusquans, get aboard the next available shuttle, and wait for the task force and the Space Marines to arrive, bemoaning our bad luck the whole way. A few appropriately sober words about Forres's noble sacrifice, and I'd be in the clear.

'We were keeping them back well enough until about twenty minutes ago,' Lanks told us. 'Then suddenly the whole swarm went on the attack, perfectly coordinated, right along our defensive line.'

'That's why,' I said, seeing movement through the smoke still wreathing the blazing warehouse. Another monstrous form was coming into view, towering over the smaller creatures around it, brandishing boneswords and a venom cannon, and at the sight of it, I don't mind admitting my mouth went dry. 'The hive tyrant took control. If you take it down, the whole swarm will be thrown into confusion.' Although why I should offer any advice liable to put me back in the firing line, I have no idea.

'We're targeting it, of course,' Lanks said, 'every chance we get. But the ones around it are just soaking up the incoming fire.' As if to confirm his words, a salvo of las and autocannon rounds ripped into the towering monstrosity; but before the majority of them could strike, the squat bulk of the creatures immediately surrounding it moved to put themselves between the incoming fire and the tyrant it had been aimed at. Barrages which would have obliterated a lesser creature rebounded harmlessly from these living shields, and a couple of nearby scavengers lumbered closer, gobbling up the 'gaunts felled by the ricochets.

'This is Commissar Cain,' I voxed on an open channel, as inspiration suddenly struck. 'Disregard the tyrant, and target the pyrovores.'

'Are you sure, sir?' Jurgen asked, as I grabbed the heavy bolter again, and began adding what little I could to the blizzard of incoming fire which suddenly began sleeting around the lumbering scavengers. Both staggered, the leading one dropping heavily to its knees, where it continued single-mindedly to search for fresh carrion, the slow oscillation of its head looking for all the world like dazed incomprehension. 'You know what happens if the guts get ruptured.'

'Exactly,' I said, peering hopefully through the sights of the bolter. 'The flammable gas it spits out meets the air, and...' I couldn't be sure if I felt the shock of detonation, the suspension of the Salamander being somewhat basic, and transmitting an inordinate number of jolts to my long-suffering sacrum at the best of times, but there was no denying the evidence of my eyes. 'That happens,' I concluded, a trifle smugly if I'm honest. Bits of charred viscera pattered around me, then the carrion storm redoubled as the second wounded fire-beast went up like its fellow, their thick chitinous carapaces converted in an instant to withering shrapnel which tore through the 'nids surrounding them.

The tyrant bellowed, staggering, wreathed in flames from the thick, combustible gel which had spattered it from the exploding incendiary beasts. Flailing blindly with its boneswords, it ripped the guts from another of the flame-spitting scavengers, which promptly went up in turn, the wounded giant at the very centre of the firestorm this time. All around us the tyranids began milling uncertainly, scuttling for shadows or charging blindly down the guns of the nearest units, according to whatever instincts ruled them in the absence of direction from the hive mind.

'Bring it down!' Lanks commanded, in awestruck tones, which I could hardly blame him for; the strategem I'd come up with more or less on the fly had succeeded beyond my wildest hopes, which had, if I'm honest, extended no further than confusing the tyrant a bit and loosening its hold on the swarm enough to aid a fighting retreat. But now it looked as if we were in with a chance of taking it down entirely.

Another hailstorm of heavy weapons fire, supplemented by a generous helping of lasgun rounds, tore into the towering creature, which by now seemed to be baking in its shell, like a crustacean in an expensive restaurant. Its formidable armour had been fatally weakened by the inferno, and even its kamikaze guardians were unable to save it this time; too busy with being broiled alive themselves to absorb much of the incoming fire, they were smashed aside like an ineffectual tackle on the scrumball pitch. As round after round of heavy ordnance tore the guts out of it, pulverising armour made brittle by the heat, the tyrant staggered, went down, and ultimately expired, with one last reflexive kick which brought the facade of an anonymous fabrication block crashing down on its scorched and battered entourage.

A cheer went up from the Nusquans, and, I must admit, I felt like giving voice myself; with the tyrant out of the way, and its control over the swarm shattered, it looked as though we'd be able to seize the initiative again. A mood of euphoria which lasted mere seconds, I may add, before Forres's voice in my comm-bead brought me back to the reality of my situation with a thud.

'What's keeping you?' she asked, and I suddenly realised that pulling back to the surface with the Nusquans wasn't going to be an option any more. The unexpected success of my gamble had given us the chance to punch through the suddenly directionless swarm, before the buried hive node could dispatch another tyrant to retake control.

'Tyranid rush hour,' I said, as Jurgen gunned the engine, and began accelerating towards the tunnel mouth he'd indicated before. 'Just asking them nicely to move over.'

'Don't take too long,' Forres cautioned, 'or we won't be here to meet you.'

'On our way,' I said. As I spoke, a demi-score of cyclists formed up around us, Nusquan pennants fluttering in the breeze of their passage, Lanks waving them on from the head of the troop. 'With an escort,' I added, agreeably surprised.

'We'll be waiting,' Forres said.

TWENTY-SEVEN

I HAVE TO admit that these unexpected reinforcements raised my spirits considerably, as I've never been averse to a few extra bodies to hide behind, and although we'd left the main battle behind us, there were still plenty of tyranid organisms standing between us and our objective. The cycles surrounding us had forward-facing lasguns built into the front fairings, which soon proved their worth, allowing us to punch through the bioforms which tried to impede our progress with surprisingly little difficulty. The vast majority of these were termagants or the larger warrior forms, which were hopelessly outmatched by our speed and the superior range of our weaponry; by the time the survivors had recovered from us getting the first shot off, we were past and away, beyond the effective reach of their fleshborers and devourers, with little in the way of retaliatory fire to worry about. Since the pintle-mounted bolter was higher than the cycles, and able to swivel in any direction, I could swing it round to pick off anything left kicking in our wake after adding its firepower to the initial punch of our charge, which further protected us against any belated return fire.

Jurgen had less opportunity to use the forward-mounted flamer, as the barrier of blazing promethium it would have laid in front of us would certainly have stopped the rough riders, even if the Salamander had been able to carry on through it without suffering too much harm. He did manage to get off a few shots from his beloved melta, however, bracing it against the rim of the driver's compartment and raising himself somewhat precariously to peer over the armour plate as he fired. Since this involved him taking his hand off the throttle I might have found the whole business somewhat alarming, had I not known that the accelerator would have been jammed fully open from the moment he fired up the engine in any case.

'Look out,' I admonished him at one point, and we swerved alarmingly, a warrior form disappearing under our tracks with a faint *crunch*, audible even over the roaring of our engines.

'Sorry sir, nearly missed the frakker,' Jurgen said cheerfully, and, to my unspoken relief, returned his attention to the controls, his desire to emulate the rough riders, all of whom were supplementing the built-in firepower of their bikes with laspistols, apparently quenched for now. Nothing else could have kept up with us, my aide cheerfully pushing the highly-tuned engine to its limits as he always did, but the cycles remained locked in formation, the riders grinning like orks, apparently relishing the sensation of breakneck speed just as much as he did.

'Good of you to tag along,' I voxed to Lanks, having matched frequencies at last, and the lieutenant waved in response, before picking off a lurking genestealer crouched on a balcony ahead of us with a shot from his laspistol.

'Least I could do after you saved our necks in the agricave,' he told me. 'Besides, I promised the commissar we'd keep the road open for her.'

'I'm sure she appreciates the sentiment,' I told him.

'She does,' Forres cut in. 'Where are you?'

'Close enough to hear gunfire,' I told her. 'I take it that's you?'

'You take it correctly,' she said grimly.

* * *

THE POWER PLANT was under siege when we reached it, a mass of chitin lapping against the great bronze doors emblazoned with the cogwheel sigil of the Adeptus Mechanicus, which had been torn from their hinges and lay at a drunken angle against the supporting buttresses. Forres and a handful of troopers were defending the breach gallantly, crouched for cover in the lee of a battered-looking Chimera, which had been parked at an angle in the archway to form a crude but effective barricade. Its power plant seemed still to be working, as the multi-laser in its turret continued to reap a rich harvest from among the scuttling abominations which threw themselves forward with the relentless determination of their kind, although the promethium tank which fed the flamer had apparently long been exhausted.

'About time you got here,' the young commissar voxed, and I bristled involuntarily for a moment before I realised she was joking. 'We've almost run out of 'nids.'

'Don't worry,' I assured her, as we opened fire in unison, tearing a huge hole in the rear of the siege lines. 'There'll always be more along in a minute.' This was undoubtedly true; faced with a fresh target, many of the foul creatures turned, unleashing a barrage of fleshborer and devourer fire against us. I ducked behind the armour plate, but a couple of the riders with us weren't so lucky, and went down hard, falling from their machines as the deadly parasite ammunition began eating them alive from the inside out; the only mercy seemed to be that the high speed impact with the floor of the cavern had left them in no condition to notice.

Able to use the flamer at last, as our escort fanned out, Jurgen triggered it with gusto, incinerating the bulk of the brood facing us, slewing the Salamander from left to right as we slowed, in order to spread the gout of burning promethium as widely as possible.

'Get inside,' Lanks urged, as the riders wheeled and turned, crisscrossing the plaza fronting the Mechanicus shrine. It was hard to be sure, but some kind of devotional mosaic appeared to have been laid there, its design obscured by scorch marks, lasgun pocks, and an inordinate quantity of dead and dying 'nids, most of which were leaking foul-smelling ichor in great profusion. 'We'll hold the tunnel mouth.'

'Sounds good to me,' I agreed, as Jurgen slewed us to a halt next to the parked Chimera. I broke open the crate, and extricated a couple of the demo charges. 'This ought to do it.' I shrugged one of the bulky satchels into place across my shoulder, and handed the other to Jurgen.

'We'll continue to hold here,' Forres said. 'With the riders securing the tunnel mouth, we'll have a clear field of fire across the whole cavern.'

'Sounds good,' I agreed, with a quick glance at the layout. The tunnel mouth was almost directly opposite the entrance to the shrine, and looked worryingly short of cover. 'Take the Salamander over there too: you can set up a crossfire with the bolter, and it'll be something solid to stand behind if the 'nids pull back any of their forces from the main cavern.' Which they probably would, once the hive mind registered that most of the creatures down here had been killed.

Forres nodded. 'Good idea,' she said, and detailed a couple of nearby troopers to move the sturdy little vehicle.

Jurgen glowered, as one of them lowered herself into the driving seat. 'Take care of it,' he instructed brusquely, as though he'd ever shown a moment's consideration for the machine-spirits of anything he'd driven.

I nodded. 'We'll be needing it later,' I said, hoping I was right.

WHEN IZEMBARD HAD briefed us, I'd formed a mental picture of something similar to the power station we'd investigated so memorably in the Leeward Barrens, albeit on a slightly larger scale; but the reality of the shrine now we'd got to it was almost overwhelming. Huge galleries had been excavated into the rock below the city, spanned by catwalks the width of highways, which carried us over humming turbine halls full of arcane mechanisms the size of small buildings. Fortunately I'd thought to bring a map-slate, which, together with my knack for remaining orientated in tunnel systems like this, was enough to keep Jurgen and I moving purposefully towards our destination.

'There's that smell again,' Jurgen said, sniffing the air with a grimace of distaste, and, detecting the whiff of sulphur myself, I nodded.

'We must be on the right track,' I agreed, loosening my chainsword in its scabbard, and unfastening the holster of my laspistol. I hadn't forgotten the way the 'nids had infiltrated the power station in the Leeward Barrens, and intended to take no chances. (Neither had Forres, I'd been pleased to note; she'd placed sentries inside the shrine to avoid being flanked in this fashion, but so far nothing had emerged from the depths of the installation. Which, for someone as paranoid as I am, provided only limited reassurance.)

Since the map confirmed our guess, we followed our noses, emerging at last into a long gallery lined with pipes and control lecterns. Jurgen looked around, and shrugged. 'Suppose this is it,' he said, completely unmoved by the grandeur of the spectacle.

'Looks like it,' I agreed, retuning my comm-bead as I spoke. Some of the controls looked vaguely familiar, although I hadn't spent much time taking in our surroundings during our pell-mell retreat from the power station in the Barrens. Something I certainly did remember, though, was the dry heat permeating everything, which was definitely present now, and the noxious smell which went with it, which by this time had grown to such an extent that I was forced to rely on my eyes and my ears to locate my aide. 'Magos, can you hear me?'

'I can,' Izembard buzzed in my ear.

'We've arrived,' I said. 'Where should we place the charges?'

Following his instructions didn't take as long as I'd feared, being simply a matter of setting the charges around a few of the pipes, linking them with det cord, and poking a few of the controls to maximise the build-up of pressure in the system before we blew the whole thing. After much debate over the relative merits of using a timer (which the 'nids could easily interfere with if the hive mind realised what was going on) as opposed to detonating the charges remotely by vox (which relied on the network of communication relays built into the city infrastructure to continue functioning despite the damage being inflicted by the fighting) we'd settled on both to be on the safe side; now, as I came to set the timer, I hesitated.

'Will two hours be enough, colonel?' I asked, knowing Kasteen would be monitoring the channel, and, sure enough, she replied at once.

'That should be fine,' she assured me. 'Your group will be the last out, apart from the units keeping the pads clear, so if you get back sooner than that we can detonate by vox from the air.'

'If the governor lets you,' I said, trying to sound as though I was joking, but not entirely sure I was. 'She seems pretty determined to keep the city intact.'

'I am the governor,' Kasteen said. 'At least if you meant what you said last time about backing me up if I declared martial law.'

'You have my full approval,' I said, for the record, knowing all our communications would be archived for later tactical analysis. If I didn't make it out of here after all, I might as well make things as easy as possible for her posthumously. 'I take it our plan didn't go down too well with her Excellency?'

'Not particularly,' Kasteen said, a wry tone entering her voice. 'Even when I pointed out that the city was lost whatever we did, and that sacrificing it now could save the planet.'

'But you won the argument,' I said, knowing her too well to ever assume otherwise.

'My gun did,' Kasteen replied laconically.

'Throne on Earth, you didn't actually shoot her, did you?' I asked, in some surprise.

'No, just drew it to make the point,' Kasteen said, to my quiet relief. Technically she would have been perfectly entitled to shoot the governor if she'd refused to step aside, but that would have involved an unholy amount of paperwork. 'Then I told Magot to make sure she got on the next shuttle.'

A conversation anyone in the vicinity of the boarding ramp would no doubt have found highly entertaining, I thought, then returned my attention to the job at hand. 'Two hours, Jurgen,' I confirmed, and we busied ourselves ensuring that the charges would explode on schedule.

'I'm done,' he said after a moment, and I nodded, watching the numbers tumble hypnotically in my own timer. 1:59:57... 1:59:56... 1:59:55...

Wrenching my attention away, I turned towards the exit. 'Me too,' I added.

'Better step it up,' Forres advised. 'There's a fresh wave of 'nids incoming. I don't know how long we can hold them for.'

'On our way,' I confirmed, and Jurgen and I ran for the entrance to the shrine as if an entire brood of genestealers had oozed from clefts in the rock, and were now hard on our heels.

THOUGH JURGEN AND I ran as hard as we could through the stark metal-lined corridors, over bridges and through caverns stuffed with technotheological marvels, I couldn't shake the grim premonition that we were going to be too late. 'Situation, commissar?' I voxed, as the crackle of lasgun fire began to echo down the passageway towards us.

'Grim,' Forres reported. 'We're being pushed back across the square. If you don't hurry, we won't be able to cover your withdrawal.'

'We're hurrying,' I assured her, my breath beginning to rasp in my throat. The great bronze doors were in sight at last, gaping vacantly, an inchoate flurry of movement visible beyond them. A moment later the full implication of that struck home; the Chimera which had been blocking the entrance had gone, Emperor knew where, leaving the way clear for the entire tyranid horde to come flooding inside if it so wished. 'Where's the bloody Chimera?'

'We needed it,' Forres said. 'You'll see.'

As we pelted through the doorway, out into the plaza, I could see precisely what she meant. The fresh cadaver of a carnifex was lying in the middle of the square, felled by the Chimera's multi-laser, which was continuing to fire at a second one. The AFV was backing up, trying to keep the range open, and I could hardly blame the driver for that; if the towering creature's snapping claws managed to get a purchase, it would rip the armour apart like tissue paper. The Salamander's bolter was joining in too, the trooper manning it firing with great gusto, the rain of explosive projectiles gouging ugly, ichorous craters in the hulking creature's carapace.

'I can get a shot,' Jurgen said, raising his melta, but before he could pull the trigger the combined fire of the two vehicles took effect, and the monster went down. Lanks's rough riders were still roaring around, picking off the smaller creatures which infested the greater part of the plaza, but there were fewer of the rapidly-moving troopers than I remembered, and several machines lay riderless on the cavern floor.

'Concentrated fire,' Forres voxed, spotting us from the top turret of the Chimera. 'Clear the way for the commissar.'

A hail of las-bolts swept the open space, taking down any tyranid foolish enough to venture out of cover, and Jurgen and I ran for it. It could only have been a hundred metres or so to safety, but it stretched out ahead of us like a landscape in a dream, where however hard you run, you seem to remain where you are.

I suppose we must have been about halfway there when the cavern floor began to vibrate beneath my feet and I staggered a little; for a moment I fancied that the explosives we'd set must have gone off prematurely for some reason, and braced myself for the pressure wave, then comprehension suddenly struck, memories of playing tag with the giant serpent among the refugee convoy flooding into my forebrain.

'Get back,' I voxed wildly, gesticulating with my arms, and glancing all around for some sign of where the hideous thing might be about to surface. 'Burrower incoming!'

The Chimera began to back up, its turret traversing in search of a target, and the Salamander followed. The cyclists turned and bolted for the tunnel too, leaving Jurgen and I painfully exposed in the middle of the plaza.

Abruptly, tiles, dead 'nids and pulverised rock exploded upwards, as a huge serpentine shape surrounded by a nimbus of crackling energy erupted into the cavern.

'Over there,' Jurgen said matter-of-factly, as though I might have failed to notice it, and cracked off a shot with the melta. A deep channel appeared, scored into the chitinous plates which armoured it, but the subterranean behemoth barely seemed to notice, surging towards the retreating vehicles. A dazzling arc of lightning shot from it, hitting the Salamander head-on, and frying the crew; then the demo charges we'd left in the rear compartment detonated, along, I imagine, with the remaining promethium in the flamer tank.

A sound, so loud that I felt rather than heard it, slammed into me, throwing me flat, and I skidded along the ichor-slick mosaic, before being brought to an unpleasant halt against the body of one of the fleshborer casualties. As I raised my head, dazed, I saw the tunnel collapse, the trygon crushed along with the wreckage of the Salamander by kilotonnes of plummeting granite. The long body spasmed for a moment, its head buried by a pile of boulders, from which ichor was trickling in a fashion which made my gorge rise.

'Ironic, that,' Jurgen said. 'With it being a worm, and all.'

'Quite,' I agreed, coughing in the cloud of dust raised by the catastrophe, and gradually becoming aware of a voice in my ear.

'Commissar,' Forres asked, her voice quite gratifyingly strained under the circumstances, 'are you all right?'

'We're alive, anyway,' I reassured her, taking a tight grip on my weapons, as the crackle and rustle of chitin echoed all around us. There was no doubt about it, we were sealed in, without hope of escape, and surrounded by tyranids. 'For the moment, at least.'

TWENTY-EIGHT

'WE CAN'T GET to you,' Forres said, as I cast around desperately for cover. The scuttling sound was intensifying, echoing from the tunnel the trygon had left, dispelling any doubts I might have had that tyranid reinforcements were indeed on the way. Fortunately, the last of the warrior forms in the cavern with us seemed to have been pulped by the collapsing tunnel, leaving the surviving termagants running for cover, but I was absolutely certain that the hive mind would lose no time in dispatching more of the larger creatures to restore control, and as soon as they arrived our brief respite would be well and truly over. 'Our weapons are having no effect on the rubble.'

'I'm not surprised,' I said. It would be like trying to knock down a hab block with small arms fire. 'But thanks for trying. We'll just have to think of something for ourselves.'

'Emperor be with you,' Forres said, more in hope than expectation judging by the tone of her voice.

'Can we get out through the power station?' Jurgen asked, trotting across to join me, his face and uniform streaked with grime, and far less savoury substances from the dead tyranids he'd evidently landed among.

'That won't be possible,' Izembard replied over the vox, consigning us to our doom in his usual dispassionate tone. 'The maintenance shafts have been sealed to prevent the tyranids from using them to gain access to the upper city.'

Then there was no time left for further debate. A trio of tyranid warriors emerged from the tunnel the dead burrower had left, their heads scanning from side to side as they absorbed the tactical situation. The termagants around us began to emerge from the shadows, bringing their weapons to bear, and so far as I could see, Jurgen and I had no more than a few seconds left to live.

I cracked off a couple of laspistol shots at the nearest of the warriors and had the satisfaction of seeing it stagger, ichorous craters appearing in its carapace; but then it recovered, retaliating with a blast from its devourer, which missed me by a handsbreadth as I dived for cover behind the downed cycle lying close to the dead trooper who'd cushioned my fall after the explosion. As the payload of acid-secreting maggots splattered against the metal, an idea struck me: an insanely risky one, but hardly less so than taking a header through a necron warp portal, and I'd emerged from that more or less intact[1], albeit thanks to the fortuitous presence of a Space Marine boarding party on the vessel at the other end. I didn't suppose for one moment that the Emperor would be quite so accommodating this time, but even the slenderest chance would be better than none.

A dazzling flash and the smell of charred flesh told me that Jurgen had picked off the warrior which had just fired at me, so I stood, heaving the cycle upright, and swung myself into the saddle. It had been some time since I'd ridden a contraption like this, but fortunately the controls were all where I remembered, and I fired up the engine with a quick stab of the finger.

'Jurgen!' I called. 'Mount up!' and triggered the lasguns in the fairing. I took one of the surviving warriors square in the thorax, thereby attracting the attention not only of the one remaining, but all the termagants it was now directing.

---

1. *Almost certainly the only human ever to have survived such a transit.*

Jurgen sprinted across to another of the abandoned bikes and clambered aboard, slinging his melta as he did so; it clanked against his lasgun, but fortunately both weapons were sufficiently rugged to withstand such minor abuse, and I had no doubt that they'd prove as effective as they always did if we needed them. 'Where are we going, sir?' he asked, as his engine roared into life.

'Throne alone knows,' I said, kicking my own steed into gear, and accelerating at a pace which would have done credit to my aide. As I did so, a volley of fleshborer and devourer rounds smeared the space I'd just left, the 'nids thrown off aim by the sudden rapid movement. It wouldn't take them long to get their eye back in, though, so I opened the throttle as wide as it would go, and roared straight for the only exit left; the trygon tunnel.

Fortunately the huge worm had emerged at an angle, leaving a steep ramp down which I plunged, Jurgen close behind. As I flicked on the headlight the smooth, rounded walls of the tunnel became visible, our destination shrouded in darkness far beyond the range of the beam.

'They're following,' Jurgen voxed, then a couple of sharp explosions echoed around us, audible even over the roaring of our engines. 'No, they're not.'

'Frag grenades?' I asked, recognising the sounds of their detonation in a confined space.

'I had a couple with me,' my aide confirmed. 'They seem to have done the trick.'

'Let's hope the rest are as easy,' I said, without much conviction.

As IDEAS GO, I'll admit, venturing into the network of tunnels dug by the tyranids wasn't one of the brightest I'd ever had, but it certainly beat the alternative. Even the discovery that we were now out of vox contact with our comrades couldn't take the shine off the fact that we were still alive, although, looked at dispassionately, the odds on our remaining so were hardly favourable. My instinctive affinity for underground warrens kept me more or less orientated with respect to the city we were leaving further behind with every minute that passed, but could do little else; the passages we followed twisted and turned, apparently at random, branching off in every direction, and I had no clue either to our eventual destination or to where the others might lead. The best I could do was to follow whichever path seemed to lead upwards, although all too often we found ourselves descending again before taking yet another fork which seemed more promising.

My greatest fear, which was hardly surprising under the circumstances, was that we'd run straight into another burrower, which, in the narrow confines of the tunnel, we'd never be able to avoid; but luck appeared to be with us in that regard. Though we encountered more than our fair share of 'gaunts and warriors, the larger beasts all seemed to be committed to the assault on Primadelving, much to my relief. Our forward-facing lasguns cut down most of the creatures we encountered easily enough, supplemented on occasion by a blast from Jurgen's melta, which he'd rested across the handlebars, and a couple of times I administered the *coup de grace* with my chainsword, striking out at one of the more resilient organisms as we hurtled past, our tracks crushing the fallen to pulp as we jolted over them.

'How long's it been, sir?' Jurgen asked, and reminded of the passage of time I glanced at my chronograph.

'Too long,' I said succinctly. The timers we'd set were still counting inexorably down, and by my estimation Forres and her forlorn hope would have made it to the shuttles by now, if any of them had managed to reach the surface at all. 'We've got about twenty minutes before the charges go off.'

No sooner had I spoken than a dull rumble made the rocks quiver around us, and I cursed under my breath. The last of the shuttles must have left the pad, and, unwilling to wait or trust to the timers, Kasteen had given the order to detonate by vox. Which I could hardly blame her for under the circumstances, as in her position I'd certainly consider us dead by now. A rising wind began to chase us down the tunnel, and I rammed the already fully open throttle hard against its stop, desperate to squeeze a little more speed out of the hurtling cycle.

'That'll give 'em something to think about,' Jurgen said, with every sign of satisfaction.

'Us too,' I said, able to picture the devastation behind us all too easily. No longer confined, the magma would burst up, and out, scouring its way through the caverns to the surface; but the noxious gases, and perhaps even the lava flow, would exploit every other conduit too, including this one. By my reckoning we had only seconds before the white-hot pressure wave tore us apart, reducing us to ashes in the process.

Then, just as I'd almost given up hope, the headlights appeared to brighten, reflecting back from blue, crystalline walls, instead of the dull bedrock we'd travelled through for so long.

'Ice!' Jurgen said, putting the thought into words, as we continued to hurtle upwards, the rumbling behind us swelling in volume with every heartbeat. 'We must be near the surface!'

'Let's hope it's near enough,' I said, an instant before my cycle plunged into a wall of snow which blocked the passage completely. Stunned and blinded, I clung on to the handlebars for dear life, somehow retaining enough presence of mind to trigger the lasguns; they fired with a muffled *crack!*, audible even through the snow clogging my ears, although whether it made a difference or not I couldn't truly say. An instant later I'd burst through into daylight and the familiar bone-freezing cold, parting company with my machine as we performed a far from elegant parabola through the air, which terminated in another snowbank. (Quite fortuitously, it occurred to me later, as if I'd hit one of the outcrops of ice I'd have suffered considerably more than the bruises and headcold which actually ensued.)

As I rolled to my feet, looking about us for enemies, Jurgen followed; although I'm bound to say he remained seated, landing with a jolt which did the bike's suspension no favours, before curving back to see how I was. On the other hand, I suppose, I'd cleared most of the snow out of his way with my head, so his egress was considerably easier.

An instant later, a plume of ash, dust, and incandescent embers

burst from the tunnel mouth, knocking me flat again, the heat beat-
ing against my face and flashing the surrounding snow to steam.
Unaccustomed as I was to feeling warm on the surface of Nusquam
Fundumentibus, I still felt a shiver at the thought of how close we'd
come to being seared to death.

'Looks like we got out just in time,' Jurgen said, his back to the
plume beside us, which, following the direction of his gaze, I could
well understand. A few kilometres distant, the whole sky appeared
to be boiling, a vast column of smoke and ash rising almost to the
stratosphere, flattening and spreading outwards as though against an
invisible roof. Dull rumblings emerged from the centre of the cloud,
which was riven by flashes of lightning, and I spat a thick gobbet of dust
from my mouth. I couldn't be certain at this distance, but something
huge appeared to be caught in the middle of the maelstrom, trying to
rise for a moment, before sinking back, burning and desiccated.

'Looks like we did,' I agreed, plodding off to retrieve my cycle,
which was looking more than a little battered by this time. Here
and there, in the distance, other plumes marked breaches in the
network of tunnels, and I resolved to give them as wide a berth as
I could. It was hard to imagine any tyranids surviving the inferno
sweeping through them, but Jurgen and I had escaped, and I knew
all too well that it was fatal to underestimate their resilience. 'Any
idea how far it is to Underice?'

Jurgen shook his head dubiously. 'It'll take at least a day on these
things. Maybe two.'

'Then we'd better get going,' I said, inspecting my machine for
signs of damage before giving up and mounting it anyway. The way
it looked now, I'd save a lot of time just looking for anything that
didn't seem broken. Then I stopped, shading my eyes, and gazing
into the distance. A bright dot, reflecting the sunshine, was circling
the ash plume, and my heart leapt with sudden hope. 'Maybe we
won't have to.'

'Looks like a shuttle,' Jurgen agreed, producing an amplivisor
from somewhere in the recesses of his greatcoat. 'Too far away to
make out the type though.'

'Who cares?' I said, and activated my comm-bead. 'Unidentified shuttle, this is Commissar Ciaphas Cain, requesting extraction. You may home on this signal.'

'We were informed of your demise,' an unfamiliar voice said. It was, however, unusually deep and resonant, even through the tiny earpiece, and I was sure I'd heard the like before. 'I will inform your regiment of the error.'

'It's a Thunderhawk,' Jurgen confirmed, as the distant dropship turned and began moving in our direction. 'The Space Marines have arrived.'

I shrugged. 'Better late than never, I suppose,' I said.

TWENTY-NINE

IF BEING PLUCKED from the snows by Space Marines had been a surprise, our reception when we boarded the Thunderhawk was positively astonishing. My time with the Reclaimers had accustomed me to the superhuman stature of the Adeptus Astartes, so that had come as no surprise, but the magenta-armoured giant waiting at the foot of the boarding ramp had presented arms as Jurgen and I approached, as though we were honoured guests.

I'd been even more taken aback once we'd boarded; instead of taking us to the Imperial Guard staging post at Underice, the dropship had lifted its nose, climbing smoothly and rapidly into space. As the sky darkened around us, and I was able to look down and see the hideous scar smeared across the face of the blue-white planet below, I tried questioning our hosts; but, though polite, they were not exactly forthcoming.

'Your presence has been requested,' the squad leader told me, easy to pick out from among his comrades by virtue of the power sword he wore, even though the iconography of this particular Chapter meant nothing to me. Beyond that he said nothing, although the mystery was swiftly solved; as we rounded the vast bulk of the orbital docks, I was able to make out a pair of vessels orbiting nearby, in close formation. One was a Space Marine strike cruiser, differing in a few details from the *Revenant*, aboard which I'd spent an eventful cruise with the Reclaimers in search of a space hulk better left alone, but similar enough to be instantly recognisable for what it was. The other ship was considerably smaller, sleek and deadly, elegant as a jewelled dagger, and this too I recognised at once.

'The *Externus Exterminatus*,' Jurgen remarked, as though the sight of Amberley's private yacht was merely an everyday occurrence.

'You're absolutely certain?' Amberley asked, over a more than welcome meal in her private quarters, after an even more welcome bath and change of clothes.

I shrugged, articulating as best I could round a mouthful of ambull steak. 'You'd have to ask the magos. But he seems pretty convinced.' I swallowed, washing it down with a sip of the remarkably pleasant vintage she'd chosen to accompany it. 'But I don't see why it matters when the 'nids got there. Most of them went up with the hive node, and the rest should be easy enough to pick off.'

'Because the first recorded contact with the tyranids was just two hundred years ago,' Amberley said, speaking slowly and distinctly, like my old schola tutors used to do when I was missing a point they thought was obvious, 'and according to your friend Izembard these have been there for millennia.'

'Maybe they've been around longer than anyone thought,' I suggested. 'Could you check the records?' If anyone was likely to have evidence to support that assumption, it would be the Ordo Xenos, the branch of the Inquisition she worked for.

'No need,' she said. 'Without wanting to bore you with the details,' which was a polite way of saying I didn't have the clearance to know, 'there have been a few incidents which might possibly be earlier incursions. But the earliest of those was in M35.'

'The ones we found had been on Nusquam Fundumentibus a lot longer than that,' I said. 'So what were they doing there?'

Amberley chewed her lower lip thoughtfully, in a manner I'd always found fetching. 'Advance scouts, perhaps. But the thing that really worries me is how many more dormant broods there might be scattered around the Imperium.'

'Who cares?' I said. 'So long as they remain dormant.'

'This one didn't,' Amberley said. 'If another hive fleet attacks, and they've got assets in place behind our lines, it could get even messier than last time.'

I shrugged. 'What are the chances of that?' I wondered aloud. 'Another hive fleet the size of Behemoth? Pretty remote, I'd have thought.' Which just goes to prove what a lousy prophet I'd make.

'Maybe.' Amberley shrugged too, apparently dismissing the matter. 'Do you think your regiment wants you back right away?'

'I'm sure they can do without me for a while,' I said. Our orders had been to remain until the planet was secure, which would take months, or even years if I was lucky[1]. It had been some time since we'd last been able to enjoy one another's company, and I was certainly in no rush to part again.

'Good,' Amberley said, favouring me with a smile I knew all too well. 'Then perhaps you and Jurgen could help me with another little matter while they get on with things here.'

[At which point the narrative abruptly concludes, with a few unflattering remarks I see no reason to repeat.]

---

1. *Though the few surviving active tyranids were swiftly dealt with, the campaign to track down and eliminate the remaining greenskins from the Great Spinal Range was both protracted and bloody; and even now the planetary defence force remains on permanent alert against a resurgence of either foe.*

ABOUT THE AUTHOR

Sandy Mitchell is a pseudonym of Alex Stewart, who has been writing successfully under both names since the mid 1980s. As Sandy, he's best known for his work for the Black Library, particularly the Ciaphas Cain series. He's recently completed an MA in Screenwriting at the London College of Communication, which left far less time than usual for having fun in the 41st Millennium, and is looking forward to spending more time in the Emperor's service now that it has concluded.

A BRAND NEW CIAPHAS CAIN MISADVENTURE

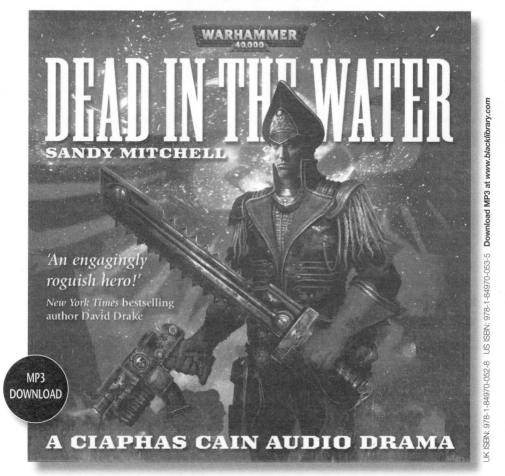

CATCH UP WITH THE ADVENTURES OF
THE IMPERIUM'S LEST LIKELY HERO

ISBN: 978-1-84416-466-0

UK ISBN: 978-1-84416-882-8   US ISBN: 978-1-84416-883-5